Visit us at www.boldstrokesbooks.com

NO EXPERIENCE REQUIRED

by

Kimberly Cooper Griffin

2019

NO EXPERIENCE REQUIRED

© 2019 By Kimberly Cooper Griffin. All Rights Reserved.

ISBN 13: 978-1-63555-561-5

This Trade Paperback Original Is Published By
Bold Strokes Books, Inc.
P.O. Box 249
Valley Falls, NY 12185

First Edition: October 2019

CREDITS
Editor: Barbara Ann Wright and Shelley Thrasher
Production Design: Stacia Seaman
Cover Design by Tammy Seidick

Acknowledgments

No Experience Required was written as a project during my year in the GCLS Writing Academy. I can't say enough good things about the WA. Writing Academy Director Beth Burnett is amazing and has curated a world-class curriculum for writers of any genre. I encourage any writer, new or experienced, to enroll in this fabulous arm of the GCLS. It will help you with the basics and provide guidance on advanced technique, but it is really the people you meet, the relationships you forge, and the breadth of experience that is shared during each of the classes that are the real magic of the WA.

During my time in the WA, I was provided with one of the most amazing gifts when I was mentored up with Radclyffe. There are not enough words to express how grateful I am for the opportunity to work with her. If not for her generosity of dedication and time to the WA as an instructor and mentor, this book would probably not have been written. Thank you so much for everything, Radclyffe.

Sandy, Barbara, and Shelley—thank you for your insight and wisdom. You grew my little story into a real book. You've also made me absolutely happy for choosing Bold Strokes Books. People are right on when they say working at Bold Strokes is more like entering a family than a new job.

Michelle Dunkley, my beloved friend and faithful beta reader, writing wouldn't be so much fun without your enthusiasm and support.

And finally, people aren't bipolar, they have an illness called Bipolar Disorder. When we stop characterizing people by their illnesses, we lessen the stigma and allow for healing.

To learn more about Bipolar Disorder, please visit the National Institute of Mental Health's page at https://www.nimh.nih.gov/health/topics/bipolar-disorder/index.shtml.

No Experience Required is dedicated to my daughter, Cassidy, who has shown me more about strength than anyone else in my life, and to my wife, Summer, who is always strong when I can't be.

No Experience Required

Chapter One

Cliff, the Gigify security guard, looked sharp standing next to the lobby desk in his freshly pressed uniform. The tired frown he'd been sporting for the last couple of months was gone, and he'd been watching for Izzy all morning to talk about it. He called out to her as she exited the elevator.

"Hey, Izzy, the gift certificate to the spa was perfect. My wife hasn't been so relaxed since before the kids were born."

Izzy was on her way to lunch but stopped to chat. "Was she surprised?"

"Heck, yeah. She thought she had forgotten our anniversary or something." Cliff chuckled.

Izzy narrowed her eyes. "What did you say when you gave it to her?"

"Don't worry. I took your advice." He hitched up his holster. Gigify took security for the high-tech campus seriously. "I didn't tell her she looked tired as hell or mention I was sick of her nagging me all the time. Instead, I just told her I appreciated all the stuff she does for the family, and I thought she might want to take a mini vacation."

Izzy raked her hands through her short blond hair and nodded her approval. "People like to feel appreciated."

"Well, thanks to you, I'm not sleeping on the couch anymore. It worked like magic. She's back to her old self now. I owe you one." He pointed his finger like a gun and clicked his tongue.

Izzy drummed her hands on the marble counter and backed toward the doors. "Remember those words when I forget my badge next time."

He winked. "Even if you do forget it three times in one week. Again."

"Hey! I told you, being forgetful goes hand in hand with brilliance. I read that in *Psychology Today!*" Izzy laughed.

One more floundering relationship fixed. Her friends didn't call her The Love Doctor for nothing. She always had the right advice at the right time, at least for everyone else. Not so much for herself. But it didn't matter. Love was for other people. She had enough issues to deal with without adding that sort of risk and complication to her carefully structured life. In the meantime, she silently patted herself on the back for helping Cliff see beyond his own Neanderthal nose for once. Maybe helping others with their love lives was her real calling in life. She could live vicariously through them.

She pushed open the glass doors of the building and stepped outside. California sunshine glinted off the glass façade of the four identical five-story buildings situated around the outdoor quad of the Silicon Valley tech company. Developers, program managers, and corporate honchos in their super-expensive jeans and ironic silk-screened tees moved along pathways among perfectly landscaped greenery and serene water features. Picnic tables and patio furniture, shaded by brightly colored canvas awnings, dotted the area. Subtle strips of rubber with texture designed to cause suction when pressure was applied were installed around the perimeter of the water features to prevent people distracted by handhelds from walking into them. The campus was home to Gigify, San Jose's largest online recruitment-software development firm, where Izzy worked as senior manager of the technical documentation team.

Izzy crossed the campus and waved her employee card in front of the card reader to the creatively named North Building, entered her PIN number, looked up at the facial-recognition reader, and pressed her thumb on the fingerprint reader. "Only one shall pass, Isadora P. Treadway," intoned a deep voice as the glass door clicked, and she pulled it open to enter the building. The approval phrase had been a fun novelty the first few times, but it got old very quickly.

Four or five people waited for their turn to perform the same sequence of events to gain entry to the Gigify commissary. It was noon straight up, and the tech masses were descending upon the sprawling space for nourishment and socialization. Indie rock strummed quietly in the background, and large television monitors played various cable programs throughout the room. She walked across the main dining room while tables started to fill with her colleagues. Thousands worked on campus, and she didn't know everyone, but many faces were familiar. She greeted several people as she passed, stopped to talk briefly with the senior director of the application performance team, and confirmed a meeting with one of the marketing managers before she made it to the café, where a cacophony of smells inundated her.

Izzy's stomach growled in response, and she paused near the mochi ice cream freezer, trying to choose what to have for lunch. Diversity and inclusion were primary objectives at Gigify. The International Café offered the usual grill fare, a huge salad bar, and varied entrees, with cultural delicacies from half a dozen countries. As if testing the resolve of dieters and healthy diners, there was even a wood-fired stove where one could get their own personal-sized pizza.

She was leaning toward the pizza when a familiar voice sang out behind her. "Hey, hey, hey!"

A tall, gorgeous Latino man strolled up to stand beside her.

Izzy shoulder-bumped him. "Hey, Hector! How are you?"

Hector grinned his million-dollar smile. "You know me. I'm chillin' like a villain. Are you having mochi for lunch again?"

She scowled. "I only did that one time, and I've never heard the end of it. It was a bad day."

Hector raised an eyebrow in clear disbelief, but Izzy didn't care. He didn't have room to judge. She had beat his time at the last San Francisco Rock 'n' Roll half marathon by over thirty minutes, and she was a slow runner. Even if she did have mochi for lunch, she could do it without remorse.

Hector was fifteen years younger than Izzy, but she loved him like a brother. Everyone, including her, warmed to Hector's handsome smile and stylish look. He always appeared put together, even after working an eighteen-hour day, which he often did. On more than one occasion they'd walked to the parking garage after a long day, he with the barest hint of a five o'clock shadow and his sleeves rolled up, she with her hair standing at various angles of attention and her clothes rumpled as if maybe she'd slept in them—and maybe she had, since she sometimes took a power nap on the couch near the foosball machine in the purple breakroom.

She and Hector had started at Gigify on the same day seven years earlier and had bonded during new-hire training. Although they didn't work in the same department—Hector was a platform developer—they worked on the same floor and often sought each other out when they happened to be near one or the other's desks. Once in a while, they had lunch together when they happened to run into each other in the commissary.

Izzy followed Hector, still unsure what she wanted to eat. When Hector stopped between the grill and the counter where a dozen prepared pizzas waited to be claimed, Izzy made her decision.

"Are you ordering to go? Or do you want to join me?" Izzy selected a tasty-looking margherita pizza.

Hector eyed her warily. "I'm craving a hamburger today. Will you be regaling me with all the details from the latest anti-meat book you've read? I seriously don't need to get grossed out and not be able to finish my lunch again. It'll force me to graze the bulk snack wall in the breakroom later. I'm doing my best to cut back on the Peanut M&M's right now."

"I'm off the vegetarianism." She picked a tomato from her pizza and popped it into her mouth.

He gave his order to the woman dressed in white behind the grill. "What? I thought you were locked in."

"I was." She shrugged. "And then St. Patrick's Day happened."

"Don't tell me. You caved to the corned beef?"

She grimaced. "Yep."

He made a face. "Seriously? That's a pretty huge jump. I mean, boiled meat is pretty much the bottom of the meat chain."

This was coming from a guy who liked menudo! She knew better than to go *there*. "No. Haggis is. Trust me. My grandmother may be from Ireland, but my grandfather is from Scotland."

She shivered, pushing the childhood memory of a Sunday dinner of haggis and neeps at her grandparents' house from her mind. Neeps. Double shiver.

"I'll trust you." Hector laughed. "Let's hold that thought. I've been thinking about this cheeseburger all morning and don't want to ruin it with carnivore guilt. As far as I'm concerned, this cheeseburger was created as is, delicious and complete with lettuce, cheese, tomato, secret sauce, and a soft, fluffy bun. It's always existed like this, and it'll make my stomach so happy."

They paid for the meals via a chip in their employee badges as they walked from the café and into the dining area. Lucky for them, they snagged a table vacated by a group of systems engineers discussing the finer points of their ongoing game of D&D.

Seated, Izzy took a bite of her pizza, expecting bitter disappointment considering Hector's look of ecstasy when he bit into his cheeseburger. She'd never enjoyed food in any form as much as Hector enjoyed his cheeseburger. Instead, she was pleasantly pleased. She finished the first piece in four bites and picked up her second.

"So, how's Jillian?" she asked through a bite, but covering her mouth with her hand. She wasn't a barbarian.

Hector's face lost all its elation. His shoulders drooped. Uh-oh. Was that a glisten in his eyes? Izzy wasn't sure she could handle it if he started to cry.

"I wouldn't know. She moved out." He put down his burger.

"What? When did this happen?" Izzy kept eating. She felt bad for him, but the pizza was so good.

"A week ago."

"I take it from the look on your face, it wasn't your idea."

"I didn't have a clue." He picked up a fry, made a face at it, and tossed it back down. The sadness in his voice pulled at her heart. "One day she was happy, and the next she wasn't."

"Did she tell you why?" She snatched his discarded fry and put it in her mouth.

"She said we didn't have anything in common, and she was sick of coming second to my friends."

"Oh." No surprise there. Anyone paying even the slightest attention would have heard Jillian's none-too-subtle remarks when Hector wasn't paying enough attention to her.

"What?"

"Nothing." Izzy concentrated on her third piece of pizza.

"I know that face," he said, pointing. "You know something you're not telling me."

She blew a breath out. "Well, I guess I saw something coming."

He crossed his arms across his massive chest. "What? And you didn't tell me?"

He was right. She should have said something. He didn't respond when *Jillian* said something, though. Why would she think he would listen to her? Besides, she hadn't thought Jillian would break up with him. Maybe threaten to, but not actually do it. Jillian was crazy about Hector.

She put down her pizza. "Wait. Maybe I could have said something, but why would I meddle in your relationship if you didn't ask me to? At the worst, I expected something would bubble up and you guys might have to have a serious discussion. I didn't expect her to move out."

Hector wadded his napkin and threw it on the table. He dropped his head and ran both hands through his hair. When he looked up, he was still perfectly groomed. How did he do that? "Well, she did. And I didn't see anything coming at all. How did you?" He pushed his hardly touched burger and fries to the side. Izzy made a note to take some Peanut M&M's to his desk later.

"It actually wasn't much of a secret." She went back to her pizza. "Anyone could see she was unhappy, especially when you were around your friends."

"When?" His brows furrowed.

Seriously? He had no clue? She dropped the remaining crust into the box and pushed it to the side.

"Just occasionally. Look, I think she was happy with you. Most of the time." Now wasn't the time to be gentle. "It's just, when you're with your friends, you forget to pay attention to her."

"Not true," he said. "I pay attention to her. I'm always aware of her when she's there."

"You may be aware of her, but when you're playing video games, you're pretty single focused. Especially when you get into your multiplayer games. Nothing registers except the screen."

"Again, not true." He pressed his forefinger against the table. "Well, maybe sometimes when it's intense. But you play. You know how it is. She knows how it is."

How could he not see it? Even now, in hindsight.

"My guess is she was more into spending time with you."

"Oh." He dropped his hands to the table and looked into the distance as if maybe he was starting to see what Izzy was telling him.

"Do you think it's final?" Izzy asked. She hoped not. Despite his shortcomings, Hector and Jillian were actually good together. Hector could get her back so easily if he simply pulled his head out of the sand.

"I don't know. I hope not. I just don't know what I can do."

Ugh. Clueless man!

"You need to make it about her for a while. Forever, if you want it to last. Make her feel special." Izzy couldn't believe she had to spell it out for him. Well, actually, she could. As long as she'd known him, women had thrown themselves at him. He'd never had to try to get a date. He'd never had to try to make something work. He hadn't built the skills. But Jillian was special. Hell, if Jillian had been into women, Izzy would have been first in line to date her—if Izzy dated, which she didn't.

Hector squared his shoulders. Hope shone in his eyes. "I'll do it. I'll show her she's the center of my universe. I don't know if it'll work, but I have to try. Thanks, Izzy. You always know what to do."

A pleasant warmth filled her to know she might have helped her friend. At least he had hope. "Just saying it like it is, Hector."

"The Love Doctor strikes again. You're better than Dear Abby or any of those other advice people out there. You should do a podcast or something. People could call in and—"

"Hey, there, you two! How's it hanging?" a familiar voice chimed in.

"Hey, Audie," Izzy said as her best friend approached.

Audie's fitted bright-yellow bowling shirt with a cat on the right breast combined with yellow and blue striped pants with the cuffs rolled up should have assaulted her eyes, but it didn't. Audie rocked her individual style with confidence, and it worked for her. Today, a spiffy hat—the kind an old man would wear, complete with a little feather on the side—topped her spiked platinum hair. She wore dramatic makeup, which would have come off as clownish on anyone else. Izzy should have felt invisible around Audie, but Audie always made her feel like the center of attention.

Audie studied Hector. "Whoa. Should I find another table? You look like someone just took away your favorite kitten and you're plotting revenge."

"Izzy was just telling me how to get Jillian back." Resolution still gleamed in his eyes.

"You guys broke up? Really?" Audie dropped into an empty seat, giving Izzy a "duh, everyone knew it was gonna happen" look.

Izzy shook her head, hoping Audie wouldn't go there.

"Yeah," Hector said, "but good old Iz had the perfect advice, as usual. I'll get her back. She won't know what hit her."

"Truth." Audie dropped a mailbox-shaped lunch box painted with various dog faces on the table. "I'll bet Iz has saved more marriages than Dr. Phil."

"Exactly what I was just telling her." Hector stood and gathered the remains of his lunch. "Well, I have to get back. It's merge day, and I have to work a couple bugs out of my code. The new intern still needs a little guidance on code reviews."

"I'm surprised you even took a lunch today." Izzy handed him the empty pizza box in response to his outstretched hand. "See ya."

He tossed the trash, waved, and strode toward the main doors.

"The new interns are here already?" Audie asked, pulling an assortment of small containers out of her lunch box and placing them on the table. "Jesus, it feels like the last group just rolled out."

Izzy didn't answer. The way Audie used the interns as a frequently refreshed dating pool made her uncomfortable.

"What do you have there?" she asked. "It looks like...I don't want to say what it looks like." Audie's lunches were never run-of-the-mill.

"Boiled eggplant. It's super good for you." Audie shook a gray, shapeless glob onto the pile of green. "You can put anything in salads."

Izzy almost gagged. "I'll trust you."

"Says the woman with the metabolism of a teenage boy." Audie tossed a lone green leaf that had fallen on the table at Izzy.

"I run." Izzy caught the leaf and started to tear it up.

"The only time I run is if I'm chased. If they're cute, I don't bother to run at all." Audie gave her a wry smile. "So, you helped Hector with the Jillian situation? God, I was wondering when he'd get a clue. That woman needs someone who will treat her like a queen."

"Like you?" Izzy asked, knowing the answer. Audie found almost anyone attractive, male or female. She was pansexual and not terribly picky. She just loved sex, and she loved people.

Audie smirked. "You know I'd never cross the lines with a friend's significant other. But if she wasn't with Hector, I'd be all over her like a bee on honey."

"I believe you." Izzy laughed. She dropped the shredded leaf into a pile on the table.

"You are amazing, you know," Audie said through a mouthful of salad greens, slimy eggplant, and some sort of boiled grains. No dressing. Gross. "You always have the perfect advice to help people with their love lives."

"I just tell people what's obvious."

Audie pointed her fork at Izzy. "There are entire industries devoted to what you do over a tuna sandwich and SunChips."

Izzy waved a hand, dismissing the comment. It was true, but she didn't want anyone thinking she had a big head about it. "It's what friends do, Audie. I listen, and I give advice. You do the same for me."

"I try, but I don't have your magic with it." Audie made a face and moved the eggplant to the side. She stabbed at her salad and then waved her fork at Izzy, pieces of salad dropping to the table. "You have a talent. Admit it."

"I like helping people. It makes me feel good." Izzy rubbed the back of her neck, embarrassed.

Audie shoveled the forkful of greens into her mouth. She made eating a salad look like work. "You should figure out a way to charge people for it."

"Yeah, right." Izzy stole one of Audie's napkins and tore a strip from it.

Audie cocked one perfectly arched eyebrow. "Why? You're providing a service."

"I can't charge my friends for advice. I'm not Lucy from *Peanuts*. The Doctor is not in. I'm a technical writer, not a therapist. They can keep their nickels." Izzy ripped a couple more strips and added them to the pile in front of her.

"Maybe not having a degree in it is a good thing. It makes you more relatable." Audie dropped her fork into her lunch box and grimaced. "I can't with this salad. I think this diet only works because it's inedible."

Izzy laughed. "Exercise, and you wouldn't need to diet."

"The only exercise I enjoy is the horizontal kind." Audie wiggled her eyebrows. "I'm serious. You need to monetize your talent."

Izzy snorted. "You're a riot. Who's going to listen to me? I'm forty-seven. I'm single. I've *always* been single."

Audie narrowed her eyes. "The best bartenders are the ones who don't drink. Besides, not true. You were with Siobhan for over a year."

Izzy laughed wryly. "Yes, Siobhan. My longest relationship, which only lasted a year because we lived in different countries."

Audie whisked her hands to the side. "Okay, your own relationship status aside, you still give the best advice of anyone I've ever known. You need to capitalize on it."

"What am I supposed to do, put flyers in the breakrooms with the tear-off thingies on them and wait for people to call me? No way." Izzy wadded up the napkin strips and bounced the ratty ball in her palm. "Besides, I like my job. I don't need another one."

Audie smacked Izzy's hand from below. The ball broke into smaller pieces and drifted down like confetti. "Hey, you're a writer. People spend a shit-ton on self-help books. You can write one of those."

"I'm not that kind of a writer," Izzy said. "I write technical documents, user's guides, white papers. I wouldn't know a thing about writing a self-help book. I'm not touchy-feely like that."

Audie took a package of Twinkies out of her lunch box, and Izzy laughed. Only Audie would have boiled eggplant *and* Twinkies in her lunch.

Audie's finger shot up, and she pointed at Izzy. "Hey, how about a user's guide?"

Izzy stopped laughing. "What? You mean like an idiot's guide to fixing your love life or something?"

"Yeah! That's it!" Audie dropped the Twinkies and spread her hands in the air as if reading a large marquee or billboard. "*An Idiot's Guide to Love.*" She nodded knowingly. "There you go. Now you even have a title. You're welcome. I expect to be the first person in the acknowledgments. It's gonna be a best seller. Mark my words."

Izzy's stomach fell. Audie wouldn't be happy until she had a book in her hands. How had she gotten herself involved in this harebrained idea?

❖

Izzy sat at her desk after lunch and spun her desk chair from left to right and back again, staring at the ceiling tiles. What business did she have writing a self-help book about finding love when she hadn't been on a date in more years than she could remember? She laughed to herself. Maybe she could write a book on how to stay *out* of love. At least it would be more in her bailiwick. Audie's suggestion was hilarious. She sighed and opened her laptop. The release notes weren't going to edit themselves.

❖

Ten minutes later, Izzy couldn't remember a word of the release document she had just read. The book idea kept slinking its way into her thoughts. She raised her hands over her head and stretched. *An Idiot's Guide to Love*. It was a catchy title, she had to admit. Something she'd probably look at if she were browsing the aisles of a bookstore. Not to buy, of course, since she definitely wasn't in the market, but just to skim to see what it was all about.

She opened a new document on her laptop. After a check to make sure none of her coworkers were around, she typed *An Idiot's Guide to Love* in the middle of the first page. She then inserted a page break, and…nothing.

She leaned back in her chair. Cool title aside, she didn't *have* to write it just because Audie suggested it. But she knew Audie. She was like a dog with a bone when she put her mind to something. She'd seen the look in her eyes, the excitement in her voice when she'd talked about it. As much as she hated to admit it, Audie's enthusiasm was contagious, and she'd always harbored a secret desire to write a book. So, why not?

She rolled her eyes.

The subject, *that* was why not.

She closed her laptop. Giving advice to her friends, as good as it was, didn't make her an expert. In fact, she was the furthest from being an expert anyone could be, an anti-expert. Love had nearly, quite literally, killed her once.

An image of her first love, Kelly, rushed to mind. Beautiful. Perfect…until Kelly had broken her heart and nearly killed her. Izzy grimaced. Since then, she'd shunned love, avoiding anything to do with dating or relationships. Siobhan had been a one-off. They hadn't dated. They hadn't been in love. She had almost no experience and, thus, no credibility. No one would buy a book she wrote on the subject.

She needed to stop with the negative self-talk. She heard her therapist's voice in her head. *What do we do when we recognize negative self-talk? We counter it with proof of our positives.* So, hey, she wasn't a recruiter either, but she'd written thousands of user's guides for recruiters about how to use the Gigify software. Proof she didn't need to *do* it to write about it. All she had to do was a little research.

The idea of writing the book was now a challenge she could get behind. She opened her laptop again and started taking notes.

❖

My name is Izzy Treadway, and I'm an idiot.

An idiot at love, to be specific.

I know what you're thinking: Why would you ever take advice from a self-proclaimed idiot?

I thought the exact same thing when my friends bullied me into writing this book. Who's going to want to listen to someone like me? A person who's spent her life avoiding love? The thing is—and not to be braggy—the one thing I happen to be pretty good at is giving advice that successfully leads to deep and lasting love. At least for other people. Maybe my lack of entanglement gives me an untarnished view into the hearts of others. Whatever it is, I bat nearly a thousand percent at giving advice that works. That's the reason why I wrote this book, An Idiot's Guide to Love. *Oh, and to get my friend Audie off my back.*

What are my qualifications, you may ask? Great question! But first, let me ask you this: is anyone actually qualified to give advice about love? It's not like there's a degree program out there to teach you the fine art of finding and keeping love. Nevertheless, I've helped countless people over the years. I'm not sure if it makes me qualified, but as long as someone needs advice about their love life, I'm willing to give it. I don't claim to be an expert—thus the "Idiot" in the title—however, to my knowledge, I've never led anyone astray.

So, take my advice. Read this book. See how it improves your love life. What have you got to lose except loneliness and heartache?

CHAPTER TWO

The scent of freshly cut grass was a pleasant sensation as Izzy ran along the greenbelt running trail she'd selected for her usual after-work run. She tried to focus on the beauty around her instead of the insanity of having agreed to write a book. She timed her breathing to the steady pace of her strides. Out, out, in. Out, out, in. The hypnotic rhythm did little to quiet her thoughts.

The book idea had taken over her mind. Wanting to write a book was one reason she'd gone into technical writing in the first place. Not that she'd seen her job as a natural progression toward her literary aspirations, but it was a way to marry her natural competency toward all things technical with her love of writing. Of course, once she'd started working, she'd put her literary thoughts on the back burner, and they'd stayed there as the demands of her work took center stage. After Audie planted the seed, however, she hadn't been able to think of anything else.

Of course, it was laughable that anyone would want to read what she had to say about love, but her friends seemed to appreciate her advice. *An Idiot's Guide to Love* would need to be about the full journey of love, from finding it to keeping it once you had it. People were always talking about how to find love. But based on the advice she gave the most, people had a hard time knowing how to nurture it once they found it.

It was all important, right? A good guide would need to span everything from finding love, to falling in love, and then keeping it. As she thought about what a good guide to love would contain, her running speed increased. This was going to be fun, even if no one read it.

❖

The first part of An Idiot's Guide to Love *is for those of you who want love but don't know how to find it. If you're already in a relationship, you may be tempted to skip to part two or part three. Don't do it. I encourage you to read from the beginning. The foundation of a great relationship starts with a solid beginning.*

We all watch the movies and read the books where people meet and fall in love. The lead actors start off all starry-eyed until they have some sort of conflict. But they always overcome it, and they end up together in the end. Their relationship is stronger than ever. Their lives are on a solid road to Happily Ever After. The simple recipe for romance, right? It happens all the time. But we all know real life is rarely like the movies or the books we read. Real life is chaos and randomness. There aren't any signs saying "start here" and "go this way." Nothing tells us "do not enter" or "destination reached." Wouldn't it be great if there were? We'd know exactly what to do. But we have to figure it all out by ourselves.

Well, I'm going to give you some advice on how to get started on your quest for love. I won't promise it won't be messy. It might even be a little chaotic. But it will get you started. And to get started, you have to take that all-important first step. You know what they say, the first step is acknowledging...something. Anyway, I'm not so good at remembering quotes. What I am good at is giving advice on relationships and love.

Chapter Three

How's the book coming along, doll?"

Izzy saw movement under the bathroom stall wall beside her. Fingers wiggled at her. Black polish with yellow smiley faces adorned the nails, and a tangle of beaded bracelets clattered on the thin wrist. She recognized Audie's voice, but she'd know the accessories anywhere.

"Don't ask." She pulled toilet paper off the roll. The backs of her thighs were numb from sitting so long. She'd been done for several minutes, but she'd been sitting there absently, trying to figure out the next chapter of the book. This little project was starting to be a major pain in the ass in more ways than one—one being Audie's nearly constant check-ins.

"Oh, but I just did."

The flush of the toilets prevented Izzy from answering right away, which was good, since she might have used a few choice words with her persistent friend. She opened her stall door at the same time as Audie, and she had to laugh.

"Are you stalking me?"

Audie waved her hand dismissively. "Please. I've been stalking you for years now. Are you just now noticing?"

"Just checking." Izzy followed her to the sinks. She washed her hands and hissed at the temperature. She glanced at Audie's reflection in the mirror. "Typical. Just when it's warming up outside, the water comes out boiling, after being ice cold all winter."

Audie wiped under her eyes and adjusted a few spiky locks of hair over her eyebrows. "I think it's to counteract the arctic air-conditioning."

Izzy dried her hands. "Hello, springtime colds."

"So, how's the book coming? I know you're writing it." Audie wiggled her fingers next to her head. "I can see the cogs and wheels spinning behind your eyes."

"I still haven't decided to do it. But I have been thinking about what I would write if I were to."

"And?"

"I don't think I can. At least not a guide. All I know is how to give advice to people about relationships they're already in. A guide has to start at the beginning—how to find love in the first place. I don't know the first thing about finding love, let alone keeping it."

"It's easy. I can help you there. Or at least get you started."

Izzy laughed. "I'm not sure you're the right person to give this advice."

Audie put a hand on her chest and raised her eyebrows. "Should I be insulted right now?"

Izzy wasn't sure if Audie was actually hurt or just acting like it. "No insult intended. What I mean is, you aren't the typical example of a person who'd read this book. You can find a date just by walking to the bathroom."

Audie swung her head proudly and used her ring finger to smooth her eyebrow. The hurt, if it was real, was gone. "As a matter of fact, I did spot a tasty morsel hanging around Hector's office."

Izzy rolled her eyes. "Let me guess. One of the new interns."

"I'm not sure, but I intend to find out. She's a little older than the normal crew. She might teach me a thing or two, if you know what I mean."

Izzy pointed at her. "See? You're definitely not the audience for the first part of the book."

"But I can share some thoughts. I haven't always been the confident huntress you see before you. I had to learn some moves."

"I am so far out of my comfort zone here." Izzy sighed and leaned her hip against the counter.

Audie patted her on the arm. "Not to worry. You're in good hands." She intertwined her hands and rested her chin on them as her eyes drifted to the ceiling. Seconds later, she bounced and looked at Izzy. "You have to let people know it's not always obvious. You gotta take chances. You need to put yourself out there and accept that it's not gonna just fall into your lap." She winked. "At least for everybody. And it can get messy sometimes. But it's worth it, right? They need to know it's worth it."

Maybe Audie could help, after all.

❖

Are you ready for romance?

You might think the first step to finding lasting love is getting out there to find it.

It's not.

The first step to finding love is opening yourself to the idea of being in love. Most people think if they're out there trying to find someone, naturally, they're open to it, right? Wrong. Going through the motions of looking for love and opening yourself to actually being in love are two very different things.

Some lucky individuals find love without any effort at all, while most of us have to work at it. And for some people, no matter how often they look, they never seem to find it. Why? Because they're not really open to it. They're cynical. They're skeptical. They're afraid. Whatever they are, they're disappointed in their efforts to find love. They grow increasingly frustrated, sometimes even bitter, when they meet person after person, but something always seems to be off. Things don't click. So they keep moving, looking for that special something, and never seem to find it.

They never find love because they have barriers around their hearts. Barriers they might not even realize are there. Not finding love becomes a self-fulfilling prophecy.

Opening yourself to love means introspection and understanding what love really means to you. It means figuring out what you need from another person. It means finding your barriers and taking them down. In some cases, the barriers are so solid, they can't be removed. They've become a part of you. But being aware of them will help you figure out how to navigate around them.

The point I'm trying to make is, looking inside and finding out what makes you the person you are is a good start to finding love. And once you figure it out, finding love will be a whole lot easier.

CHAPTER FOUR

S weet!" Izzy sang to herself as she backed her Tesla into the only
open slot of the row of charging stations in front of Whole Foods.
"Gus, this is our lucky day. An open charger at the grocery store on a
Saturday evening. The stars must be aligned for us today. What do you
think?"

Gus, Izzy's Australian heeler-Lab mix, leaned over and licked
Izzy's face as she unbuckled his restraining harness. He hopped across
the console and followed her out of the driver's door and sat next to
Izzy as she hooked up the charging cable. Gus didn't need a leash. He
was a good dog, but Izzy clipped one onto his collar after she grabbed a
reusable grocery bag from the car, and they made their way to the store.
San Jose had leash laws; besides, not all other dogs were as good as he
was, and she wanted to keep him safe.

Izzy spotted a familiar face as they neared the front entrance.
"Hey, Gus, your friend Lucy is here." A large square of artificial turf
was situated next to a row of water dishes and bone-shaped handles
mounted to the wall. Gus's ears perked up, and his tail wagged as if he
hadn't just spent the last hour running all over the dog park with Lucy,
who was lying next to a half-full water dish. The fourteen-year-old Lab
was pooped. At six years old, Gus still had a ton of energy left, even
after an earlier five-mile run and an hour of nonstop frolicking at the
dog park. Izzy gave them each a treat and headed into the store.

Air-conditioning and the unique health-food scent of the market
assailed Izzy's senses. Young men with thick beards and overly thin
women in hemp yoga attire roamed the aisles. Izzy headed over to the
produce bins to pick out a small variety of seasonal apples.

"Are those good?"

Izzy looked up as she reached for a Gala. Across the mounded display of shiny fruit, a pretty woman dressed in a loose T-shirt, warm-up pants, and flip-flops smiled at her.

Izzy smiled back. "I like them. They're nice and sweet." She barely acknowledged the flare of attraction that warmed her chest when the woman looked at her.

The woman picked one up and studied it. "You seem to know what you're doing."

Izzy laughed. "Me? No. I usually buy what I know. Gala, Granny Smith, Fuji, Braeburn, and Honeycrisp."

"You had me fooled." The woman tossed back her hair.

"I'm just an amateur apple shopper." She pointed to the produce manager. "She's the expert."

The woman looked to where Izzy pointed, and Izzy turned toward the cashiers. The produce manager knew her stuff. She'd give the pretty woman some good apple advice.

Even for a Saturday evening, the store was busier than usual, with lines at all of the cashiers. Izzy got in line at the express register and read the magazine headlines as the shoppers ahead of her rang up their groceries. She picked a magazine featuring a chicken coop on the cover. Maybe she could produce her own eggs. She thumbed through the magazine while the guy a few people in front of her rang up his kambucha and meatless hot dogs.

"Ooh, Casanova! Did you get her number?"

A familiar voice sounded just before an arm wrapped around her from behind.

"You truly are stalking me!"

Audie let go and shifted her basket. "If I were stalking you, I'd use the keys you gave me to your house and hide in your shower. But answer the question. Did you get her number?"

"You scare the hell out of me, you know that?" The line moved forward, and Izzy put her apples on the belt. "You lost me. Whose number?" Izzy knew who she was talking about. She just didn't want to get into another conversation with Audie about the pointless exercise of flirting when it wouldn't go any further anyway. No one wanted damaged goods.

The guy behind them gestured to Audie to put her stuff on the belt as well. Audie looked him up and down and smiled. "Oh, aren't you cute, letting me cut in line." The guy smiled back, and Audie put her basket on the belt.

Now Audie was another story. Izzy had no doubt Audie would

have left with the guy's phone number if Izzy hadn't been there. Izzy snorted. "You're unreal."

Audie winked at the guy and turned back to her. She gestured toward the produce section. "The apple lady. I saw you talking to her. I watched from afar so as not to interrupt your pickup moves."

Izzy rolled her eyes. "I wasn't picking her up."

Audie grabbed her forearms. "I know. I saw everything. She was picking you up."

Izzy looked around to see if anyone was listening. The guy behind them definitely was. She lowered her voice. "She was not!"

"She most certainly was. The watching, the laughing, the hair flip. She was into you, my friend. Are you blind?"

Izzy made it to the cashier and paid for her produce while the cashier bagged it.

"She was asking me about fruit. That was all. Just one shopper to another. I referred her to the produce manager." Izzy glanced toward the apple section as she thanked the cashier. The apple lady was doing the hair-flip thing talking to the produce manager.

"She was interested in more than apples, my friend." Audie paid for her groceries, and they walked out of the store.

But I'm not. Audie knew it, too. Yet it didn't keep her from hoping Izzy would someday jump into the dating pool. "Well, it looks like the produce manager is giving her what she's looking for. Just know it could have been you." She gathered Gus, who was lying next to Lucy, where she'd left him.

Izzy rolled her eyes at Audie. "Stop it."

"What am I gonna do with your mama, Gus?" Audie knelt in front of Gus, who sat up, wagging his tail vigorously. "She isn't even open to obvious flirtation, let alone love."

"Tell your Auntie Audie she's a nut, Gus."

Audie stood and patted Gus's head before lifting her grocery bag. "You're going to have to figure this stuff out if you plan to write your book, you know."

"I think I can write it without having to live it. You're the one who said I gave great advice." Izzy swung her bag of apples.

"It's true." Audie followed her into the parking lot. "I wonder where your knowledge comes from."

"Common sense, mostly." Izzy stopped next to her car.

Audie kept walking but responded over her shoulder. "Common

sense is overrated when it comes to matters of the heart." She waved. "Anyway, see ya, wouldn't wanna be ya!"

Izzy put her groceries in the backseat of her car as she watched Audie get into her little red convertible Volkswagen and drive away. Gus jumped into the Tesla and took his spot on the front seat.

She mulled over what Audie had said as she unplugged the charging cable. She'd decided to write the book, was excited about it. She even had some ideas about what to put in it. But maybe she needed to think more like a person who would be reading the book. She could be open to it without actually doing it. Couldn't she?

❖

Dating means different things to different people. For some, it means meeting various people to see what's out there before settling down. For others, it's all about the variety, period. Still others are looking for their soul mate.

What are you looking for? Are you in it for casual companionship? Or are you looking for your Happily Ever After?

Either way, figure out what you're looking for before you throw yourself out there. You shouldn't try to figure it out on the fly. Otherwise you might be stuck in the awkward position of saying no to a second date with a person who just spent a whole month's salary trying to impress you.

It's not just a matter of figuring out what color eyes you prefer or what turns you on in bed, although that's important, too. It's also about knowing what motivates someone. Sometimes, knowing what you don't want is a start to figuring out what you do want. A good way to do this is to make a couple of lists: one for what you want in a potential love interest and one for what you don't.

I have this friend, we'll call her "Audie." Now, Audie is a free-spirited person. To know her is to know how not picky she is. She loves all kinds of people, and she's attracted to what's on the inside. The outside doesn't matter to her at all. Or at least that's what she thought. It turns out, Audie has certain piercings in delicate places that can easily get tangled if her partner also has similar piercings. She learned this the hard way and had to make a call to a very good friend (me), who helped her out of an exceptionally embarrassing situation. Believe me, this experience traumatized everyone involved. Now, Audie would rather not date a person with piercings in those particular places—and she still owes her very good friend (me), big time!

The moral to the story about my friend Audie is this: you may think you're pretty open-minded about who you date, but there's always a deal breaker.

Chapter Five

Izzy stood in front of the wall of snacks in the orange breakroom absently tapping an empty biodegradable cup against the counter and staring at the food but not seeing it. Ideas for the first few chapters of the guide were streaming through her mind. What were people looking for in a relationship?

All of her research said to narrow your options before you go out there. Otherwise you'll end up dating a lot of frogs before finding your prince or princess. It made sense. Compatibility was key. Back when she started college, she doubted she saw much past a pretty face and a nice smile. Kelly's face came to mind. Maybe she'd had bad luck with Kelly because she never really took the time to decide what she wanted. She shook her head. She didn't want to dwell on that particular hell from her past, so she pushed the thoughts from her mind. It was twenty-five years later, for Christ's sake. She'd survived and learned, which was what mattered.

Now, what would she look for in a partner? She didn't have a "type," but she did have some fundamental preferences. Someone with a good sense of humor, for one. Not just someone who appreciated a joke or two, but someone who would make her laugh. And her dream girl—if she were interested in one, which she wasn't, thanks to Kelly— had to be perceptive and intuitive. People who always seemed to be oblivious to the needs of those around them drove her crazy. Smart was a no-brainer. Looks didn't matter too much to her. Although she wanted someone who was active, she didn't care if they were overweight as long as they could go on bike rides with her and take hikes. Of course, all of this was theoretical. She wasn't interested in dating anyone; she just needed to go through the exercise of how she'd figure out what her dating requirements were so she could write a book about it.

"Hi, um, do you know where I can get a cup like that?"

The voice roused Izzy from her musings. She turned, and her eyes refocused. A woman she didn't remember seeing around campus was standing next to her, pointing to the empty cup she held. Izzy's stomach did a little flip. She would have remembered seeing this woman before. She was striking—a little taller than her, with luxurious, long, black hair pulled back from her face in some sort of tie but hanging free down her back. Her eyes were large and dark, almost black, but sparkling with light. Izzy mentally shook herself.

"Hmm? I'm sorry. What did you say?" Izzy hoped the woman didn't think she was checking her out. Even though she sort of was. She might avoid relationships, but she wasn't dead inside.

The woman backed up a step. "Oh, I'm sorry. Are you a developer? Did I interrupt some sort of creative zone just now? I'm so sorry."

Izzy laughed. "No. I'm in the tech writing group. I was thinking about what I was writing. It wasn't going well, so I'm glad you interrupted. The cups are in the drawer over there." She pointed to a credenza.

The woman opened the drawer and selected a cup from the stack. "Ah. I was afraid I had to bring my own or something. The new-hire orientation is pretty emphatic on the reuse, repurpose, recycle thing." The woman used air quotes to emphasize the company's environmental mantra.

Izzy laughed. The company was a bit militant about the use of plastics on campus. "They're biodegradable, so you're safe. Never bring a single-use bottle into this campus, though. We'll run you off with a pitchfork."

The woman's beautiful eyes grew large, but amusement flashed in their depths. "That was definitely my takeaway."

Izzy held out her hand. "I'm Izzy Treadway. So…you're new."

"Jane Mendoza." The woman took her hand. Her hand was soft with a firm grip. "I'm a summer intern. I started yesterday."

"An intern?" Not that she was judging, but she was. If Izzy had to guess, she put the woman in her early thirties. Most interns were usually college students.

"Weird, right? I skewed the median age chart for this round of orientation. I'm actually a professor over at Bay Shores, and I'm shadowing the intern program this summer. Quite a few of our students intern here, and I wanted to know more about it firsthand so I could provide better guidance to those interested in Gigify. So, here I am."

Jane had a nice smile.

"Here you are," Izzy said, smiling back. "How do you like it?"

"So far, I love it." Jane pulled her hair over her left shoulder. The gesture was casual, but Izzy was reminded of classic screen stars.

"Which team are you working with?"

"The development team."

"Interesting." Was this the "tasty morsel" Audie had been talking about? The description was an understatement—and a bit rude, if Izzy really thought about it.

"I teach IT systems and have a remedial coding background, but I'm no expert. My mentor is teaching me as we go along. Do you know Hector de la Cruz?"

She *was* the woman Audie had mentioned. Hector took an intern under his wing every summer, and they almost always landed a job in a great firm, if Gigify didn't immediately hire them upon graduation. Jane was lucky she ended up with him.

"Yeah, I know Hector. Is this a possible career change?"

Jane scanned the snack wall. "It's a fun diversion for the summer, but I like teaching."

Izzy gestured to the wall like a game-show host. "Welcome to the bane of my existence. The bulk-snack wall. We have one in every breakroom on each floor. Wherever you go, there they are. Name your poison."

"I don't think it's a coincidence they tell you about the fully stocked breakrooms and the daily boot camps in the same breath during in-processing. This could be a temptation my thighs should live without," Jane said. But she placed her cup under the spout of Peanut M&M's.

Izzy knew right then that they would be friends.

Jane turned the dispenser knob, and three candies plopped out.

"There's an art to the pour," Izzy said. "Would you like the tutorial?" She'd been about to leave because she had a meeting in five minutes. But Jane was so...interesting.

Jane stepped aside. "By all means."

Did Jane just look her up and down? A warm rush flowed across Izzy's body, and her hand shook when she reached for the dispenser.

The unit was a low-tech, crank-and-pour apparatus. Izzy cleared her throat and steadied her hand. "A full turn is too much. Just a half click to the right, and the chute stays open. The magic is in the perfect rotation of the knob."

Jane put her hand over her mouth but continued to watch.

A steady flow of candies poured out, and Izzy suddenly worried about her choice of words. She focused on the cup she held. Was "knob" a dirty word? *Stop it!*

She snuck a look at Jane, who was watching her, not the cup. She was smiling, but she looked friendly enough. She watched the volume in the cup increase until it was three-fourths full, and her head suddenly filled with static. Too many thoughts to keep track of. She was doing it wrong or acting weird. A familiar voice injected paranoia where healthy people usually didn't feel it. Oh no. She was veering into the noisy headspace she tried so hard to stay away from. The warm flush she'd felt a second ago turned into a hot panic. *Stop it!*

She did a counting exercise to calm her thoughts and checked in. None of the thoughts were spilling from her lips. She was breathing fine. She was just showing the new intern how to use the machine. *You're good. It's good.*

Jane's smile seemed natural. She smiled back and transferred her attention to the cup again.

Was she being an asshole by assuming Jane wasn't capable of figuring it out herself? *She probably thinks you're a control freak. No. You're a regular person, showing the newbie the ropes. Stop it!*

With a hand feeling nothing like her own, she rotated the knob one click to shut the chute and stop the stream. She shook the cup to level the candies.

Or maybe she thinks you're a show-off. Show-offs were usually trying to gain approval. Is that what you're doing? Stop it! Reboot!

The voices in her head fell silent. The reboot always worked.

A perfect pour. Perfect control.

She handed the cup to Jane. "Bam! Maximum product volume without causing spillage and waste." Her voice sounded fine. None of the residual tightness in her chest snuck out.

Jane showed no sign she was aware of the five-second war occurring in Izzy's mind. She accepted the cup of colorful candies and rested her hip against the counter. "I give you a solid ten for execution, a ten for dismount, and a nine point five for presentation."

Izzy frowned at the imperfect score. "Only nine-point-five for presentation?"

Jane tilted her head and pursed her lips. "You failed to execute the customary bow at the end. I had to deduct."

Is Jane flirting? No way.

Izzy pretended to consider the constructive criticism. "I have to accept it. I came with my best, but my best wasn't good enough."

She was not flirting. It was just a quick-witted response she was known for. Besides, flirting was for people who dated, not her.

"Well, there's always the three p.m. slump to try again," Izzy said as she filled her own cup with candies.

"Three p.m. slump?"

Izzy turned the handle. Another perfect pour. "It's a scientific fact that office workers have a period, usually around three p.m., when they crave either sugar or caffeine or both."

"I've never heard of it. But if I think about it, that's about the time I always go for my afternoon latte," Jane said, popping an M&M into her mouth.

"I read it on the internet, so I'm pretty sure it's true," Izzy said. She shook her cup and selected a candy. Not enough reds, but she didn't intend to estimate the percentage of each color in this pour. Audie appreciated her occasional flares of OCD, but the newbie didn't need to be aware of them.

Jane made a serious face. "I believe you."

"I admit, I'm using science to justify my addiction. Peanut M&M's are my downfall when it comes to snacking at work. I just can't walk by the breakroom without getting a refill." Izzy shrugged. Her meds caused her to gain weight if she wasn't careful. She made a mental note to go for a longer run later.

"Why don't they have celery sticks instead?" Jane popped another candy into her mouth.

"We have those, too." Izzy gestured toward the refrigerators. "Cheese sticks, fruit, chips, soda—whatever will keep a developer hopped up on sugar and caffeine and from looking for greener pastures."

"We get overpriced pizza slices in the quad and noodle cups in the vending machines."

Izzy realized Jane was eating all the blue M&M's first. She leaned against the counter. What the hell? She was already late for the meeting with Hector. He'd get over it. "I remember those days. I went to Bay Shores for graduate school."

Jane looked up from her cup and smiled. "Maybe we can go watch a softball game together sometime. I know the coach."

Izzy nodded at the idea, but she probably wouldn't go. Jane was most likely someone she'd want to be more than friends with, and she couldn't have that. Even if she got past the rejection once Jane got to know her, all her relationships ended one way or another. She couldn't chance what that could do to her. She tried not to let her disappointment show. It was her lot in life to be single. She'd gotten used to it. That was why she always stopped a flirtation before things got too far. Thankfully, before her thoughts began to circle too quickly, the phone she'd left on the counter vibrated.

It was Hector.

We're in the Popeye conf. room

She sighed. She should have known; this close to release meant she couldn't blow off the meeting.

"Well, it was nice talking to you, Jane from Bay Shores. I hope we run into each other around the campus." Izzy backed out of the breakroom as she spoke.

"Me, too, Izzy from Gigify," Jane said with a wave.

One of the first steps after you've decided what kind of person you're looking for is to let people know you're on the market. For those just starting to get their feet wet, it may feel safer dating people you know as opposed to strangers. Even a friend of a friend might feel like a safer choice than going at it blind. Once you let folks know you've started dating, you might be surprised at how many people will want to hook you up with someone they know who's looking, too. Sure, you'll get a few "nice people" your great-aunt Beatrice would like you to meet from church or the son or daughter of a friend from bridge club. If you're lucky, friends might set you up with people who at least share some common interests.

Letting other people know you're on the market isn't always about announcing it or wearing it in big letters on a T-shirt. You may be more comfortable meeting people somewhere you go all the time, like the gym or a sports team. Believe it or not, many people meet their significant other at work. Think about it. You're probably there more than you're home. You're also surrounded by people who have at least one important interest in common. So, it's highly likely you'll meet at least a few coworkers who could be dating material. Just be careful. Dating someone from work can get awkward. Many companies have fraternization policies because of this.

Chapter Six

The staff meeting adjourned midafternoon, and as the team trickled out of the conference room, Izzy walked over to the credenza near the door and grabbed a small bunch of grapes left over from the lunch her boss had ordered in. There were leftover sandwiches, too, and the cookies were singing her name, but she refused to give them eye contact. If she didn't see them, they didn't exist. She'd already had an embarrassing number of Peanut M&M's courtesy of Hector, who had joined the meeting for the last hour to give a presentation on the latest release candidate so they knew what to expect as far as documentation went after the final sprint merged.

She tossed a grape into her mouth and leaned against the credenza, turning her back to the noisy cookies. Everyone had left the room except her and Hector.

"When you were dating, what did you do to meet people?" she asked him.

Hector eyed the sandwiches. "The normal stuff, I guess."

"Bars and clubs?"

Hector inspected a ham-and-cheese sandwich. "Yeah. I did the club thing. But clubs are mostly for hookups."

"Just hookups?" She glanced back at the cookies and looked away. No. She was stronger than her desires.

Hector leaned against the credenza. "Everyone knows you don't usually find a serious girlfriend at a club. It's too loud to get to know someone. Clubs are all about sex." He took a big bite of the sandwich. "And getting drunk," he said as an afterthought through the food in his mouth.

"Where did you go to meet women for more than just a hookup?"

She had to look away when he answered. Seeing half-masticated food churning in his mouth was disgusting. Unfortunately, the move forced her to look at the cookies.

He took another bite. "Anywhere else, really. The mall. At school. At the grocery store. I once asked a woman out when I was getting my tires rotated. She had arms like a professional weightlifter. I had to break up with her because she could beat me in a wrestling match. I can't date a woman who can hold me down."

She swatted his arm. "That's the most misogynistic thing you've ever said."

He took another bite and smiled, lettuce dangling out of the corner of his mouth. "I'm a pig, I know."

"True on so many levels." She picked up an oatmeal-raisin cookie. Raisins were a fruit. It had to be better for her than the chocolate-chunk cookie or the sugar cookie. They were all as big around as her face. She'd only eat half of it.

"How did you meet Jillian?" She broke off a piece of the cookie and put it in her mouth.

"At a dance club in Oakland."

"I thought you only hooked up at clubs." She took another nibble. God, it was good.

"Jillian is the little sister of a friend. He brought her to the dance club so I could meet her. I wasn't expecting much. In fact, I almost didn't go." He lowered the plate he was holding, and his eyes went all distant. "But when I first set eyes on her, bang. She was it for me."

She could almost forgive the food in his mouth. Almost.

Hector picked up the second half of his sandwich. "Why are you asking me all this?"

"Research for the book. If I told you I was looking for a date, would you try to set me up with one of your friends?"

Hector set the sandwich aside and rubbed his hands together. "You want me to pimp for you, Iz? It could be a thank you for you saving my relationship with Jillian."

She picked at the cookie. "This is purely hypothetical for the book. I've been doing some reading and found most people meet their partners through introductions from friends."

Hector looked disappointed, and then his expression grew thoughtful. He picked up his sandwich again.

"If I *were* to set you up with one of my friends," he said around a hunk of bread, "who would it be?" He thought and chewed. "None of my sisters bat for your team. I do have one cousin we have suspicions about. She's good at softball, likes to wear ballcaps. But she has a rotation of greasy biker boyfriends, so it's probably an androgynous millennial thing." He poked her with his elbow. "Sorry, Iz. I actually think you'd like her."

This was getting weird. "Again, it's only hypothetical. I'm not looking. Thanks anyway." She popped the last bite of the cookie into her mouth. Where had the rest of it gone? She rubbed her hands on her chinos.

"You got my hopes up." Hector finished his sandwich, and they left the conference room.

Izzy swiped another oatmeal cookie before she could stop herself. *You're weak, Treadway. Weak!* She told herself to shut it as she took a bite of the new cookie.

"Well, I'm not looking."

She hit the elevator call button and they watched the numbers above the elevator light up as it landed at other floors. She regretted her terse response. She wasn't sure if it came out that way because she was mad at herself for taking two cookies or if she wished Hector wasn't so keen to find her a girlfriend. Probably both.

Hector didn't seem to notice. "If you change your mind, just say so. I know a lot of people."

"I won't change it, but I'll tell you first if I do."

"How's the book going, by the way?"

"I have an outline and a couple chapters written so far."

"Sounds like a good start."

"Yeah, but it's harder than I thought it would be."

The elevator doors opened, and they got in. The door was closing when an arm shot between the doors, and the sensors opened them again. Izzy winced. What if the sensors failed? When the doors opened, Jane was standing there. Izzy's stomach lurched, and the elevator hadn't even moved.

"Fancy meeting you here," Jane said, pushing the same number Hector had already selected. She looked at Izzy with a shy smile. "You're right about the three p.m. slump. I'm trying not to think about M&M's."

"You can't fight science." Izzy's stomach did another little flip. It could have been the elevator rising this time, but she didn't think so.

"When you put it that way…" Jane smiled. She faced them from the other side of the elevator, hugging a laptop to her chest.

She was so pretty, but something else about her made Izzy's stomach flutter.

"Do you know each other?" Hector's eyes bounced with amusement between them.

"We met in the orange breakroom the other day," Izzy said.

"She showed me how to dispense the snacks without an avalanche." She winked at Izzy, and Izzy winked back. Izzy never winked. What the hell was going on?

"Goddam Peanut M&M's," Hector said. "They're addictive."

Jane touched her arm with her soft, warm hand, a nice contrast to the air-conditioning in the building.

"I heard you're writing a book," Jane said, an excited gleam in her eyes.

"You did?" Izzy looked at Hector.

He shrugged. "Audie and I were talking about it this morning at my desk. I didn't think it was a secret."

Was it? Not really. But having more people know about it put a little more pressure on her. The bad kind of anxiety shot through her. Not the kind she got from looming deadlines or reviews with her boss but the kind she felt when she wasn't sure if she could keep it together. She used her breathing exercises to keep it from spinning out of control. "I'm just getting started."

"Audie said it was going to be a best seller." Jane squeezed her arm and let her hand drop.

Izzy blushed. "I have to actually finish it first." Her chest already felt tight with anxiety, now add excitement. A lethal combination for her. She reminded herself to just breathe.

Jane bounced. "What's it about? Do you have a title yet?"

"*An Idiot's Guide to Love.*"

The elevator deposited them at their floor.

"You're writing about love? Interesting," Jane said.

Izzy immediately second-guessed the whole idea. Who was she to write about love? It was stupid. "I know. What kind of expert could I be?"

They were near the orange breakroom. Jane put a hand out, stopping her. Hector continued into the room. "Not at all. It's a great idea. Is it a self-help book?"

Izzy tried to ignore the flush she knew had crept to her cheeks. "Yeah, but interesting, you know?"

"How'd you get the idea?" They walked into the breakroom. Hector was making a cup of coffee. "She gives great advice. Half the people on this floor have come to her for her wisdom. She's the love whisperer." Hector snapped and pointed at Izzy. "Hey, you can use that for your book title. *The Love Whisperer*. It's catchy."

Izzy laughed. "You'll have to run it by Audie. She's pretty set on *An Idiot's Guide to Love*."

As if conjured by the mention of her name, Audie walked into the breakroom with a cup of coffee. "I heard my name. Tell me you were saying something scandalous about me."

"Was it 'Audie' or 'idiot' you heard?" Hector looked highly amused at his joke.

"If it was 'idiot,' I would have known she was talking to you, smart guy." Audie slapped the bill of Hector's San Jose Sharks ballcap.

Hector laughed and readjusted his hat. "We were just talking about Izzy's book."

"You're already generating buzz." Audie's eyes landed on Jane, and a look settled over her face.

Izzy had seen that look before. Audie was interested. Izzy didn't know why she had the urge to stand closer to Jane. What was this? High school?

Audie held out her hand to Jane. "You're new. We haven't been formally introduced. I'm Audie."

"I'm Jane." Jane shook her hand.

"She's interning with Hector this summer," Izzy said.

"Aren't you a little...mature to be an intern?" Audie asked.

Izzy cringed. One of Audie's not-so-endearing qualities was her use of the new interns as a dating pool, even though she was old enough to be their mother. Most of the time they ignored her. But sometimes, Audie got involved with one of them, and then it was uncomfortable for everyone around. The only thing saving Audie from being reported for sexual harassment was that she was exceptionally respectful about consent. Izzy had to give it to her—she was confident and charming. *But, still, ew!*

Hector laughed. "Smooth, Aud. And on that note, I have a meeting. Jane, I'll see you in an hour to go over test cases."

"Sounds good," Jane said as he walked away.

Audie's eyes stayed on Jane, who slowly withdrew her hand from Audie's. "So, you're an intern." Audie leaned against the counter and put a wooden coffee stirrer in her mouth.

Jane had a playful sparkle in her eye. "A mature intern, yes."

Izzy was impressed with the ease in which Jane took the borderline rude comment. Why was she getting so irritated at Audie? Was she jealous? She had no reason to be.

Jane gave Audie the condensed version of how she'd come to work at Gigify for the summer, and as much as Izzy enjoyed talking with both of them, she really didn't want to continue analyzing her reaction to Audie.

"I've been in a meeting all day. I have to get to work on a few docs," she said, interrupting the discussion. She backed toward the breakroom door.

"Oh." Jane looked at Izzy and then back to Audie. "Yeah, me, too."

Jane and Audie followed her out of the breakroom, but when she reached her desk, they stopped and continued talking. Great. She couldn't get away.

"I'm so behind on these documents." She opened her laptop, hoping they'd take the hint.

Audie was single-focused, though. "How does your partner feel about you working here this summer?"

Izzy shot a look at Audie before she could stop herself. She wanted to apologize for her classless friend.

"I don't have a partner," Jane said.

"Do you ever date your students?" Audie asked, ignoring Izzy.

Izzy thought she was immune to Audie's lack of filter, but this was getting uncomfortable even for Audie. "Audie! I can't believe you just…" She turned to Jane. "I'm sorry…I'm…" She searched for words. "I don't know what I am." She leaned back in her chair.

Audie raised her hands. "What? It's research. For the book. I'm helping you out, Iz. You need to know how people meet other people." Audie turned back to Jane. "How do you meet people, you know, for dating?"

Yeah, sure. For the book. Izzy gave up.

"Is this research for your book?" Jane asked Izzy.

Audie answered for her. "She needs as much information about dating as she can get."

She wanted to strangle Audie but shot her a look instead. She didn't care if Jane was watching.

"For the book," Audie added quickly.

Izzy was done with this conversation and was getting ready to tell them to leave.

"I mostly meet people through friends," Jane said.

Audie was relentless. "By people, do you mean male people, female people, or both?"

Izzy held in an embarrassed groan even though she wanted to know.

If Jane was offended, she didn't show it. "I find it refreshing you didn't assume. I date women."

It shouldn't matter to her, but a little buzz filled Izzy. Women, huh?

"So, your family and friends set you up with women?" Audie asked with a knowing nod.

Jane laughed woodenly. "My family definitely does *not* set me up with women."

Audie winked at Izzy. Izzy narrowed her eyes. What was she winking at her for?

Audie set her gaze on Jane. "Oh, so you meet them at work, places like that?"

Shameless. Shameless. Shameless.

Jane held a hand up. "I have a rule not to date anyone from work. It's easier to keep it professional."

A wave of relief rushed over Izzy.

"No exceptions?" Audie asked.

When Jane shook her head vehemently, Izzy hid a smile.

"I was involved with a coworker for a couple years. Our breakup was brutal, and it was hard to keep it from bleeding into our professional life. Since then, no exceptions."

"It must have been hard to see them at work afterward," Izzy said.

"She was in a different department, thankfully. But she teaches media. She gets asked to represent the school on air quite a bit, and it still kind of knocks me back a bit when I turn on the television and see her."

Izzy was enthralled with this personal tidbit, but even better, it seemed to take the wind out of Audie's sails.

"Well, I better get back to work." Audie sighed.

As if Izzy hadn't been telling her the same thing for the last ten minutes!

"I guess I better get going, too." Jane took a step backward. "Izzy, if you need anyone to do research or beta reading, let me know."

Izzy smiled. "I'm good as far as research goes. The internet is an amazing thing." It was a lie, her being good about the research, but she refused to dive into her dysfunction with a beautiful stranger.

Jane rolled her eyes. "Oh, yeah. Because the internet is always right."

Was she teasing her? "Don't worry, Professor. I'll find primary sources to back up my internet searches."

Jane touched Izzy's arm. "I mean it. I think it would be fun to help. In academia, we help each other out."

"Thanks, I'll let you know." Izzy's arm tingled where Jane touched her.

❖

Online dating sites are a popular place to meet people in this age of technology. They can be a safe and unintimidating way to get your feet wet as you ease into the business of dating. You can even think about it as online shopping—for romance! A quick search for dating sites will provide a huge list of online apps designed to suit everybody, and from the relative safety of your living room couch, you can shop for potential dates. Whether you're looking for a one-time hookup or your future spouse, the internet has the app for you.

Be careful, though. The relative anonymity of online dating apps can result in some interesting surprises and, in some cases, can lead to safety issues if you aren't careful. So, trust your gut. If it doesn't feel right, it probably isn't.

Chapter Seven

The light from the Mac display was the only illumination in the room as Izzy did a search for dating websites. She was tucked into bed with Gus pressed firmly to her side, his head on the pillow beside her, and her cats Fat Bob and Prince on the other. It was a snuggle fest, and it was a good thing she was single because there wasn't enough room in the bed for another person.

Earlier that evening at bowling league, the team had given her a ton of advice on the ins and outs of online dating. Like Hector and Audie, they had been a little *too* eager to provide her with guidance. What was it with her friends wanting to hook her up? She took a deep breath and entered the criteria in the web browser.

Holy crap! She found so many sites, and some were pretty wild. She pulled up the first website that didn't look like a foray into kink. Not that anything was wrong with kink, but it wasn't her particular cup of tea. The site didn't make it easy to just look around. They required a profile before she could even see what the website looked like. She didn't want anyone to notice her while she checked things out. Would she be a fraud if she created a fake profile? Well, yeah. Fake was the very definition of a fraud. She groaned. Okay. She'd create a profile so uninteresting, she'd fly under the radar.

First things first. A username. Should she use her real name or a pseudonym? She couldn't think of a good pseudonym to suit her. TechChick was taken, and NymphoHoney was just not her style. Feeling like a total bore, she considered several derivations of her full name before she settled on "I. Treadway." It didn't give her true identity away, and she wasn't required to load a picture, so she didn't. The bare minimum was the name of the game if she was just there to poke around. A message popped up telling her a profile without a picture severely limited her chances of finding dates. Good. That was exactly what she wanted, so she ignored it. Next, she had to fill out a questionnaire. The first question irritated her, and it only got worse as she read the next ones. Who cared about the color of a person's eyes? She liked both athletic and curvy women. How could she pick just one? Each question drove her irritation level higher. When she reached the end and hit save, she felt judgmental and shallow, but, finally, she could progress to the browsing section.

She'd chosen the free option, so she was allowed to scroll through the database with restricted access. She could wink at people, but she couldn't message them directly unless they initiated contact. She also couldn't see full profiles, only the first five lines of their "About Me" section. She also found, unless she paid, she couldn't really communicate much with anyone, not that she wanted to. But this was research. The site had a monthly fee option, or she could go a full year for seventy-nine dollars. She had to admit it was a good deal, but how many people did this for a full year? She decided to fork over the monthly fee to see more of the profiles.

An hour later, Izzy was still scrolling through profiles, the experience strangely compulsive. She learned which of them drew her in and which ones didn't. Some were written well; others were barely legible. Others were so charming she wondered why they were still on the site. Her digital notepad filled up with the notes she took.

A small eye with long eyelashes appeared in the corner of her screen. A wink! Someone was winking at her! She didn't even have a picture up, and someone was winking at her. Should she ignore it? The user name, FemmeFatale, seemed somewhat ominous, but she was curious. With an apprehensive tickle in her stomach and reminding herself this was all for the book, she clicked on the profile and saw a photo of a woman with her dog. She looked friendly enough. She hovered the cursor over the wink button for a moment before she winked back. Seconds later, a message appeared in the instant-messaging window.

Hi, there, I. Treadway.

Hi, she typed back.

FemmeFatale: *I noticed you don't have a picture. Are you shy?*

I. Treadway: *A little.*

FemmeFatale: *The cool thing about being online is you don't need to be shy.*

I. Treadway: *How so?*

FemmeFatale: *You never have to meet the person you talk to if you don't want to.*

I. Treadway: *True.*

FemmeFatale: *So, what are you doing right now?*

I. Treadway: *Talking to you.*

FemmeFatale: *Ask me what I'm doing.*

I. Treadway: *Okay. What are you doing?*

FemmeFatale: *I'm touching myself, thinking about—*

Izzy clicked out of the profile and hit the block button. This was supposed to be the *tame* dating site. What had she gotten herself into? She closed her computer and placed it on her bedside table. In the shadows of her dark bedroom she thought about the interaction. Part of her felt bad for the abrupt way she had left the conversation with FemmeFatale, but what was the woman thinking? The internet brought people closer together but also introduced a virtual distance, making people feel as if they could do things they never would in person. She'd worked in technology most of her career. She used social media all the time. But this online-dating thing had revealed an aspect she'd never really considered. It took a while before she finally fell asleep.

❖

There are countless ways to meet people. Ask your coupled friends how they met, and you'll probably get different answers from each of them. Take my friends Rhonda and Jean. They met while skydiving in Dubai. Two years later, they were married during a jump at 12,000 feet above the California desert. I was invited to the ceremony, but the only way you could get me to jump out a plane would be if it was on fire, and even then, I'd take some time to consider the options.

Anywho—even though most people will tell you they go to bars or clubs to find romance, it's usually not where people meet the people they end up with. Bars and clubs are noisy, and unless you read lips, it's hard to get to know someone when you can't hear what they're saying. Before a bunch of you go running to flood my social media with your stories of meeting your Happily Ever After at a bar, I'm not saying it's unheard of. I'm just saying it happens far less often than you'd think.

So, bars are out, and you don't skydive. Where do you go to meet people? Unless you're a hermit, you meet people every day—at work, waiting in line at the grocery store, volunteering at the pet shelter—all day, every day. Use this interaction to meet potential dates. Of course, you'll want to make sure it's appropriate because you'll probably run into the person again. But it's also a way to meet people with the same interests as you.

CHAPTER EIGHT

Izzy's headphones were on, and she was banging out a knowledge article for the latest software release to the synthesized brilliance of her Pandora 80s station when a yellow Peanut M&M dropped onto her keypad. Then a blue one. She looked up and saw Hector leaning over the cubicle wall above her. His great big smile was infectious, and she dropped her headphones to her neck and smiled back. Billy Idol's "White Wedding" continued to play from her shoulders.

"Damn girl! You're gonna go deaf with your music on so loud."

"Hey, Hector." She ignored his comment. He was one to talk. His car vibrated with the bass he cranked when he arrived every morning. She stretched. A quick glance at the clock on her monitor told her she'd been writing for four hours straight. No wonder her neck was stiff and her shoulders were tight. She'd have to go for a run later to get rid of some of the tension. How she'd fit it in was a mystery, since she had four more articles to write after this one.

Hector tossed an M&M into the air and caught it in his mouth. "It's quittin' time. We're getting ready to head over to Lefty's to celebrate the release. You wanna go?"

Izzy grimaced and ran her tongue across her front teeth. "That's a great way to break a tooth, you know."

"It'll look great with the love handles I'm working on." He slapped his nonexistent paunch. "You gonna come, or what?"

She leaned back in her chair. He always asked. She rarely went. "I don't know, Hec. Your release celebration means an avalanche of work for me. I have a bunch of articles to hammer out by Friday, when the public release is announced." She and he both knew work was only part of the reason.

He gave her a pathetic, hangdog look. "Please? You'll get it done. You always do. Come for an hour. We're getting ready to head over right now. You can pick it up later tonight if you want to."

She really did love that he always asked. Her tight shoulders told her she needed to take a break anyway. She sighed. "Sure. Why not? Let me just close this one out and send it for review. I'll meet you over there in less than fifteen." The look on his face was its own reward. So much for that run.

He drummed a short beat on the cubicle wall. "Sweet! See you soon!"

Ten minutes later, Izzy finished the article and shut down her laptop. As she gathered her things, guilt bubbled up inside her. Gus. She hated leaving him home alone for another hour or so, especially since she knew she'd be working extra hours the rest of the week. Then she remembered the dog-walking company had taken him to the dog park down the street from her house that day. He also had the doggy door. It wasn't a terrible thing, she told herself, even as she made a mental note to swing by Petropolis to get him a new elk antler on the way home.

Lefty's was just across the street from the Gigify campus, and it took Izzy only a few minutes to drop off her laptop at her car in the parking structure and head over. The warm air provided a nice contrast to the air-conditioning inside the building. It was still light out, with sunset a few hours away. Part of her wished she was going home for a run, but Hector's smile when she said she'd join them was enough to keep her from flaking out on him.

The little bar, a square, one-story building, featuring a flashing neon sign lighting up the whole area when it clicked on at dusk each night, had been in the same location for at least thirty years. It sat in the middle of a smallish blacktop parking lot surrounded by several much larger, much newer, business buildings. Neon beer signs gave it a festive look. At one time, Lefty's had been a biker bar on the far outskirts of town. However, with the boom of Silicon Valley, it was now right in the middle of things, and the bikers had been squeezed out when all the tech geeks had taken over. Izzy would have loved to see the early days when the first programmers in their short-sleeved button-up shirts with pocket protectors had ventured into Lefty's for a drink.

Visions of the geeks and bikers sitting shoulder to shoulder at the bar made her laugh.

She opened the big wooden front door and walked into the dim pub. Not much had changed after the bikers left. Although it was a non-smoking establishment, like all public buildings in California, the air hinted at ancient cigarette smoke and spilled beer. The décor was still predominantly Harley-Davidson inspired, and the front wheel and handle bars of a chromed-out classic soft tail was mounted on the center of the wall behind the bar, flanked on each side by mirrored shelves of liquor. The bartenders dressed like bikers in leather vests and chaps.

Izzy spotted Hector and his group over in the far corner near the bar, and she weaved through tables to meet them. The noisy bar was crowded three people deep watching the Giants game on a couple of huge TV screens mounted at each end of the bar.

"I wasn't sure you would actually come. I saved you a seat." Hector shouted as he took his backpack off the seat to his right and pulled the chair out.

She smiled apologetically. "I almost didn't, but you asked so nicely."

Hector pretended to be offended. "I'm always nice!"

The other developers at the table groaned and laughed.

He glared at everyone around the table. "Well, at least when the release is on schedule and we're not dealing with any major risks."

Ganesh, who was sitting across the table, raised his beer bottle. "Here's to a release going out on time for once."

The rest of the developers at the table clinked their bottles and glasses together.

Izzy picked up an unclaimed water glass and clinked it along with the rest.

Hector laid his hand on her shoulder. "We have to get you a drink. What are you having? Arnold Palmer? 7Up?"

Jane appeared behind Izzy and put a bottle of beer from a local brewery on the table in front of her. "Oh." She sounded hesitant. "I was at the bar when I saw you come in and…well, I can get you something else."

Izzy took a sip from the bottle. "Beer is great. Thank you."

Why'd she say that? She couldn't remember the last time she'd had a beer. Wine was more her style, but even that was rare. She rarely drank alcohol, but when a pretty woman bought her a drink…

Jane looked relieved and pushed a stray hair behind her ear. "For a second I thought I'd committed a huge faux pas."

Was Jane's hair different? It wasn't pulled back like she usually wore it. It looked soft and…wait. Jane had asked a question. "Um, not at all. Besides the calories, alcohol interacts with a medication I'm on. But I do partake every once in a while. Tonight's a perfect night for it. Thanks again."

Jane sat in the empty seat next to Izzy and looked her up and down. Izzy blushed.

"You surely aren't worried about calories, are you?"

"At my age, I can't afford not to be." Jeez, she sounded like Hector and Audie, with all this talk about calories. But her mouth wouldn't stop. "Plus, the medication also has a side effect of weight gain. I stay ahead of the double whammy by running." Seriously. She needed to stop.

Jane sipped her beer. "I thought you looked like a runner. I wish I didn't hate it so much. Exercise is a wonderful medication on its own."

At least Jane hadn't asked about the medication. She had no idea why she'd even offered the information. Being bipolar wasn't something she talked about much. Most people didn't understand enough about it. All they knew were the jokes and bizarre behavior some people exhibited when they weren't medicated properly. But Izzy had been on medication for a long time, and people would never be aware of her condition if she didn't tell them. For her, it was an invisible illness, and she liked to keep it that way. Tonight was no different. "I agree. Exercise and a good night's sleep are the keys to a wonderful life."

Jane raised her bottle. "Here's to good sleep and exercise. I'm glad you're here. Hector said you don't usually come to these."

Izzy bumped Hector's arm. "Hector probably didn't tell you my job kicks into overdrive when yours finishes. So, I'm usually working longer days right about now."

Hector returned the arm bump and leaned forward to see Jane. "Don't let her fool you. Izzy works long days all the time. She wants to make us all look like we're slacking off."

"I noticed," Jane said. "Last week we were putting in twelve- to fourteen-hour days, and she was here before us and still here when we left most days." Jane looked at Izzy. "I don't know how you do it. Lester was pissed at me."

"Lester?" Hadn't Jane said she dated women?

"My dog. He knows he's the boss."

Izzy already liked Jane, but she liked her more for being a dog person. "I bring Gus in with me on long days. He has a bed under my desk."

Jane sipped her beer. "Lester doesn't understand the long days. My schedule at the university isn't as taxing as the one here. This has been an adjustment for him."

Ganesh leaned across the table. "Izzy takes better care of Gus than I take care of my kids. He has a bandana for every occasion, and she has the mobile groomer come out at least once a week. He's the nicest-smelling animal I've ever let kiss me on the lips."

Izzy grinned. "What can I say? He's a passionate dog."

"He's a lucky dog," Ganesh said.

"I baby my boy, too," Jane said. "I think I'll bring Lester into the office and see how he does. I already planned to take him to the dog park this weekend to make up for all the long days."

"Gus and I go to the one by the university all the time."

"We usually go to the one closer to my house, but the one by the university is nicer. We should go together some time."

Izzy started to politely decline, but something overrode the warning signals going off in her head. Before she knew what happened, she and Jane had made plans to meet up at the dog park by the university. It wasn't like it was a date, right? Besides, she had Gus to think of, and he loved the dog park. It would be selfish *not* to go.

❖

Nature is full of elaborate mating dances. Just tune in to the Animal Channel, and you'll see birds with brilliant plumage strut for each other. You'll witness the great clashing of antlers and horns as large mammals rut with one another. You'll see solitary reptiles come out of hiding to impress each other with feats of strength and agility, all for the purpose of trying to attract a mate. This ritual is such a part of the natural world, you sometimes don't even know it when you see it. Take a cat who rubs its face against yours. It isn't just being affectionate; it's rubbing its scent on you, claiming you. You had no idea you were leading your cat Twinkles on when you allowed him to rub on you, did you?

When it comes to humans, though, some people like to think humans invented flirting. They don't like to think an act so exciting is actually an instinct. But flirting is a dance of give and take, the very beginning of the mating ritual. When you flirt with an interesting person and they flirt back with you, you know they're interested. It's an integral part of who we are. Never mind the same exciting performance acted out between two humans is the same performance acted out when the female praying mantis gives in to the male praying mantis, mates with him, and then rips his head off. But I digress...

Chapter Nine

Sunshine warmed Izzy's back as she sat on the wrought-iron bench, watching Gus play with a couple of golden retrievers. Saturday mornings were busy at Afton Hollow Dog Park. She'd arrived a little early for her meet-up with Jane after she took Gus on a short run. Now, she was just hanging out waiting for Jane while Gus played. He was running circles around the two dogs while they crouched and barked, feinting attacks at him. He was in canine heaven.

Izzy, however, was battling a world-class case of the jitters, bordering on terror. What had she been thinking, making plans with Jane? It wasn't a date, but no way could they be friends when her heart raced every time she saw Jane and thoughts of Jane invaded her mind at odd hours each day. She sat forward, prepared to leave, but she really didn't want to, did she? It would be rude, and Gus was having fun. But more than that, she really wanted to see Jane. She sat back and took several deep breaths as she tried to distract herself from the feelings she needed to not have.

The retrievers looked as if they could be litter mates, but they belonged to two different people, a man and a woman who had arrived separately. They stood several feet apart, watching their dogs play. The woman alternated between watching her dog and her phone. The man alternated between watching his dog and the woman. The woman appeared unaware of the man's gaze, but she played with her hair and looked like she might be aware of being watched. It wasn't long before the man moved closer and started to talk to her.

Izzy was out of earshot, but she observed them with interest, amused by their complex interaction. Even from here, she could tell they were flirting.

The man petted his dog affectionately but distractedly as he spoke to the woman, their dogs being the common interest bringing them together, aside from their obvious attraction to one another. They laughed as the dogs played between them until, in their exuberance, they ran into the woman, who teetered, throwing out her arms to catch her balance. The man moved quickly, grabbing her elbow and saving her. It was the perfect scenario for them to establish their need for one another. The woman pushed her hair behind her ear and glanced up at the man through her eyelashes, laughing. The man pushed out his chest, and Izzy expected him to pound it like a mighty silverback gorilla.

Izzy had been exceptionally aware of flirting since she'd started writing the chapter about it in her book. Before then, she was clueless. She didn't know how to flirt, and she never knew when someone was flirting with her. Direct and to the point were more her style. All the hair playing and coquettish talents displayed by the woman were beyond her.

Her friends hadn't been much help either. Hilde said buying someone a beer at a bar was classic flirtation, and Heidi said smiling a lot and laughing at someone's jokes was the best way to flirt. Shawna suggested touching when talking was a sign someone was flirting with you. But Izzy dismissed all of their ideas when she simply used herself as context. She touched people all the time when she talked, and she wasn't flirting. Buying someone a drink and listening to them when they talked was just a nice thing to do.

"You got here before us."

It was a pleasant surprise when Jane sat next to her, pulling her from her thoughts.

"Who do we have here?" Izzy asked, talking to the handsome white dog at Jane's feet. He had a red bandana tied around his neck and was one of the cutest bulldogs Izzy had ever seen.

"This is Lester." Jane leaned forward to scratch the husky dog's neck with both hands.

Clearly jealous, Gus came bounding up and started sniffing Lester.

Jane reached a hand out to Gus and ended up with a palm full of Gus saliva. She laughed. "This must be Gus."

"The one and only. Be careful. As you can see, he's vicious."

Jane looked up, confused. "He seems so sweet."

Izzy laughed. "I'm just kidding. He's super friendly. If someone broke into my house, he'd probably show them straight to the valuables, but only after licking them to death."

"Of course you were joking." Jane rolled her eyes and pushed a couple stray hairs behind her ear. A slight blush crept over her cheeks.

Was Jane nervous? She wasn't alone. Izzy was about to leap out of her skin.

Hiding her feelings, she scratched behind the bulldog's ears. "Your mama is so funny!"

"Lester, do you want to go run around with Gus?" Jane asked. She detached his leash and gestured toward the open grass. Gus took a few excited leaps toward the center of the park and glanced back. Lester looked up at Jane before he ambled after him. Lester appeared sedate compared to Gus, who ran back and forth between Lester and the open grass.

The man with the retriever walked by the bench with his dog, and Izzy searched for the woman. She was near the exit with her dog, holding hands with another woman. Izzy laughed to herself. She'd gauged the situation all wrong. Judging by the guy's expression, he had, too.

"Our boys seem to get along," Jane said.

Izzy returned her attention to the dogs, who were playing. "Gus has never met someone he doesn't like."

"Lester mostly can't be bothered with other dogs. I was a little surprised when he followed Gus. Normally, he just sort of strolls around the park and comes back after he's done. As you can see, he's not one for much exercise."

Lester was sitting out in the grass while Gus ran circles around him.

"He looks quite muscular to me." Izzy turned away from Jane and rolled her eyes, feeling like a dork. Muscular? Really?

"He could stand to lose a few pounds. Then again, I've never seen a trim English bulldog." Jane wrapped Lester's leash around her hand and kept clasping and unclasping the hook. Maybe Izzy wasn't the only nervous one.

"I've always loved bulldogs." Why was she finding it so hard to find something interesting to say?

They watched the dogs play.

"How do you like working at Gigify?" Izzy finally asked after a few minutes of wondering what to talk about.

Jane seemed to consider the question. "I love the company, and I love the team." She tilted her head back and forth. "But the work is pretty intense. I'm enjoying learning new things and honing my coding skills, but I've gotta be honest. I don't think I'd want to do it longer than the summer."

"That's longer than I'd last. Programming is definitely not my idea of fun. How do you keep your eyes from crossing after staring at a screen all day?"

Jane smiled at her. "Isn't that exactly what you do, writing tech docs all day?"

Izzy thought about it. "Well, yeah, I guess so. Writing is different, though."

Lester ambled back to the bench, and Izzy reached to pet his head. He turned and nuzzled into her hand with a rumbly groan.

Jane smiled at her. "He seems to like you. Normally, he just ignores everyone."

Izzy slid off the bench to the ground. She scratched his neck, which he responded to by pressing his head into her lap. "You like to snuggle, boy? I don't blame you. Your mama is super pretty."

Had she seriously said that aloud? Heat rose to her face. Fortunately, her position on the ground in front of the bench hid the blush from Jane. Fortunately, Gus saved her when he came back to the bench and dropped his head into her lap to get some affection for himself.

Jane laughed. "Looks like someone's a little jealous."

"He's not used to sharing me," Izzy said over her shoulder.

"Does he get jealous of your girlfriends, too?"

Izzy smiled to herself. *She knows I date women, too.* One less thing she'd have to navigate if they became friends. "I've never introduced him to a girlfriend."

Jane sounded puzzled. "Oh, you haven't had him for long then?"

Izzy snorted. "He adopted me at the pet fair at AT&T Park five years ago. It was love at first sight."

Jane seemed to think it over. "So, in five years, you haven't introduced him to any girlfriends?"

Izzy focused entirely on Gus. "I don't really date."

Jane was quiet for a moment, and Izzy could almost hear her thoughts. Why was she writing a book about love, then? What was wrong with her? What awful social issue made women stay clear of her? She wanted to explain, but she wouldn't. It would just prove to Jane how damaged she was.

"I hope this doesn't come out wrong—"

"But why am I writing a book on love if I don't have a clue how to do it myself?" Izzy said for her. She laughed. "Let me know the answer if you have it, because I keep asking myself the very same question."

Jane laughed with her. "Not what I was going to ask, but I guess it's a good question, too. I was going to ask how in the world someone like you avoids dating."

Someone like you? It sounded like a compliment coming from Jane. Maybe it was. "It's easy. I don't ask people out."

When she glanced over her shoulder, the little wrinkle between Jane's eyebrows was adorable, but Izzy could see the questions brewing behind her pretty eyes. It was hard to keep her wall up with this woman.

Jane clicked the clasp on the leash with renewed fervor. "I imagine you get asked out all the time, though."

Izzy untangled herself from the dogs and pushed herself up onto the bench. "Contrary to popular belief, not very often. Actually, never." The wall was crumbling, and her stomach churned.

"Impossible to believe." Jane put her hand on Izzy's arm. It felt like she was pressing warm sunshine into her skin, and her stomach settled.

"I just don't put myself out there for that kind of thing, I guess."

Jane patted her arm. "Well, if you did, you'd get scooped up in a heartbeat."

Izzy struggled to find a response to Jane's comment. She was saved when Jane squeezed her arm and pointed at their dogs, who were blissfully playing again.

"Aw! They love each other!"

❖

Back in the day, some people liked to keep a little black book. It was one way of keeping track of the people you were interested in. Nowadays, while it's easier to connect with people via various channels of social media, it may become more difficult to manage things if you're talking to, or dating, people you've met in various ways. Unless you're a serial dater and only date one person at a time, how do you remember where you met someone?

You could be like one of my friends (Audie, you know who you are) and just go with the flow. If you forget where you met someone, you ask. If you accidentally call a date by the wrong name, you laugh it off. Being direct totally works for her. It's part of her charm. But other people aren't as comfortable with this kind of thing. Me? It would bother me no end if I couldn't recall something important like where I met someone. I like to remember birthdays and favorite foods. I'm old-fashioned like that. So, I'd probably use a spreadsheet or at least some sort of electronic notebook where I compile and reference notes about people I'm dating.

So, whether you're old-fashioned or more on the cutting edge of dating, technology can be your friend.

Chapter Ten

Another document sent for review. Izzy closed her laptop, tossed it onto the bed, and rubbed her eyes. The room fell into shadowy darkness when the light from her screen went out. Eight p.m. already? How had it happened? Another Saturday spent working. At least she'd completed the last document. How long had it been since her queue had been empty? It called for a celebration. Visions of the ice cream she'd picked up at Trader Joe's danced in her head. A snore drifted up from the warm, furry mound pressed against her leg. She had to make a choice: ice cream or puppy snuggles? Was there really a choice?

She turned on the television, settling on a house fixer-upper episode she'd already seen. With its raised sink basin and glass-enclosed marble shower, it had inspired her to remodel her own guest bathroom, which was still not complete after almost six months. The sense of accomplishment from clearing her queue evaporated at the reminder. All she needed to do was replace the vanity counter. She did these projects herself on principle. She was handy, having grown up with a father who was a general contractor and brothers and sisters who had followed in his footsteps. But she never seemed to have the time. Projects always seemed to drag out.

Comforting her bruised pride with justifications, she picked up her personal laptop to message her brother Teddy to ask him to give her some references for a contractor. What would she do when he offered to do it himself, as she knew he would? She didn't want him to, but not because he'd tease her. That was a given she couldn't avoid. Mostly, it was because he was busier than she was, and she didn't want to put pressure on him. He and his husband had their hands full with five kids. But he was the sweetest of her brothers, and his teasing wouldn't go beyond the call or text thread she started. However, her three other brothers—Max, Grant, and Patrick—would give her unbearable, long-term grief, though not as much as her sisters Amelia and Viv would. She couldn't win. Teddy it would be. And she'd stand her ground on using the contractor.

She was just about to open the message app when she noticed the icon for the dating site blinking. Her email had been lighting up with notifications for days, but she'd ignored all of them so far. She still hadn't put a picture up, so she couldn't imagine what her "suitors" could be interested in.

Three messages and several winks. Interesting. The first message began with, "Hey, Baby." She deleted it without reading another word. She wasn't anyone's baby. The second one was from a woman whose profile picture featured her holding an automatic rifle. She deleted it. The third was an email from the site coordinator providing a list of potential connections the site algorithm had selected based on common interests.

She looked at the list of suggested connections. What kind of women would the site try to match her with? She hovered her finger over the delete button, but curiosity and a justification that she was doing research won out. She looked through the matches. Some of them seemed normal. Normal? What was "normal"? The first profile was Stacey from Santa Clara. Stacey was a nurse and forty-seven, just like Izzy. Oh, she was a runner, too. She and Stacey liked a lot of the same things. She enjoyed reading, but she liked to go out and do things, too. She appeared to be intelligent and active, an alluring combo. The more Izzy read, the more she liked Stacey from Santa Clara—until the last sentence. Stacey didn't like dogs. Bye-bye, Stacey from Santa Clara.

The next profile was a definite miss. The woman was twenty-three and looking for a sugar mama. She wrote it right there in the profile. "Seeking sugar mama." What was a "sugar mama," exactly? She had to look it up. Once she did, she knew she definitely wasn't into that kind of thing.

The next profile was better: Anaya, forty-four, from Cupertino. She looked familiar. A little buzz filled her stomach. Strikingly pretty. Long dark hair. She was a project manager from a local software-development company. They'd have things to talk about. Nothing in her profile raised any flags. If Izzy really *was* ready to date, and not just doing research, she might actually contact Anaya. Izzy ran through the remaining seven profiles in the list, most of which were completely off-target. One other was close, but she lived all the way over in Santa Cruz. Someone would have to be awfully special in order to make her want to drive to Santa Cruz for dating. And since it was just research, it was a no-go, too.

Izzy was just about to log out of the website, when she received an instant message from the app. Curious, but a little wary after her first experience with instant messaging, Izzy clicked on the blinking icon at the bottom of the page. It was Anaya from Cupertino. The little buzz of excitement flared in her stomach again.

It intrigues me when people don't post pictures. Who are you, mysterious I. Treadway?

Izzy considered the message for a moment, wondering if she should answer. What would she say? She considered playing it coy. She typed *I is for Intriguing*, but she deleted it and sent, *Hi, Anaya. I is for Izzy* instead.

Hi, Izzy. Is that short for something?

Isadora. My mom wasn't thinking about my future reputation when she picked it.

Was she flirting? She didn't even know she knew how. More interesting, she wasn't even nervous. Ah! The anonymity of the internet!

Isadora is a beautiful name. Quite noble, in fact. Anaya seemed even more familiar as they chatted.

Thank you.

So, why don't you have a profile picture?

I'm new to all of this. I haven't picked one out yet.

Picking the right picture is the worst. It's hard to figure out what you want others to see.

Your picture is lovely.

And it was. Then it struck her. Anaya looked quite a bit like Jane. Not in a twin-like way but close enough. The photo had even picked up on a playful glint in her eyes similar to Jane's. The buzz in her stomach dialed it up a couple notches. If Anaya was remotely like Jane, she'd be pretty awesome.

Thank you. I wasn't fishing for a compliment, I swear.

I didn't think you were. It's a lovely picture.

My sister took the picture on our birthday a few months ago.

Your sister and you have the same birthday?

LOL. We're twins.

Izzy smacked her forehead. Duh. So smooth. *You look happy.*
It's a rare picture that catches me genuinely smiling.

How weird would it be if Anaya was Jane's sister? There was more than a passing resemblance. Jane was almost always smiling, though. Why was she thinking about Jane? *Identical or fraternal? You don't usually smile?*

While she waited for Anaya to respond, she looked to see if Jane had a profile on the website. There were several Jane Mendozas, but she couldn't find one for the Jane she knew. Of course she didn't. A woman like Jane wouldn't need one. Besides, what would she have done if she found one? It wasn't as if she wanted to date her. Well, "want" wasn't the right word. "Should" was better. She didn't date. Period. Kelly had cured her of that. God! Could she just stop thinking about Kelly? She pushed thoughts of Kelly away to focus on the more pleasant, but still slightly confusing, thoughts about Jane.

A ding sounded when Anaya's response arrived.

Fraternal. My sister Rayann is much prettier than me. As
far as smiling goes, I do. All the time. But smiling for
pictures makes me self-conscious.

So, no connection to Jane. It was probably for the best. It would make work a little uncomfortable if she found out she was chatting up her sister. Why? She wasn't sure. It just would.

I find it hard to believe your sister could be prettier than you.
You have a beautiful smile.

She sent it without editing herself. Her thoughts about Jane made her forget her self-consciousness, which was the only way she could justify being so bold. She regularly gave compliments, but not usually to total strangers on dating websites who might take her remarks differently than they were intended. Like they meant something more. Because they didn't.

Thank you, Izzy. You're very kind.

Izzy hesitated. The buzz was completely gone. Did she want to continue talking to this pretty stranger? It wouldn't go anywhere. She rubbed the center of her chest. The familiar tightness was back. She did have research to do. *Just being honest, really.* She searched her mind for a way to say good night.

Well, thank you anyway.
You're welcome.
Will you send me a picture? Maybe just a quick selfie, so I
can see who I'm talking to.

She did *not* want to send a picture. *I'm a mess. I took a run earlier, and I have hat-hair.*

I don't care what you look like. I just want to see your eyes.

Her anxiety spiked, but why did she care? It was just research. She took a quick picture of herself with the camera on her laptop. Her hair actually wasn't as bad as she thought. She sent the picture before she could second-guess herself.

If that's a mess, I want to see you when you clean up. You have such warm eyes and a beautiful smile.

Izzy was embarrassed. *Thanks.*

I want to keep chatting with you, Izzy, but I have an early morning tomorrow. Can I message you again?

Izzy thought about it. Messaging wasn't a big deal, right? Until it turned to something more. She bounced her leg. She had complete control over whether it turned into anything else.

Sure. I don't come on here much, though.

We'll see how it goes, then. Good night, Izzy.

Anaya's profile went to inactive.

Izzy breathed out and rubbed her face. She was sweating. Had she really just chatted someone up on a dating website? She wasn't sure how she felt about it. Izzy scrolled through the message thread to make sure she hadn't made a fool of herself. Instead, she came off as more confident than she thought.

Proud of herself, she tossed the laptop onto the bed and got up for some ice cream.

Gus didn't even notice.

Ready to go out on a date? You've done the prep work, gotten to know some people, and have an idea of what you want, so it's time!

To get started, there are mainly two kinds of people: those who do the asking and those who wait to be asked. Some lucky people are in the middle and are good with both. If in the middle describes you, awesome! If you're the type to do the asking, that's also good, because the ball is in your court. The hardest part is figuring out how you're going to do it.

If you're the type who waits to be asked, well, it might be a little trickier. And if you're super shy, you could end up doing a lot of waiting before someone notices you're interested in being asked out. It's okay, though. It just requires a little more maneuvering on your part. You'll need to let the person you want to date know you wouldn't mind going out with them if they asked. You can do this subtly or you can do it brazenly. This advice goes back to the chapter on flirting. However you decide to do it, you just need to make your availability and willingness clear.

Chapter Eleven

How's the chapter on flirting going, Iz? Did you finally get it kicked out, or do you need a demonstration?" Izzy, Audie, and Jane were at the pick-up window of the Traveling Bean, which was parked outside of the Gigify campus. They waited for their coffee orders before finding a table in the shade.

Izzy rolled her eyes. "I'm good, thanks."

A passel of software engineers sitting at a nearby table looked at Izzy with interest, and one laughed and nudged the one to his left. She knew them from random meetings, but not personally. A bubble of self-consciousness rolled in her stomach. Were they talking about her writing the book? Or did she have a booger hanging from her nose? She rubbed her nose.

Regardless of whether Izzy was comfortable with it or not, most of the company knew she was working on the book because of Audie. Aside from explaining what it was about and why she, of all people, was writing it, Izzy was mostly okay with it. Folks were interested and eager to give their insight, which made things easier for her when she was delving into subjects outside her experience. The acknowledgments section was going to be a novel of its own!

"You sure you don't need to see a demonstration of an expert at work?" Audie's eyes were focused on something behind Izzy. Was that drool glistening on Audie's lips?

Izzy looked over her shoulder. Ah! The company-sponsored cross-fit class. She should have known. They were in the middle of their morning routine. Izzy could see the instructor in her mind's eye, looking all sporty in her micro shorts and sports bra, all six of her abdominal muscles tanned and defined, glistening with sweat as she marched between her students telling them to give her another ten super-hard cross-fitty somethings.

"What? Are you gonna go interrupt them in the middle of their workout with a subtle 'How *you* doin'?'" Izzy asked.

Jane laughed, and a buzzy, happy tremble flitted through Izzy's chest at the sound.

"Give me some credit here." Audie gestured toward the group. "She looks like she's thirsty. I'd take her a bottle of water and my phone number. It's all in the interest of research, though. I'd be helping you out."

"I'm sure you would." Izzy took her coffee from the barista. "But I finished that chapter a week ago. I'm on the asking-someone-on-a-date chapter now."

It had also been a week since her online chat with Anaya. The more she thought about it, and despite the acid reflux it seemed to cause, the more she talked herself into actually doing the things she wrote about. She could call it field research. Who was going to listen to her advice if she couldn't speak from experience? Plus, there was something about Anaya. She snuck a look at Jane. They really could be twins. Maybe. Whatever it was, she was ready for the next step. A gurgle of anxiety trembled in her stomach.

"The chapter you're talking about sounds super interesting and fun." Jane accepted her mocha from the barista. A dollop of whipped cream slid down the side, and Jane licked it up before it dropped.

A tremble of another sort echoed a little lower in Izzy's body, and she forced her gaze away from Jane's pink tongue licking the whipped cream from her plump lips. *Stop it! All this book research has turned you into a horny coed!*

"I can give you tips on the asking-someone-on-a-date chapter, too, Iz." Audie was looking at her now. Had Audie watched her objectify Jane and the whipped cream?

"I think this chapter is going to be harder than the flirting one. I'm not sure I've actually asked someone out on a date before. It's been so long since I've even been on one."

She said she wasn't sure, but she was. She and Kelly had never dated per se. They'd just sort of fallen into bed together after a softball game. Their relationship had consisted of several months of urgent sex and times between when she thought about nothing else but getting Kelly into bed again. Lust and love had hit her hard at the same time, but they hadn't ever really dated.

She hadn't dated Siobhan, either. They'd met at a company conference in Las Vegas, and their rooms had been next to one another. After one of the dinners, they'd walked back to their rooms, and when Izzy was unlocking her door, Siobhan had kissed her. She'd been too shocked to do anything other than respond to her body, which really, really liked what Siobhan did to her. Siobhan had gone back to Ireland the next morning. Long-distance didn't work very well, and after a year of never seeing each other, they both had agreed it wasn't working and they'd remained friends.

God. Thinking about it all made Izzy's stomach ache.

Suffice it to say, Izzy had no experience at all with dating, and the mere thought of it made her physically ill.

She watched Audie dump several packets of artificial sweetener into her coffee, stir it, and then put the wooden stirrer into her mouth. "It's easy. You just ask someone if they want to do something you both enjoy doing."

She said it as if it were the easiest thing in the world. And for her, it probably was. Izzy didn't know the first thing about asking someone out on a date. The prospect terrified her. "What if you don't know what they enjoy? What if they say no?"

Audie chewed on the stirrer. "You find out during the flirting. If they flirt back, they'll probably say yes. And usually, you get to know a little about someone."

"Eating is always a good choice," Jane said. "Or coffee. Meeting up during the day doesn't come with all the pressure, and you can leave after a short amount of time if it isn't working out."

Izzy tipped her cup toward Jane. "Good idea."

"Oh, boy. Are you thinking about asking someone specific out? Like, a *real* person?" Audie put her cup on the table and looked at her expectantly.

Jane put her cup down, too, and looked at her.

Izzy wasn't sure she appreciated the disbelief.

Both of them watched her so avidly, clearly waiting for the answer, Izzy suddenly felt a little scared. "Maybe. I haven't made up my mind."

"Who?" they asked in unison.

Izzy stared at her coffee cup, glanced up at them, and went back to staring at the cup. "A woman I've been talking to online."

She glanced up again to gauge their responses. Jane wore a weird expression, and Audie looked amused.

Audie pointed at her. "You didn't tell me you were talking to someone online."

Jane looked at her phone. "I have to get back for a meeting."

"We still on for lunch today?" Izzy asked as Jane got up.

"I'm not sure. It depends on what work Hector has for me." Jane sounded a little distracted. "I'll let you know."

Izzy watched Jane walk back toward the building. Her thick, black braid glistened in the sun.

"Who's this online woman?" Audie nudged her arm. "How long have you been talking to her?"

"Only a week. She seems really nice."

Audie wiggled her eyebrows. "You've been trolling the dating websites?"

"Trolling?" Izzy shot a look at her. "I don't even know how to troll anything. It's solely for research."

"Oh, yeah. Research."

Audie didn't believe her, she could tell.

❖

Later that evening, Izzy sat at her desk in her home office and logged into her personal email. She hadn't mustered the courage to log into the dating website since her last chat with Anaya. What if Anaya saw her online and messaged her? She'd made up her mind to ask her out on a date, but it didn't mean she wasn't terrified of it. She needed a little time to get there.

Nestled in among the email from various organizations she donated to was a notification from the dating website that she had an unread message from Anaya.

She froze. Excitement in her gut mingled with paralyzing fear. She sat there staring at the email for several minutes before selecting the link taking her to the app to view the message. Her fingers moved with numb effort.

Why was she so scared?

She knew exactly why. She was venturing into perilous territory. She breathed out. This time would be different. She was going in with knowledge and no expectations. It was only research. She could protect herself.

She read the message, and all of her anxiety fell away. A single unassuming line. *Hope to see you online sometime soon!—A.* So normal. So unthreatening.

A subtle ding sounded, and the instant message icon lit up.

Hey, Izzy! How was your day?

It was Anaya. A pang of excitement flared along with a little of the anxiety she'd built up over the last few days.

Good. How was yours?

I finally finished a big project I've been working on, and it closed under budget and on time. It's a pretty big deal. So, it was a really good day.

Congratulations!

Thanks! How would you like to meet me somewhere for a celebratory drink?

Anaya had turned the tables.

Sure. When?

Her fingers were numb again.

Tonight? Unless you have something else going on or something.

Tonight? She couldn't. It was too quick.

I don't have anything planned.

Her fingers had typed it without her knowledge.

So, you'll meet me?

Sure. It sounds fun.

What spirit had possessed her? While Izzy wondered what had gotten into her, Anaya suggested a sports bar, and they agreed on a time. The crush of anxiety she felt was normal, right? She could barely feel her legs when she got up to go find something to wear. Was she really going out to meet someone she'd met online? Every terrible outcome of the impetuous meeting tried to swamp her mind. *Stop it. Stop it. Stop it,* she chanted to herself. This wasn't real life. It was just research.

She went through the motions of changing her clothes in a numb fog.

❖

Izzy pulled into a space in the parking lot at the Handlebar and turned off her car. Was she really there meeting a woman she had never met in person before? She was nervous. Beyond nervous. Terrified. She fought back an urge to message Anaya to tell her something had come up, and she had to cancel. No. She said she'd be there, and she would. She would go in and tell her she could stay only an hour. That way, if she wasn't having a good time, she had an excuse to leave. And if they hit it off, they could always arrange another meeting. Cool. She had a plan.

Izzy opened the car door and got out before she could lose her nerve. The bar was crowded. The Giants were playing, and there were quite a few patrons in the bar wearing jerseys. She looked around and saw a woman similar to Anaya's profile picture sitting at a tall table in the center of the room and talking to a server, who was laughing. A good sign. She approached the table.

Anaya's face lit up. She was prettier than her picture.

"You came!"

The warm greeting eased a little of Izzy's anxiety, but all she could manage in way of a response was "Hi." She felt conspicuous just standing there.

Anaya didn't seem to notice. She pulled out the stool next to her. "You look just like your photo."

Izzy sat. Why wouldn't she look like her picture? "You say it like you're surprised."

Anaya pushed her long hair over her shoulder. "I sort of am. Maybe one in five people looks anything like their profile picture."

She wondered how many people Anaya had dated from the website. "Really?"

"Really."

"I sent you an unedited, unrehearsed selfie the first time we messaged."

"You have no idea how many people pretend their photos are casual snapshots that just happened to come out great. They totally posed or edited them."

"The picture I sent was definitely not posed. You got the real me, hat hair and all."

"Well, *now* I know. Before, it was a crapshoot."

Izzy suddenly felt a little dizzy. If she had even thought people not being the person they said they were was a possibility, she knew she wouldn't be here now. She sat on her hands so Anaya couldn't see them shaking.

Anaya flipped her hair over her shoulder again, and Izzy wondered if it was a nervous habit. She didn't look nervous otherwise.

Izzy adjusted her stool so she was facing Anaya more directly and wondered how many times Anaya had met with people from the dating site to be so jaded about the photo thing. "Well, you look exactly like your picture."

Anaya smiled, and she had a little dimple just like Jane. But the more Anaya talked, the less she reminded her of Jane.

"I think I told you my sister took it. We were on our birthday trip to Iceland."

A nice, neutral topic. Izzy's insecurity started to fade. "How was Iceland? I've always wanted to go."

Anaya's eyes gleamed with memories.

"It was fantastic. There's so much to see. The people are nice. Oh, and they drink like there's no tomorrow. Speaking of which, do you know what you want? It's happy hour for another five minutes, so you should order two of whatever you choose."

No drinks tonight. Definitely not on a first meeting with someone. "I can't stay long. I have a thing in about an hour."

Anaya didn't seem bothered by the news and waved the bartender over.

"Willy! Get the lady a drink!" Anaya leaned close. The smell of whiskey on her breath wasn't the turn-off she thought it would've been. "Get two anyway. I'm buying, and I'll drink whatever you don't. I'm celebrating the closure of the project from hell."

Izzy ordered a soda water. Anaya looked surprised, but Izzy didn't feel the need to explain her medical history. Not when she barely knew Anaya. One mention that she was bipolar, and people quickly distanced themselves. If things went well and they became friends, maybe she wouldn't turn tail and run.

"Tell me more about this project you're so glad is over," she said.

Anaya flipped her hair once again. "I don't want to bore you. It's technical. Suffice it to say, it's over, and I'm super glad."

Izzy arched an eyebrow. "I'm a technical writer. It's my job to understand techy things."

A smile lit up Anaya's expressive face. "I knew there was a reason I liked you. I'm in software."

Common ground. That was good. "Me, too. So, try me. Tell me about your project."

Anaya described the project, and the conversation moved on to trips they had each taken. Izzy looked at her watch. An hour had passed in what felt like minutes, and Izzy was surprised she didn't want to leave.

Anaya looked at her with a frown softened by the three more drinks she'd had in the meantime. "I don't want you to go."

Izzy took a sip of her club soda. "I can stay a little longer."

Anaya's frown turned to a giddy smile. "Yay." She clapped. Then suspicion clouded her expression. "Hey! You only said you had another thing to have an excuse to leave. In case I was some weirdo. Am I right?"

Izzy hesitated. "It's true."

Anaya laughed with a twinkle in her eyes, again reminding her of Jane. *Stop that!* She forced herself to focus on Anaya, who was describing herself.

"I'm actually quite boring. I work. I run. I watch sappy rom-com movies in my jammies. Infrequently, I join a friend for drinks. I don't have a secret life as a serial killer." She grabbed Izzy's shirtsleeve. "Not one I admit to, anyway." She quickly fell into peals of laughter. "As you can see, I wouldn't be able to hide it if I did."

Izzy laughed harder than she had in a long time, and it felt good.

"You lied about one thing. You *are* a weirdo." Izzy felt a little drunk herself, even though she'd had nothing stronger than soda water.

"I am. I really am." Anaya wiped her eyes.

"Anaya!" A tall guy appeared behind her, hugging her.

"Jake!" Anaya turned around in her seat and hugged the newcomer back. "This is my friend Izzy. Jake lets me beat him at trivia all the time. Izzy is helping me celebrate the end of the project from hell."

Jake high-fived her. "The dreaded project is over? Sounds like we need a round of shots!"

He waved to Willy, who came over already armed with a bottle of Fireball whiskey and three shot glasses, which he poured and pushed in front of the three of them before Izzy could say she didn't want one.

"To good friends and the end of shitty projects!" Anaya called out as she lifted her shot.

Izzy raised her shot, and she and Jake tapped their glasses to Anaya's. Instead of drinking hers, Izzy took a sip of her soda water. Anaya downed hers and winked at her and downed the other.

❖

Has this ever happened to you? You're interested in someone in your circle of friends. You think they might like you in the same way, but you're not sure. They're attentive. They laugh at all your jokes.

They call to see how your Aunt Phyllis's hernia operation went after you mentioned how worried you were. They bring you miso soup when you don't show up for the weekly potluck because you have the flu. It's more attention than you received from your last three relationships combined. You start to think they might be romantically interested in you. But their behavior is so subtle, you start to think you might be reading into things.

One afternoon, they ask you if you want to go to a movie. It's just you and them. They say they want to spend some one-on-one time with you! Could this be it? You've waited so long!

The theater is mostly empty when the movie starts. It's a comedy. You sit shoulder to shoulder and look at each other often during the funny parts. Their hand lingers when they grab your leg at a particularly funny part. You grab hands at another funny part. You spend the rest of the movie wondering if they will take your hand again, and you can't concentrate on the storyline, but you laugh in the right parts and continue looking at them to share in the humor.

The movie ends. You don't want the date to end. Is it a date? You try to work up the nerve to ask if they want to get a cup of coffee, but before you ask, they say their dog has been at home alone for most of the day, and they need to get home. Is it an excuse? You wonder how to say good-bye. While you debate between a hug or a kiss, your friend goes in for the hug. You hug them back, and the hug is longer than the one when you greeted. Your cheeks even touch. They pull away but hold both of your hands and say they want to do more things with you like this, just you and them. You turn to leave, but they turn and ask about your Aunt Phyllis. You tell them Aunt Phyllis is doing great.

I can totally understand your confusion over the mixed signals. It's so unnerving not to know if someone is interested in you the way you might be in them. It takes so much energy to try to read their actions.

The good news is, there's an easy way to figure this out. It's a simple method I'm surprised more people don't use. I think this advice will be well worth the price of this guide. Ready for it?

Ask them.

CHAPTER TWELVE

The Gigify commissary was bustling with the lunchtime rush. A group at a table nearby stood to leave, and Izzy took the table, motioning Jane and Audie to follow.

"How do you always find rock-star seating?" Jane shook her head in amazement.

"If I told you, I'd have to kill you."

Jane laughed, and Izzy smiled at the melodic tinkle of it. It was a nice break from her obsessive thoughts about the impromptu meeting with Anaya churning through her mind all morning. Her mind had been like a little dog, chasing every detail around, and she couldn't stop it. It happened every time new things occurred in her life, but none of the practiced coping mechanisms were helping—not meditation, not redirecting, not writing it down to deal with later. None of them. She hadn't tried the reboot yet, but that was just for dire situations.

Audie slid into the seat next to Izzy at the round table. Jane chose a seat on her other side.

Audie shoulder-bumped her. "You look like you have something on your mind, my friend."

She could always count on Audie to notice and be direct about it. "I do."

Audie took a bite of her salad. "Is it the book? Or is it work? Because if it's work, you know I am so not your girl."

Jane patted Izzy's arm. "I could help with the technical-writing thing."

Izzy loved how quickly Jane offered to help. She was so nice. So was Audie, but Audie didn't make her stomach flutter.

"It's nothing work related." Izzy took a bite of her pizza and covered her mouth to continue while she chewed. "It's about dating."

Audie smirked and pushed her sleeves up. "You definitely came to the right place. Lay it on me. What do you need to know?"

"What technically constitutes a date?"

Audie steepled her hands in front of her, a wizened benefactor of knowledge. She cleared her throat. "It's when someone asks another person to do something together at a pre-designated time in the future."

Izzy threw a napkin at her. "Smart-ass! I'm wondering if impulsively meeting someone at a restaurant or bar is technically a date."

Audie picked up the napkin and tossed it back. "What do you think?"

"I don't know." Izzy picked at her pizza. "I should know this stuff because I'm writing about it, but I'm learning as I go."

"Did someone ask you to meet them somewhere? Is that where this is going?"

Audie sounded surprised, and Izzy didn't appreciate the lack of confidence. She glanced at Jane, but Jane was studying her lunch.

"You say it as if I'm not capable of it."

Audie only smirked back. When she looked at Jane for reassurance, all Jane did was keep picking at her salad.

"Just last week you were questioning it yourself. What's changed, dare I ask?" Audie asked.

Izzy wasn't sure she wanted to give too many details just yet. She hadn't worked out how she felt about it. "Well, I met up with someone from one of the dating sites."

Jane continued to pick at her salad, but Audie slammed down her fork and twisted her fingers in her ears.

"I think I heard you wrong. I thought I heard you say you met up with someone from a dating site."

Izzy wanted to throw her pizza crust at her. "Shut up. You heard me right."

Audie picked up her fork. "Holy Shih-tzus! You're quicker than I thought you'd be."

She knew Audie would overreact. But that was how Audie was about everything, she reminded herself. She waved her hand breezily, even though she felt far from casual about the whole thing. "It was just a quick hookup. Nothing major," Izzy said.

Audie's eyebrows disappeared under her spiky bangs, and Jane finally looked up from her salad.

Audie pushed her lunch to the side. "Do you mean hooked up in the biblical sense?"

She realized her poor choice of words. "Hooked up for a drink, nothing more. A spur-of-the-moment thing. We met at a sports bar and hung out for about an hour and then called it a night."

"How was it?" Jane asked. She was staring at her salad again.

Izzy watched her for a second, but Jane didn't look up. She seemed preoccupied.

Audie didn't seem to notice Jane's distraction. "I need deets, my friend. This requires a full expository presentation."

Izzy struggled to describe Anaya without comparing her to Jane. "She's all right. Nice. Smart. It was loud in there, and it was hard to hear, but she seemed like a cool person."

"And..." Audie waved her fork impatiently. A piece of lettuce flew off and landed unnoticed on the back of a developer sitting at the next table.

"And what? That's it." Izzy plucked the lettuce from Amit's T-shirt.

Audie let go of a dramatic sigh. "And...what did you wear? What did she wear? Where did you go? What does she look like? Did you like her? Were there sparks?" Audie fired off her questions like a machine gun. "But most importantly, did you make plans to meet up again?"

"Jeans. Business suit. The Handlebar. She's attractive. She seems nice. As you know, I'm clueless about sparks." She paused in her answers to give Audie a meaningful stare. No way was she going to get into a discussion about why sparks weren't in her bailiwick right then, in front of Jane. This was new territory for her. She was shaking in her boots. She had no idea how to navigate this new territory. Thankfully, Audie's mouth was full of salad, and she didn't press. "As far as meeting up again, we didn't get a chance to get into it. A friend of hers showed up, and I left before they did."

Audie flashed a knowing smile. "Ah. The old-friend defense."

She was clueless. "What?"

"It's when you arrange ahead of time to have a friend show up with an escape plan in case the date doesn't go well."

"It wasn't a date, and the friend showing up seemed like it was unexpected."

The knowing smile returned. "They all do. Do you want to see her again?"

Did she? She kind of did. And her anxiety wasn't masquerading as a heart attack but more like she was about to go bungee jumping. That meant something. "I'm not sure what I want. Part of me wants to just let it go because it's such a hassle. But part of me wants to see how it could go. I guess I should just play it out for research, if for nothing else."

Audie nodded knowingly but gave her a half-smile. "I support the research."

Jane didn't weigh in.

Izzy pushed her uneaten pizza aside. "All this stuff makes me nervous. I've started running more."

Izzy snuck a glance at Jane. Audie knew all about her condition. She knew she ran more when she was trying to avoid an episode. But she hadn't mentioned it to Jane, and she didn't seem to pick up on it. When Izzy looked back at Audie, her eyes had softened. She got it. Izzy was grateful her best friend was always there for her when she needed it. Gratitude flooded her. She could always count on Audie when it mattered most.

"I think you look great even without all the running," Jane said. It was the first time she'd seemed interested in the conversation. "Why do women think they need to change themselves in order to make people like them?"

Izzy didn't know how to respond. Jane thought she was running to be more attractive for dating. That was funny.

But before she could answer, Jane stood and smiled. "I meant it rhetorically. I gotta go. I have a lot of work to do."

They watched Jane leave the table.

Izzy started to clean up the remains of her lunch. "She was a little preoccupied. I hope we didn't bore her with the mundane talk about my nonexistent dating life."

Audie looked at Izzy, shook her head, and laughed. "Yeah. That's exactly what it was."

There was something more to it, and it seemed Audie knew what it might be, but Izzy was already overwhelmed, so she didn't ask.

❖

Picking the location for a first date is an important decision. A lot hangs on it. Not only does it make an early first impression, but it might end up being the much-repeated first-date story of a lifelong romance if things work out.

There's a lot to consider when you pick a location. How was the date initiated? Is it a blind date? Do you know the person very well, or did you just meet them? Was the date requested after a period of casual conversations, or was it a spur-of-the-moment thing? Is the situation formal, or is it casual? Do you want it to be a surprise? Do you have a budget to work within? Are you feeling romantic, adventurous, or just horny?

Once you know the location, deciding what clothes to wear is easier. Something to keep in mind is it's always polite to let your date know what you'll be wearing. No one enjoys feeling under- or overdressed.

Chapter Thirteen

Izzy cut the sandwich she'd just made for dinner in half and picked up her laptop to take into the living room, where she planned to work on the book. She was writing the chapter about planning for a first date, something she had no experience with, since she'd never actually asked someone on a date or officially been on one.

What she'd seen on television and in movies seemed overly angst-ridden. Would they, or wouldn't they? Should I, or shouldn't I? All the what-ifs. Why didn't people just be straightforward about what they wanted and accept the response when it was given? Easy peasy. Maybe that should be the focus of the chapter. She'd underscore the need to be direct. *Follow your gut. Leave the games and silly head trips out of it.*

Happy to have a grasp of the subject, she got situated and opened the laptop. Instead of opening the manuscript, though, she clicked on her browser icon and logged on to the dating website. She'd been doing this more often since meeting Anaya in person. Most days, they managed to catch each other online at the same time, and they messaged each other. Anaya was easy to talk to, and Izzy looked forward to chatting with her online. It filled her with anxiety to imagine asking to see her in person again, but she figured she needed to just do it. Tonight was the night.

Anaya's profile icon was outlined in green, indicating she was active, and Izzy was about to say hello, but Anaya was quicker.

How's your day been? Did you finish all the work you said you had the other night?

Izzy smiled. She hadn't told Anaya about the book she was writing, but being in similar career fields, she had told her about the mountain of documents she'd been working on.

I did. I was even able to get off work at a decent time today and take Gus for a run.

Did you see the sunset?
It was beautiful.
I was wondering. Do you want to go on a real date? Nothing
*   fancy. Coffee or something. Someplace where we can*
*   actually hear each other talk?*

She shouldn't have been surprised, but she was. She'd been ready to ask Anaya out. They *were* chatting each other up on a dating website, after all. Still, she was taken off guard.

It's not a big deal, Anaya typed.

She'd taken too long to respond. The cacophony of thoughts in her mind quieted, and simple anxiety curdled her stomach as she read Anaya's words.

Anaya sent another message.

Unless you want it to be, that is. I suck at this part. I just
*   want to see you again. To check if you're as cool as I*
*   remember from the last time. I had a few drinks. Who*
*   knows if my memory is as good as it should be?*

Izzy typed her response before her mind glitched out again.

Sure. How about coffee on Saturday?

It's a date!

There was no ambivalence in the reply, Izzy thought. Relief swept through her before a new wave of anxiety blew in.

Was this still research, or was she really dating after swearing off it forever? How had this happened?

The new chapter could wait. She got up to go for a run.

"So, I have a real date," Izzy said while her coffee brewed, and she watched Jane select a perfect apple from the fruit bowl in the orange breakroom. She loved to watch Jane select fruit. It was always a process, and more often than not, Izzy found herself craving the piece of fruit Jane picked out. Today, Jane looked extra serious in her selection. Izzy pried her eyes from Jane and watched the coffee drip into her Wonder Woman cup.

"With who?" Audie was leaning against the counter watching the silent newsfeed on the giant TV monitor in the corner of the room. "Is it the woman from that dating site you met at the bar the other night?"

Izzy concentrated on the last drops falling into her coffee cup. It was a mixed bag, sharing information about this scary adventure with other people. They might have opinions. They might have input. It was hard enough handling her own thoughts about it. But doing it all on her own was even scarier. "Yeah. She asked me out to coffee this Saturday. She called it a date."

Jane harrumphed, and Izzy turned to look just in time to see her toss the apple back into the fruit bowl with a frown. The fruit was obviously subpar today. Jane went over to the bulk wall and filled a cup with Peanut M&M's.

Audie broke a stem of grapes from a bunch. "The dating-site lady likes you." She popped one of the grapes into her mouth with a grin.

"How do you know that?"

"Because she asked you to coffee." Audie pushed another grape into her mouth.

Audie ate her grapes as if it was a side note. She didn't do it the same way Jane did, as if they were individual parcels requiring attention and analysis. Izzy always knew if the grapes were tasty when Jane's eyes went half-closed and out of focus as she ate them.

"What does that have to do with anything?" Izzy poured half-and-half into her coffee.

Audie sighed as if the answer were obvious. "It's not another bar. Or her place. Coffee means she wants to talk. She wants to get to know you better. She must already like you, since she met you in person already. It means she's not trying to get you into bed right away."

"It could also mean she just wants to be friends," Izzy said. She poured a couple drops of agave into her coffee.

Audie sighed. "Did she call it a date, or did she call it a meetup?"

"She specifically asked if I wanted to go on a 'real date.'" Izzy leaned against the counter and stirred her coffee. She probably looked way more relaxed than she felt.

"Yeah, she likes you."

"I have some work to do," Jane said. The candies clattered in her cup as she spun around and walked toward the breakroom door.

"Okay," Izzy and Audie said in tandem and watched her leave the room.

"Did she seem grumpy or something to you?" Izzy wondered if she should follow Jane to ask her if something was wrong.

"Or something," Audie said.

"I think she's working too hard."

Audie looked at her with a half-smile.

"What?" Izzy sipped her coffee.

"If I didn't know better," Audie said, "I'd say she was a little jealous."

"Of me and you?"

Audie swatted her arm. "You're so dense sometimes. No, idiot. Of you and dating-site lady."

Izzy thought about it. Jane didn't date people she worked with. Even if she did, she was far too beautiful to be someone's research project. The idea was laughable.

She snorted.

"There's no way she's jealous of Anaya. Jane and I are friends."

Jane looked deep in thought in front of her computer, and the desks on either side of her were empty when Izzy leaned against the low cubicle wall in front of her. Her stomach fluttered at the smile Jane flashed when she looked up and saw her there.

Izzy propped her elbow on the cubical wall and rested her chin in her hand. "That's nice to see."

Jane tipped her head to the side. "What?"

"Your beautiful smile." Had she really said "beautiful"? *Yikes!* Oh well. She pressed on, knowing she couldn't take it back. "You've seemed preoccupied lately, and I've missed it, that smile. I came to check on you."

Jane's smile faltered, and her eyes darted to the side. "I've had a few things on my mind."

"You want to talk about them? I'm a good listener."

Jane tilted her head to the other side and looked at her. Izzy could see the cogs spinning, but Jane hesitated so long, she thought she wasn't going to open up to her. It was silly to have brought it up at the office anyway. Maybe if she suggested dinner or something. Just the two of them. No pressure, no interruptions.

But Jane's shoulders dropped a little, and she leaned back in her chair. She stared at her hands, which were in her lap. "It's family stuff." She looked up at Izzy briefly before glancing away. "Among other things."

"Ah. Family stuff." With such a large family, Izzy knew how that went. "Wanna talk about it?"

Jane seemed to search for a way to start. "My folks are getting old, and my dad just seems to be getting crankier as the years go by."

Izzy was thankful her dad was exactly the opposite. The tough contractor was softening up in his old age. But this was about Jane, not her. "I hear it's not uncommon."

"My mom expects me to come over for Sunday dinner every week. So, I go, and I get to listen to him rant about politics and…things. It's just getting to me, I guess."

Izzy went to her parents' house for Sunday dinners at least once a month, too. She cherished her mom and dad. It was awesome that Jane was close to her parents. But it sounded like things were getting strained.

"We had to make a no-political-discussions zone at my folks' house during the last election," she said. "It was bad. We all vote Democrat, but we were split during the primaries."

Jane's eyes grew distant, and Izzy wondered if she'd said something wrong. She was about to ask when Jane issued a single, humorless laugh.

"I wish it was just politics."

The look on Jane's face made the hair on the back of Izzy's neck stand on end. She was probably overreacting. "Nothing's worse than political arguments," she said, trying to joke the tension away.

Jane's eyes went hard in a way Izzy had never seen. "Have you ever had to put yourself between your father and mother so he couldn't hit her?" Izzy didn't know what to say and Jane looked away, rubbing her shoulder. "I can't believe I just said that."

"Are you okay?" Izzy asked.

Jane rubbed her shoulder again. "It's just a little bruised. It was my fault anyway. My mom was trying to change the subject from 'the gay issue,' as she likes to call it. My dad calls it something far more politically incorrect. I should have let it drop."

Izzy felt like she might be sick. She thought it strange Jane had been keeping her sweaters on even when they were outside beyond the chill of the office air-conditioning the last couple of days.

Looking uncomfortable, Jane sat up straighter. "Seriously, I don't know why I told you this."

"Is your mom safe?"

"Yeah. When I'm not there she's great at keeping the conversation neutral." Jane lifted her eyebrows. "Years of practice."

"Well, if you ever need any help, I'm here for you." Izzy moved around the desk and put a hand on her shoulder. "Even if it's just to talk."

Jane looked at her as if she wanted to say something but had second thoughts.

"Seriously. I'm here if you want to talk about it."

Jane smiled, but Izzy thought she might cry. Instead she took a deep breath. "None of this is new, but I appreciate your worry."

Now that you're going on a date, you can feel relatively confident the person you're with is interested in you. But how interested are you in them? Where do you want this date to go? At this point, it's a good idea to think about the possibilities. Are you already hoping this is just the first of many dates? Are you still trying to figure out if you like the person in a romantic way? How far are you willing to take a first date if it goes well? Will it be a smile and a thank-you ending? A kiss? More? What if it doesn't go well? Do you stay until the end, or do you have an exit strategy?

Regardless of your hopes and expectations, you should be prepared to handle a list of the most likely of possible outcomes.

CHAPTER FOURTEEN

Izzy was early, and See You Latte was busy, which didn't surprise her. She'd never seen the coffee shop *not* busy. At least the line was short. While she waited for her order, she thought about her conversation with Jane the day before and kept her eyes peeled for a table to free up. As luck would have it, when the barista handed her the bhakti chai latte she'd ordered, a table near the window cleared, and she hurried to get it before someone else grabbed it. She was brushing away scone crumbs when Anaya walked through the door. They saw each other at the same time, and Anaya greeted her with a hug.

"Is it okay? I'm a hugger." Anaya released her and smiled.

Izzy wasn't a big hugger. She hugged her family on occasion and sometimes her friends if the situation called for it.

"Totally okay," she said and meant it.

"Good. Because I like you, and I'll probably spontaneously hug you a few more times today."

Izzy didn't know how to respond. She pulled out a chair. "Let me get you coffee. What's your poison?"

Anaya picked up Izzy's cup and sniffed it. "What you have smells amazing. I'll try that."

"Okay. One extra-spicy bhakti chai coming up."

Izzy ordered the drink and a couple of scones—a chocolate-chip and an orange-cranberry to be safe. As she waited for the latte, she started to worry Anaya wouldn't like scones at all. What would she do if Anaya didn't want one? She could eat them both, but would Anaya think she was a glutton? Would it be worse than if she left a scone uneaten? Would it make Anaya feel bad? Her brain started to ramp up the inevitable hectic chatter. *Don't start. Don't start. Don't start.*

She chanted silently. The chatter slowed, and she concentrated on her breathing until the chai was ready.

"I'm so glad you got something to nosh on." Anaya eyed the scones when she got back to the table. "I'm starving." She looked up at Izzy with a grateful smile. "Oh, and thank you. I should have bought since I invited you."

"You bought drinks the other night. Take your pick. I'm good with either. I can always go back for something else. They have lots of other pastries and things." Izzy slid the plates to the center of the small table, the uncertain voices trying to start up again.

Anaya took the scone closest to her, the orange-cranberry, and broke a piece off, popping it into her mouth. "Yum!"

The chattering voices stopped. Then she wondered what Anaya meant about who should buy. "Are there rules?"

Anaya sipped her chai. "Rules?"

"About who buys on a date. You said you should have bought."

Anaya laughed. "I suppose some people have rules, but you'll figure out quickly I'm not a rule follower."

Izzy found the mischievous gleam in Anaya's eyes intriguing. Maybe her revelation should have alarmed her, because people without rules often behave unpredictably. But Anaya's candor gave her a sense of safety.

They spoke about travel and running, and before Izzy knew it, two hours had gone by.

Anaya stretched. "I saw you look at your watch. I think the scones have worn off. I need some real food."

Izzy was right there with her. "There's a Thai restaurant next door. I could go for a late lunch, if you're free." She'd surprised herself at how easy it had been to ask. No stress. No overthinking it. Her time with Anaya had also kept her mind off Jane.

"Sounds great. But only if you let me pay."

"For a woman without rules, you sure like to throw them out there." The teasing came easy. She was enjoying herself, and being around Anaya was fun.

Anaya winked at her. "I'm pretty versatile, actually."

Izzy was clueless about flirting, but even she knew Anaya had uttered a not-so-subtle innuendo. The realization gave her a little buzz, followed by a huge surge of insecurity. When was Anaya going to figure out she was different? Would it be better if she told her up front? *Stop it! Stop it! Stop it!*

Lunch was another two hours, and Izzy enjoyed the conversation. Unlike the coffee shop, the restaurant wasn't exceptionally busy, and the wait staff didn't try to rush them off as soon as they were done with their entrees.

Finally, Anaya took Izzy's wrist and looked at her watch. "I hate to say it, but I have to get going."

"Yeah, me, too." Other than getting back home to Gus, Izzy really didn't have to leave, but she didn't want Anaya to think she didn't have a life.

Anaya picked up her phone and opened a new contact page. "I'm tired of watching your profile all the time, waiting for you to log in. Can I have your number?"

Izzy wished she could be as direct and confident as Anaya. The buzz in her stomach moved to the rest of her as she entered her info. For the first time, it drowned out the fear.

"I guess our first official date went well, if you're asking for my number now," Izzy said. It was a joke, but had she sounded like a dork? *Stop it. You don't need to overanalyze everything.*

"I'd say it went well. Better than well, actually." Anaya saved the info Izzy had entered.

Izzy felt her own phone vibrate in her back pocket.

Anaya looked up through her long lashes. "I just texted you. Now you have my number."

Izzy stood there, outside of the restaurant with Anaya, and wondered how to say good-bye. What was the protocol after the first official date?

She didn't have much time to wonder. Of course, Anaya knew exactly what to do. She stepped close and gave Izzy a hug. This one was longer than the first one hours ago.

❖

You did it! You went on a date, and you didn't die!

Now what?

Do you want to see them again?

If your answer is no, the kind thing is to break it to them gently as soon as possible. I get that it doesn't feel good to hurt someone's feelings, but it's worse to lead someone on just because you don't want to let them down. It will hurt way less if you do it at the start. Sure, they'll probably get the point if you don't call them or answer their calls. But if you ask me, it's not nice to keep someone hanging. Some people are good at rejection, and some are not. The main thing is to be kind and direct when it comes up.

If you enjoyed the date, however, and you suspect the other person did, too, there is absolutely nothing wrong with telling someone you like them. Sure, you chance finding out they aren't into you, but wouldn't you rather know sooner than later?

So, my advice is, if you want to see someone again, tell them. Contrary to what you see in movies and television, there is no specific time frame to wait. You can tell them when you say good night from the first date. Or you can tell them sometime in the future. There is no rule governing the right time.

Now, there are always going to be dates that fall somewhere in the middle. Maybe fireworks or instant attraction didn't happen, but you wonder if they will, given some time. Maybe there are other complications. What do you do then?

Unfortunately, you're kind of on your own when this happens, and you'll have to figure out what you feel, what you need, and whether the other person can give it to you. It requires major introspection, but more than that, it requires good communication and honesty. You can do it. I know you can.

Chapter Fifteen

Izzy squinted into the brilliant sunlight. The Bay Area gloom had receded, warming the day enough to make her consider taking off her *Rick and Morty* hoodie. She, Audie, and Jane were at the Traveling Bean again. It was becoming a habit for them to take a break mid-morning each day. Sometimes Hector came along, but not today. It would have been nice if it was just her and Jane so she could check in with her, but it seemed like Jane was feeling better today.

Audie doctored her tea with sugar and lemon at the pick-up window, flirting with Tarin, the owner of the coffee truck. Audie flirted with everyone, but with Tarin, it was more reserved. Izzy suspected Audie really liked her.

"How'd your coffee date go with Anaya?" Jane slid into one of the chairs in the shade of a nearby oak tree. "Did you get what you needed for the book?"

"It was fun. It ended up going long, so we stretched it over lunch, too." She pulled a couple of chairs over to Jane.

"Oh." Jane sounded strained. "Are you hitting it off with her?"

Izzy wondered if Jane didn't approve of the research Izzy was doing. Was it one of the "among other things" she had referred to when Izzy had checked on her the other day? Maybe Jane thought she was toying with people's feelings—a worry Izzy sometimes had herself. She couldn't blame her. Maybe she'd think differently if she knew she had really enjoyed the date and was thinking about going on another one, one that wasn't just for research. Either way, Izzy didn't want Jane to think badly of her.

She smiled to reassure her. "I think so. I really enjoy her company."

"Are you talking about your date this weekend?" Audie sat with them and took a sip of her tea.

"Yeah. I had a good time," she said. The best thing was the sense of relief over not getting all spun up at the disruption of her orderly life and the idea that maybe she wasn't quite as damaged as she thought she was. Maybe she *could* manage a relationship. Maybe not now. In the future. Something casual, though. She still couldn't risk losing herself like she had in the past.

"You sound surprised," Audie said, cocking her head.

She thought about it. "I thought it would be more work. I'm still not really into the dating thing, but this doesn't feel awkward like I imagined it would."

"Good. If it feels like work, it's probably not going to work out. Are you planning to see her again?"

"I think so." The answer came so easily, it surprised her.

"You didn't set one up at the end of the one on Saturday? Have you at least followed up with her?" Audie asked.

Izzy leaned forward, cradling her coffee cup in her hands between her knees. "What do you mean, follow up?"

"You know, called her or texted her to tell her you enjoyed the date, to see how she was doing, and to tell her you want to see her again. You have to keep the juju alive."

Izzy sighed. Of course it couldn't be easy. She started to second guess following through with asking Anaya out again. "All of a sudden, it's feeling like work."

Audie sat back in her chair. "It's not work if you like her."

"How do you do it?"

"I always follow up. I don't like to leave them hanging." Audie flashed a mischievous grin. "Why wait to see them again if you hit it off? If the date doesn't go so well, I'll try to let them down gently, but either way, I get back to them soon after the date."

Izzy was curious. "Do you text them? Message them? Call?"

"Usually, I call. It's more personal." Audie sat forward and winked at her. "But, if it goes really well, I roll over and tell them in person."

Izzy laughed. "You're a dog."

"I know. But a sweet, cuddly dog. Arf! Arf!" Audie laughed.

Izzy turned to Jane. She was quiet again, and she missed her ready smile. "How about you, Jane. What's your MO?"

After a pause during which Izzy thought Jane wasn't going to answer, Jane shifted in her seat.

"I don't know. I guess, I'm a little shyer about it. I have a hard time taking the initiative in this kind of thing."

Izzy found it hard to believe. She was so beautiful. "So, you usually wait to be asked?"

Jane tilted her head. "Yeah, I guess I do."

"I'm sure you don't have to wait very often, though." She took a sip of her coffee. "I'll bet you have a line of women lighting up your phone."

Jane stood. She smiled, but it wasn't as bright as the one Izzy had seen last. "I guess you'd lose your bet, then. I need to get back."

Izzy and Audie got up to walk back with her. Audie didn't seem too bothered by Jane's abrupt change of subject, but Izzy could tell something was wrong. She wanted to get her alone, to check in, to make sure she knew she meant it when she said she was there for her. But she'd already told her as much, so she'd wait until Jane reached out to her.

Izzy's concern for Jane lingered through to the afternoon, especially when Jane blew off lunch to work on bugs in the new release. She didn't want Jane to think she was prying, so calling Anaya to thank her for the coffee-lunch date seemed like the perfect distraction. At least her worry about Jane had minimized her anxiety, so it didn't seem as daunting a task as she thought it might be.

Nevertheless, her finger hovered over Anaya's number for a few minutes before she could muster the courage to press it. They'd never spoken on the phone before. What would they talk about after she thanked her? They'd had no trouble finding things to talk about Saturday, but she was drawing a blank now. It was so much easier to chat online. Maybe that was what she should do. She started to open the website. No. Too cheesy.

She took a deep breath and pushed the number.

The phone rang once, and Anaya picked up. She didn't get a chance to change her mind.

"Hey, Izzy! I was just about to call you."

Anaya sounded happy to hear from her. A good sign. She relaxed a little. "Oh, yeah?"

"Yeah," Anaya said. "I had fun on Saturday."

"Me, too. I just finished the last of the leftover pad thai I took home."

Anaya's laugh carried across the phone line. "I finished the green curry yesterday. What were we thinking ordering so much just for us?"

"Our eyes were bigger than our stomachs, as my mom likes to say." Izzy leaned back in her chair and gathered her courage. "I'm glad you liked it. Hey, besides telling you I had fun, I was also calling to see if you wanted go out to dinner sometime this week." She held her breath. What the hell was she doing?

"I'm free Wednesday."

Izzy's shoulders relaxed, and she spun in her chair. She looked up and saw Jane standing there. She smiled and indicated she'd just be a minute. "Wednesday's perfect. I'll message you the details."

She said goodbye, but when she looked up, Jane was gone, probably because she didn't want to intrude. Izzy stood and to see where she'd gone and spotted her walking away.

"Hey, Jane!"

Jane kept walking as if she hadn't heard her, and Izzy jogged to catch up.

"Hey, busy lady!" she said from a couple steps behind her.

Jane turned around, but kept walking backward. "Meeting. I'm late. Talk later?" Her smile didn't make it to her eyes, and she was walking in the opposite direction of the conference rooms.

"Sure. No problem."

Izzy stopped where she was and Jane disappeared behind the next corner.

In some ways, second dates are easy. You've already spent time with the person. You can assume there's mutual interest, otherwise one or both of you would have found a way to avoid a second date. You've learned some of the other person's interests, so you have things to talk about. You're probably more relaxed around each other.

On the other hand, a second date means there may be an expectation of things progressing between you. If you're not one to hop into bed with someone quickly, there might be some anxiety about how to deal with possible pressure to go faster than you're comfortable. For people who are good communicators, this might be a good time to set some ground rules around expectations. For people who have trouble communicating, this part can get a little uncomfortable.

The best thing you can do here is understand what you're ready for at this point. Do what feels right to you and figure out a way to say no when it doesn't feel right. A good person will understand and won't pressure you.

What if it's you who wants to make the move toward more? Simple. Tell them. But, remember, the same thing applies to you. A nice person understands if the other person wants to take it slower.

CHAPTER SIXTEEN

Gus followed Izzy from room to room as she tried to figure out what to wear on her second date with Anaya. She'd left work early to make sure she had enough time to get ready, but Gus, who was a perceptive boy, not only knew she was getting ready to leave him again, but that she was nervous as hell, second-guessing, for what seemed the hundredth time, her decision to ask Anaya out. Izzy tried not to get impatient when he ended up underfoot once again.

She dropped to the floor and ruffled his neck. A cloud of fur rose. It didn't matter how often she groomed him; the fur was everywhere. It was one of the reasons she rarely wore black. "Gus, my man! You know you're my favorite." She looked around to make sure the cats weren't close by. "It's a work night, and I'll be home early. How about I take you to the dog park tomorrow? Sound good?"

Gus's ears perked up, and he tilted his head. His head whipped to the front door, where his leashes hung.

Oh, no. She'd said the magic words. Now he thought they were going there. She was such an idiot. Redirection. "Who wants peanut-butter bombs?"

Gus danced in a circle on his back legs, already starting the tricks she made him do in order to get treats. He was such a smart boy!

Izzy got up and gave Gus a couple of treats and ran him through his trick routine, mixing it up so it wasn't always in the same order. Once they were done, she filled one of his chew toys with real peanut butter and left him in the kitchen to work on it, hoping she would have some guilt-free time to finish getting ready.

The restaurant they agreed on was nice, but it wasn't formal. She laid out several outfits, ranging from casual jeans and a button-up shirt to the tailored women's suit she'd had made for her niece's wedding. Jeans seemed too casual, and the suit, while she really liked it, was a little too dressy. She opted for a pair of taupe linen pants and a white, flowy peasant shirt that tied in the front. It was a softer look than she usually wore, but she wanted to be pretty. A pair of flat sandals completed the outfit. She spent more time on her hair and even put on a little makeup. Audie would have been proud of her. Hector would have made fun. What would Jane think?

She felt good—better than she had in days. Excitement about the evening overshadowed the tiny bit of anxiety that gnawed at her. She was probably experiencing a bit of hypomania, but after the insecurity and anxiety this whole dating thing stirred up, the mania felt good—which she had to be careful about. The depression side of the cycle would come, too. But that's what her meds were for, right? It was all the nature of her disorder. She had it under control.

She decided to take the light rail to the restaurant. Parking downtown was usually a mess. Besides, having a train schedule to adhere to was a good way to control the end of the evening.

The restaurant was a couple of blocks from the train station, and Izzy was pleased to find she'd timed it right. Anaya was already there, waiting at the bar. She told the host she had reservations and threaded her way to the bar.

"You look amazing," Anaya said when Izzy caught her eye. She rose and wrapped Izzy in a hug. "You smell amazing, too."

Izzy blushed. "Thanks," she said when Anaya let go of her.

Anaya slid back onto her barstool. "I came directly from work, so I had a drink while I waited." Anaya waved the bartender over. "What can I order for you?"

Izzy waved the bartender away. "I might have a glass of wine with dinner. The host is waiting to seat us. Do you want to bring your drink to the table?"

"Sure. I'm starving. Let me close my tab."

Anaya took Izzy's hand as the host showed them to their table, and Izzy looked around to see if anyone was watching them. When no one seemed to notice, she reminded herself that things had changed a lot since the last time she'd been in a relationship.

"You look really nice," Anaya said, leaning toward Izzy as they settled across from one another in the booth. "I really like the way the shirt ties up the front. It's alluring and shows just enough skin." Anaya rubbed the center of her own chest when she spoke, her eyes riveted on Izzy's chest. "It makes me want to untie it."

Izzy blushed at the comment and didn't know what to say. Thankfully, Anaya's eyes met hers again.

"Have you ever been to this restaurant before?" Anaya asked.

Izzy opened the menu so she didn't have to watch the desire dance in Anaya's eyes. Things felt so different from their coffee date, and she wasn't sure she was ready or even able, to respond to Anaya's spoken and unspoken suggestions. "A few times with friends. The ravioli is really good, but I hear the steak is the best thing on the menu."

Anaya reached across the table and stroked the back of her hand with a finger. "Have you tried it yourself?"

Izzy cleared her throat. "No. I'm one of those people who orders the same thing every time. I had the ravioli the first time I was here, and I've had it every time since."

Anaya took Izzy's hand, forcing her to look up from the menu. She brushed a fingertip along the lines of Izzy's palm. "I hope you're a little more adventurous in other aspects of your life."

Izzy shivered at the touch. Her mind short-circuited. Regardless of her earlier confidence, she was so far outside of her realm of experience and comfort, she didn't know how to respond. She normally didn't pick up on sexual innuendo, but Anaya wasn't even trying to be subtle. "I'm just not much of a foodie, so once I land on a good thing, I stick with it."

The server appeared, and she tried to pull her hand out of Anaya's, but Anaya kept hold of it.

"We'll have a bottle of the Bocelli Sangiovese." The server left the table as she continued to stroke Izzy's palm. "It's lush and smoky. I think you'll like it."

Izzy swallowed hard. "I wasn't planning on drinking tonight."

"I promise you'll like it. If you don't, more for me."

Anaya's eyes were mesmerizing, the swirls she was making in Izzy's palm with her fingertip adding to the effect. Normally, she would have been bothered by someone ordering for her, especially alcohol, but the strangeness of the situation made her feel almost removed from her body.

Anaya leaned forward and stared. "You have such beautiful eyes."

Izzy fought the urge to squirm. "Thank you." She looked away. It was impossible to return Anaya's intense stare.

"When you look at me like that, they do something to me."

Izzy wasn't sure what Anaya meant. How was she looking at her?

Once again, the server saved her from having to answer by appearing with the wine. Anaya let go of Izzy's hand to look at the menu, and the weird feeling of being mesmerized receded.

Anaya raised her glass when the server left the table with their dinner order. "To the beginning of something wonderful, I hope."

Izzy lifted her glass and forced a smile. Everything about Anaya seemed to be exaggerated tonight. She craved some distance. Was she just being too sensitive? She tried to focus on something about Anaya she liked. Her smile. She had such a dazzling smile.

Anaya reached across the table and brushed Izzy's collarbone with her index finger. The continued moves into her personal space were overwhelming, and Izzy didn't know how to respond. A long time ago she'd enjoyed this kind of play with Kelly. They'd been so young and uninhibited, and Kelly had been so open about her desire, which had made Izzy feel daring and carefree. It had been wonderful, like a powerful drug. Now, Izzy felt like retreating. The touches were too much, too soon. Her chest was tightening.

"I'm so glad I took a chance on your pictureless profile." Anaya sat back in the booth, swirling the wine in her glass before she took a drink.

The physical distance allowed Izzy to breathe a little easier. She pretended to sip her own wine and thought about the good time they'd had Saturday, wishing she could recreate it. "Me, too."

Anaya's forehead furrowed. "Usually, people who don't have pictures are just voyeurs. I don't respond to their messages, and I certainly don't message them. But something in your profile summary was so open and honest, it made me want to know more about you. Now that I know you're a writer, it makes sense. You're an artist. I'm definitely drawn to artists." Anaya laughed. "See what I did there? I'm *drawn* to artists."

Izzy laughed, too. Anaya seemed more like her Saturday self in that moment. "I'm a technical writer. I'm afraid there isn't much art in it."

"There's something there maybe you don't realize." Anaya tipped her empty wineglass at her.

"I'll take your word for it."

Anaya refilled her glass. "This wine is from his vineyard, you know. Bocelli's. The opera singer. You know his work, don't you?"

Izzy wasn't an opera enthusiast, but she'd heard of him. "Some."

Anaya leaned her head back against the booth and closed her eyes. "I love to listen to him when I'm at the beach at night, listening to the waves crashing on the sand."

"Sounds nice." Izzy took a sip of water. "I love the ocean but don't go nearly enough."

"Have you ever made love on the beach at night, Izzy?"

Izzy choked on her water.

"I surprised you." Anaya laughed. "It was an honest question. There's something so romantic about the crashing waves and opera. A warm night. A beautiful woman. You can't do anything else with that combination but make love, don't you agree?"

"It sounds nice," Izzy said between coughs.

"Maybe when we get to know each other better, we can take a weekend at the beach," Anaya suggested.

Izzy couldn't tell if she was just painting a nice possibility or whether she was being literal. Either way, she was moving a little too fast for Izzy's comfort.

The server came with their food, saving her from answering.

Anaya filled her glass again. How had she finished it so quickly? Izzy's first glass was still full, but Anaya didn't seem to notice. She had to put her hand over the rim when Anaya tried to top it off.

Anaya smiled. "More for me."

The food looked great, and Izzy was glad to have something to distract them from the direction their conversation had taken.

Anaya took a bite of her steak, and her eyes rolled back. "I can't believe you haven't had this steak. It's fantastic. Like an orgasm in my mouth."

Izzy nearly choked again but didn't respond, concentrating on her ravioli. She was surprised she could even taste it through the smog of anxiety taking over. It wasn't as fantastic as Anaya's steak, apparently, but it was as good as she remembered.

"Here. You have to try this." Anaya held a forkful of food toward her.

Izzy had just put some food in her mouth and held up her finger. Anaya continued to hold the fork with steak on it in front of her mouth as she chewed, and Izzy became self-conscious. She swallowed the ravioli before she was completely ready, and she had a hard time swallowing. At the same time, Anaya moved her fork closer, so Izzy had no choice but to open her mouth and allow her to stick the food in. The whole thing was awkward with an air of false intimacy, and Izzy covered her mouth with her hand to chew in private while Anaya watched her with an expression of anticipation. Izzy couldn't taste anything through her embarrassment, but she nodded and tried to smile even as she chewed and chewed in an effort to get the steak down without choking.

"Isn't it the best thing you've ever tasted?"

Izzy held up her finger as she continued to chew and finally swallowed it. "It's very good," she lied.

"How's the ravioli?"

"It's good."

"Can I have a taste?"

"Oh, yeah. Sure." Izzy pushed her plate across the table so Anaya could reach it.

"You do it," Anaya said. "It's sexy when a woman feeds me."

Izzy didn't know what to do. She'd never fed an adult before, and she sure as hell hadn't felt sexy as Anaya had watched her chewing the steak. Still, she pulled the plate back, cut a ravioli in half, and scooped it up. Anaya opened her mouth and leaned toward her, gazing at her. The moment felt forced and anything but sexy, and Izzy felt trapped in the weird game-play. Halfway to Anaya's mouth, the food fell off the fork and onto the table.

Anaya raised an eyebrow. "I make you nervous. I like that."

Izzy put her fork down and raked her hands across her face.

"Here. I'll help you." Anaya took Izzy's hand and put the fork back into it. Then she guided Izzy's hand, spearing the other half of the ravioli, and delivered the food to her own mouth.

"Mmm!" Anaya chewed the ravioli while staring into Izzy's eyes.

Izzy couldn't look away, but not because she enjoyed the moment. Quite the opposite. She was almost repulsed.

"I have to go to the bathroom," she said, wiping her mouth with her napkin and sliding out of the booth.

All the stall doors were open, and the bathroom was empty. She locked herself in a stall, leaned against the door after she locked it, and tried to think of excuses to leave. She had to get out of here. Maybe she could claim her stomach was upset.

Hadn't she learned her lesson with Kelly?

She shook her head. Nothing about this situation resembled her time with Kelly, so why was she thinking about her right now? Maybe it was the sensation of extreme surrealism. Maybe it was the feeling of trying to be someone she wasn't. Her head felt staticky, and things she hadn't thought about in years were coming back to her. Her relationship with Kelly had quite literally been a crazy time for her. She'd just started college, Kelly had been her first real girlfriend, and as it turned out, her last, if she didn't count Siobhan—which she didn't. Being with Kelly had started out as the best time of her life and ended as the worst.

At first, being in love for the first time has been bliss. Several months of toe-curling, walking-on-air euphoria. Her spiral into hell had started when she'd come back from using the restroom after making love to Kelly, and she'd overheard Kelly say "I love you, babe" to someone on the phone.

Izzy pressed her fingers against her eyes, remembering everything about that moment: running back to the bathroom to be sick, crying uncontrollably, lying to Kelly about her lunch not sitting well in her stomach.

Days of turmoil had followed as she'd alternately provided excuses for Kelly and felt cheated on, until the confrontation, when Kelly finally admitted she was planning to move away to be with her former girlfriend at the end of the semester. An ache had consumed her then, and she'd started planning ways to escape it. She stole her roommate's prescription sleeping pills, a handful of pain medication, and a bottle of Jack Daniel's, which she used to wash the pills down, and curled up on her bed in her dorm room, ready to be freed from the pain. But she'd woken up in the hospital when a person in green scrubs shoved a tube down her throat and filled her stomach with a thick concoction of charcoal, making her heave and retch.

She'd spent a month locked up in a behavioral-health hospital, where she was put on a suicide watch and diagnosed with bipolar disorder. She remembered moving from her school in Ohio back home to San Jose in a lithium fog, where she put college on hold to focus on fixing herself. Numerous med adjustments during months of intensive outpatient psychotherapy where she'd battled suicidal ideation were also hazy. Years of therapy and rebuilding her shattered self-confidence had followed, during which she swore to herself she would never fall in love again and risk repeating the hell she had finally escaped.

She'd had no indication she was bipolar before she'd met Kelly. The blush of new love had camouflaged the mania at first. But then the crush of the breakup had plunged her into the abyss of depression. That's when the cycling began—amazing highs followed by debilitating lows. And always the anxiety. Medication treated much of the symptoms, but it took intensive therapy and hard work to learn the coping skills designed to help her manage her fluid emotional states and chaotic thought processes. It had taken most of her twenties for her to level out, and in the mysterious ways of the human mind, she had blocked most of the bad stuff. Until now, when snippets of that time kept sneaking in.

What the fuck had she been thinking? Why had she risked triggering this personal hell? She needed to get out of here.

"Izzy?" Anaya's voice echoed against the marble walls.

Izzy hadn't heard the door to the bathroom open, and she held back a groan. The stall walls went all the way to the floor, so Anaya couldn't see her, but she was the only one in there, so it was obvious where she was. "Be right out."

She flushed the toilet, even though she hadn't used it, and opened the stall. Anaya was right there, blocking her exit.

"Thank goodness. Are you okay?" Anaya touched Izzy's arm. "You left the table so quickly, I thought maybe you had gotten sick."

"To be honest, my stomach—"

"This is like a little private room." Anaya put her hand in the center of Izzy's chest and pushed her back into the stall.

"What are you doing?" Panicked, Izzy already knew.

"This." Anaya cupped Izzy's face and kissed her.

Shock paralyzed Izzy. Even if she could have found it in herself to move, it would have been difficult with Anaya leaning against her, holding her captive against the wall. Anaya's mouth was soft at first, her kiss was gentle, so Izzy allowed it, hoping Anaya would finish and let her leave. But the kiss grew firmer, Anaya's breathing became rapid, and her tongue sought entry into Izzy's mouth. Anaya wrapped her arms around Izzy, pressed harder against her, and pushed her thigh between her legs.

Still, Izzy didn't move. She just stood there and let it happen.

Anaya's lips moved across Izzy's cheek and down to her neck. "Izzy, I want you. Come home with me tonight."

Izzy put her hands on Anaya's arms, ready to push her away. "I…I can't. Not tonight."

Anaya kissed her neck. "Please. I don't usually plead, but I will. There's just something about you. You make me so ready. And your kisses, God, your kisses."

Izzy would have laughed if she wasn't so shocked. What kisses? Anaya had done all the kissing. "I can't, Anaya. I need to go home tonight. I took the train."

"I took a cab. We can go to my house. You'll love it there."

Izzy gently pushed Anaya away from her and, to her relief, Anaya took a step back. Anaya's eyes were dark with desire.

"I have to go home to my dog."

"We can go to your house, then."

Anaya tried to kiss her again, but Izzy turned her head. Undaunted, Anaya began to kiss her neck.

Izzy tried to slip away. "Anaya, I can't. Not tonight."

Anaya whimpered against Izzy's neck, and the vibration made Izzy shiver. It wasn't passion, but Anaya must have thought it was.

"Here then. Right here. Put your hands on me." Anaya took Izzy's hand and guided it up her skirt.

Izzy no longer felt like she was in her own body, and she observed herself laughing and stepping away. "We're in a public bathroom."

Anaya grabbed for her. "I can be quiet. It won't take long. I'm so ready."

Izzy sidestepped out of her arms. "Anaya, our dinner is getting cold." She opened the stall door and stepped out.

"God. I forgot we had food." Anaya laughed and straightened her clothes. Then she grabbed the door and closed it. "I'll meet you at the table. I have to pee."

Izzy didn't even wash her hands before she rushed back to the table. What a mess. Nothing had prepared her for this, but she didn't need experience to know Anaya was coming on way too strong. Any resemblance to Jane was wiped away. The two were nothing alike, and she felt bad for ever thinking differently. Why was she even dwelling on it now? The numbness left her, and her chest went tight again. She was having trouble breathing. An uncomfortable buzz filled her head as thoughts and emotions spun around, spiraling up her anxiety level. She was on the verge of a panic attack, and just the possibility jacked it up even more. Self-recrimination raced through her mind, and she couldn't remember any of her coping exercises. She needed to get out of here, but more than anything, she needed someone to ground her.

She looked toward the bathrooms to watch for Anaya and slid her phone out of her pocket. She didn't know what else to do. She called Audie.

The phone only rang once, thank God. Good old Audie. "'Sup? Aren't you supposed to be on your big date?"

Izzy held her hand over her mouth and the phone and spoke quietly.

"I am. But she wants to sleep with me! Help!" She looked around. No one seemed to be listening.

A whoop sounded across the line. "You go, girl!"

"It's not a good thing!" she whispered between her teeth.

Audie giggled. "Why not? Wait. Never mind. I forgot who I was talking to."

"How do I get out of it?" Laughter cackled through the speaker again, and Izzy almost had to hold the phone away from her ear. "It's not funny, Audie. I'm freaking out."

"Just tell her you don't want to."

"She's not taking no for an answer."

"What do you mean?" Audie's voice grew serious.

"I mean, she's being really insistent. Really, really insistent. She followed me to the bathroom and, well—"

Anaya came into sight and stopped at the bar on her way back to the table. At first, Izzy wondered if she was just chatting with the bartender, but the bartender gave her another drink, which she guzzled.

"Are you still there?" Audie asked.

Izzy slid low in the booth. "I think she's an alcoholic."

"What?"

Izzy kept her eye on Anaya as she paid for the new drink. "I'll tell you about it later. I just need to know what to do to get out of this."

"Do you need someone to pick you up?"

"God, yes. If you could, I'd be forever in your debt."

As Anaya finished her drink and walked toward their table, Izzy was surprised she wasn't weaving after so much alcohol. She wanted to hang up the phone, but she needed Audie to come pick her up. Besides, abruptly hanging up would be suspicious.

"I'm in Vegas for that design conference."

Izzy's stomach dropped. "I forgot you were out of town." What was she going to do? And now Anaya had seen her on the phone. Great.

"I'll call Hector and send him over. You're at the Bull and Bear, right?"

Izzy's hopes rekindled, and she sat up in the booth. Anaya made it to the table. "I'll see you when you get back to town, Mom. I have to go."

"Oh, is she back?" Audie whispered through the line. Izzy was relieved Audie caught on so quickly, but she didn't know why she was whispering. Anaya couldn't hear her over the phone.

"Yes. That's right." She rolled her eyes and mouthed the word "Mom" as she pointed at the phone when Anaya raised her eyebrows.

"Okay. Okay. I'm calling Hector right now," Audie whispered.

"I love you, too, Mom. Hugs to Dad! I hope he gets home soon." Izzy ended the call and slid her phone back into her pocket.

Anaya smiled as she slid into her seat. "Did you miss me?"

Izzy laughed, not knowing what to say.

"Your mom called?" Anaya took a sip of her wine.

Did Anaya really believe it or was she on to her?

"I normally wouldn't have answered, but they're getting on in years, and when one of them calls, I usually answer to make sure everything's okay." Technically true, but she felt bad for misleading Anaya.

"You're such a thoughtful person." Anaya leaned forward with her wineglass, her voice a little slurred. "It's one of the things I find extremely attractive about you. One of many, many things."

"Well, I…uh…" Izzy didn't know what to say, and she found it hard to look Anaya in the eye.

"I like that, too." Anaya gestured with the glass as she spoke, and a slosh of wine stained the white tablecloth. "You always get so flustered when I compliment you. It's so cute."

"I'm not good with compliments." It was the truth.

"I think you'll get used to it." Anaya winked. "When I find a woman attractive, I make sure she knows it. And you, Izzy, are a very, very attractive woman."

"Uh, thank you. As are you." She didn't want to egg her on, but as much as Anaya was making her feel uncomfortable, she *was* a beautiful woman.

"You're so far away." Anaya slid from her side of the booth and pushed herself into Izzy's side.

Surprised, Izzy moved over to make room, but Anaya just pressed closer. Izzy felt trapped.

Anaya pinched one of the ties of Izzy's shirt and tugged playfully on it. The loose bow slipped free. Izzy wore a camisole under the shirt, but the move felt uncomfortably intimate. The tightness in her chest increased, and she breathed heavily, probably giving Anaya the wrong idea. Sweat beaded in her hairline. She fought for clarity.

"Um, tell me about the project you just finished." She needed to distract her until Hector could get there.

"That's boring." Anaya smiled and put the end of the string in her mouth and then used the wet end to draw circles on the skin of Izzy's cleavage.

Izzy looked around the restaurant to make sure no one was watching and tried to think of a way to distract her. "I…uh…I like to hear about the things intelligent women do at work. It…um…it turns me on."

Anaya pulled back and grinned. "It does? I'd read the stock report to you if you told me it turned you on." She took Izzy's hand and traced the lines in her palm as she described the project she'd worked on over the summer. Izzy had a hard time listening as Anaya intermittently kissed her neck and played suggestively with her fingers. Izzy kept looking toward the door, hoping Hector would be there.

Anaya had reached the part where she had made the final project presentation to her CEO, and her hand was creeping up Izzy's thigh. Izzy was almost in a panic and had no idea how to distract her any longer.

"Izzy, is that you? I was over at the bar, and I saw you, and oh… Did I interrupt something?"

Izzy looked past Anaya and was surprised to see Jane standing at the end of the table. Her messenger bag hung from her shoulder, as if she'd just come from work. Why was she here? Part of her was happy to see her; she just wished it was under different circumstances, and she didn't have a drunk woman pressing her up against the wall.

"Jane!" she said with genuine surprise. God, had she ever been so relieved to see someone. "No, no, we're just having dinner. This is… my friend, Anaya."

Jane held her hand out to Anaya, who was forced to slide away from Izzy to shake it. "Nice to meet you. Anaya? What a beautiful name."

Seeing them together, Izzy noticed Anaya and Jane looked nothing alike. Anaya had nothing on Jane.

Anaya looked at Izzy and then back to Jane. "Thank you. Nice to meet you, too."

Izzy looked past Jane for Hector. She couldn't ask Jane to join them. She didn't even want to. She was, however, grateful for the interruption. Jane's presence eased the tightness in her chest. She could finally breathe again. How much longer would it take Hector to get there?

Jane repositioned the strap of her bag, and her face fell. "I was supposed to meet Hector here to get some personal advice, but he just called and said he couldn't make it."

Was Jane here to talk about her problems with Hector? A pang of jealousy shot through her. She wished Jane would confide in her instead.

"I hope Hector had a good excuse to stand you up," she said.

Anaya leaned across the table to get her glass.

Jane gave Izzy a meaningful look over Anaya's head. "I think he had a previous commitment with Audie."

Oh! Oh! Oh! Now she understood! Jane was here instead of Hector. She opened her mouth and closed it, unsure what to say.

Jane continued. "I needed someone to talk to, and you were on a date, so I asked him. I had no idea you were coming here. This is awkward."

Izzy was confused at first and then realized Jane was concocting a plausible excuse for her to be here. Good. It could work, if only she could get rid of the buzzing in her head to think more clearly.

"Is everything okay?" She hoped Jane would have a good excuse to get her out of here. It had to be a good one, or Izzy would look like a real shmuck. Anaya, drunk or not, was pretty sharp.

At that moment, Anaya turned to Izzy with a questioning look, and Izzy knew what it meant. Anaya wanted to continue their date—in private. Izzy searched for something to say.

Jane sagged as if she were suffering a great amount of heartache. "It's Bruce. It's always Bruce." Her voice cracked just a little at the end.

"Ah, yeah. Bruce is a huge problem." Izzy played along, shaking her head as if she knew exactly what Jane was talking about.

Anaya looked between Jane and Izzy. "Who's Bruce?"

"My husband."

Izzy almost choked. She took a sip of her water and tried to compose a serious face.

Jane lowered her shoulder, and the strap from her bag slid off so she could put it on the floor in front of her. "He and I have been having problems, and it's gotten pretty bad. I don't know what I'm going to do." Jane looked as if she were about to cry. She lifted her bag again and pulled the strap over her shoulder. "Oh, jeez. Listen to me. I shouldn't be bothering you while you're on a date, Iz. I take up too much of your time with this as it is."

Izzy was impressed. Jane really looked upset.

Anaya put a hand on Jane's arm. "Are you okay?"

Izzy was touched because Anaya looked genuinely concerned. She almost wished it wasn't all a lie.

"It's just so embarrassing. He's been cheating on me." Jane slid into the other side of the booth.

Anaya leaned forward, listening.

Jane held Anaya's gaze and gestured at Izzy. "Izzy—my best friend, the sister I never had—has been listening to me with all my doubts, but I finally got proof."

Anaya took Jane's hand. "How'd you do that?"

Jane's face collapsed, and she dropped her head into her hands. "I walked in on them tonight!"

Anaya's eyes grew wide. "Another woman?"

Jane shook her head. "Worse!"

Anaya looked skeptical. "Worse?"

"My brother Wyatt!"

Izzy knew it was a made-up story, but even she gasped.

"Oh, no!" she and Anaya said together.

"Oh, yes. And with the baby only a week old…"

Anaya squeezed Jane's hand. "Wait. You just had a baby? I never would have guessed."

"Little Lester—he's named after my great-grandfather—was premature, and I bounce back quickly." She rubbed her belly. "At least I did with the first six babies. I have a few pounds left to go."

Izzy chewed her lips to keep from laughing. She was glad Anaya was sitting beside her and not across from her.

Anaya looked incredulous. "You have seven kids?"

A sob tore through Jane. "Four girls and three boys. God, I don't know what I'm going to do!"

The performance Jane was putting on was a masterpiece. Izzy almost forgot it wasn't real.

Anaya patted Jane's hands. She had hold of both of them now. "Where are the baby and the other kids now?"

"With my mom. We live with her, ever since Bruce lost his job last year." Jane looked at Izzy with frantic eyes. "She doesn't know about Bruce and Wyatt. She'd kill him. I can't go home."

Izzy sat forward. "You can't!" She hoped she sounded a fraction as convincing as Jane.

"What are you going to do?" Anaya asked.

"I don't know. I don't have anywhere to go." Jane pulled away from Anaya and slumped back into the booth, covering her face with her hands.

Izzy pounded the table. *Too much?* Anaya didn't seem to notice, and Jane still had her hands over her face. "You have to stay with me. We'll figure out what to do."

Jane dropped her hands. Tears streamed from her eyes. "Oh, no. You're busy. The kids and I couldn't impose." Jane stood to leave.

"Where else will you go?" Izzy motioned for Anaya to move so she could get to her friend. They both slid out of the booth.

Jane turned to leave. "I'll figure it out. You've done so much for me."

Izzy grabbed the strap of Jane's bag to stop her from leaving. People at the closest tables were looking now. Because it wasn't real, Izzy didn't mind like she normally would. "I insist."

Jane stopped and turned. "Are you sure? I don't want to ruin your date."

Anaya rested a hand on Jane's shoulder. "You can't be alone tonight." She was buying it—hook, line, and sinker.

Anaya convinced Jane to sit back down while Izzy paid the bill. They walked out of the restaurant while Anaya called a car service.

Anaya's driver must have been just around the corner because the car arrived within a minute of them leaving.

Anaya opened the car door and took Jane's hands in hers. "Things will get better."

Izzy was almost free and clear, and the ball of dread in her stomach was starting to dissolve. "Thanks for din—" But a passionate kiss cut off her words.

Anaya eventually drew back and caressed her check. "You're a great friend. I'm not surprised. Take care of her tonight. We can pick up where we left off soon, okay?"

And with that, she climbed into the car and was gone.

Izzy stood there clutching her stomach with one hand, watching as the car turned onto the boulevard and merged into traffic. She felt almost faint with relief.

"She's really into you."

Izzy turned to Jane and blew out a long breath.

"How did you…I mean…why did you…" She was standing on the sidewalk, alone with Jane, and couldn't seem to get her thoughts to flow properly. The buzzing in her head had stopped, and now she just felt weak.

Jane, on the other hand, looked full of energy. "That was fun. I haven't done improv since my high school drama days. I think Ms. Navotny would have given me an A for tonight's performance."

Izzy still wasn't sure what to feel at the moment. Relief, confusion, guilt—a swarm of emotions churned within her. It was great to see Jane upbeat for a change, especially since she'd been so preoccupied the last several days. Izzy smiled. "You were brilliant! How did you get roped into this?"

"When Audie called Hector, I was just leaving work with him and a couple of others after working on a regression. He had to meet his girlfriend somewhere, but he asked if I could save you from the clutches of some wild woman. My train goes right past here, so here I am."

"I owe you big-time."

Jane scowled. "It looked like I showed up just in time. I think she was about to try to undress you right there in the booth."

"You should have been in the bathroom earlier. I really thought she was going to..." Izzy shivered. She'd never been scared of a woman before. "I can't even think about it. Just thank you so much for rescuing me."

"Glad I could help."

Jane started walking toward the train station, and Izzy fell into step with her. "I'd offer you a ride, but I took the train, too."

Jane patted her laptop bag. "It's okay. I catch up on my shows on the train."

Izzy snuck a glance at Jane. She'd really missed seeing her smile. "Thank you again. You did a great job in there. If I didn't know better, I'd have thought the whole story was true."

Jane took a bow. "Four years of high school drama."

"A true Academy Award performance."

"Thanks. You weren't too bad yourself. I could see you holding back laughter in the beginning, but you really got into it at the end."

"You were pretty convincing. I almost believed you."

They were quiet for a moment. And then, Jane stopped. Izzy turned around to see why. The smile was gone.

"You know what she was doing in there wasn't okay, right?"

"She was coming on a little strong. She was really drunk. She had at least three drinks, plus most of a bottle of wine."

"Drunk or not, she was sexually harassing you. You said no, and she wasn't listening. It's not okay."

They were walking again.

"I honestly never thought a woman would ever be so...so disgusting. You know? It was scary. And disappointing."

Jane's pace picked up; she was nearly stomping. She'd switched from smiling to angry in a blink of an eye. "Why didn't you tell her? You were just sitting there letting her paw all over you."

Izzy jogged a little to keep up. "Are you mad at me?"

They'd made it to the train station and were walking up the ramp to the platform. The anger on Jane's face fell away, and another expression Izzy didn't know how to read replaced it.

Jane peered down the tracks. "I'm not mad at you. I just...I don't know...I just feel a little angry how you..." Jane looked at Izzy briefly, bit her lip, and glanced down the tracks again. "Never mind."

Izzy really wanted to know. "What? Tell me, Jane."

Jane stared at her and looked away again. Izzy started to think she wouldn't respond.

"It's just, how could you be attracted to that...*woman.* She's disgusting, and here I am, and you don't see me." Jane glanced at her and dropped her eyes. "So, I guess it's out there now."

Izzy moved so she stood in front of Jane, forcing her to look at her.

Jane gazed at her then. Her eyes were fierce but soft at the same time.

They faced each other on the platform, and Izzy didn't know what to say. But a gentle breeze was blowing Jane's hair, and she looked so beautiful.

❖

Oh, the first kiss. Sigh. Is there ever anything better than the first kiss? Fireworks and weak knees. Butterflies and electric shocks. All the good things you've imagined and more. So much more. There's no effective way to describe what a first kiss is like, except it's beautiful and powerful, and there really is nothing like it in the world.

CHAPTER SEVENTEEN

A rush of wind surrounded them, and a train pulled into the station. Another rolled up seconds later on the opposite side of the platform facing the other direction. The platform bustled around them as passengers exited and boarded the trains, but Izzy wasn't paying attention to anything but Jane, who was staring at her with a special look in her eyes, holding Izzy captive.

The platform emptied, and the trains they should have been on left the station, moving in opposite directions, but they continued to stare at each other. Izzy was paralyzed, unsure what to do, except she knew she didn't want to break the crystalline bubble they found themselves in. Jane stepped closer, their toes nearly touching. A buzz filled Izzy's stomach. Jane's eyes fell down and to the right, and warmth wrapped around her hand as Jane intertwined their fingers. Izzy studied Jane's eyes, which were the most amazing amalgamation of different shades of brown. She'd always thought them to be so dark as to be nearly black, but the brown was warm and the colors so subtle, they seemed infinitely deep and full of mystery.

When Jane's gaze came back up and landed on hers, Izzy was almost startled. But then her eyes dipped to scan Izzy's mouth, and she could almost feel the warmth of Jane's gaze sear her skin. Izzy stared at Jane's lips. How would they feel if she were to kiss them? She couldn't think of anything else. She traced the lines of Jane's lips with her eyes and knew how soft they'd be, how pliant they'd be, and she felt like she was falling in a slow, gentle arc. The ground seemed so far away, and the world seemed to fade until only Jane and she existed, floating in that crystalline bubble.

When Jane's face moved toward hers, Izzy moved forward; strands of Jane's hair blowing in the breeze tickled her checks. Jane's lips teased hers for a moment before their mouths found each other. She couldn't breathe, but she didn't need to, because everything had shrunk away until only the warmth of Jane's lips on hers, and nothing else, filled her consciousness.

Time vanished as they kissed. Izzy couldn't tell which of them pulled away first, but their parting was slow and gentle. They stood there panting, staring into each other's eyes. Izzy's hands were tangled in the hair at the base of Jane's neck, and she stroked the soft skin beneath her fingertips. Jane's hands cupped her jaw, and Izzy dipped her head to nestle into them.

The wind picked up as a train pulled into the station.

Jane shut her eyes and sighed. "My train."

Another train pulled in across from it.

"And mine." Izzy slowly removed her hands from Jane's soft hair and stepped back.

Jane's hands slid from Izzy's face, and she kept one up in a sort of wave, a slight smile on her lips.

They watched each other walk to their trains and board. Izzy took a seat on hers, and through the glare on the windows of the train across from her, she watched Jane take a seat, too. Jane's gaze upon her was not as physical as her hands, which had warmed her cheeks, but heat filled her just the same.

The doors to her train closed, and the train started to pull away. Soon the trains were rolling away from each other in opposite directions, the heat of Jane's kiss still imprinted on Izzy's lips.

What had just happened?

One of the most exciting times in life is falling in love.

One of the most terrifying times in life can be falling in love, too.

The euphoria of new love is a terribly powerful thing. It makes people do weird things. It reveals things about people they didn't know existed. If a person isn't prepared, it can cause all sorts of chaos. Remember how out-of-control high school was? Most of it was the hormones surging through everyone's rapidly developing bodies, but oftentimes, the trigger for the drama was the process of young people falling in love for the very first time.

New love ruined friendships, caused bad choices, interfered with getting good grades, and threw peer groups into wild disarray. It was tumultuous and exciting, and most of the time, people look back and have a good laugh—or a good cry, depending on how things turned out. But more often than not, when something blew up in high school, it had to do with love—or what we thought was love back then.

The point is, falling in love is an interesting time, and when you're going through it, it helps to understand what's going on so you can navigate the ensuing wild ride. At this time big decisions might come into play, and thinking things through can be tough.

CHAPTER EIGHTEEN

Izzy rolled over and stretched before shutting off her alarm. She hadn't slept much the night before, having been so keyed up by the kiss, wondering what it meant, steeped in her new knowledge of the scent of Jane's hair, the softness of her lips, the warmth of her hands.

Having heard the alarm and knowing what came next, Gus was up and by the side of the bed, his tail thumping against the mattress as he waited for his morning scratches. As tired as she was, Izzy had to get up and take her morning run.

When things got chaotic at work or in her life, a run always seemed to help her release some of the mania. It also helped when she felt herself dipping into depression. The endorphins helped steady her. In addition to her meds and a consistent sleep schedule, running was a priority in managing her bipolar symptoms. Gus seemed to enjoy it as much as she did.

Once they were outside, she performed some cursory stretches before starting off at a trot, heading to a nearby park. She wasn't a fast runner, but she fell into a steady and easy cadence as she took in the early morning air scented by the distant ocean and dew-enshrouded foliage lining the path. The route she chose was an even five miles, which they could complete in just under an hour, giving her plenty of time to get ready for work.

Once she hit her rhythm, her thoughts soon drifted to last night. Tightness filled her middle as she remembered the feeling of Jane's lips against hers. All the drama with Anaya seemed insignificant now. Izzy increased her pace as she played back the minutes on the platform.

The kiss changed everything. She couldn't think of Jane as just a friend anymore. She was so much more. But what did it mean? And, more importantly, how did Jane feel? Was it possible it hadn't been as earth-shattering for Jane as it had been for her? The thought made Izzy stumble, and she stopped with her hands on her knees, panting on a street she'd already run down. So deep into her reverie, she'd completed her loop and was several blocks into a second loop. She considered turning back, but before she had made up her mind, she was running again, with Gus looking up at her with his happy smile.

"Guess we're doing ten miles this morning, buddy," she said through deep breaths. "Good thing we don't have any meetings first thing."

She turned up her music and matched her pace to the drumbeat of Outkast belting out "Hey Ya!"

No one knows exactly when people first started referring to the stages of intimacy using the euphemism of American baseball, but it seems to have caught on around WWII. And people, especially in American culture, have used it ever since.

First base is the tentative first touches, the long stares, the stomach-dropping moment when you let the other person know you like them, and the elation of incendiary first kisses when you find out they like you back. The experience usually includes holding hands, embraces, maybe even some face-touching, and running fingers through your partner's hair.

Some people round right through first base on their way to second—or farther on their first date. Others take their time, waiting for the third or fourth date for a first kiss, sometimes longer. Either way, the first kiss is generally regarded as the classic thermometer for chemistry between two people and the very definition of first base.

CHAPTER NINETEEN

Since she was late, Izzy drove in to work. Traffic was light, and within fifteen minutes, she leaned out the driver's side window of her Tesla, waving her employee badge in front of the card scanner to enter the underground parking garage. She was just rolling up the window when her phone vibrated in the cup holder in the center console, and the Bluetooth connection chimed on the hands-free display on her dashboard. Audie. She was glad the window was up. On a normal day, Audie tended to say inappropriate things, but on the day after Izzy's date, there was about a hundred percent chance of it, and Izzy didn't want the speakers of her car to broadcast her business to anyone who might be walking through the garage. Izzy's precaution paid off. Before she even said hello, Audie's voice boomed through the Tesla.

"Where are you? Tell me you're in a naked hibernaculum. I've gone by your desk three times already to see how your date went last night, but no Izzy. Please tell me this is because the rescue mission was a false alarm, and you woke up in a strange bed on the other side of town and decided to call in sick so you can stay horizontal with the scary beauty."

Izzy groaned. Scary beauty was right. She backed into one of the charging stations in the parking garage. "I thought you were in Vegas."

"When you called, I was in the airport getting ready to board my return flight. So, was I right? Did you go home with the hottie from the dating site?"

"No, I did not. But Jane came to save me, not Hector." Izzy tapped her fingers on the steering wheel as she thought about Jane.

"Hmm. He didn't tell me he was going to delegate when I spoke to him."

Izzy imagined the discussion between Audie and Hector, their commentary about her nonexistent love life and how it could change with the right woman. She thought about Jane again and then shook her head.

A dramatic sigh issued from the car speakers. "You mean I've been stalking the closed door to his office all morning for no reason, when all I had to do was interrogate Jane about the reconnaissance mission? I just saw her. At least *she's* in a good mood today. Why doesn't anyone tell me anything? Why aren't you at work, then?"

Izzy heard something in Audie's voice that she guessed might be worry. Audie knew all about Izzy's bipolar issues. "I just pulled into the parking garage after running a few extra miles this morning."

Audie chuckled. "Ah, I see. Were you running off the tension, so to speak? Do you have a case of blue balls?"

"Disgusting. I'm not even going to respond."

Audie laughed. "Hurry up and get up here. I need to hear all about your disastrous date."

She transferred the call to her phone to continue and got out of her car. "I'm in the parking garage. I'll be up in a few minutes."

"Cool! I can't wait…Damn!"

"What?" Izzy held the phone to her ear with her shoulder and removed the plug from the charging station so she could power up the Tesla.

"I just checked my calendar. I'll be in a meeting for the rest of the day."

"Let's do lunch, then." Izzy plugged her car in and grabbed her laptop bag.

"They're bringing lunch in. Curse this day! I'll hunt you down if I get out early. Otherwise, I'm coming over for a beer tonight, and you're going to spill the details. I'll bring the beer since you never have any at your place."

Izzy laughed and hung up. When she got to her desk, she didn't even take her laptop out of her bag. She just dropped the bag onto her chair and headed to the other side of the floor. She hadn't made up her mind about what she was going to say, but she refused to sit at her desk with the awareness of Jane's proximity taunting her until they somehow bumped into each other. Butterflies filled her stomach.

When she neared Jane's desk, all of the developers, including Jane, were standing in the corner huddled around a huge monitor. It was the morning scrum, when they prioritized their work for the day. Disappointed, and not wanting to interrupt, Izzy was just about to turn around to go back to her desk when the group broke up and started to filter back to their desks. Jane saw her and smiled. A surge of anticipation overcame her. She stood by Jane's desk and watched her approach. She really liked the way Jane walked.

"Hey, there." Jane came to a stop right in front of her with a shy smile.

"Hey." Izzy's mouth was dry. Standing this close to Jane, she could smell the herbal scent she remembered from the night before.

They stared at one another. Izzy's brain had fallen into a recursive loop consisting of memories of their kiss, followed by questions about what it meant, back to the kiss, ad nauseum. There was no room for words.

"You got home safely last night?" Jane finally asked.

"The train station is only a block from my house." Izzy had no idea how she accessed words from the contention in her brain.

"It's close to my house, too," Jane said.

Were they really talking about the train? Jane must have thought the same thing because she rolled her eyes and laughed.

"The train is the last thing on my mind. You wanna get some coffee?"

"Sounds perfect." So, she wasn't the only one.

"Come on." Jane picked at her sleeve, pulling her toward the breakroom.

Izzy fell into step beside her. She would have followed her anywhere.

When they arrived at the orange breakroom, a couple of guys on Izzy's team were playing air hockey at the far end of the room, and Xiying from the security development team was putting a bag in the restaurant-sized refrigerator. The thwack-thwack of the plastic strikers hitting the puck on the air hockey table rang through the room, as did brief blurts of competitive smack talk from the two document-control managers.

"See you at the weekly interlock meeting, Izzy," Xiying said as she passed Izzy and Jane on her way out the breakroom.

"Sounds good." Izzy watched Xiying leave and almost wished she would stay to distract them. Jane's presence, inches away from her, was like a solid thing pressing against her, and all she could think about was last night. But she definitely wasn't ready to talk about it. She had to move, put some distance between them.

She walked to the espresso machine and, with a shaking hand, selected a cup from the stack next to it. Several cups came up at once, and she had to restack them. Finally, she got her cup under the spout and started to brew a cup of coffee. During her struggles, Jane went to the Peanut M&M's and filled a cup. When she came back, she leaned against the high counter island across from her and popped one of the candies into her mouth. Wasn't she even a little nervous?

Jane smiled. "I'm stress eating."

Maybe it wasn't one-sided. Jane was stressed in what way? Stressed they kissed and shouldn't have? Or stressed they'd kissed and wondered what was next? Stressed about something Izzy hadn't yet thought about? God, she was so out of her element, and the tension was making her insane.

"Why are you stressed?" Izzy leaned against the counter next to the machine. How did she manage to sound so casual? This wasn't casual. Audie would have high-fived her for being so cool. That was on the outside, though. Inside, Izzy's guts were roiling.

"I think you know." Jane looked away from Izzy. Was that a crack in her façade?

The espresso machine burped out the last of the coffee, and Izzy turned to take the cup from under the dispenser and put a new one in its place for Jane. The distraction gave her a moment to catch her breath because, for some reason, she was having a hard time breathing. God, it seemed like she was always having a hard time breathing lately.

"Oh." Her heart beat like a hammer in her chest. Were they really going to talk about this here at work? Could she handle it?

With a loud hoot of victory, a clatter came from the air hockey table, and the thwacking of the puck stopped.

"Championship defended once again!" Quan pumped his fist in the air.

"Not for long, buddy!" Jack slapped Quan on the back.

Quan looked at Izzy, raised his fists in the air above his head, and started humming the theme to *Rocky*.

Izzy waved and two guys exited the breakroom, discussing the finer points of the game. They had no idea Izzy was about to faint from whatever was going on with the herd of buffalo in her stomach. How did they not feel the power of whatever was happening between her and Jane in front of the espresso machine?

Izzy turned toward the coffee machine to check the progress of the brew.

"Izzy." Jane's voice was close to Izzy's ear. When Izzy turned, Jane was right there, inches away. She put her hands on Izzy's shoulders. Izzy stared into those infinitely deep chocolate eyes and opened her mouth to say something, but Jane's lips were suddenly there, pressed to hers. Her body responded with an intense heat that coalesced into a fireball in her middle. The kiss was everything. Nothing around them mattered. Jane's mouth tasted of chocolate and peanuts.

Izzy opened her lips, inviting Jane's tongue into her mouth. She reached up to cradle Jane's face, sinking her fingers into her hair, kissing her without restraint. They leaned into each other. Jane's hands slipped to her chest, twisting into fists holding the fabric of her T-shirt. Izzy had never felt possessed like this, nor had she been so willing to be possessed. She abandoned all control and kissed Jane back, releasing all the pent-up confusion of the last ten hours, allowing herself to be swept away by the soft press of Jane's body and the pliant lips sliding against her own.

Voices in the hall just outside the breakroom pulled Izzy from the haze of desire that had descended upon her. She quickly pulled away, dropping her hands from Jane's hair. Her back banged into the counter, and she turned to pick up one of the coffee cups just as Hector and one of his developers walked into the room. Hot espresso splashed over Izzy's hand.

"Shit!" she said, grabbing a paper towel. She barely felt the sting of the burn, but it gave her an excuse to keep her back to the doorway while she pulled herself together. Oh Lord, what a *kiss*! A tingle ran up Izzy's spine.

"Hey, smooth moves! You still thinking about your date last night?" Hector laughed as he came up beside her and grabbed a cup, thrust it under the spout, and pushed the brew button. "I need details. Let's catch up at lunch, okay?"

Izzy turned around and exchanged a look with Jane. "Sounds good." She definitely planned to omit some details.

Hector turned his attention to Jane. "Do you have a minute to chat about the sprint we were talking about in the scrum meeting this morning? Monica has an idea we want to work on."

"Sure." Jane looked completely normal. Her beautiful clear skin was the same as it always was, and Izzy saw no sign of their interrupted kiss. Izzy handed Jane one of the cups of coffee as she started to follow Hector out of the breakroom. The look Jane gave Izzy over her shoulder was the only thing indicating they'd shared a moment capable of melting the countertops in the room. The desire in her eyes burned like a simmering caldera.

If the chemistry is right and the attraction is there, second base is almost inevitable. It's just a matter of getting there. Second base is a hand slipped under a shirt, that skin-to-skin touch, exploration above the waist, the grinding of hips, the titillating promise or hope of something more. Second base is a safe place to hang out if you want to get to know your partner better outside of the bedroom before "going all the way."

Second base is foreplay, heavy petting, the buildup of desire. If your partner doesn't spend much time at second base and wants to move directly to third or beyond, you can get a good idea of how they will be when you have sex. If that's what you're into, great. But if you're looking for something different and you want some buildup before you get busy, you're going to want to make this preference known early on, or you're going to set yourself up for frustration down the road.

CHAPTER TWENTY

The morning flew by for Izzy. Her mind was on Jane and their kiss as she went through the motions of her job. Somehow, she made it through a meeting right before noon and was relieved when Hector told her he couldn't join her for lunch after all. The issue he'd been looking for Jane to discuss kept both of them from taking a break. Glad to have some time alone to think, Izzy grabbed a sandwich and took it back to her desk, where she tried to submerge herself in reviewing a stack of documents.

By three o'clock, she had finally settled into her normal rhythm and was engrossed in some edits when she felt a presence behind her. She knew who it was immediately because heat spread across her body. When she turned, Jane was standing with an apple in her hand and a smile on her face.

"I've been heads down for hours. I need a break. Want to go for a walk?" Jane took a bite of her apple.

Izzy swallowed hard. How had she never noticed how sexy Jane was when she ate? "Is that all you've had today?"

Jane's eyes were on Izzy's lips, and Izzy's heart thumped.

"Hector had pizza brought in."

Izzy dragged her eyes from Jane and closed her laptop. They headed toward the sidewalk that looped around the campus in a sort of landscaped greenbelt. They'd taken breaks and walked this path a few times before, but it was different now.

When they were out of earshot from the building, Jane stopped.

"Things were pretty intense in the breakroom. And last night. I just had to say it, to get it out on the table."

Jane's expression was open, vulnerable, and Izzy was relieved to see that Jane seemed as affected by the kiss as she was. She glanced away before she closed the distance between them again. When she looked back, she saw what appeared to be insecurity on Jane's face and wanted to make it go away.

For a writer, she was having a difficult time finding words. "It was awesome," she said. Pathetic and insufficient as the words were, they were true, and she was relieved to see Jane's expression of insecurity fade.

Jane slid her hand up Izzy's arm, and a flash of the same excitement she'd felt when Jane had led her to the breakroom flared within her. She wanted another kiss, and it scared the hell out of her. What was happening? Her controlled life was in jeopardy, and she couldn't stop the threat. More interestingly, she didn't want to.

They started walking again. Jane's hand fell back to her side, and Izzy thought about reaching out to hold it, but she couldn't bring herself to do it.

Jane's voice was quiet. "I wasn't sure if you were okay with me kissing you."

"I kissed you back." In fact, she wanted to kiss her now, hide behind a tree and kiss her until they both turned into puddles. Where was her sense of control?

"But I started it. I didn't know if you were just being nice."

Izzy snuck a glance at her. "I definitely wasn't just being nice. Does it matter who started it? Maybe I did."

"I'm pretty sure it was me. I've been wanting to do it for weeks."

"Really?" Izzy stopped walking. "Weeks?"

Jane turned and walked backward, smiling while she gazed up through her eyelashes at Izzy. "Really."

Izzy jogged to catch up with her. "How come you didn't say anything?"

"You were interested in Anaya the Playa."

"It was just research." Jane's raised eyebrows forced her to be more truthful. "At least at first. I got a little curious on a personal level at the end, but you saw how that went." She ran a hand over her face.

"Audie never said anything to you?" Jane asked.

"Why would Audie do that?" Izzy asked. Wait. Audie *had* suggested Jane was jealous. Izzy had to concentrate to keep up their pace.

"Both she and Hector have known I find you attractive." Jane pushed her hair behind her ear and looked at her feet as she walked.

"They did?" And they never said anything! They were *her* friends.

It would have been nice to know this. She had no idea what she would have done with the information, but still!

"They indicated it was up to me to make the first move, that you'd never do it. But I was too shy, and you seemed to be having fun meeting new people."

"I wouldn't exactly call it fun." Izzy looked over at Jane, who glanced at her and then away.

"You seemed to enjoy it."

Izzy couldn't tell how Jane was feeling. "It's for my book."

"Are you sure that's all it is?"

"Mostly," she said. But not this thing with Jane. Oh, no. The two kisses with Jane had flipped her for a loop. She was still buzzing with them. She wanted more, even if it was scary. She'd gotten carried away with Kelly all those years ago, and look where that had gotten her. It didn't stop her from craving Jane, though. Not even a little bit.

They were heading back to the building, but Izzy wasn't ready to go back to her desk. Not the way she was feeling. As they passed the parking garage, Izzy didn't check to see if anyone was watching. She took Jane's hand and led her to the gate, badging in.

"Where are we going?" Jane sounded surprised.

"Shortcut." Izzy wasn't sure why she was doing this. To the right, a stairwell led to the upper level. Izzy walked them to the first landing, where they had a little privacy. She backed into the corner. The lighting was dim, and the cement was cold against her back. The musty smell of the underground mixed with car exhaust was familiar as she pulled Jane against her and kissed her.

Jane immediately leaned into her, breast against breast, hip against hip, thigh against thigh. Izzy wrapped her arms around her, splayed her hands against her back. The kiss was impatient and deep. Izzy lost herself in it, her world telescoping to just the two of them. Jane's skin was warm, her lips full and luscious. Izzy nibbled on Jane's lower lip and then traced a path along the edge with her tongue before pressing her mouth firmly against Jane's, pushing a hand into the thick strands of Jane's hair.

When Jane untucked the bottom of her shirt and slid her fingers along the exposed skin of Izzy's waist, anticipation coursed through her. A trail of heat flared across her skin as Jane slid her hand behind her and caressed her back. Izzy's nipples swelled, and she dropped her hand to Jane's ass, pulling her against her, wanting to feel the pressure of Jane against the ache erupting between her legs. Izzy wadded a handful of

Jane's dress in her hand. She wanted to pull it up and feel Jane's skin, but somehow, she still had a grasp on decency.

Izzy had little to no sense of time or place as they kissed.

Music started to play. Izzy registered it as Jane's phone but didn't care. Jane didn't seem to, either, and it silenced after a moment while they continued to kiss. Despite her earlier attempt at decency, Izzy found her hand under the hem of Jane's dress and inside the back of Jane's panties. Jane's skin was smooth and warm under her hand. She ached to find Jane's center.

Jane put her other hand under Izzy's shirt, and both of her hands wandered across Izzy's bare skin until they were just under her breasts. Izzy moaned, wanting her to move them up and possess her aching flesh.

The music started again, and Jane groaned, breaking the kiss. Izzy's heart was racing. Jane eased back and reached into the top of her dress and pulled out her phone. God, she was so sexy!

She made a face. "It's Hector. I'm late for a meeting."

Izzy laughed. She tucked her shirt back in as Jane smoothed her dress and hair.

"Is it important?"

"It's just a one-on-one. He's supposed to walk me through some test outputs."

"He'll forgive you."

"Not if he knew what we're doing. Do I look as disheveled as I feel?" Jane laughed nervously and pushed her hair behind her ears.

"You look perfect. Beautiful," Izzy said as she moved a single strand of hair from Jane's forehead. It was true. Her naturally full and wavy hair was gorgeous, and her clothes were in place.

Jane smiled and put her fingers on her lips. "I feel like anyone could look at me and figure out exactly what we've been doing."

"If they did, they'd be jealous of me for getting to kiss you." Izzy smoothed her shirt into her waistband. "Is my shirt okay?"

"It's fine, but I'm not sure people will think that's your lipstick."

Izzy laughed and wiped her mouth. Jane grabbed her wrist and gently pulled her hand away. With her other hand, she rubbed a spot at the corner of Izzy's mouth. When Jane's eyes landed on hers, their gaze locked. Izzy was sure she was about to kiss her again.

"Your meeting?" Izzy reminded her.

Jane seemed to gather herself.

"Oh, yeah." She looked at her phone. "I am so late. I'll text him."

As Izzy and Jane made their way out the garage, the sunlight made Izzy squint.

"I won't need any sugar or caffeine to get me through the afternoon slump," Izzy joked as they neared the main doors to the office building.

Jane laughed and ran a hand down Izzy's arm, sending tingles throughout her. She was in trouble.

The air-conditioning was chilly against Izzy's hot skin when she keyed the card reader and opened the doors to let them inside. Without a word, Jane peeled off toward a conference room on the first floor as Izzy pushed the button to summon the elevator.

A sudden shot of panic hit Izzy as the door slid open. She looked over at the front desk. Rhonda was talking to a delivery driver, and Cliff was nowhere to be seen. That meant no one was watching the live camera feeds from around the campus—especially the parking-garage stairways. Thank God!

Third base is a tricky base. It's where a lot of action occurs, but the players can still officially retain their amateur standing, if you catch my meaning. There's a certain gravity or weight to the situation when you go past third base, but if you stay there, it's easier to remain uncommitted. Even so, people often have a hard time knowing when to stop there or keep rounding toward home plate. The thrill of motion can send a player rounding toward home before they know what they're doing. Third base has always been more about preserving some sort of purity while also getting away with something titillating.

Third base is exciting. You've gone past passionate kissing and tentative touching, and you're exploring each other with crazy abandon. Some among us will want to debate the "penetration equates to sex" aspect. "Penetration of what with what?" some may ask. Others will want to consider the multifaceted nuance of gender identity and sexual orientation. The bottom line, third base tends to be a place where you haven't quite gone all the way in whatever fashion you prefer to have sex. For some, it will be genital manipulation, even orgasm. For others, that constitutes home plate.

Either way, third base is a pretty wild place.

Chapter Twenty-one

Thoughts of kisses and residual tingles of hands on bare skin kept Izzy from concentrating on her work when she got back to her desk, and although she kept an eye out for Jane, she didn't see her the rest of the afternoon. When five o'clock came around, she decided to go home. She took the long way to the elevators so she could swing by Jane's desk. No laptop. Her chair was pushed in.

She popped her head into Hector's office, and he looked up from his computer.

"Hey, Iz. I've been meaning to tell you sorry about last night. Audie called me just as I was leaving to go pick up Jillian for a date. You were right about making it all about her." He winked.

"No problem. Jane saved the day. Speaking of, have you seen her? Did she leave?"

"She got a call during our one-on-one saying her mom was in the hospital."

"Is she okay?"

"I'm not sure. I guess she took a fall. Jane left so quickly, I didn't get many details."

Izzy said thanks, pulled out her phone, and was dialing as she got on the elevator. The call went directly to voice mail, so she left a message.

She had no idea what to do next except wait for Jane to call her back. So, she went to the underground garage to get her car. The smell of the garage evoked memories, and Izzy shivered. She'd never enter the garage again without thinking about Jane's hands on her.

Izzy pulled into her driveway without recalling the drive home. Jane's lips occupied all of her senses. She was lucky she'd navigated the famous traffic mess of San Jose's rush hour without incident being so distracted.

A quick look at her texts while walking into the house showed that Anaya had sent her a message. Dread filled her chest. She had to let her know she couldn't see her anymore, but how was she going to do that? Yet when she read the message, she found that Anaya had solved the issue for her, saying Izzy's life seemed too complicated, and while she enjoyed their time together, maybe they should just be friends. The tightness in Izzy's chest disappeared instantly.

Smiling with relief, she tossed a family-sized frozen chicken pot pie into the oven and went into her room to change into running clothes, Gus dancing around her feet. She was in the bathroom when her phone rang.

Hoping it was Jane, she was a little disappointed when she found a message from Audie.

"Hey, Iz, I know I said I'd come over for a beer to hear all about your miserable date, but I'm gonna be at work for another hour or so, and I'm tired from the Vegas trip. I'll take you to lunch tomorrow so I can hear all the gory details. Hope we're cool. *Ciao, bella!*"

Izzy was relieved. She needed time to think, and she wasn't sure she was ready to talk with anyone, especially since she hadn't even talked to Jane about what was happening between them. She still didn't know where they stood. Jane had made it obvious she'd been thinking about Izzy for a while now, so it wasn't one-sided. But what did it really mean? And was Izzy ready to explore where this could go? Also, where was her normal anxiety? She inventoried her emotions. No tight chest. No difficulty breathing. No racing thoughts…well, no *negative* racing thoughts. Instead, a pleasant sense of anticipation and excitement zinged through her body every time she thought about Jane.

As if to tell herself she couldn't get away with coasting through this kind of shake-up, Izzy started to wonder if she was suppressing her normal emotions to avoid the sense of chaos that came with letting a person even slightly into her heart. Because that was what it was, right? She was playing with the idea of pursuing something with Jane. Familiar anxiety flooded her.

"For fuck's sake!" she said to herself. She needed to get out of her head. "Come on, Gus. Let's go for our run while dinner cooks."

She finished getting ready, and Gus was already waiting at the door with his harness and leash in his mouth.

"I think you like running more than I do." Izzy scratched his head and attached the leash.

They headed toward a nearby park that had a perimeter path just under a mile long. It was the perfect route, especially since Izzy had been on autopilot for much of the evening, and it was probably safer if she took a path that crossed only one street.

They made two laps and headed back home to check on dinner.

The house smelled great when she entered. With twenty minutes to go on the timer, Izzy jumped into the shower.

She was toweling off when her phone rang again. Expecting it to be Audie changing her mind about coming over, she felt her heart pound harder when she saw Jane's name displayed on the caller ID.

"Hey, you." She hoped she sounded relaxed.

"Hey, you." Was that nervousness in Jane's voice, too?

Izzy dropped the towel onto the counter and hand-combed her hair in the mirror. "I went by your desk on the way out of the office. Hector said your mom fell. Is she okay?"

"I just dropped her off at home."

Izzy wanted to know more about it, but Jane didn't offer, and she didn't want to pry. "I'm glad she's okay."

"She'll be okay in a few days." Jane sighed, sounding tired.

"How are you doing?" Izzy asked.

Jane chuckled. "I'm a bit distracted, to be honest."

"About your mom?"

"I'm angry about that. I'm distracted by you."

Izzy wanted to ask what she meant by the first statement, but it didn't seem like Jane wanted to discuss it, and the second statement made her heart pick up its pace.

"Me, too," Izzy admitted. She was smiling into the phone, glad she wasn't the only one in this condition. She could think of nothing other than feeling Jane's warm skin under her palms and tasting her lips.

"What are we going to do?" Jane's voice was almost a whisper.

Izzy leaned against the counter in the bathroom. "What do you want to do?"

"Tricky question."

Izzy could almost see Jane's raised eyebrow and half-smile as she teased her. She wanted to ask if she could see her right then, but she was afraid she'd sound too needy. Was it smart, anyway?

A siren sounded outside of Izzy's house, and Gus, who was curled up on the bathroom rug, howled. It echoed through the small room.

"What's all the commotion?" Jane asked.

"Sorry. An ambulance went by the house, and Gus likes to join in." Izzy used her foot to ruffle the fur on Gus's side. "Right, my protective boy?" He wagged his tail once and dropped his head to his paws.

"That's cute," Jane said, and a siren wailed on Jane's end, too.

"Sounds like emergency vehicles are deploying all over the city," Izzy said. "Are you still near the hospital?"

Jane exhaled loudly. "This is embarrassing. I'm in my car. Just down the street from your house, actually."

Izzy chuckled. "Are you stalking me, Jane Mendoza?" There was a big sigh on the other end of the line, and Izzy imagined Jane burying her face in her hands.

"Kind of. God. You're going to get a restraining order. After I dropped my mom off, I took Lester to the dog park and knew you lived around here. I got curious and googled your address and saw how close I was. So, the next thing I knew, I was going past your house and—" Jane blurted out one quick sentence.

Izzy heard her take a deep breath. A buzz crept across her skin. Jane was so close. She realized she was still naked from the shower. "Why didn't you stop?"

"At your house?"

"Yeah. Why didn't you knock on the door?"

Another sigh came across the line. "I chickened out."

"Why?" She was pretty sure she knew.

"I'm not sure. That's a lie. I'm nervous about what's going on between us."

"Yeah, me, too." Izzy glanced at herself in the mirror. "Do you want to come over and talk about it?"

Jane paused, and Izzy wasn't sure what answer she wanted to hear more.

"Yes and no."

Izzy didn't expect that answer and laughed. Well, she'd already offered, and she could smell dinner was nearly done. "Come over. I made dinner. Nothing fancy but enough for two. Are you hungry?"

"I am."

"So, you'll come over?"

"I'm already parking in front of your house."

Izzy walked into her bedroom, suddenly in a hurry. "I'll be at the door in a couple of minutes. I have to put some clothes on."

Jane gulped on the other end of the line. "See you in a few, then."

Minutes later, clad in shorts and a T-shirt, Izzy opened her front door and found Jane and Lester standing on the stoop.

Gus ran circles around them.

"It smells incredible in here."

"I can take credit only for turning the oven on and taking the pot pie out of the box before tossing it into the oven." Just as she spoke, the timer went off, and Jane followed her into the kitchen. Izzy silenced the timer and opened the oven to take a look. A wave of delicious aroma billowed into the kitchen. "It looks like it'll be about five more minutes," she said as she closed the oven again. Nervousness pinged around in Izzy's stomach. "I don't have much to offer along the lines of beverages, but do you want some water or a cup of coffee?"

Izzy leaned against the counter and twisted the corner of the dish towel she'd picked up when she opened the oven.

"Water's fine."

Izzy draped the dish towel over her shoulder and poured them each a glass of water from the filtered tap, and they walked into the living room and sat on the couch. Izzy was careful to sit at the very end to keep some distance between them, although she was totally aware of Jane on the other end.

"So, your mom is okay?"

Jane's brow furrowed. "Okay is a subjective word."

"You sound angry."

"I'm pissed that she lies to the doctors when they ask what happened. I'm pissed that my dad just stands there, acting like he's concerned when she leaves the emergency room in another cast with an eye swollen shut. He had the nerve to call me to come pick them up because they were taken to the hospital in an ambulance. That was a first. He must have freaked out because she was unconscious."

"What happened?"

Jane frowned into the hand she placed over her eyes. She looked angry, exhausted, scared, sad…and a whole lot of other emotions. Izzy wanted to hold her.

"He pushed her down the back steps when she asked him about mowing the lawn."

"Oh…" Izzy didn't know what to say.

Jane put her water on the table and stared at it. "I don't know why I'm telling you. I'm just mad. At both of them. I really came over here because I wanted to get my mind off it."

"It's okay. Can I do anything to help you feel better?"

Jane looked up at her, and a shy smile played across her lips. "Just being near you helps."

Izzy smiled back when a volley of squeaks came from the corner of the room. The dogs were playing with Gus's toys, including a canvas Darth Vader squeak toy and his prized unicorn.

Izzy sipped her water. "Gus definitely likes Lester. The unicorn stuffy is his favorite. He sleeps with it."

Gus got excited when he heard his name and came over to Izzy for a pet, but in the process, his tail knocked over Jane's water.

"Oh, no! I'm so sorry!" Jane quickly righted the glass, but the entire contents had already escaped, covering the table, and were now dripping onto the wooden floor beneath it.

"It's only water." Izzy used the dish towel she'd draped over her shoulder to sop it up. While doing so, she had slid over on the couch, and she was now sitting right next to Jane. Once the water was sopped up, she started to move back to her end of the couch, but Jane reached over and took her hand, stopping her.

The soft warmth of Jane's hand on her wrist surprised Izzy, and she stared at it for a moment before looking up. Jane's eyes had the same expression she'd seen in the train station. She couldn't look away. Again, she wasn't sure who started it, but they were kissing. And before long, they were back to where they were in the parking garage. Jane's hands were under Izzy's shirt, and Izzy pulled her onto her lap. An annoying voice tried to invade her mind, telling her this wasn't a good idea, but the sensations buzzing through her and her overwhelming attraction for Jane easily overrode the voice. She welcomed the presence of mania, which only amped up her excitement.

Without breaking the kiss, Jane straddled her, pressing into her, and an exquisite ache filled Izzy. She slipped her hands under Jane's skirt, cupping her ass and pulling her closer. The satin fabric of Jane's panties was soft under her fingers. Their kiss was slow, deep, exploring. Jane's kisses sent tremors through her, feeding the throbbing pulse between her legs. Izzy slid her hands under the band of Jane's panties and massaged the muscles beneath her palms. Jane's hips began to rock, and she shifted to the side so her legs straddled Izzy's thigh. Jane's leg between Izzy's put pressure against the throbbing at Izzy's core, which intensified exponentially as Jane's rocking grew faster and harder.

The experience of growing so aroused so quickly was an absolute first for Izzy. Without warning, a flash of brilliant pleasure burst through her; she went taut and threw her head back as waves of warmth flowed through her. She kept her eyes squeezed shut as she gasped for breath, and Jane's soft lips pressed against her throat. Explosions of erotic sensation originated between her legs, coalescing in the places Jane kissed. She shuddered. "Oh God, please."

Jane's lips closed over hers, silencing her, and Jane's hips moved quickly. Izzy's thigh was wet where Jane's center moved against her bare leg. She squeezed Jane's firm backside and pulled her against her, harder, helping her keep contact. Suddenly, Jane's back arched and she lifted her head. She had her eyes wide open, staring at Izzy with a laser-like intensity. Her mouth formed an "O," and a long moan slipped through her beautiful, full lips, swollen and glistening. A thrill pierced Izzy, causing her to shiver as Jane's movements slowed, and she felt as if they were dancing. Jane collapsed against her, dropping her head to rest against Izzy's shoulder. Izzy held her and kissed the side of her face, not caring about Jane's thick hair tickling her. The soft, warm dampness against her leg held most of her attention. Had they really just done what they did? Fully clothed?

Jane turned her head so her face was close to Izzy's neck. Small puffs of breath tickled her sensitive skin.

"What just happened?" Jane asked. She dragged her fingertips up Izzy's arm.

Goose bumps rose in the path of Jane's fingers, and Izzy shivered. A surprised giggle nearly escaped her, but she kissed her instead, their kiss unhurried and full of words Izzy didn't know how to speak.

Jane reached up and traced the side of Izzy's face.

"I can't believe we just…you know…" Jane's voice was husky, lower than Izzy had ever heard it.

"Did you…" Izzy tilted her head.

A slow smile etched itself across Jane's face. "Oh, yeah. Right after you."

Izzy smiled back. "I've never done that before. I mean, fully clothed."

"God, I want to touch you right now." Jane slipped her hand into the front waistband of Izzy's shorts.

Izzy gasped, and Jane's fingers were teasing the top of her panties, trying to move them aside. A throb ripped through Izzy again, and she rolled slightly away to allow Jane more room to do whatever she planned to do. Her toes curled in anticipation as Jane's fingers slid beneath the edge of her panties, skimming her...

The fire alarm started to chirp, and through the fog of desire gripping her, Izzy became aware of a burnt smell.

"Dinner!" she said, trying to get up. Jane's hand in her pants prevented her from moving, and a huge smile stretched across her face. She kissed Jane. "I'm so sorry!" Jane laughed and removed her hand, and Izzy regretfully got up to check the oven. The pot pie was toast.

Jane was a few steps behind her.

A cloud of smoke filled the kitchen. Fortunately, there wasn't any fire. Just a pot pie with a blackened crust.

"Let's open some windows." Jane was already tugging at the sliding-glass door.

Izzy turned on the oven fan and carried the burnt dish out to the back patio to take the smoke outside. Jane waved a magazine at the fire alarm to stop its chirping. After a few minutes, the smoke cleared enough to silence the alarm, and by then, the voices in Izzy's head were telling her she'd let things go too far. Fortunately, the emotional high was still quite strong, and Izzy was easily able to quiet the voices—mostly.

"That was exciting," Jane said.

"Sorry. I should have reset the timer."

"I guess we lost track of time." Jane moved closer to Izzy.

"We sure did." Izzy wrapped an arm around Jane's waist and pulled her close. They kissed for a minute or two before Izzy reluctantly pulled back. "Maybe almost burning the house down was a sign."

"A sign of what?" Jane looked confused.

Izzy felt stupid, but everything happening between her and Jane, as exciting and sexy as it was, was starting to scare her. "A sign telling us to maybe put on the brakes a little bit."

Jane's eyebrows rose. "Really? Because I thought we were just getting started." She nibbled on Izzy's earlobe, and it felt so good, Izzy couldn't help but tilt her head to show Jane just how much she enjoyed it. She had to work hard to remember what she'd been saying.

"Um..." Had she been talking about signs? Izzy shivered when Jane ran her tongue along the outer edge of her ear. Signs. Yes, signs. They needed to slow down. Jane's tongue was soft and hot. They didn't have to *stop*. Just go slower. Even as she thought it, a tremor of apprehension wove through the elation of being in Jane's arms. "We… we haven't even gone on a proper date yet."

What a weird thing to say, like she was some sort of stodgy old man. But she felt Jane smile against her neck.

"Are you saying you'd like to date me?"

The vibration of Jane's voice, low and breathy near her ear, sent tremors along Izzy's spine. She closed her eyes and tried to stuff the apprehension away. "Yes. A date."

Jane stepped back so they were no longer touching. "Then ask me."

Without the heat of Jane's body pressed against her and without soft lips teasing her, Izzy was able to think beyond the haziness of desire, and her unease grew. She focused on the beautiful woman in front of her, the softness in Jane's eyes giving her courage. "Will you go out with me tomorrow night?"

Jane stepped closer with a slow, sexy smile.

Izzy's stomach fluttered with anticipation…or was it trepidation?

"Yes. But just for the record, proper dates are overrated," Jane whispered before teasing Izzy's lips with the tip of her tongue. Izzy gave in to another deep kiss and slid her knee between Jane's legs. Tension began to build in her lower belly, and any unease melted into the background.

The doorbell rang.

"Ignore it," Jane said, increasing the pressure of her thigh between Izzy's legs.

Izzy didn't intend to answer it. She ground against the taut muscle of Jane's thigh, so close. Jane slid her hands under Izzy's T-shirt and ran her fingers up the sides of her breasts. Izzy threw her head back, and Jane kissed her neck. Jane pinched one of her nipples through the fabric of her bra. Izzy gasped. A tremor began in her center. Izzy closed her eyes.

"Izzy? Are you okay? It smells like something has turned to charcoal in here." Audie's voice sounded from the living room.

Izzy and Jane jumped away from one another, and Izzy stepped back, her bare leg grazing the edge of the open oven door. Fortunately, the door had been open long enough to cool somewhat, but the shock of it against her leg caused her to overbalance, and she stumbled to catch herself, ending up on the kitchen floor.

She wasn't hurt, but the surprised look on Jane's face caused her to laugh out loud, and Audie found the two of them doubled over in laughter when she came into the kitchen.

"What happened in here?" Audie asked, staring at Izzy on the floor and then at the open windows and doors.

Izzy, out of breath from laughing, pulled herself up to standing. "It looks like we're going to have to order pizza."

And then there's the seventh-inning stretch.

Everyone is different. Have I said it before? It's true. Some people are "all or nothing, jump right in, don't look back" kind of people. Some people are "one toe at a time" kind of people. And some people fully intend to go into it one toe at a time but find themselves doing a triple gainer into the deep end before they realize what happened. I realize I just mixed sports metaphors, but you know what I mean, right? It's all good. It's just better if you know what kind of person you are before you start second-guessing everything you do.

The thing is, people go at their own pace, and each situation will affect their actions, sometimes producing surprising outcomes. There is no perfect numbered list, like they publish in those magazines in grocery-store-checkout racks. "10 Steps to Landing Your Dream Lover." Really?

Anyway, the best advice you can use is this. If you listen to your heart, you'll do well.

Chapter Twenty-two

It was Friday night, date night, and Izzy stepped out of the shower. The cold water had felt good. She'd gone for a run after work, but her skin had been hot all day thinking about what had happened on the couch the night before. She and Jane had barely talked all day, but their looks at each other the few times they crossed paths could've started fires. Izzy had alternated between aching for more to terror to do it again. The back-and-forth was exhausting. Now she was getting ready for the date and the amped-up rate of toggling was beyond ridiculous.

After last night, she told herself this date would not end with them in bed. Her libido, on the other hand, told her to shave her legs and wear cute underwear. She stared at her reflection and reminded herself they needed to go slow, take their time getting to know each other. God, she was nervous, mostly in a good way. But if she wasn't careful, she could find herself in—No! She didn't want to think like that. She just had to keep an eye on her emotions. Elation was a tricky beast. She was already feeling it, and she had to step back and wonder if it resulted from the normal pheromones and excitement of a possible good thing, or if she was tipping into the danger zone where racing thoughts and sustained mania lived? She was so tempted to let the elation take over, much like it had the night before. It felt good. But she had to be wary. She needed to remind herself to sleep, eat well, exercise, and take her medicine on schedule.

She leaned against the bathroom counter and shook her head. If she just stuck to her schedule, she could let the elation run its course. Going slow would help her manage all this. She took a deep breath and went into her room to get dressed.

A few minutes later, she rolled up the sleeves of her favorite button-up shirt. It was soft cotton, and the lavender looked good over the white T-shirt she wore under it. With her favorite jeans and new suede slip-on shoes, she felt just the right amount of casual for the restaurant she'd picked for them.

With rush hour over, the drive over to Jane's house didn't take much time. They lived only five miles apart, but rush hour could make the difference between a twenty-minute drive and an hour-long one. Sometimes, Izzy wondered what it would be like to work in a place where she didn't have to factor in the drive time to reach places. But her family lived here, and aside from the driving commute, the crowds, and astronomical price of housing, San Jose was a great place to be. She didn't mind the urban crowds. She owned her own home. Her house was a straight shot on the train from her work. She had it good here.

Jane's house was in an older part of town Izzy loved but had little reason to visit. Her instructions had Izzy find a red gate with her address on it, which opened to a narrow sidewalk flanked with wooden fencing running alongside the side of a massive Victorian house. The fence on either side was draped in a vine sporting a plethora of sweetly aromatic white trumpet flowers. Walking down the path, she felt a little like she was in a fairy tale, venturing into a magical realm.

Jane's house was an ivy-covered granny flat with lots of windows. A water fountain gurgled under a front window.

Izzy knocked on the front door, and Lester barked on the other side of it.

Jane's voice followed. "Hush, big man. It's your friend Izzy."

The door opened, and Izzy's heartbeat increased. Lester looked at her with a friendly doggy smile, his tongue lolling out the side of his mouth. Izzy patted him on the head, but her eyes were riveted on Jane.

"You look awesome." Jane's appearance deserved a more eloquent comment, but Izzy couldn't think of one. Jane glanced down at her pale-yellow sundress with small blue flowers and then up with a shy smile. She always looked good but normally wore her hair back or in a ponytail. Today her hair was loose. Izzy could almost feel her fingers slipping through the long strands.

"You clean up nice, too. But I already knew that from when I rescued you from Boozy McHandsy," Jane said.

"Boozy McWhat?"

"The woman you went out with who wouldn't take no for an answer?" A crease appeared between Jane's eyebrows.

Was that jealousy in Jane's expression? "Yeah. Fun times."

Jane pushed her hair over her shoulder. "You and I have way different ideas of fun."

Izzy reached up and moved a lingering strand of hair. "I was thinking about the platform when we were waiting for the train, actually."

Jane's eyes dropped to Izzy's mouth.

Izzy's stomach fluttered with anxiety and something else.

The side of Jane's mouth rose. "Oh, yeah. Fun is an understatement, then."

A cat weaved between Jane's ankles, and they both looked down.

"Who's this?" Izzy asked, bending to pet the black-and-white-spotted cat.

"This is Juliet. You will now be her favorite person ever because you scratched behind her ears."

Izzy stared at Jane. God, she wanted to kiss her. Another nearly identical cat rubbed against her leg.

"And who is this?" Izzy asked.

"Romeo. They're brother and sister." Izzy raised an eyebrow and looked up at Jane again as she petted both cats. "I know. But it's purely familial love between them, I assure you."

"Are they allowed outside?"

"They're inside cats. They'll sit in the doorway and sometimes venture out to look around, but neither of them seems interested in exploring beyond the front stoop."

"My cats are indoor cats, too."

"I didn't see them when I was over the other day."

Izzy stood. "Fat Bob and Prince. They were running on only twenty-three hours of sleep and couldn't be bothered to meet guests. If you had been there when they were awake, you would have had a cat lap blanket. They love company."

"Speaking of company, why are we still on the porch? Come in. Where are my manners?"

Jane stepped aside, and Izzy wanted nothing more than to go inside and see where Jane lived. But if she did, they might start kissing. A wave of butterflies filled her stomach. If they started kissing, she'd probably have no willpower, and they'd miss their reservation. Not to mention her vow to not wind up in bed this time.

"I'd love to, but we should leave. Our reservation is in twenty minutes."

Did disappointment cloud Jane's eyes?

❖

Jane rolled down the window of Izzy's Tesla, and fragrant night air filled the car. It was late, and the heat of the summer day had transitioned into a pleasantly cool night. Izzy glanced at her passenger and wished she wasn't driving so she could watch her hair blowing in the wind and her beautiful skin glow in the lights from the car's computer display.

The date had been better than she'd hoped, and she'd expected it to be wonderful. Their conversation over dinner had been engaging, the live music after dinner had been perfect, and the walk they'd taken after dinner, hand in hand through the flower garden in a local park, had been just right. It was now past midnight, and even the ride home was something out of a fairy tale.

When they arrived at Jane's gate, Izzy got out of the car to walk Jane to her door. After she opened the gate, Jane took her hand, and they strolled along the walk toward her little flat.

Jane reached out and cupped one of the white trumpet flowers in her hand, and a sweet fragrance rose in the air. "I had a truly wonderful night tonight."

"I did, too. Thanks for humoring me and going on a date with me."

Jane looked at her, the light from the moon reflecting in her eyes. Izzy's stomach did a cartwheel, a frequent sensation she'd experienced throughout the night any time Jane looked at her.

"I wasn't humoring you. I looked forward to this all day."

"Me, too," Izzy said. They'd made it to Jane's door, where Jane held both her hands in hers, and Izzy looked at them. "I wish the night wasn't over. I really enjoy being with you."

Jane stepped closer and let go of Izzy's hands. She put her hands on Izzy's chest near her collarbones and leaned close. "It doesn't have to end," she whispered and kissed her.

The kiss was light and teasing at first, and Izzy returned it, enjoying the feel of Jane's teeth gently nibbling on her bottom lip. Soon, though, the kiss became a deep exploration, and Jane's hands were at the nape of her neck, tracing a line of fire across her back.

When they took a breath, Jane held her close.

"I should go home," Izzy said.

Jane's smile was bright in the moonlight. "But you want to come in."

Izzy laughed. "I do, but I think I should go home."

"What if I say I don't want you to go home?" Jane played with the hair at the back of Izzy's neck, and tingles ran up and down her spine.

Izzy swallowed. "Then I'd say you're making it hard to stick to my plan."

"What plan is that?"

Jane kissed her again, letting her lips linger on the corner of her mouth. Izzy had a hard time remembering what they were talking about.

"My plan of taking it slow."

Jane ran her fingers along the open vee of Izzy's button-down shirt and slid them along the neck of the T-shirt beneath. Her fingers felt hot against Izzy's skin.

"Do you always go slow?"

Izzy ran her hands over the soft skin of Jane's arms. She didn't really want to get into the details of how she hadn't been with anyone special since Kelly, and that was why it was important to go slow. Her thoughts started to buzz and she took a few deep breaths. The pressure in her head eased a little. "Not always."

"Why do you want to go slow now?"

"Because I don't want to screw it up."

Jane kissed a trail across Izzy's jawline and nibbled on her ear. "I never understood how going fast is a bad thing. If it feels right, how can it be a bad thing? Besides, technically, we've known each other for several weeks. Doesn't that count for anything?"

Her logic almost made sense. Izzy shivered as Jane sucked gently on her ear lobe. Her resolve was almost gone. "You have a point."

Jane kissed Izzy's neck. "So, you'll come in?"

Izzy's thoughts were buried in a haze of desire, but she hesitated. If she went in, they would definitely take their relationship to the next level.

She was still trying to organize her thoughts when Jane kissed her, driving all reason out of her mind.

❖

Home plate, also known as scoring, is the full-on culmination of sexual togetherness. Or something like that. Some people are happy with staying at third base. There's plenty of gratification in the kind of things you can do there. And, honestly, one could see the idea of home plate as being the apex of heteronormative bias. After all, not everyone enjoys penetrative sex, and some who do, don't use an appendage attached to their partner, either organically or with straps, to accomplish it. So, basically, home plate is more of an understanding that all physical barriers have been removed, at least at a sexual level, than it is a specific sex act. If it happens at third base for you, well, baby, you've scored with a triple, which leaves you with more energy to go a little longer. You go, you!

Some people go from first base to home plate in one interaction. Others take a lot longer to get from first to home. It depends on the people, their particular values around sex, and the level of attraction between them.

Chapter Twenty-three

Izzy wasn't sure how she arrived at the foot of Jane's bed, but there she was, heart pounding, legs weak and shaking. She didn't have words for the kiss she'd just experienced or the desperate need surging through her. Jane stood before her, wrapped in her arms, trembling. Izzy was dazed, and she dropped her gaze to the lips she'd just been kissing, fully intending to do it some more. But when she moved her head in their direction, Jane put her hands on Izzy's chest and pushed her back so she was sitting on the bed, so that Jane was standing before her. She reached out to pull Jane into her lap, but Jane had other plans.

She stepped back and slid one of the straps of her dress from her shoulder, tossing her hair back. Izzy looked up into Jane's eyes, and their dark-brown beauty swam with a sexy intensity Izzy had never experienced. The gaze penetrated her with an electric heat, filling her entirely, and the beauty before her immobilized her.

Jane pushed the strap all the way off and ran her fingers under the top of the dress to the other strap, sliding it from her shoulder. The top of the dress fell down until the soft cotton revealed a luscious expanse of cleavage and the top half of a lacy white bra. Izzy used her fingers to trace the lines of Jane's collarbone and ran them down until they rested on the little pink rose sewn into the center of the fabric between Jane's breasts.

Jane captured Izzy's hand and placed her fingers under the lacy garment. The back of Izzy's fingers brushed over Jane's erect nipple. Jane sucked in a breath while Izzy held hers. Jane pulled Izzy's hand from the garment and kissed Izzy's palm before slowly turning around.

"Unzip me?" Jane looked back at her over her shoulder, and Izzy complied, moving Jane's hair to the side. All thoughts of going slow had vanished, and the desire cascading through her completely eclipsed the anxiety that had plagued her. She kissed a small constellation of freckles dotting the space between Jane's shoulder blades while she slowly lowered the zipper. The dress fell away, and Izzy stepped closer, encircling Jane's waist with her arms. She kissed Jane's neck and pressed against her from behind, flattening her hands against Jane's stomach, moving them up until they were resting just below Jane's breasts. Jane let her head fall back, and Izzy pressed kisses against her warm skin until Jane turned in her arms and kissed her.

God. What a kiss. Feeling Jane's skin, warm and soft beneath her hands, Izzy grew dizzy as she pressed her lips against Jane's and traced the soft skin of her inner lips with her tongue. As their kiss deepened, Izzy ran her hands in random patterns over Jane's shoulders, down over her hips, and up along her spine. She couldn't get enough of touching her. She couldn't get enough of kissing her.

Jane unbuttoned her shirt and pushed it off. When Jane's hands slid under the bottom of her T-shirt, Izzy gasped, and Jane pushed the shirt up and over her head.

"No bra. Sexy." Jane dipped her head and put her mouth around one of Izzy's nipples. The sensation shot straight to Izzy's groin. A moan poured out of her while she tangled her hands in Jane's hair, throwing her own head back as Jane's tongue played across her chest.

She untangled her hands from Jane's hair, skimming her fingers along Jane's back until she found the hook to her bra and unclasped it. Jane stood back and pulled the undergarment off.

"God, you're beautiful," Izzy whispered. Jane's full breasts, tipped with dark nipples, swayed with Jane's breathing. The matching lacy white panties Jane wore contrasted gorgeously with Jane's light-brown skin and rode low across her hips, just below her slightly rounded belly. In the dim light of the room, she looked like a painting.

Jane moved close and unbuttoned Izzy's jeans, pushing them down with Izzy's panties. Izzy stepped out of her clothing as well as her slip-on shoes and pulled Jane into her arms. Jane responded with a long kiss and pulled Izzy onto the bed. A startled cat jumped away, but Izzy barely noticed, the feel of their naked skin against each other the center of her attention. Jane rolled her onto her back and covered her with her body. Izzy ran her hands up and down Jane's sides, pausing to cup the sides of her breasts, filling her hands with their softness. She gently rolled Jane's nipples between her fingers and thumbs before taking one of them into her mouth. Teasing the firm flesh with her lips, she then ran her tongue around it before sucking and gently nibbling it. Jane straddled her thigh and pressed against it. The damp warmth of Jane's panties revealed how excited Jane was, and Izzy slid her hands into the back of Jane's panties, pushing them down. Jane rose and removed them, kicking them off the bed.

"Is there anything you don't like to do?" Jane asked as she lowered her head to tease one of Izzy's nipples.

"I don't think so," Izzy said. Her voice trembled with need.

"Well, don't hesitate to let me know if you want me to stop. Or if you want more of something." Jane sucked on Izzy's nipple while she pinched the other one.

"Oh, God. Like what you're doing now? I love that."

"You do? Good. Because I love your breasts."

Jane rubbed herself against Izzy's thigh, and Izzy held her ass, pulling Jane harder against her. Jane moved her leg up placing it between Izzy's leg, and Izzy's hips rose and fell in the rhythm Jane had started. Between Jane's artful attention to her nipples and the pressure of Jane's leg on her center, a throbbing pulse started to fill Izzy.

"I could come like this again." Jane's mouth was near her ear now, and soft lips closed around Izzy's earlobe. "But I want you inside me when I come with you." Jane reached back and took Izzy's hand, sliding it between her legs.

"I'm left-handed," Izzy said, exchanging hands. She smiled and kissed Jane as her fingers teased through the damp hair between Jane's legs, dipping into the warm wetness.

Jane lifted her head and gasped. "I knew that," she said just before she kissed Izzy.

Izzy explored the slick folds around her fingers, tracing the edges and slipping between them to tease the opening. Jane guided Izzy's fingers, moving her middle and forefinger against her clit. Izzy pressed it, getting to know Jane's body, taking in the way it responded to her touch.

"That's it. Yes." Jane moaned and pushed against Izzy's fingers.

Jane moved Izzy's fingers around and over her clit a few times, showing Izzy how hard she liked to be touched, and then Jane let go, dropping her hand back to the bed to support herself as she rocked over Izzy on her hands and knees. Izzy moved her other hand to Jane's breast and pinched the nipple while she rubbed Jane's clit. She dipped her fingers into Jane and slid her fingers back over the sensitive area. Jane moaned, and wetness covered Izzy's hand. Jane's hips began to twitch more aggressively, and when Izzy slid her fingers into her, strong muscles wrapped around her fingers. She hooked them and stroked the front inside of Jane's wall. Jane cried out and shook in Izzy's arms before she dropped her head onto Izzy's shoulder and lowered herself onto her. Izzy left her fingers inside Jane, the muscles gently contracting against them. She wrapped her other arm around Jane and held her until Jane caught her breath.

It wasn't long before Jane eased Izzy's fingers out of herself and slid down to rest between her thighs, focusing her attention on Izzy's pleasure.

❖

What happens after you've had sex for the first time?

Some people are come-and-go kind of people, and some like to bask in each other's company after making love for the first time. It's a delicate situation. Feelings come up and surprise you sometimes. It would be great if we could know exactly what we want before the situation arises so we could tell each other how we want to handle the post-coitus period, but even when we do, we usually don't feel comfortable telling each other, preferring to play it by ear.

Most important, the last thing anyone wants is to wake up alone after they fall asleep in someone's arms. That's just rude.

CHAPTER TWENTY-FOUR

The light from the streetlight in the alley illuminated the room enough for Izzy to make out most of the furnishings in Jane's room. She was on her side, and Jane was spooning her from behind. Jane's gentle breathing was even and deep as she slept. The press of her breasts against Izzy's back was intensely erotic, and she wanted to move against their soft weight. They'd made love for hours, and Jane had finally pleaded exhaustion, falling asleep a moment later.

This won't last.

A tremble of anxiety lodged itself in Izzy's chest at the sudden thought. She should be content in the aftermath of their lovemaking. It had been incredible. But maybe it had been too soon. Had it? She felt as if they went from kissing to bed so quickly. She reminded herself they'd known each other for several weeks, during which her attraction had grown. Her sex still pulsed with desire when she thought about how things had escalated so quickly once they had kissed. Yet her chest was tight and felt as if it was getting tighter as she tried not to focus on how she was breathing. As much as she reveled in Jane's naked skin molded against her back, something like claustrophobia started to descend. She needed to get out of bed.

She lifted Jane's arm and rolled slowly out of bed. Immediately, she missed the warmth of Jane's body. She watched her sleep, wrapping her arms around herself against the chill of the night.

Looking around, she had absolutely no memory of the layout of the house. She'd been utterly distracted by their kisses when Jane had led them to the bedroom. No bathroom connected to the bedroom, and on her way out of bed, she tripped over a large animal. Jane didn't stir at her whispered surprise, and Lester barely acknowledged her clumsy pets of apology as he dropped his head back onto his paws and started snoring again.

Out of bed and moving, she felt the tightness in her chest start to subside.

The hallway was dark, but seeing a doorway directly across from the bedroom, Izzy reached inside and flipped the light switch, pleased that it was the bathroom. She quickly slipped inside and shut the door. Her refection in the mirror looked just like her, even with her hair standing on end looking like she'd just rolled out of bed after a night of making love. She smiled at the thought. The knot of anxiety lodged in her chest eased a little more. She ran the water and splashed some on her face, then dried off and sat on the toilet. As she peed, she wondered what was next. Should she stay the night? The tightness in her chest increased. Her knee bounced. Jane hadn't said what she expected. Was this a one-night thing? Or was it something more to her? Izzy hadn't thought it through. She'd spent so long closing herself off to romance. Was she open to it now? She knew she wanted more of what they'd just done. The whole thing. The dinner, the talking, and definitely the sex. But what about Jane?

This probably won't last.

The tightness in her chest was back. She dropped her head into her hands and took several deep breaths. She straightened her back and let her head drop and took a few more. It helped.

Izzy finished in the bathroom as quietly as she could and returned to the bedroom. It took a moment for her eyes to readjust to the dark, but when she got back to the bed, both of the cats were settled on the empty side. Jane was asleep on her stomach with the sheet pulled up to her waist. Her bare back was beautiful in the light coming in from the window, her long, dark hair fanned out on the pillow. A thick strand draped over her face, and Izzy slowly moved it, her fingers barely touching Jane's soft cheek. She was like a beautiful sketch drawn by an Italian artist. Izzy couldn't help but stare, filled with desire and tenderness. She started to move the cats to get back into bed when doubt crept in again, and the tightness squeezed her. She was exhausted. Had Jane meant for her to spend the entire night? Maybe she was supposed to leave. Indecision filled her. Should she at least gather her scattered clothing?

"Are you going to just stand there and stare at me like you're a

heavenly goddess sent to watch over me and protect me in my sleep?"
Jane hadn't moved at all. Izzy had thought she was still asleep.

"I could stand here all night and watch you sleep."

Jane rose on one elbow. "You can't possibly stand there naked
and beautiful and me not have my hands all over you. Are you going
to make me get up, or are you planning to get into bed and make love
to me again?"

The tightness in Izzy's chest disappeared, and she lifted the
covers, forcing the cats to jump off. She slipped into bed and scooted
over until she was next to Jane, who had rolled to her side facing her.
Jane's warmth washed over Izzy, and she sighed. She ran her hand
along Jane's side and bent to kiss the warm skin of Jane's shoulder.

"When you got up, I thought you might be leaving."

"Did you want me to?"

Jane ran a hand along Izzy's arm. "Not if I have a say in it. I want
to make my world-famous omelet for you in the morning."

"It's settled then." She sounded more confident than she felt.

Jane moved closer, and Izzy kissed each of her eyes and then her
mouth. The kiss started slow but quickly became more, and Izzy was
swept away once again.

❖

*People have all kinds of mornings after. There's the "how do I get
out of here without hurting their feelings" morning after. There's the
"I slept so hard I must have drooled, and they saw it" morning after.
There's the "I haven't slept enough, but I don't care" morning after. I
could go on and on. The thing about mornings after is getting past the
uncomfortable feeling of not being in your normal routine whether you
wake up in a new bed, or in your own, with a new person. The movies
always seem to show the beautiful costars waking up with big smiles
and big kisses. But in reality, ordinary mortals have morning breath,
pillow hair, full bladders, and the unforgiving brightness of morning
sunlight to contend with.*

*Some people try to get around these unpleasantries by getting up
early and sneaking to the bathroom to freshen up. Others accept the
dishevelment, cuddle carefully, and shyly excuse themselves to use the
bathroom.*

So, basically, the type of morning after you'll have depends on the person you have the night before with. You will always experience some sort of insecurity. Just know the other person has the same insecurity you have. It's best to just go with what feels right to you and check in with the person you wake up with.

Chapter Twenty-five

Sunlight slanted in through the bedroom window and crept across Izzy's face, waking her from a deep, dreamless sleep. Her hips, her inner thighs, and her glutes protested as she rolled to her back and stretched like a lazy dog. When she reached over for Jane, she encountered a warm furry body. A quick scan of the bed and the room told Izzy that, aside from the two cats who were curled together on Jane's pillow, she was alone. The rich scent of coffee promised that Jane wasn't far away, though.

Izzy extracted herself from the tangled sheets and swung her legs over the edge of the bed. They'd certainly made a mess. She smiled. Raising her arms over her head, she stretched again, enjoying the announcement of muscles she hadn't used in an extremely long time. She found her jeans and shirt on the floor at the foot of the bed and pulled them on, tucking her panties into her pocket. The cats watched her with unaffected gazes from their fur-limbed huddle. Were they used to overnight guests?

This isn't going to last.

She shook her head to stop her inner voice. *Let me just have this moment!*

She straightened the bed around Jane's cats and scratched behind their ears, knowing she needed to get back to Gus and her own cats. They'd be okay for food, but they were definitely not used to being home alone all night.

The coffee smelled good, but her bladder told her to make a pit stop before she did anything else. A little mouthwash would be nice, too. A plastic-wrapped toothbrush, the type dentists gave away at appointments, lay on the bathroom counter next to a tube of toothpaste.

When she finished in the bathroom, Izzy wandered down the short hall to the small kitchen, where she found Jane at the stove wearing a short, flowered robe. She slipped up behind her and wrapped her arms around her waist, nuzzling her neck.

"Good morning, gorgeous," she murmured between kisses.

Jane put down the spatula she was holding and pressed into her, bending her head to the side to give her access to her neck. Izzy grazed her lips along the warm skin. God, she smelled so good.

"It *is* a good morning," Jane said, turning and wrapping her arms around Izzy's neck. "A very, *very* good morning."

Jane kissed her with all the intensity of the kisses they'd shared throughout the night, and heat filled Izzy. She slid her hands into the robe and let her hands wander over the bare flesh of Jane's back.

Jane pulled away, panting. Izzy tried to coax her back, but Jane laughed and retied her robe.

"I'm going to burn your omelet. You were supposed to sleep until I woke you up with kisses and breakfast in bed."

Izzy pulled out the front of her shirt and pretended to fan herself. "Your kiss woke me up. But if you want, I can go back and pretend to sleep."

Izzy leaned against the counter while Jane slid the omelet from the pan onto a plate beside two pieces of toast and a sliced orange. Izzy's stomach growled. It smelled like heaven. Jane handed it to her and picked up an identical plate.

"Too late. The moment has passed, and breakfast is ready."

Jane set her plate on a tray with a carafe of coffee and two yellow ceramic mugs, and led Izzy to a small, wrought-iron table on the patio near the fountain. The gurgling water blocked the sounds of nearby traffic, and the little yard was partitioned off from the main house by a tall trellis with vines growing all over it. More of the fragrant white trumpet flowers hung interspersed with the vibrant green. A pergola with a mesh sun block over it protected them from direct sunlight. The summer morning was already warm.

"It's beautiful out here. Have you lived here long?" Izzy settled at the table where Jane had already placed napkins, silverware, and things to doctor their coffee. She spread her napkin over her lap.

"About five years. It's perfect for just me and the animals. I've been thinking about buying something, though. At my age, it seems like I should own my own home."

"There's something to be said for being able to call someone to fix your garbage disposal or toilet when something goes wrong." She took a bite of her omelet. "This is so good!"

Jane smiled. "Omelets are my specialty." Her brow furrowed. "I hadn't really thought about not being able to call someone to fix things."

"You just need the right friends. I'm pretty handy, but between my dad, my sister, and my brothers, I have plenty of options if I need to call someone when something breaks."

"Your family lives nearby?" Jane asked.

"Yep. All of them, aside from my nephew Travis, who's in the air force and stationed in Germany. My mom and dad are here, as are all seven of my siblings, the rest of their twenty-seven children, and eleven grandchildren."

Jane's eyebrows shot up over the edge of her coffee mug. "Wow! You have a huge family!"

"It can be a little much at times, but I wouldn't trade it for the world." Izzy had a sudden image of introducing Jane to her family. A pleasant flutter in her stomach was followed by a major rush of apprehension. Her knee started to bounce, and she had to force herself to hold it still. Too much. Too fast. *Slow. Slow. Slow. Stop!* "Do you have any brothers and sisters?"

Jane's eyes lowered, and she took a sip of her coffee. "One of each. Leticia and Alejandro. They both live out of state."

Izzy had expected Jane to close down when the topic of her family came up. However, while her shine dulled a little, Izzy didn't think she was completely shut down. "Are you close to them?"

Jane looked up at the sky. "Not as close as we used to be. My sister married a military guy, and they moved out of the country when he got stationed in Japan. My dad was not at all happy about her marrying a marine—especially a non-Latinx marine. And even worse, she got pregnant before they were married. The situation put a lot of stress on the family for a while. Then I came out of the closet, taking the spotlight off her and triggering World War III." Jane started stacking their breakfast dishes on the tray.

Izzy helped clear the table. "Oh, no. Are they better about it now?"

"We don't talk about it."

"About any of it? Or just some parts."

"Any of it, really. At least my mom and dad don't. They barely acknowledge Leticia's husband, but my mom dotes on their two kids— as much as she can with them living in Oklahoma now. As far as me being a lesbian, my dad went ballistic when he found out, and now it's a don't-ask, don't-tell situation."

"How are your brother and sister with it?"

"They're cool. In fact, my sister got into a huge fight with my parents about their refusal to acknowledge it. It's been a big part of the distance between everyone. My brother doesn't come home. I haven't seen him or his family in five years."

Izzy followed Jane into the kitchen, carrying the coffee carafe. "It must be hard."

"At times. I don't think about it much. Or talk about it. I'm not sure why I am now."

Jane seemed a little sad, and Izzy hated it, even though it took her mind off her own anxiety.

"You know what I'm thinking about?" Izzy placed the carafe on the counter and took the tray from Jane's hands, setting it beside the carafe.

Jane's eyes resumed a little of their earlier twinkle. "What are you thinking about?"

"I'm thinking this robe has been taunting me all through breakfast."

"Oh yeah?"

"This part here especially." Izzy traced the opening on her chest, sliding her finger between Jane's breasts and pulling when she reached the tie around her waist. It came undone easily, and the robe dropped open.

Jane's chest rose with quick breaths, and she took Izzy's hand, leading her out of the kitchen. They didn't make it to the bedroom. When Izzy stopped to kiss her in the hallway, the walking stopped and the groping happened, and the next thing Izzy knew, she had her fingers inside Jane, grateful the wall was there to hold her up.

❖

Sleeping together is usually seen as a serious step in any relationship, regardless of the length of time it took to get there. But does having sex with someone mean you're dating? Good question. It depends on who you are. Some people are comfortable with casual sex. Other people consider sex a sacred act. The answer depends on the people involved and how they view the act of sex. It's always good to communicate your views to the person you're considering having sex with.

Like everything else, communication is key. Am I sounding like a broken record here? Communication. Communication. Communication. I can't say it enough. It's the most important thing in any relationship. No one reads minds. If you expect anyone to anticipate your every need or desire, you're setting yourself up for failure.

So, when it comes to determining whether you actually are in a relationship or still just having fun with someone, just ask. It's the fastest and safest way to figure it out.

CHAPTER TWENTY-SIX

Midmorning on Monday, Izzy and Jane entered the elevator and headed to the Traveling Bean coffee truck. They were supposed to meet Audie, who was probably already there, and Hector was just a few minutes behind them. They needed the caffeine, since neither of them had gotten much sleep over the weekend. They were the only ones on the elevator, and Izzy stole a quick kiss before she thought about Cliff watching the video feed at the front desk. She had no regrets and waved at the camera.

Jane looked over her shoulder. "What are you waving at?"

"Cliff in security. I forgot about the camera when I kissed you."

"Oops! We said we'd be discreet." Jane put her fingers over her mouth. She looked like a kid caught stealing a cookie.

"You mean like you were when you attacked me in the breakroom last week?" Izzy teased. Flares of anxiety occasionally hit her when she thought too hard about what was happening between them, but the newness and excitement were keeping her on an endorphin high, and she felt better than she had in years. It could be mania, but blaming it on endorphins kept her anxiety from tipping into the red zone.

Jane swatted her arm as the elevator doors opened. Cliff was nowhere to be seen, and the receptionist was just walking up with a replenished candy bowl.

"Do you think we should tell Hector and Audie?" Jane whispered as they headed out the main doors.

Izzy thought about it. "What do you think? I have no experience with this kind of thing."

Jane shrugged. "You know them way better than I do."

"An official announcement would be weird, but we shouldn't hide it from them. Let's just act normal around them and let them figure it out." Izzy bumped against Jane as they walked and grinned.

Jane gave Izzy a playful push. "Well, they won't figure it out at work, then. Because it's not like we're going to be pawing all over each other here."

Izzy pretended to straighten an invisible tie. "That would be unforgiveably unprofessional."

They both looked over at the parking garage, then at each other, and laughed.

"I'll never go into a parking garage and not remember your mouth on my—"

"Shut up!" Jane said, and the push wasn't as playful this time, even though she still smiled.

"You two are far too chipper for a Monday morning," Audie said as they approached the food truck.

"It's a beautiful day. What's not to be chipper about?" Izzy asked.

Audie pointed a wooden stirrer at her. "See what I mean? It's Monday. You need to ease into it. How can you sustain the same kind of energy through the rest of the week if you start like that on Monday? There are rules."

"I forgot the rules," said Izzy, pretending to frown. "I meant to say 'meh.'"

"Better." Audie put the stirrer into her mouth and leaned against the truck.

"What's better?" Hector came up beside Izzy.

Izzy put a hand on Hector's shoulder. "Our broken spirits and utter despair."

"Huh?"

"Audie is not having any good moods today. She says they're reserved for later in the week."

"Did someone not get laid this weekend?" Hector asked. His eyes were on Audie.

Audie rolled her eyes, and she accepted the coffee the barista handed her. It was a barista Izzy had never seen, a young man who looked as if he was playing hooky from high school.

"I think she's just being cranky because Tarin isn't working today," Izzy said.

"No one makes a vanilla latte like Tarin." Audie didn't deny Izzy's statement.

They spent the rest of the break teasing Audie about her crush on Tarin. Izzy stole a few glances at Jane, but no one seemed to sense anything had changed between them, which was a relief. Seeing Hector bait Audie gave her a little trepidation about giving either one of them fuel to do the same to her.

❖

A few hours later, Audie appeared next to Izzy's desk.

"Hey, do you know where the design-review meeting is supposed to be? I forgot my laptop, but I'm pretty sure it's on this floor." Audie tapped her fingers on the top of the cubicle wall; her bad mood from the morning seemed to have left.

Izzy consulted her online calendar. "Yep. It's in the corner conference room. We'll be a little early, but I'll go with you."

The conference room was empty when they arrived. They took seats across the table from one another.

"You look all sorts of happy today. What's up?" Audie asked.

"I had a good weekend," Izzy said.

"What was so good about it? Did you meet a new woman online or something?"

Izzy snorted. She'd told Audie the whole story about Anaya when she'd dropped by last Thursday. "I think I'm done with online dating. I spent most of it with Jane, actually." She knew Audie would be curious, but she just realized she wanted someone to know.

She was right. Audie squinted. "I see. What did you two do?"

She decided to be casual about it, not make it seem like a big deal. It was probably a futile attempt since Audie always seemed to pick up on things, but it was worth a shot. "Let's see. We went to dinner and saw some live music. Oh, and we watched a movie."

Audie pointed at her. "You slept with her, didn't you? I knew I noticed something different. And it wasn't just you. Jane is all giddy with sex energy, too. You two are totally getting it on!"

Izzy looked behind her at the open conference-room door. "Yes. We slept together," she whispered.

Audie got her phone out and typed something into it.

"What are you doing? You're not posting this on social media, are you?"

Audie kept her eyes on the phone. "Of course not. I'm texting Hector to tell him I owe him twenty bucks."

"What?"

"About a month ago he bet me you'd be dating Jane by the end of the month. I said it wouldn't happen until at least the end of next month. I was banking on your inability to pick up on when a beautiful woman is throwing herself at you."

Audie finished texting and put her phone on the conference table.

Izzy was speechless. "You were betting on this? How did you know? I didn't even know."

"Of course you didn't. You never do."

"What do you mean never? This is the first time—"

"Tricia in human resources."

Izzy looked over her shoulder at the door. "Where?"

Audie looked confused. "What do you mean where?"

Izzy was confused. "You said Tricia was here."

"No. I said Tricia has been hitting on you for nearly three years."

"She has not!"

Audie grabbed her head in frustration. "Okay, you just made my point."

"What point?"

"Tarin," Audie said after a pause.

Izzy snorted. "Now you're just smoking crack. You have a thing for Tarin, not me."

"I didn't say you had a thing for her. I'm saying *she* has a thing for *you*, or at least she did."

Izzy flapped her hand in dismissal. "Ridiculous."

"Girl, she told me herself." Audie leaned back, crossing her arms over her chest.

"I don't believe it."

Audie smiled and looked away. "Ganesh."

"Ganesh? Now I know you're crazy. I'm certain Ganesh isn't into me. Number one, he's married. Number two—"

The chair to her right was pulled out, and Ganesh sat next to her. "My wife would be pleased with your honor toward our marriage, Izzy." The deep lines around his eyes were creased, and his sixty-seven-year-old eyes glistened with amusement.

"I meant Ganesh was behind you." Audie snorted into her closed fist.

"Oh, Ganesh." Izzy reached to touch his arm and thought better of it, dropping her hand to the table. "You walked in at an awkward moment. Audie was—" Ugh! She didn't want to explain. "She was just pulling my leg." She turned back to Audie, who had her head on her arms, and her shoulders were shaking. "I hate you," Izzy said to her as others began to enter the room.

"We haven't even started talking about action items yet, Izzy," Hector said, sitting at the end of the table.

Audie just laughed harder, and Izzy sat back in her chair with her arms crossed and glared at her.

❖

Ah, the age-old question: What is love?

Poets and songwriters have been asking this question for centuries. How do you know when you fall in love? For some, it's a gradual thing. They're going along feeling good about being with a certain someone, and then one day it just dawns on them they don't want to spend another day without that specific person in their life. That's when they know they're in love. For others, it's a whack-you-in-the-face kind of thing. They're minding their own business, doing their own thing, and then they meet someone and, bam, they're in love. No warning, no buildup, it's just there.

What about love at first sight? Is there such a thing? Some people don't believe in it, but others swear by it. Who are we to judge?

Whether it's the gradual dawning, the smack-you-upside-the-head kind, or the tentative journey toward a golden ring, all anyone knows is it's different for everybody, and you know it when it happens to you. If you have to ask, you probably haven't experienced it.

Chapter Twenty-seven

When Izzy arrived at her parents' house, the street was already lined with cars. As she walked up the front walk, a swarm of the little ones ran from around the side of the house, chasing one another. A few of them waved and yelled, "Hi, Aunt Izzy!" as they ran past her and continued around to the other side of the house. They were all careful not to trample the flowers lining the front sidewalk. No one wanted to be on the receiving end of Grandma's anger if any of her dahlias were harmed. The youngest of the crowd, Aldo, trailed after the pack and stopped in front of Izzy, holding his hands up for her to pick him up. Of course, she did, and he gave her a slobbery kiss before going rigid, which was his signal to put him down. When she did, he took off running after the others. She looked around for parental supervision, and one of her four brothers waved at her from the corner of the house before running after the kids. She had no idea how her brothers and sisters kept up with all the children. She loved having them all around, but she was grateful none of them were hers.

She let herself into the house and said hello to a few of her nephews and nieces who were lounging on the couches in the living room playing on their phones. Madison was the only one who leapt up and gave her a happy hug, while the others just waved.

"Maddie, you've always been my favorite." She gave a meaningful glare over Madison's shoulder to all of the others, and they laughed as they got up to give her hugs, too.

She walked back to the kitchen and said hello to another brother, who was making a salad, and his wife, who was at the sink helping one of their little ones wash his hands.

"The army is in the back, Iz," her brother said as he tore up a head of green lettuce. She went out through the French doors to the backyard where everyone was hanging out. Most of her four brothers and three sisters were already there, as were a number of her nephews and nieces and their kids. The backyard was peppered with groups of people sitting in stackable, white plastic chairs and blankets spread on the grass for the babies.

As she knew he would be, her father was standing at the built-in barbecue grill all of them had built for him ten years ago. He was wearing the apron that said "I Got Crabs in New Orleans" she'd brought back for him last year from a business trip to Louisiana. He'd nearly peed his pants when he read it. Her mother, who didn't think it was *that* funny, was standing next to him at the counter, handing him hot dogs and hamburgers. The smell of cooking food made her stomach growl. Her identical-twin brothers stood near, chatting with their parents, and turned to look at her at the same time. They both smiled and waved. She could always tell them apart, but even their kids would sometimes go to the wrong dad.

Her mom put a package of hot dogs on the table next to the grill and met her halfway across the patio, giving her a hug.

"When do we get to meet Jane?"

She'd told her mom about Jane earlier in the week. The conversation had been hard to bring up, and she'd felt like she was having a heart attack, but her mom would have felt slighted if she'd found out from someone other than her.

"She had a thing to do with her parents today. I'll ask her to come to next week's dinner."

"Her parents can come, too. Three more won't make a big difference."

Izzy didn't want to get into Jane's issues, especially since she didn't really know the whole story. What she did know made her not like them—especially Jane's father.

Two of one of her brother's kids ran out of the house and across the patio.

Her mom gestured toward the yard. "Are you sure you want to subject Jane to this? We might scare her away."

Izzy smiled. "She's been warned, but she said she's not scared. Let's see how she does."

"So, it's going good?"

Butterflies fluttered in her stomach at the thought of Jane. "Yeah, it's going well, Mom. Better than well, actually. Fantastic."

"Are you girlfriends?"

Izzy had been wondering about this herself. "I don't know what to call it. We're not just dating. I'd say it's kind of serious." Maybe it was because she was talking to her mom and her defenses were down, but panic shot through her when she admitted how she felt. She looked to her mom for grounding.

Her mother beamed. "Well, whatever you call it, I'm so glad. You deserve someone special."

Her mother's statement left a lot unsaid. Top of the list was her fear Izzy would never find love because of her bipolar illness. Her mom hated for her to be alone.

Izzy watched the children run around the yard. "It's a little early."

Her mother shifted to stand in front of Izzy so she was forced to look at her. "I see love in your eyes, honey."

Love? No way. It was way too early for love. Wasn't it? "We've only been together a week or so."

Her mother put her hand on Izzy's shoulder. "The heart doesn't work on a designated time line, Isadora."

"I know, Mom, but you know me. I like to take it slow."

Her mother flicked the dish towel that had been draped over her shoulder at Izzy. "Slow is an understatement. But I understand. I just don't want you to be overly cautious to the point of never getting there. You know what I mean?"

"I know, Mom. But I can't help it."

They were quiet for a moment, watching the rest of the family do their thing.

"You've been stable for a very long time. You may never have another episode. We've read the books. Some people have one bad period and never go through it again."

They'd had this conversation several times in the past. Her mother was the eternal optimist, and Izzy was the eternal pessimist, just waiting for the next episode to sweep in and clobber her.

"Other people have to regularly check themselves into the hospital to adjust meds even when they try to manage everything just right, Mom."

Her mother rubbed a hand on Izzy's arm. "Other people. Not you, honey."

She'd tried not to think about it the last several days since she and Jane had started seeing each other. But it was out on the table now, so she had to face it. "It's not me *now*. But it could be me. Who knows what can trigger it again?"

Her mother twisted the corners of the dish towel.

"You're so careful. You'll know if you're starting to show signs of an episode. It's not like you'll snap. You'll show symptoms before it gets bad. You know what they are. You'll catch them and adjust accordingly."

Izzy grimaced. "But what if the adjustment is too painful?"

Her mom knew exactly what she was scared of most. "You mean, what if being in love causes the episode itself, and you need to leave the relationship?"

"Yeah, I guess that's exactly what I mean."

Her mother stepped in front of her again. "Would you rather be so careful you never know, honey?"

"I'm not sure, Mom. Maybe I need to think about her, too."

Her mom took a moment. "Why don't you let her decide for herself?"

She hugged her mom. "You always sound so logical."

"It's what a mother does, honey."

As Izzy drove home, she thought about the conversation with her mother.

Love? Ha! Strong attraction, sure. Deep-like, for sure. But love? No way!

But…maybe.

Shit! She'd missed her exit. She drove to the next off-ramp and backtracked, the question continuing to niggle at her. Was it possible she might be falling in love with Jane?

She'd spent most of her adult life protecting herself and others from her illness, scared she'd lose control and hurt someone or herself— mostly herself, to be honest. But, aside from her hospitalization and a few times where she'd had to adjust her medications, her illness hadn't posed a real issue. And even during those times, she'd only had to monitor her reactions to things to make sure she wasn't feeling or acting outside of her own comfort zone. However, the illness had always been on the forefront of her mind, predicating her actions, reining in the way she led her life. And in all that time, she'd kept a safe distance from anything that could possibly rock her carefully controlled life, which included keeping a safe distance from possible romantic relationships. One bad relationship and subsequent episode had barricaded her from taking a chance again. After all this time without incident, was she really okay continuing to live her life at a distance from love?

She thought about Jane, and her heart beat harder. The last week had been amazing. She wanted nothing as much as she wanted more time with Jane. And it hadn't been scary. Anxiety-ridden? Yes. But, she hadn't spent any time at all worrying about acting badly or losing control of her emotions. She'd actually been enjoying where her emotions took her, mostly. The only time she felt fear or out of control was when she stepped out of the moment and analyzed herself to make sure she wasn't moving into a mania in which she might lose herself. And when she tested herself and imagined how she would react if Jane rejected her, she felt as if she could find herself on a precipice of the abyss she'd been in all those years before. But even in the normal scope of things, wasn't the thought of losing something like love supposed to make a person feel depressed and maybe a little out of control? Besides, what was normal anyway?

Love? There was that word again. Was she really in love with Jane? Without hesitation, a part of her screamed, "Yes!" while the analytical part of her tried to dissect what love really meant. A warm rush of feeling filled her, and she realized she'd answered her own question. Yes, she was in love.

An immediate panic emerged.

Was it too quick? The wary part of her tried to put on the brakes. But she'd known Jane since the start of the summer. Izzy's mind wandered to that first day in the orange breakroom. She'd been enthralled by Jane ever since, and she hadn't even known it. She'd looked forward to seeing her at work every day. She'd sought Jane out in the halls at work and watched the clock every day until it was break time or lunchtime. Truth be told, Izzy had been taken with Jane since the first day she'd met her. How had she not figured it out until now? Probably because she'd been so busy keeping up the barrier she erected between her and the world.

As she turned onto her street, her phone rang, disrupting the hyper-analytical path her thoughts had taken. She was relieved. The display on her dash said it was Jane.

"Hey, beautiful," she said with a smile.

"Hey, yourself."

"How was dinner at your parents'?"

Jane sighed. "Superficial and tense, which equates to a good day in the Mendoza household."

So much was implied in that statement. Izzy was glad Jane felt comfortable enough to be open, as slight as it was, but she didn't feel comfortable pressing for more details. "I thought you would be tied up with them until much later."

"I did, too, until I realized I had better things to do."

Jane's throaty voice sent shivers down her back. "Like what?"

"Like you."

"You have a dirty mind," Izzy said, but she loved it.

"I know. I know." Jane sighed as if resigned to the fact. "But really, I was sitting there, trying to be engaged, and all I could think about was how much more I wanted to be with you."

Izzy's pulse raced to think she might see Jane. "Where are you now?"

"Driving down the 101 near the San Mateo bridge."

"Do you want to come here?"

"If you're up for it."

"Of course, I'm up for it." Izzy pulled into her open garage. When she entered the house, Gus danced at her feet, waiting for her pet him. She threw her keys onto the counter and rubbed his head.

"I can hear Gus being all excited to see you." Jane laughed. "I'm going to swing by my place and pick up Lester. Can I spend the night?"

"We have work tomorrow. But I'm definitely okay with it if you are."

"Don't worry. I'll let you get your beauty sleep."

"You know me so well."

"I've seen you when you haven't had enough sleep."

Was Jane alluding to something? She wanted to ask, but she decided to let it slide. "I love sleeping next to you," she said, instead.

"Me, too."

The house was clean so she didn't need to do much to prepare for Jane's visit but load her breakfast dishes into the dishwasher and change the sheets.

She performed one last check around the house and noticed her medication dispenser on the bathroom counter. It was an elaborate, multi-compartment unit that held seven days' worth of medication. Since she had to take medication three times a day—in the morning, at noon, and at bedtime—the dispenser was an easy way to make sure she stayed on top of it, since missing a single dose could affect her mood for days.

She slid the dispenser and all of the medication bottles into a vanity drawer. She'd have to eventually bring up her condition to Jane, but it hadn't come up yet.

The doorbell rang forty-five minutes after the call. They watched television and then went to bed. After making love, Jane fell asleep, and Izzy held her, thinking about the conversation with her mother and her thoughts in the car on the way home. The feelings she had for Jane washed over her. If she wasn't in love, she had no idea what love was.

❖

You're still wondering if it's love. You're spending all your free time together, and still, it isn't enough. It's like you want to crawl into their skin and merge with them. Wait. Too much? Maybe it's just me. Anyway, things are going really well, and it's obvious you're no longer just dating. What you have is getting pretty serious.

What do you do now?

This is the time when many people start spending the night regularly at one or the other's place. Maybe you start to carry a toothbrush and a spare change of clothes with you when you visit. You might offer a drawer for them to keep their stuff at your house. Heck, you might even be thinking about living together. Besides getting to spend more time together, there are certain economic advantages to combining your households.

Regardless of the living situation, though, this is also the time when most people want to declare some sort of exclusivity, whether it's monogamy, rules for their polyamory, or just plain laying down some sort of expectations of one another when it comes to sharing the object of your heart.

Right about now, things are getting real, folks.

CHAPTER TWENTY-EIGHT

Izzy probably would have just put the water bottles back in the cooler rather than stand in the long line if it wasn't for the dogs. She was already filled with guilt for having to purchase the single-use plastic bottles, but they'd already used all the water they brought. With temperatures hovering at the hundred-degree mark and the water fountain not working at the dog park where Jane and the boys waited, she needed them. At least the air-conditioning in the store felt nice. She fanned herself with her ball cap and waited in the slow-moving line.

After she paid for the water, Izzy jogged across the street. Heat radiated from the dark pavement. It would definitely be a short stay at the park. Jane wasn't at the bench where she'd left her, but she spotted her throwing a tennis ball for an unfamiliar chocolate Lab. Gus darted around the dog as it charged with singular focus for the ball. A woman she didn't know stood next to Jane, and they chatted as if they knew each other. The woman put her hand on Jane's arm and left it there. A flare of annoyance rose in Izzy. The touch implied a familiarity she didn't like. Jane subtly stepped back out of the woman's reach, and Izzy chided herself for her jealousy.

Izzy stood by the bench, wondering if she should join Jane and the woman, but Jane looked over her shoulder and saw her. The smile on her face erased the last vestiges of Izzy's annoyance, and she walked over to them. Jane gave her a quick kiss and took one of the bottles of water. "You're a goddess! I'm on the verge of heat stroke."

"The line was a mile long. It's half-priced Slurpee day."

Izzy smiled at the woman standing next to Jane while she poured water into the collapsible dish they'd brought for the dogs. Lester took a couple laps of it, and Gus drank like he'd been in the desert for a year. She offered some water to the Lab, too, who was nosing toward the bowl.

"Come on, Sheba. You have your own bowl." The woman moved the other dog's bowl next to the one Gus and Lester shared.

Izzy offered her hand to the woman. "Hi, I'm Izzy."

The woman took Izzy's hand. "Bethany."

Jane shook her head. "Where are my manners? Izzy, Bethany is an old friend of mine. She works with me at the university."

Izzy noticed Jane didn't tell Bethany how she and Jane knew each other. Had she already explained the situation? Or was she unsure what to call her. Girlfriend? Lover? Coworker? They all applied. Which did she prefer? Ugh. She was overthinking things again.

Bethany slowly let go of her hand. "Nice to meet you, Izzy."

"Same here." Bethany's eyes were a stunning light brown with a golden ring around them. Her radiant smile was just as striking. Izzy had to admit the woman's presence was almost palpable. Not that Izzy was attracted to her. She was too polished for Izzy, almost *too* put together. She looked familiar, though. Izzy tried to place her.

Bethany rested her hand on Jane's shoulder. "Did you just call me old, JM?"

"You know what I mean!" Jane swatted her hand away.

"What do you do at the university?" Izzy asked. The feeling of unease returned. This beautiful woman was obviously familiar with Jane, almost flirty. She didn't know if she was jealous of the longer tenure of their relationship or of the way Bethany was always touching Jane.

Bethany petted her dog. "I teach film and media."

"She's responsible for most of the news anchors on air these days," Jane said.

Jane sounded proud of Bethany's accomplishment. And then it hit her. This was the girlfriend Jane had told her about, the one who had inspired Jane's no-dating-coworkers rule because of their brutal breakup. They'd obviously moved past all that.

Bethany clasped a leash on to Sheba's collar. "Speaking of which, Sheba and I have to get going. I have a panel to be on for Channel Seven's five o'clock news tonight. They're debating the gender pay gap at the university."

"Sounds interesting," Izzy said, even though Bethany had been directing her comments to Jane.

Bethany flashed her brilliant smile. "Maybe. If I hadn't already discussed it a dozen times before. It's all talk, talk, talk."

Jane squatted and said her good-byes to Sheba, who ate up the attention with kisses of her own. When Bethany walked away, Izzy found she was even jealous of the way Jane said good-bye to Bethany's dog.

"So, that's your ex, huh?" Izzy said after Bethany disappeared into the parking lot.

Jane's eyebrows rose. "How'd you know?"

"You told me and Audie about your ex who taught media and appeared on local television."

Jane's brow furrowed. "I did?"

"Yeah. When Audie asked if you dated coworkers."

Jane rolled her eyes. "Oh, yeah. Audie is something else, with all her intimidating coolness. I'm afraid it made me an oversharer. I'm surprised you remembered."

She'd called Audie intimidatingly cool. Izzy held back a scoff. She'd never tell her, though. She'd be insufferable. Izzy tried to jettison her jealousy and kissed her instead. "I remember everything about you."

Jane raised an eyebrow and gave Izzy another peck. "I'll have to be more careful."

They held hands and watched the dogs play. The earlier question about how Jane would introduce her to a new person rolled around in her mind. Were she and Jane exclusive now? It seemed important to know these things. Asking seemed so scary, though.

"So, I was wondering…" Izzy said before she could stop herself.

Jane looked at her from the corner of her eye. "Wondering what? Whether I like dark chocolate with caramel or nuts? Yes. Yes, I do."

Izzy loved her silliness. And there was the love word again. Stop it! Quit overthinking things! "Good to know. And coincidentally, I do, too. We were meant for each other."

"I already knew that. This new discovery is just a bonus." Jane gave her a quick kiss on the cheek. "Tell me. What were you wondering?"

Now she really had to finish her question. *Here goes nothing.* She took a breath.

"I was wondering what it is we're doing." There. She got it out. "Are we a 'thing'?"

Jane's expression grew serious. "I would definitely say we're a thing."

It was such a good answer. The best answer. But scary, too. It meant things, things Izzy wasn't sure she was ready for. She took Jane's hand and stared at it as she spoke. The whole dog park receded from her awareness; this was such an auspicious moment.

"I don't want to make things weird, but I just want to call dibs on you. You don't have to get a tattoo or anything—unless you want to—but I sort of want to tag you somehow to say you're mine. You know, when other women come around and see what a catch you are."

Jane put her face close to Izzy's. She wore a sweet smile. Izzy laughed.

"You think I'm a catch?"

Izzy squeezed her hand. "The best kind of catch. What I'm saying is, I really don't want to share you."

Jane tossed her hair over her shoulder. "Oh, I see. You want to know if I plan on dating other people."

Izzy put her foot on a tennis ball they'd brought with them and rolled it back and forth. "I'd like to be the only one you date, yeah."

Jane put her foot in front of the ball to stop Izzy's nervous fidgeting. "Okay, as long as I'm the only one you date. I'm not jealous or anything, but I could cut a chick if she started chatting you up."

Izzy looked up and put her hand on her chest. "You'd cut a chick for me? That's so sweet!"

Jane pursed her lips. "Well, in my mind, I would cut a chick. In real life, I have an aversion to blood. Oh, and violence. But definitely in my mind, I would cut a chick. And it wouldn't be pretty!"

Izzy swung their hands between them. An excited bubble rose in her stomach. She had a little anxiety, too, but she chose to ignore it. "So, it's settled. We're a thing, and we're not dating anyone else."

Jane looked like she was excited, too. She hugged their hands to her chest.

"Deal. Do we spit on our hands and shake on it to make it official?"

Izzy put her hand on Jane's shoulder and pulled her close. "I think a kiss will be better."

❖

Whoa! You're in love!
True love!
Ultimate, pure, and unfettered love!
You feel it in the deepest parts of you. Your heart is wrapped around this new person and you're bursting with it. You've never felt this way

before, and every moment is infused with sunshine and happiness. Feelings of bliss, of walking on air, fill your days. Your nights are imbued with passion. Nothing will ever be the same, and nothing will ever mean so much. You've reached the pinnacle of happiness.

Now what?

Now comes the hard part if you haven't already done it. Now you have to tell them. This part is all you. It's up to you to come up with the best way to tell your beloved you love them. Maybe you'll shout it out during an intimate moment. You could just declare it honestly over a cup of coffee. Or perhaps you're a romantic and need to plan the perfect moment. Whatever you chose, it will be perfect.

Chapter Twenty-nine

Jane and Lester spent the night at Izzy's every night that week. They didn't plan it that way. It just happened. And Izzy liked it. She liked it a lot. She liked getting ready for bed with Jane. She liked sleeping next to her all night long. She liked waking up in the morning with Jane curled up around her or nuzzled into the crook of her arm. She liked standing next to her in the bathroom brushing their teeth. She liked fixing Jane toast and filling two to-go mugs with coffee each morning.

"I'm going to hate when school starts again, and we don't get to ride into work together every morning," Jane said. It was Friday as they sat shoulder to shoulder on the train. She was looking out the window at the college campus across the highway. School started in less than two weeks.

A small ball of dread grew in the pit of Izzy's stomach. "I've been trying not to think about it. At least we'll be able to ride partway together."

Jane turned to look at her, and heat rose in Izzy as it did anytime Jane did that.

She had it bad.

"Yeah. But I need to spend some time with Romeo and Juliet. I can't just give them a few minutes a day as I run in to get a clean set of clothes and check their food situation. The neighbor girl has been going in to play with them for a while each day, but Romeo gave me the cold shoulder yesterday when I dropped by. I think they're getting resentful."

Izzy didn't want to be jealous of the cats, but she was. They demanded Jane's time, but she wanted more than she was already getting. If the truth were told, she wanted all of it. The cats deserved their time, too. Izzy wouldn't love Jane the way she did if she didn't want to spend time with her cats.

There was that word again: love. It was coming up more often since her mother had planted the idea. She refused to dwell on it. Things were going too well.

Time together was the main issue now.

"They can come over, too, you know," Izzy said.

"How do you think they would get along with Fat Bob and Prince?"

"Fat Bob probably wouldn't even notice another cat unless it was trying to eat his food. I'm not sure about Prince. I think he'd be okay, but he was a kitten when I brought him home to be Fat Bob's brother, so I don't know how he'd react to another cat. What about Romeo and Juliet?"

"They went with me up to my aunt's house when I was taking care of her during her breast-cancer treatment last summer. My aunt has three cats, and aside from Romeo puking in my shoe for a week straight in the beginning, they all got along."

"I guess there's no way to know unless we try," Izzy said. And just like that, Jane and her zoo started spending most nights at Izzy's house.

Izzy couldn't be happier.

"You can't tell me you didn't notice the sex scenes were a little too choreographed." Jane tossed the empty tub of popcorn they had shared into the garbage receptacle as they left the theater, and Izzy held open the door.

The theater was nearly deserted, and a pimply faced usher was sweeping the closed concession area. Late shows at the independent theater weren't usually so dead, but it was a weeknight, and the film had been showing for a few weeks already. They'd shared the theater with one other couple, who had still been wrapped around each other when the credits started to roll. Izzy couldn't blame them. The movie had been sexy, but she preferred pawing all over Jane in the privacy of their home rather than getting all hot and bothered in a semi-public place and not being able to satisfy her cravings. At least she hoped those two young women didn't go that far in the dim theater. The pimply faced usher might get an interesting education he wasn't expecting.

"The love scenes were lovely. I enjoyed them," Izzy said.

"I couldn't help but think it was just a way for the male director to get off, filming his own fantasies of what he thinks two women do when they make love."

"Not everyone does it the same. That's just how those two characters did it."

"Come on! The kissing? Women just don't do battle with their tongues like that."

"Okay. Agreed. Some of the kisses were a bit much with the strings of saliva and tongue wars. But I think they were just trying to be cinematic. Imagine having a camera two inches from your face and a director watching every gesture."

"The sex was just as bad. The women clearly took on gender-typical roles. One was the man and one was the woman."

"They both looked like women to me." Izzy pulled her collar and fanned herself to make Jane laugh, which she did.

"They *were* beautiful."

"You just have to let yourself enjoy the intent of the scene, which was two exceptionally beautiful women enjoying each other in a particularly intimate, and visual, way." She cleared her throat. "And stimulating."

"Oh, yeah! Another thing. They came together all the time."

"We've come together before."

"But not every single time. The director is absolutely not in touch with how real women's bodies work. We don't get wet at the drop of our panties."

Izzy looked at her sideways. "You do."

Jane pushed her shoulder. "I think we're an exception. In my past, it wasn't always so."

Izzy did a fist pump. "Yes!"

Jane pushed her again. "Don't get a big head about it!"

"Too late. I'm a love machine, and my lady can't get enough of my awesome moves."

Jane giggled. "Anyway, we were talking about the movie."

"Ah, yes. The movie."

"It's not accurate, and I think it sets unrealistic expectations for women."

"I liked it." Izzy took Jane's hand.

They had nearly reached the train station and were taking a shortcut between two buildings. Music, or more accurately, the deep vibration of bass from one of the brick buildings filled the space and pulsed through the alley. Izzy stopped, and Jane, who had taken an additional step, looked back, her eyebrows raised in a question. She looked so beautiful silhouetted in the light coming in from the distant parking lot. Izzy's heart nearly burst, and a feeling welled up in her, filling her throat with emotion.

"What?" Jane asked.

"Did we just have our first argument?" Izzy asked.

Jane looked at her with an amused smile. "I believe we did."

"We need to kiss and make up."

Jane looked around to make sure they were alone and moved closer. "Like this?"

Jane kissed her and clumsily shoved her tongue into Izzy's mouth. Izzy laughed and pushed her away.

"Gross!"

"See? Not sexy. But this," Jane moved back in. She cupped Izzy's jaw with both hands and slowly drew her close. Her eyes were suddenly serious and dark, the minimal light in the alley filling them with secrets. "This is sexy."

Jane's sudden switch to seductress bewitched Izzy.

Jane's breath was light upon Izzy's mouth before her warm lips pressed against Izzy's. Her tongue fluttered along the inside edge of Izzy's bottom lip before she sucked on it. She pulled back just enough to smile at her before she moved back in and kissed her hard.

Izzy walked her backward toward the brick wall and pressed Jane against it. They were in the shadows so she cupped the sides of Jane's breasts through her T-shirt, her thumbs stroking her nipples through the thin fabric, feeling them come alive under the thicker cloth of her bra. Jane moved one of her hands behind Izzy's neck and wrapped the other around her waist, grabbing her ass, pulling her closer. Izzy pressed her leg between Jane's, and she ground into her, the fast beat of the music from the dance club setting the tempo.

Izzy pulled her head back just enough to look into Jane's eyes. "Tell me. Did the movie turn you on even a little bit?"

Jane panted. "Maybe a little bit."

Izzy pushed her hand into the front waist of Jane's shorts, and Jane gasped. Izzy snuck her hand into Jane's panties, and plunged her fingers into Jane's silky depths. She was so wet, so ready.

"Just a little?" Izzy whispered, pulling her fingers out to stroke her clit.

"Hurry. Just hurry." Jane moaned and threw her head back.

Izzy slid back into her. Jane's shorts constrained her hand, and she couldn't move exactly like she wanted, but it didn't seem to matter. Jane was writhing, spreading her legs, giving her as much access as she could, and Izzy stroked her clit hard and fast. It didn't take long at all before Jane was shuddering, and her breath was coming in shallow gulps. Izzy slowed her strokes as Jane's body started to relax.

"Fuck," Jane said.

Izzy giggled. "That's the first time I've ever heard you curse."

Jane panted and looked from side to side. "It's also the first time I've ever had sex in an alley."

Izzy pulled her hand out of Jane's pants and stepped back to let Jane straighten her shirt, which had risen to her ribs. The expanse of soft skin visible made Izzy's fingers tingle.

"Me, too. That's a lot of firsts for one night. First argument, first curse, first sex in an alley."

"I hope all our arguments end like this," Jane said.

They laughed and Jane looked up. "Oh, God." She pointed to a point near the alley's entrance, where a small electronic device was mounted high on the wall.

Izzy squinted to see. A shot of alarm hit her, and then a trill of excitement swept it aside. "A camera. How embarrassing." But she wasn't embarrassed. Not really. Even so, she averted her face and laughed. Facial recognition was a reality.

"Well, maybe some lucky person will get to see what it looks like when two women have real sex."

"I'm down with that. As long as it doesn't show up in some meme somewhere."

❖

Izzy got ready for bed. She slid her pill dispenser out of the drawer and lifted her medication out, trying not to make too much noise since Jane was right outside the door. She took her meds, placed the pillbox back in the drawer, and got into bed next to Jane, who was reading a book. Izzy lay on her side with her head propped up on one hand, watching Jane.

A feeling so huge it threatened to burst her skin filled her. On the outside, she probably looked serene—if not a bit stalkerish, what with the staring—but on the inside, she was in turmoil. A feeling of necessity was boiling in her. She loved her.

It was too soon to say anything, though. They'd been together only a short while. Plus—she thought about the pillbox in the bathroom—she needed to say some other things first.

The cats were lying in a heap near the foot of the bed, and the dogs were lying in their beds next to the dresser. Things were so very domestic. It just felt so right, what was happening between them. What would happen if she let down her barriers? They were mostly already pretty much down. She felt safe with Jane. Her real fear was her own chemical makeup going out of whack and causing chaos.

"What are you staring at?" Jane didn't look away from her book, but her mouth was turned up in a half-smile.

She was so pretty. Smart. Kind. A jumble of responses caught in Izzy's throat.

Jane turned to look at her, and still Izzy couldn't speak. Jane's head tilted to the side, studying Izzy.

Izzy could only stare back.

Jane lowered her book. "You're making me feel self-conscious."

Izzy cupped Jane's cheek, rubbing her thumb along her chin. Jane closed her eyes and smiled. "I have to tell you something."

Jane opened her eyes and scanned her face. "Should I worry?"

"I don't know." Izzy sat up.

Jane sat up, too. "Lay it on me, then."

"Well…" Izzy picked at the comforter. "I guess you could say I come with a little baggage." The nerves hit her hard, and she had a difficult time continuing, unsure how to finish what she had to say.

Jane took her hand and held it in her lap. "Who doesn't?"

"True." Jane's response made her feel better. "But I guess I should disclose my baggage so you have the opportunity to make decisions."

Jane, traced the outlines of her fingers. "What kind of decisions?"

Izzy blew out a breath and watched the cats curl around each other at the foot of the bed. "I take medicine for depression."

Why did she minimize her condition? It wasn't just depression. She was bipolar. Amplify the depression part and throw in a bunch of mania and a side order of psychosis when things really got bad. Saying she had depression was like saying she had a stubbed toe when the whole leg had been blown off.

"Half the world is taking antidepressants these days." Jane must have noticed how nervous Izzy was. She put a hand on Izzy's shoulder and waited for Izzy to look up. "I don't want to diminish your situation, Izzy. It's just that you're probably one of the most even-keeled people I've ever known."

If she only knew. But, for some reason, even though she was so close to telling her the whole story, Izzy couldn't come right out with it. "The medicine works," she said instead.

"If it makes you feel any better, I took antidepressants for a short time several years ago when I first came out. I had a hard time dealing with my father's reaction. As dean of students, I also work with students who deal with depression and more. It sounds like you're managing it."

"I have been since I was in my early twenties. My situation isn't situational, though. It's clinical. I'll be on medication for the rest of my life."

Jane leaned forward and gave her a kiss. "You'll have to try harder to chase me away. I'm glad you told me, though."

Izzy wanted to tell her the rest, but all of a sudden, it seemed as if she was making too big a deal about it. "Some people are uncomfortable with this kind of thing."

"I'm not sure why. I think more than half of my friends are taking antidepressants. Maybe some mental illnesses are kind of scary, but most are just like any other illness and treated effectively by the proper care and or medication. It makes me mad how our society treats this kind of thing, attaching this stigma to it."

Irritation whipped through her. It wasn't Jane's fault she felt qualified to school her, of all people, about mental illness. She probably thought she was being reassuring, and in a way, she was. She let it go. "I think people are afraid of what they don't understand. When meds don't work or people don't manage their illness well, the symptoms can be pretty scary."

Jane squeezed her hand. "You're the least scary person I know, Izzy."

"Like I said, the meds work for me."

Jane dropped the book onto the floor beside the bed and snuggled into Izzy, who scooched down so they were lying together again. Jane ran her fingers along Izzy's bare arm. "Were you afraid of telling me?"

"Yeah." She shivered as Jane's strokes drew goose bumps on her skin.

Jane kissed her shoulder. "Why?"

"Because of everything we just talked about."

Jane propped herself up on her elbow and looked into Izzy's eyes. "Well, it doesn't change the way I feel about you one bit."

Jane kissed her, and all conversation ceased when the kiss grew insistent.

❖

There's never enough time in the day when you're in love. Am I right?

When love enters the picture, all you want to do is be together. But real life competes for time, too: work, family, friends, various obligations. Eventually, it becomes obvious you're spending all of your available time together, and you decide it would be more convenient to live together since all you're doing is going home to feed the cats, water the plants, go through the mail.

Sometimes, it's more of an economical decision. Why pay for two households when you're spending most of your time at just one of them? One of you might live closer to work or where you both like to hang out. Maybe you've been needing to get a roommate, and moving in together solves the problem.

Occasionally, living together never even comes up. Some people are particular about their freedom even when they're in love with someone. All kinds of relationships are out there, and you don't need to judge folks, especially when they're happy.

Take some advice, though: make sure you talk about it before you make the big move. Nothing is worse than finding out the love of your life hasn't told you their Great Dane insists on sleeping in the bed with you.

Chapter Thirty

Jane tossed her car keys onto the island countertop. "I think my cats are planning a mutiny."

Izzy flipped the sandwich she was making and lowered the heat under the pan. It was early November and the cooler weather called for grilled-cheese.

Jane took off her hoodie and hung it over a barstool.

"What do you mean?" Izzy came around the kitchen island and wrapped Jane in an embrace, kissing her. The kiss lingered, and when Jane playfully bit her bottom lip, a pang of arousal shot through her. She pressed Jane against the counter and slid a hand up the bottom of her tank top. Her skin was so warm. So soft.

Jane gently removed her hand and stepped back. "You were cooking something."

"Oh, right!" Izzy ran back to the stove, removed the pan from the flame, and placed the sandwich on the plate she had waiting on the counter. She cut the perfect sandwich in half—crispy on the outside, all melted cheese on the inside. But her mind wasn't on the sandwich. "What were we talking about? You're dangerous to have around when I cook."

Jane laughed. "Um, my cats. They're not happy." She took a bite of the sandwich Izzy put in front of her. "This is sinfully good."

"The secret ingredient is gruyere, and the trick is to butter the bread on the outside *and* the inside." She took a bite of her own sandwich and moaned.

They ate in silence for a moment.

Izzy finished half her sandwich. "What are the cats doing to show they're not happy? They seem okay when they're here."

"It's subtle, but I've noticed signs of displeasure."

"Like what?"

"Well, they hide when I bring the kennel out. They hate the car ride, I think."

"Maybe they need more treats?"

"They turn their backs on me when I leave the house now. Before, they wanted love. And Romeo has taken to sitting on my keyboard when I'm on my computer. Also, Juliet puked in my slipper yesterday."

"Subtle," Izzy said. She'd hate it if Fat Bob turned his back on her. "Well, except the puke. That's pretty direct."

"I know, right? Seriously, I think they're feeling neglected, and I feel bad." Jane finished her sandwich, rested her elbows on the counter, and covered her face with her hands.

Izzy refrained from touching her, afraid she'd get carried away, and it looked like Jane really needed to talk about this. "What do you think we should do?"

"I don't want to stop doing what we're doing."

Izzy tried to think of a solution. "Maybe we could go to your place more often. We don't always have to be here."

Jane seemed to think about it. "My place is out of the way, though."

As if they sensed a major decision was being made about them, all four cats appeared in the kitchen. Romeo and Juliet wound around Jane's feet. Prince jumped into Izzy's lap, and Fat Bob flopped onto his back on the floor at her feet. Izzy dug her toes into his furry belly and scratched Prince's head. The purring in the room was loud.

"Look at them," Jane said, petting Prince's sleek back. "No matter if we stay at my house or your house, we'll have a feline displeasure issue. Plus, my house is so small. We'd basically be on top of each other."

"I don't mind being on top," Izzy teased.

Jane swatted her. "Of course, you don't. But seriously, I have to figure something out. It's not fair to leave the cats alone so much."

She covered her face with her hands again, and Izzy felt bad for Jane's obvious turmoil. She had an idea, though.

"You bring them here most of the time, but it seems they hate the ride. But maybe..." Izzy grew nervous about suggesting her solution, but she'd been thinking about it for a while now. "But maybe you could all move in here. You spend so much time here, and I love having you here, and I hate when you aren't here, and I know it's so soon, and you have a lease, but I really think..." She was rambling. She couldn't help it. Now that it was out there, she wanted it to happen—to have Jane with her all the time.

Jane peeked out from between the fingers covering her face. Her movement was slow, and Izzy couldn't read her expression. It was too soon. She knew it. She shouldn't have—

"I was thinking something similar, too."

"It's too soon. It doesn't have to be immediately. But maybe… wait. What?" She realized what Jane had just said. She looked up, and Jane was staring at her. God, her eyes were gorgeous. "You have?"

"Yes. My lease is up next month. I was just going to renew it, but I started thinking about how we were doing so well together and maybe, well…" A few seconds later, she continued as if she were steeling herself. "Is it too soon, though? We've only been seeing each other for…how long?"

"Five months." A little less than five months, but Izzy wasn't going to haggle.

"But how long is long enough?" Jane asked. "Is there a rule?"

"Funny you should ask. I've been researching this topic for the book. People have done studies, and the results are all over the place. But most things I found on the internet say six months is about the right time to start considering it."

Jane scoffed. "Well, the internet is always right, right?" Her eyes were bright with humor, which was a good sign.

Izzy held up a finger in the pose of a politician. "The truthiest truth"

They laughed then, Izzy wondering if hers sounded a little maniacal, but it was a real laugh, releasing the tension. She wiped her eyes and held her aching belly.

Jane wiped her eyes, too. "We've been seeing each other for only five months. We'd be flouting the six-month rule if we shacked up now."

Izzy threw up her hands in revelation. Prince jumped from her lap. "But I have a wacky idea."

"What is it?"

It seemed when she'd taken the leap, she'd jettisoned all caution. She felt good. "Let's do what we want. Screw the internet. Let's be the crazy outliers."

"You think we should?" Jane sounded unsure again.

Izzy had never been so sure about something in her life. "I do." She couldn't believe *she* was the one doing the convincing.

"I don't know."

Jane said the words, but her eyes said she did know, and a giddy buzz flared in Izzy's belly.

Jane continued, but Izzy knew she had her. "It feels like a drastic thing to do just for a pair of neurotic cats."

"Well, if the truth has to be told, the cats are not the main thing driving this for me. I mean, they're important, for sure. But it's more about being with you more." Izzy pulled Jane to her and hugged her tight. "I love…your company." Izzy had almost told her she loved her but amended her statement at the last minute. They were talking about living together, and she still couldn't say it.

"I love your company, too."

The low timbre of Jane's voice so close to Izzy's ear tickled, and she shivered.

"I sense a 'but' coming up," Izzy said, nuzzling her face into Jane's neck.

Jane leaned back but not so much to break the embrace. She searched Izzy's eyes.

"*But* moving in together is a big deal," she said.

Izzy wanted to reassure her, but any hesitation she had was gone, and she was all in on it now. This *was* a big deal. She should be scared, but she wasn't. "True. I just know I want to spend as much time with you as I can. We feel right together. I think we should give it a shot."

Jane smiled "I do, too. But what if I have a terrible habit, and you begin to hate me for it, and then you regret it?"

Izzy couldn't think of a single thing Jane could do that she would hate, except chew ice, but she already knew Jane's teeth were too sensitive for that. They could negotiate anything else. "Have you been hiding any bad habits from me? Come on. Lay them on me. Now's the time. Test me. I'm pretty sure I can deal with them, because everything you do is pretty amazing."

"I have you so fooled!" Jane laughed. "How about you? Have you been hiding any from me?"

Apprehension built in her. She still hadn't told Jane she was bipolar. It wasn't a bad habit; it *was* a pretty big deal. Now was her chance to bring it up. But she didn't want to spoil the mood. She would tell her in time. Yet she hadn't had any symptoms or episodes in forever, so maybe it wouldn't be a thing anyway.

"I'm an open book, lady. What you see is what you get," Izzy declared. It wasn't a lie, not really.

"Well, I like what I see," Jane said, trailing a finger along Izzy's collarbone and down into the V of her polo shirt. "Okay, let's do it!"

Glee bubbled throughout Izzy. "Really? Just like that?"

Jane's wandering fingers stopped. "Are you already having second thoughts?"

"Me? No way!" Izzy hugged her tight. "Not at all. This is fantastic!

She'd switched from nearly constant-anxiety mode to things-couldn't-be-better mode. They were two extremes on the same continuum, and neither was optimal, but she'd take the one that felt better over the other any day.

❖

You've made the big step, and you've moved in together. It's awesome! It's fun! You're sharing space with another person. You have a good time finding places for all your stuff. You realize you have two of everything—two sets of silverware, two bathroom scales, and two teapots. It's time to downsize. Yard-sale time!

Optimizing cupboard space is only part of the process, though. The hard part is yet to come. You have to start thinking like a single unit, acting like a single unit, making decisions like a single unit. You have schedules to sync, routines to establish, expectations to work out.

Communication has never been more important. It isn't as easy to hide bad habits when you're sharing the same space. During this period, secrets have a way of showing themselves. So, this is the time to come clean with anything you might have on your mind.

CHAPTER THIRTY-ONE

Izzy stood near the driver's door of her car in her garage. She balanced a sweet-potato pie in her hand, and over the roof of her car, she watched Jane place an identical pie on the passenger seat of her own car.

"You'll be at my parents' house at four o'clock, right?" She selfishly wished Jane was going with her instead of over to her own parents' house first. Izzy still hadn't met them and wasn't sure she ever would. Jane hardly spoke about them, and when she did, she didn't reveal much. What little she had disclosed wasn't great. And every once in a while, she'd think back to that day in early summer when Jane had rubbed her arm. And the day Jane picked her mother up from the hospital. Izzy wasn't eager to meet them, but it felt weird not knowing much about that side of Jane's life, especially since Jane had come to several Sunday dinners with Izzy's family, who adored her.

"Mom is anal about eating exactly on time, so we'll be finished with dinner way before four o'clock. I'll help my mom with the dishes, and then she'll probably do needlepoint while my dad switches channels between the games and the Westminster dog show. I'll just hang out with them for a little while, and then I'll head over. I'm thinking I'll get there by three thirtyish."

"Mom says dinner's at four, but it never starts on time, so you'll probably have some extra time if you need it."

Jane jangled her car keys. "I seriously doubt I'll need it. I can only take so much channel switching. I can't promise I'll be hungry, though."

Izzy's stomach growled at the thought of a turkey dinner with all the fixings. "We'll have plenty of food, either way. Grant, Patrick, and my dad have been smoking turkey since yesterday."

"I'll try not to fill up too much. The way they were talking about it last weekend, it's going to be the best turkey I've ever eaten."

"It is. I promise."

"I'll see you in a little bit." Jane blew her a kiss.

"Can't wait."

Izzy watched Jane pull out, and she followed her until the interstate, where Jane went one way, and she went the other. It was their first holiday together, and she was excited.

❖

"Where's Jane?" Amelia's voice was low so she wouldn't wake the sleeping infant in her arms.

Izzy's oldest sister sat in their father's recliner in the den where it was relatively quiet, and she rocked her newest grandchild, Simone. Izzy couldn't wait to get her hands on the baby. She was only nine days old and was Haley's first baby. Izzy shouldn't have favorites, and she'd never tell anyone she had one, but Haley and she had always had a connection.

"I swear. You all like Jane more than you like me." Izzy was kidding. She loved that her family adored Jane.

Amelia smirked. "Insecure much, little sis?"

Izzy laughed. "You're just the tenth person to ask where she was."

"And…"

"She's at her parents' house, but she'll be here for dinner." Izzy gently lifted the baby from Amelia's arms and cradled her. Her tiny nose was perfect, as was every part of her. She kissed her little head and stood, rocking back and forth. Simone stretched but didn't open her eyes.

Amelia got up from the recliner and sat on the edge of the big desk near it. "Why didn't you go over there with her before you came here? You don't have to help Mom cook every year."

Izzy slipped her pinkie finger into one of Simone's small fists. "I wasn't invited. I haven't met her parents yet."

Amelia crossed her arms. "You haven't? Jane's been here several times."

"First of all, our family is pushy and greedy. We obviously don't have enough family members, so we need to absorb everyone we meet. Second of all, Jane's parents aren't okay with Jane being gay, so I'm not sure how me meeting them will go down. I'm not in any hurry, and Jane doesn't seem to be, either."

Amelia snorted. "You're kidding me. So, she has to divide her life in two just to make them happy? How do you feel about it?" Amelia sounded pissed, and Izzy loved her for it.

"I feel sorry for Jane, mostly. It's a stress on her family. Her brother and sister barely see her parents because of it. Neither of them came for Thanksgiving."

"Are her siblings gay, too?"

Izzy shook her head. "Jane doesn't talk about it much, but the best I can figure, they just don't like the way their parents make Jane deny her life in order to please them."

Amelia seemed to ponder that statement. "No offense against Jane, but it sounds like her brother and sister have bigger balls than she does. Shouldn't she stand up for herself, too? I mean, her brother and sister are being more of an advocate than she is for herself."

Izzy agreed, but she also knew Jane had other reasons. "She's afraid of what would happen to her relationship with her parents."

Amelia covered the baby's ears. "Maybe her parents need to face losing all three of their kids to understand what bigoted assholes they are." She uncovered the baby's ears. "That's just my opinion, though."

Izzy smiled, filled with love and gratitude for her family's unwavering support. But everyone had their own journey. "I guess Jane needs to figure it out on her own."

Amelia put her arms out to take the baby. "Well, if I was with someone who wouldn't introduce me to their parents, I'd have a problem with it."

Izzy placed Simone in Amelia's arms and leaned over to kiss her little head. "Maybe I'll bring it up when we've been together for a little longer."

"You need to have the hard conversations when they're new, Izzy. Otherwise, they can get out of control before you know it."

Amelia sat back in the recliner, and Izzy had a flashback to when Amelia would read to her when they were kids. Her sister was right.

"I'll keep it in mind. I'm going to see if Mom needs another pair of hands."

Amelia cleared her throat. "Hey, Iz?"

Izzy turned back. "I promise I'll talk with her. When the moment's right."

"Actually, I need to talk to you about Haley."

Concern immediately filled her. "Why, what's wrong with Haley?"

Amelia trailed a finger along Simone's little arm. "I'm not a hundred percent sure, but I think she might be having a bipolar episode."

A cold wave washed over Izzy. Haley being bipolar was news to her. "What? Where is she?"

"She and Josh are still at home. I brought the baby so they could talk through some things. I'm hoping they'll come over later."

"Are they okay? What makes you think she's bipolar, let alone having an episode?"

"I'm not sure. She's been acting erratic, and Josh is pretty frustrated. One minute she's going, going, going, and the next, she won't get out of bed. She swings between elation and depression. I thought it was all the pregnancy hormones, but she hasn't leveled out since the baby came. It seems worse. She's all over the place. Today, I went over there before I came here, and she was inconsolable about not being a good mom." Amelia pushed her hair back, tears shimmering in her eyes. "Nothing I said helped, and when Josh tried to talk to her, she just went off on him."

"Maybe it's postpartum depression. Has she talked to her doctor about it?"

"She doesn't want to. Josh is trying to convince her to see someone."

Izzy couldn't imagine sweet Haley going off on anyone, especially Josh. "Do you think she's a danger to the baby?"

Amelia's expression was pensive. "I don't think so, but you never know. You hear about all those moms in the news who do terrible things, and no one ever suspected anything was going on."

"Do you think Josh can keep an eye on it?" Josh was always so steady. If anyone would take care of Haley, he would.

"I do. But I was hoping you could talk to her, too, and see maybe if you think she has the symptoms you had when you—"

The door opened, and their mother appeared in the doorway. "I thought I'd find you two back here. Look who's here." She stepped aside, and Jane was there.

Izzy went to her and gave her a hug. She was glad to see her but anxious to finish the conversation about Haley without Jane there.

"It was exactly how I described it. After dinner, Dad turned on the television, and Mom pulled out her needlepoint. I'm not sure they even registered that I left."

Her mother's brow furrowed. "Maybe you all can come here next year."

Jane glanced at Izzy and then back to Izzy's mom. "You're so kind. I'll run it by them."

Izzy knew she wouldn't.

Izzy's mom glanced around the room. She tipped her head at Izzy and Amelia. "You two look so serious. Were you talking about Haley?"

Izzy glanced at Jane. She didn't want to talk about it, not with Jane in the room.

Amelia stood and shifted the baby to her shoulder. "I was just asking Izzy to check in with Haley to see if—"

Izzy interrupted her. "I'll definitely have a talk with her. Postpartum depression is a serious thing and—"

Amelia put her hand on Izzy's arm. "Like I said, I think it's more than just postpartum depression."

Their mother looked worried. "Poor baby. It sounds like she probably needs to be checked for—"

"Let's not jump to conclusions." Izzy put her arm around Jane's shoulders and stepped out of the room. The noise of a house full of people surrounded her, and she felt a little less anxious. "We need to see what the doctor says before we assume anything. I'll talk to her. See if I can get her to go."

Her mother followed them and rubbed a circle on her back. "You and Haley have always been as thick as thieves. She'll probably listen to you."

Amelia stepped around them and looked at Izzy like she used to when they were kids and she knew Izzy was up to something. Izzy walked around her. "Well, Josh is with her now. Maybe he'll be able to make her feel better today, and they'll wander over here."

Their mother walked toward the kitchen. "In the meantime, dinner's almost done. Izzy and Jane, can you please help me set out the food?"

Izzy was grateful for the excuse to end the conversation. She took Jane's hand, and they followed her mother to the kitchen.

Her brothers and sisters were setting up folding tables and placing them near the great table in the dining room. It sat twenty, and additional folding tables were set up in the adjacent living room. With nearly sixty people there, it would be tight with all the extra tables, but the family was expert at fitting everyone in.

"You guys have this down to a science, don't you?" Jane said, looking around.

Izzy helped by spreading a tablecloth over one of the tables. "I used to think it was crowded when it was just us kids. But as the family has grown, we somehow still make everyone fit."

"We have to serve it buffet-style, though," her mother said, coming up behind them with a bowl of dinner rolls. "So, if you girls could set the food up on the kitchen island and get the plates and silverware down, we can feed this army in about ten minutes." Her mother pointed to two of her brothers. "Can you get the kids rustled up and their hands washed?"

One of her sisters was stirring a pot on the stove and turned around. "The gravy's done, and the rest of the rolls have only about two minutes left."

Another sister came into the room, grabbed a stack of serving platters from the counter, and headed back outside. "Dad's taking the turkey and briskets out of the smoker, Mom."

It was organized chaos, and Izzy loved it. She turned to Jane, who was smiling. She handed her a plate of cranberry sauce and told her where to put it.

"Perfect! Everything's done at the same time," their mother said. She plucked the lid off an electric roaster on one of the counters, revealing a huge and perfectly browned turkey. In what seemed to be an effortless move Izzy had seen countless times, her mother lifted the giant bird onto a silver serving tray and placed it in the center of the kitchen island. Izzy and Jane set bowls of perfectly whipped mashed potatoes, steaming corn on the cob, green bean casserole, roasted Brussel sprouts, potatoes au gratin, cranberry sauce, apple and walnut stuffing, and caramelized sweet potatoes next to the turkey while Izzy's mother carved the meat.

One of Izzy's nephews ran into the kitchen. "Grandma! Where are the pies?"

"Some are still in the oven, but the others are in the garage on the picnic table."

The little boy flashed one of his radiant smiles and started to run from the kitchen.

"The door is locked, and I have the key!" his grandmother shouted after him.

The boy stopped short, dropped his head, and shook it before he looked back at her with a meek smile. Then he giggled and ran off in the other direction.

"Last year, Mom had all the desserts sitting on a table in the mud room, and a group of the boys sampled every one of them before dinner. No one found out until we went to bring them in," Izzy explained to Jane.

Jane laughed. "Hilarious! I hope there won't be a test. I still can't remember what kids go with what parents."

Izzy laughed. "Don't tell them, but I get confused, too. Thus, the liberal use of nicknames, like buddy, sport, princess, and booger."

One of her sisters placed a bowl on a table. "Okay, the rolls are done, and I've put them and the gravy on the tables. Are we ready to eat, Mom?"

"As soon as the briskets are here." As if on cue, the French doors opened, and trays of smoked brisket and the much-bragged-about smoked turkey were marched in. "And here they are! Let's get the group gathered."

Their mother went from room to room to round up everyone. Izzy leaned out the back doors to call in any kids who were still outside, then went back to the den to get Amelia. When she entered the room, Amelia was pulling a blanket up over the baby, whom she'd placed in a traveling crib.

"Dinner's ready, Amelia," she said and turned to leave.

"Hey, Iz, hold up."

"I know, I know." She knew Amelia was going to corner her about their earlier discussion. Amelia always saw through her.

"You haven't told her, have you?"

Izzy sighed. "Not completely."

Amelia waved her hand. "What does 'not completely' mean?"

Izzy picked at the door frame. "I told her I take medicine for depression."

Amelia took her hand. "But not the rest?"

"It just hasn't come up, and it never seems like the right time." It was an excuse, and she knew it.

"Are you planning to?"

Izzy looked her in the eye. "Of course. I just have to figure out how to do it."

Amelia squeezed her hand. "Listen, Izzy. I know it's hard for you. But you have such a good handle on things. It's an illness, and you manage it better than most. Isn't it about time you stop acting like you're ashamed of it?"

Izzy looked at the floor. "I'm not ashamed."

"You act like you are."

She wasn't ashamed; she just didn't like telling people about being bipolar, or, rather, she didn't want people feeling sorry for her or, worse, afraid of her. "I just don't go blurting it out to everyone. I wouldn't if I had hypertension or diabetes or some zillion other illnesses. It's just not who I am."

Amelia crossed her arms over her chest. "Do you remember when you first came out?"

Izzy immediately became defensive. "Being gay is not even remotely the same." She knew Amelia didn't mean to compare being gay to an illness, but she felt a little cornered.

"I'm not saying it is. Hear me out, though."

She blew out a breath. "Okay…"

"Do you remember how you felt when your friends were getting all boy crazy, and you weren't, but you didn't say anything because you were trying to figure things out?"

It was so long ago, but when Amelia reminded her, it felt like yesterday. "Yeah…"

"Remember how much of a relief it was when you decided to just be who you were, and you didn't have to worry about someone finding out or misinterpreting something?"

Where was this going? "Yeah. I remember."

Amelia snorted. "God, I remember when Max and Teddy came out. Max went through it a lot like you did. But Teddy waited so long after Max, even though he knew all along he was gay. But he thought Mom and Dad would think he was just trying to be like Max. Remember? He was a nervous wreck, always afraid someone would out him. He lost all that weight, and his hygiene went all to hell."

Izzy groaned. "Oh, jeez, don't remind me. You would smell him before you saw him sometimes."

They both laughed.

"What I'm trying to say is, this is a lot like what we were talking about earlier about Jane and her parents. If you let this go on too long, it could become a much bigger thing than it needs to be."

Amelia always seemed to understand things and could explain them in a simple way. She sighed. "I hear you, big sis. I'll find a way to tell her."

Amelia smiled. "Good. Now we better get in there, or we'll be left with nothing but green bean casserole and the turkey butt."

You've met that special someone. You've exchanged those three wonderful words. The hard work is over. You survived all the scary parts about putting yourself out there. Now it's time to coast, right?

To put it bluntly—not even close.

Chapter Thirty-two

Izzy's fingers were flying across the keyboard. The words were coming easily, and she was making better progress on the book than she had in several weeks. Two chapters cranked out already during this session, and she was well into the third. It might not be impossible to get this thing done, after all. A touch from behind made her turn around. Jane looked awesome in leggings and her Gigify hoodie.

"You wear my sweatshirt better than I ever have," Izzy said, spinning her desk chair around and pulling Jane into her lap. She slid her hands under the edge of the top and caressed the smooth skin of Jane's hip.

Jane ran her hands through Izzy's hair, which was already a mess since she hadn't brushed it yet. They kissed, and Izzy wanted to take Jane right back to bed. The writing was going well, though. Maybe she could find her groove again after they made love. Jane's lips were velvety soft. The skin under Izzy's fingers was warm. She moved her hands up and cupped Jane's breasts through the taut fabric of her sports bra. Jane's nipples grew hard against her touch.

"Oh, no, you don't." Jane broke the kiss and grabbed her wrists, removing her hands from beneath the hoodie.

"What?" She was going for an innocent tone, but it came out sounding amused. Jane let go of her wrists, and Izzy tried to get her hands under the thick fabric again.

Jane employed evasive tactics and giggled. "You know what's what. The sun is shining, and it's warm. I was thinking we could spend a little time outside today rather than staying in bed the entire weekend. Again."

Izzy kissed Jane's neck. "I was just thinking the opposite, actually." She looked at her watch. "We've been out of bed for two hours already.

Wouldn't you like to get naked with me for a little while? We can enjoy the sun this afternoon."

Jane turned her head to let Izzy trail her lips across her neck. "Well, the sun can wait for a little while, I suppose."

Jane didn't stop her from sneaking her hands under her shirt this time, and Izzy trailed kisses across her jawline to kiss her lips. Jane put her hands on Izzy's throat and caressed Izzy's jaw with her thumbs as their tongues touched, and their lips moved together.

Izzy leaned forward. Jane rose from her lap, and they stood together without breaking the kiss, which was getting hotter as the seconds progressed. The old leather couch in Izzy's office was only a few steps away, and they moved toward it as Izzy pushed Jane's sweatshirt up her torso, revealing the purple sports bra underneath. The tight fabric pressed Jane's breasts together, and Izzy ran her tongue through the deep cleavage before she kissed the rounded flesh above it.

They fell onto the couch with Izzy on top. Izzy pulled down Jane's leggings and swept her fingers though the wet warmth between Jane's legs. She teased Jane's swollen lips and kissed a trail down her body until she was nestled between her legs. She wasn't in the mood to go slow. She lowered her head and ran her tongue through the same wet path her fingers had just traversed. Her own sex clenched as the sweet tang of Jane filled her mouth. The rigid swell of Jane's clit rose under Izzy's tongue, and Izzy played with it for a few seconds before she wrapped her lips around it and started to suck. Jane's hips rose off the couch, and Izzy wrapped her arms around her legs so she could keep from being bucked off. Her lips worked Jane's clit, which grew firmer in her mouth. Jane held nothing back. She spread her legs and held Izzy's head, letting her know what she needed. The power Izzy had over Jane's pleasure made Izzy's sex clench as she felt Jane get closer and closer to orgasm.

"I'm gonna…" Jane never finished the sentence, as her back arched, and she shuddered under Izzy's mouth. Izzy slowed her movements in time with the slowing of Jane's breathing, and finally, she rested her cheek against the silky soft skin of Jane's inner thigh. She ran her hands along her legs and abdomen, relishing the feel of Jane's skin, absorbing its warmth.

"Come up here." Jane pulled Izzy up so Izzy was lying on her. Her voice was low. "Why do you still have your clothes on? Take them off."

"Yes, ma'am." Izzy stood. Her clothes were off in seconds, and she straddled Jane. Jane slid her hand between Izzy's legs. Her fingers pushed into her, and Izzy rocked above her as Jane's fingers filled her. She leaned forward so she hovered above Jane, raising her hips to allow Jane room to move her arm, and soon Jane was moving in and out of her in a delicious rhythm.

Izzy shifted her weight to her left arm and used her right hand to rub her own clit while Jane's hand continued to pump between her legs, and her other hand played with her nipples. Her orgasm built quickly. She didn't even try to stretch it out. As soon as she felt the first surge of spasms, she urged it on with her own fingers. Hard thrusts with her hips to bring Jane's fingers against the front walls of her vagina took her over the edge, and her muscles clenched around Jane's fingers. She shuddered with the massive release of pleasure as she rocked through the burst of fire raging through her. As the pulses eased and her muscles relaxed, she eased down until she was lying on Jane. They were both panting, and a thin shimmer of sweat coated them. Where their skin connected, it glided over each other, and Izzy squirmed a little, enjoying the sensation. Jane's fingers slipped from her, and she instantly missed the feeling of being filled by Jane.

"I love making love with you," Jane said next to her ear, causing her to shiver.

"I think that's what you call fucking, my love," Izzy said, rising to see Jane's face. The arm holding her up shook slightly. The brilliant orgasm had temporarily sapped her strength.

Jane's face broke into a slow smile. "Well, then, I love fucking you."

"I love fucking you, too." Izzy moved a strand of hair from Jane's face. "I also love how your one eyebrow goes up when you say 'fucking.'"

Jane scrunched her eyebrows. "It does?"

"Yeah. This one," Izzy said, tracing the perfect arch of Jane's right eyebrow. "This eyebrow is in collusion with your filthy language."

Jane laughed. "What?"

"Anytime you curse, this eyebrow gets all archy. It's like it's daring anyone to call you out for using such foul words."

Jane wriggled her eyebrows. "I had no idea."

"Try it. Say something dirty."

Jane blew a stray hair away from her mouth. "Like what?"

Izzy helped move the stubborn hair away. "Anything."

Jane thought a moment. "I honestly can't think of anything to say spur-of-the-moment."

"Oh, I think you can," Izzy teased.

"Seriously! I can't."

Izzy narrowed her eyes. "Say, fuck me until I scream."

Jane laughed and then reset her expression. She tried to look serious. It almost worked, except her eyes sparkled with amusement. "Fuck me until I scream, Izzy."

Jane's eyebrow twitched but didn't arch like it had before. But the way she said it made her voice deep and sultry, and Izzy felt the low timbre of it deep inside. She shivered.

"Ooh la la," she said and wiggled against Jane.

"It didn't move, did it?" Jane sounded pleased with herself.

"A little."

Jane ran her hands down Izzy's back. "I'm not going to be able to curse without being aware of my eyebrow now."

"I'm glad I could enlighten you on this very cute thing you do." Izzy wrapped her arms around Jane, squeezing her as she relaxed against her. "I could stay naked with you all day. I think I'm getting addicted."

"Me, too," Jane said, squeezing Izzy back "I have to go see my mom today, though."

"Oh, yeah?" Izzy said. Would Jane finally ask her to go? She wanted to get some more writing done, but it would be nice to at least meet some of Jane's family.

Jane trailed her fingers in lazy patterns over Izzy's back. "I'll only stay for a couple hours. Just long enough to have lunch with them and to sit with my dad while he watches the ball game."

Did she not want Izzy to come? Or was she waiting for Izzy to ask to come along? "I was just going to write a bit today."

"It will probably be nice to have the house to yourself."

Now it was obvious. She wasn't invited. Izzy was disappointed. "I kind of like having you around, skulking about and all."

"I'll be back around two, and I'll skulk around for the rest of the day with you. How about that?" Jane indicated she wanted to get up.

Izzy pretended she didn't notice and continued to lie on her. "Sounds like a fine idea."

Jane put her hands under Izzy's shoulders and pushed gently. "I need a shower before I go."

Izzy settled against Jane even more, willing gravity to make her heavier. "Yeah. You might want to wash all this sex off you before you go out and about."

Jane lifted Izzy's head and stared into her eyes. "I can't have people knowing I've been fucking my girlfriend."

Izzy laughed and pushed herself up. "See? You can't do it! You can't make your eyebrow stay still when you use dirty language."

Jane took the hand Izzy offered. "Remind me not to play poker with you. Come take a shower with me."

Izzy let Jane guide her toward their room. "Okay. I think you've become a nymphomaniac. Not that I'm complaining."

Jane looked over her shoulder at her. "You're awful."

Izzy's heart melted. Jane was so beautiful. "Awful sexy, you mean."

"That, too."

When you love someone, everything is awesome. Every day is Valentine's Day. You can't wait to be with each other. You get butterflies when you think about them. Nothing feels as good as how you feel when you're with them. You want to do anything in your power to show them how much you love them.

While it's tempting to change things in order to accommodate your new relationship, it's important to not lose yourself in it. Eventually, things calm down. The newness will wear off, and life will return to something like your old life. But if you've changed everything, you won't have anything to settle back to, and you'll begin to miss some of the things you enjoyed doing before you got together. This is when things can get dicey. You don't want to start resenting your lover because you don't have any time to yourself, do you? And you sure don't want to blame them for causing you to neglect your friends.

The best thing you can do is maintain some of your individual activities and don't let your friendships suffer. You'll be happy you have them when the new-love smell wears off.

CHAPTER THIRTY-THREE

The last coat of paint was finished, and Izzy stepped back to look at her handiwork. She couldn't take all the credit. Max and Teddy had helped quite a bit. The paving-stone walkway had gone in that morning, and last thing to do was the touchup paint. The new shed they'd built in the backyard looked great, and they had hardly any injuries to show for it.

"What did I do to deserve you?" Jane wrapped her arms around Izzy from behind.

Izzy hugged Jane's arms to her and grinned like a fool. "Do you like it?"

"I love it. I've never had my very own studio."

"Well, you haven't been able to do your stained glass since you moved in here. This will let you set up all your equipment and supplies."

Izzy had stayed up most of last night painting the inside and installing shelves, and then she'd risen early to finish it. She knew she should have gone to bed at a more reasonable time, but once she'd started, she couldn't wait to get it done. And now she was. It was worth it to see Jane so happy. Plus, she wasn't too tired. She'd get back on a regular sleeping schedule soon.

"I've never had my own personal studio before. The little corner in my landlord's garage at my last place was awesome but a little cramped. This is awesome!"

"Well, as far as a twelve-by-ten shed will let you spread out. You get to be as messy as you want to be. You know why? Because this is your space."

Jane kissed her. "You're the best girlfriend ever!"

Izzy grinned. "I think I'll have a T-shirt made up to remind you when I forget to put the paper roll on the toilet roll thingamajig."

Jane spread her arms to take in the entire shed. "This gives you a get-out-of-jail-free card for the rest of the year."

"Awesome!" Izzy started to celebrate and then realized she'd been duped. "Hey! There're only three more weeks left in the year!"

"Three whole weeks of no worries about leaving me in a delicate state in the bathroom. Sounds fair to me."

"Maybe I'll build one of those toilet-paper-roll-holder stack things after I finish this." Jane looked confused so she explained. "You know, those cutesy decorative things you put near the toilet meant to hold a bunch of rolls? They disguise the fact that they're there to contain toilet paper and are not, in fact, a whimsical piece of bathroom decor."

Jane ticked one eyebrow up. "Oh. Like the classy outhouse sculpture at your grandma's? Right next to the magazine rack full of National Rifle Association magazines? Under the corncob mounted behind the glass inscribed with 'break in case of empty roll'?"

"Exactly!" Izzy said.

Jane tapped her chin in consideration. "A plausible solution. Or you can simply replace the roll. Just a thought."

Izzy laughed and leaned back to kiss Jane.

The screen to the back door slid shut, and both of them looked in the direction of the noise.

"Hey, Haley!" Izzy said, and she and Jane went to meet her on the back porch. "Where's the baby? Is Josh watching her?"

Haley wrapped her arms around herself and didn't even smile when she saw them. "The baby is the only thing anyone talks about anymore. It's like I've become invisible," she said.

A heavy stone of worry filled Izzy's stomach. This wasn't the Haley she knew. Her sister's words over Thanksgiving echoed in her mind.

"You know you're still my favorite." Izzy gave her a hug. Haley just stood there and didn't hug her back. "Babies are like getting a new toy. They even have that new-human smell."

"Oh, I love to smell the tops of baby heads," Jane said.

Haley flopped her hand toward the house. "She's asleep in her car seat in the living room. She sleeps all the time. Thank God. I'm not sure I could manage it if she were always awake."

"I'm gonna go in and stare at her," Jane said, skipping into the house. Izzy would have laughed at her if Haley didn't have her so worried.

"Do you take naps while she sleeps?" she asked.

"I try. All I want to do is sleep all the time." Haley looked down at herself in disgust. "That and eat ice cream, as if I need to gain any more weight."

Izzy took in her niece's appearance. She didn't look like her usual cheerful self. She looked listless and drawn.

"You're beautiful, Haley." Izzy draped an arm over her shoulders and led her into the house. She had an idea. "Ice cream sounds good. Jane, would you mind watching Simone while Haley and I go to Cow Licks for a couple of cones? I promise to bring back some lemon caramel."

Haley barely registered the suggestion for ice cream. The old Haley would have danced at the suggestion. This Haley simply shrugged.

"Exclusive baby snuggles just for me *and* ice cream? Absolutely! Take your time!" Jane started to unbuckle Simone from her car seat.

"You are such a baby freak," she said with a laugh.

The baby stretched but didn't wake when Jane lifted her carefully from the seat and cradled her in her arms.

Jane kissed Simone's forehead. "Babies happen to have the purest energy on the planet. Can you blame me for wanting to soak it up? Just look at her. She's gorgeous."

Izzy could easily see Jane with babies of her own. She was such a nurturer. The thought made her smile.

Izzy quickly changed from her paint-splattered clothes, and she and Haley walked to the ice cream shop. When they arrived, the smell of fresh-baked waffle cones filled the air.

They ordered. It was always the same for them. Mint chocolate chip for Izzy and butter pecan for Haley. They took their cones to a small café table for two in the corner of the shop, far enough away from the rest of the tables to not be overheard. The bright sunshine and cloudless day gave the impression it was warmer outside than it was.

The ice cream was perfect, adding sweetness to the tension surrounding Haley. "So, your mom says you've been a little down since the baby came," Izzy said.

"I guess." Haley stared at her ice cream and took a tentative bite. She looked like she wanted to cry.

"What's up?" Izzy tried to keep her tone light. Maybe Haley would open up. "Do you think it's hormones? Lack of sleep?" If they needed to pretend until Haley was able to talk about it, she'd do it.

Haley wiped her tears away, then dropped her face into her hands. Izzy took the melting ice cream cone from her. Haley rubbed her eyes, reminding Izzy of when her niece was a toddler and was overwhelmed. She placed the cone on a stack of napkins she'd taken at the counter, letting the paper absorb the melting ice cream. Haley didn't seem to notice. Her eyes were unblinking and unfocused.

"I'm not sure I can do this, Aunt Iz." It was almost a whisper.

"Do what, sweetie?" Izzy reached across the table and cupped her elbow.

"Anything, really." A sob shook her. "It's so hard. I'm an awful mom."

"What makes you think that?"

It seemed almost rude to keep eating her ice cream, but they didn't have any more napkins to use, and it seemed ruder to get up to toss it while Haley struggled, as if it would call more attention to her breakdown. So, Izzy kept on eating without tasting, and she held on to Haley's arm, wanting to ground her while she wondered if Haley would answer.

Haley leaned back in her chair, wiped her face with both hands, and took a deep breath. When she finally looked at Izzy, her eyes were like lasers. Accusation, fear, challenge poured from them. The quick shift was familiar, reminding her of herself when her meds needed to be adjusted.

"I don't want to say it. You'll think I'm a terrible person." Haley held her chin high, her expression cold and challenging.

"I'd never think you were a terrible person, Haley."

The intensity of the stare diminished some, but it was still there. It would be easy to misunderstand. She could easily think Haley was angry at her. For what? Making her think? Making her feel? Making her say it out loud? It wasn't her fault, but Izzy would allow her to throw accusation at her. She had firsthand experience at how this felt. There had to be a place to focus the pain, the anger, the confusion. Otherwise, she would explode into a million little pieces, and each piece would continue to feel and grow, and—

"Everyone always talks about falling in love with their baby the first time they saw them. Not me. All I felt was fear and emptiness." The volume of her voice rose as she spoke, gathering intensity. "I thought it would go away. But it's only gotten worse. Every day, it gets worse. I'm so afraid I'm going to ruin this baby. All I want to do is run away, or…" Haley didn't finish, but Izzy felt a rush of cold run through her. Haley's voice dropped to a whisper. She stared at the table, all challenge gone from her expression, a haunted shadow replacing it.

"She doesn't deserve me. She should have a real mother who loves her and wants to be with her." Tears streamed from her eyes.

Izzy dropped the last few bites of her cone on top of the melted mess on the napkins and held Haley's arms with both hands. "You love her. You *are* a real mother, sweetie."

"You have no idea what I mean!" Haley shouted, and then her shoulders immediately dropped. Her face seemed to crumple in on itself. Tears rolled down her cheeks unnoticed. "I'm sorry. So sorry. I'm a terrible person."

"It's okay. It's okay. I love you. You aren't a terrible person. You're having a hard time. You can say or do anything, and I will always love you, always be here for you." Haley wouldn't remember her exact words. Izzy knew. But it was important Haley knew she would always be there, would always be safe.

"I know, Aunt Iz. You're the only one who really understands me. I know you understand why I know I'm a terrible person."

To acknowledge or dismiss Haley's words would be equally unproductive, so Izzy chose not to do either. She wanted to know what Haley meant earlier.

"You said you 'want to run away or…' Or what, Haley?" The options were terrifying, knowing how she had once been where Haley might be going. Her jaw was aching from clenching her teeth. Old memories played at the edges of her mind. This was about Haley, not her.

Haley took a stuttering breath. "I don't want to say it."

"Why not?"

"It's terrible."

She rubbed Haley's elbow. "We've never had secrets before. You can tell me." Did she really want to hear, though?

"It's horrible, Aunt Iz. Don't make me say it." Haley's voice was barely audible. Snot dripped from her nose into her lap. She didn't acknowledge when Izzy pulled her hand into her sleeve and wiped it away.

"Haley, do you think about doing something to the baby?" The question had to be asked. Haley snapped her head up, the angry expression back, and she glared at her. The shifts in emotion were jarring. Izzy felt the echoes of whirling, overpowering emotion skidding through her head, the sizzle of lightning-fast changes, the frustration of not being able to control them, the guilt of being mean to others, the indignant response of not giving a shit, the judgment—They were only memories, she reminded herself. This was not about her. Haley needed her. "I know you wouldn't—"

"No! No! I would never do anything to hurt her." Haley put her hands over her face and rested her elbows on the table. "Never!"

Relief washed through Izzy, but it was short-lived. "Then what? What do you think about that could be so awful?"

Haley's hands were still over her face. Izzy waited. "I think Simone and Josh would be better off without me. People would be better off if I disappeared."

The darkness of the thought overpowered Izzy for a moment. The inky darkness of complete and utter despair almost paralyzed her. She struggled away from it. It wasn't hers. It wasn't in her. It was a memory. Old and distant, but it was still there, still as powerful at it had been when she had wrestled it all those years ago. She didn't believe it any more. But Haley didn't know, couldn't see it. Not yet.

"I know you might think it. I know it feels real to you. But trust me, it's not true. None of us would be better off without you. We are better *because* of you. We love you."

Izzy dragged her chair around the table and wrapped Haley in her arms. Haley went limp and leaned into Izzy's embrace. A thousand memories of holding this precious child in her arms filled Izzy with a love unshakable and huge. No one, no *thing* was going to hurt this girl!

Haley's body shook. Warm tears soaked through Izzy's shirt, but she held on to Haley until the shaking subsided and the sobbing stopped.

The young cashier behind the counter came over and quietly left a napkin dispenser on the table. She cleared the glob of melted ice cream and soggy cones and left to wait on a new set of customers. Izzy pulled several napkins from the dispenser in the middle of the table and offered them to Haley, who blew her nose and wiped her eyes without escaping from Izzy's arms. A long sigh warmed the wet material on Izzy's chest.

"I got snot and tears all over you." Haley rubbed the wet material. "People are staring."

Izzy smoothed Haley's hair and kissed the top of her head. "We don't know them, and worse things have been on this shirt. I have two cats and a dog, remember?"

A muffled, half-hearted laugh rose, followed by a tremulous sigh.

"I need help, Aunt Iz. I think I need someone to fix me."

Izzy leaned back and looked into Haley's eyes. "I'd like to take you to a doctor. Will you let me?"

This was the tightrope her mother talked about, the one she'd said she'd walked with Izzy. No pushing, no convincing, no discussion. When a person was in an episode, logic did not exist, and ideas were fleeting. Emotions ruled every decision and rolled around on an erratic tide, changing for no apparent reason. The idea had to be her own; otherwise, Haley was likely to push back or change her mind, and they might not have another chance to change it.

Haley blew her nose again. "I know as much as any doctor. In fact, I know more, since it's my mind we're talking about here. I'm smart enough to tell them what they want to know to get them off my back. I'm not sure a doctor can help."

Izzy resisted the urge to argue. She understood the futility of using logic against a person with bipolar illness and the delusion of being all-powerful, all-knowing. "Talking might help, though."

"I've been fooling my ob-gyn all this time, haven't I?"

"You have?"

Haley sat up and took a deep breath. "Sure. She 'checks in' on me to see if I'm doing okay. If we're doing okay. I just talk about Simone, say the things she wants to hear. She has no idea of the other things I'm thinking, what I'm capable of. I have her completely fooled."

Again, the allusion to her doing something drastic. Had she been fooling her, too? A hard pit was expanding in Izzy's stomach. "I guess you can continue fooling your doctor, but if you want help, you might consider being open about what's going on with you. It might be helpful."

Haley raised her hands and then flopped them down again. "What if there's no way to fix this, Aunt Iz? What if I'm just a terrible person?"

"You aren't a terrible person." She struggled to get through to her. "You know how I have to take medicine to even things out? And how I have to go to a therapist to check in?"

Haley rolled her eyes. "No offense, Aunt Iz, but this is worse. You've never been like this."

Oh, if only she knew. But right now was about Haley. She needed to know there was hope. "Oh, honey. It's not a competition. You just haven't seen it. My medicine keeps me on track."

"You're bipolar, right? Is that what this is?" Haley asked.

She had a pretty good idea, but she knew enough to get a doctor's diagnosis before asserting anything. "I honestly don't know. But I do know you don't have to feel like this."

Haley crossed her arms over her chest and leaned back in her chair. "I don't know how I *can't* feel like this. I've always felt like this, but I never showed it. I just don't know how not to show it now. Maybe it's the hormones."

The sense of certainty of uncertain things came back to Izzy, and she hated it. The false sense of knowing for sure something was the way it was, the claustrophobic closeness of all of it rushing back to her all these years later. She couldn't be in Haley's mind; she didn't want to. But she had to help her. Hope was the strongest thing she had right now. "Our minds are frighteningly powerful things. But trust me, if you work with a therapist, you'll figure out how to control it."

Izzy had. Mostly.

Over time, everything, even new love, loses its shine when it becomes familiar. It doesn't mean it's not awesome. It just means euphoria can last only so long before it starts to become just a normal part of your life.

Some people simply ease into the next chapter of their relationship without a pause. They like the predictability of knowing exactly where they stand and being able to take their partner for granted. It's just there one day, the comfortable way of being with the person you fell in love with. Contentment. Ease. Trust.

Other people miss the thrill of how it used to be as soon as they realize the newness has worn off. They long for the days when their heart would race at the mere sight of their beloved. Contentment to them is a sign of a relationship in decline. They miss what they used to have at the beginning. A feeling of wanting something else begins to seep in.

This can be a critical time. You can chance it and just see how things shake out. Or you can try to keep the sizzle alive. I vote for keeping the sizzle alive.

CHAPTER THIRTY-FOUR

The light from the computer screen lit up the corner of the living room. Most of the lights in the house were off, and only the lamp next to the couch where Izzy sat was on. Gus and Fat Bob snuggled on the seat of the couch next to Izzy, who sat with her legs folded under her and her laptop on her lap. The words were flowing from her fingers as Izzy finished typing a chapter of the third section of the guide. She was two-thirds done! She couldn't wait to find out how it ended. It was easy to write about comfort and warmth and feeling like part of a couple. It was a lot like how she and Jane were, and it felt good to write about it.

A hand on her foot made her look up. Jane stood there, her hair tousled from sleep. Izzy hadn't even noticed her come into the room. A rush of affection flooded her, and she thought about lying next to Jane in their bed with the warm comforter enveloping them in its cozy cocoon and the soft feel of Jane in her arms.

"Hey, babe."

Jane stifled a yawn. "Honey, are you going to come to bed sometime soon? It's late, and you have work tomorrow."

"What time is it?" Izzy checked the clock on her computer screen. "Oh, jeez! It's past two a.m. I just got into the writing zone and lost track of time."

Jane rubbed her eyes. "You have the most energy I've ever seen in a person. You stay up like this and still go running in the morning and after work. How do you do it?"

Izzy closed her computer. She wasn't tired, but she really should try to get some sleep. "Good genes, I guess." She knew it wasn't good genes. More like a mild case of mania. The thought slightly concerned her, but she also knew it was just part of the cycle. The question was, how far into the cycle was she? Just getting started? Or near the end?

The fact she was even questioning her state of being meant she needed to check in.

❖

Light jazz floated from hidden speakers in the comfortable waiting room just outside of an office in the three-story Victorian-style house. The place had been remodeled to accommodate several small offices, most of them used by therapists. The two stuffed chairs in the room flanked a round, antique end table. In front of the chairs was a matching coffee table featuring a stack of current magazines: *People, The New Yorker, Business Week, Cosmopolitan, Parents, Time,* and *Psychology Today.*

Five minutes early, Izzy ignored the magazines, convinced that if she selected one, it was a test factoring into her therapist's assessment of her. She trusted her therapist with her life but didn't believe her when she'd laughed about the idea when Izzy had asked about it. Izzy tapped her fingers to the music and tried to empty her mind. She liked to start her sessions without an agenda. Important things surfaced if she didn't try to guide the session. In addition to checking in about the late nights writing, she figured the trip to the ice cream shop with Haley would come up.

The door opened, and her therapist, Tori, poked her head out.

"Hey, Izzy. Come on in."

Izzy suspected Tori was bored with her by now. After twenty-two years, Tori knew just about everything about Izzy. Theirs was like a long marriage—comfortable and familiar. The longevity of their relationship defined their discussions, even though they were one-sided. The book project had spiced things up a little recently, however, and Izzy enjoyed the spark it added to their time together.

Izzy chose one of the chairs across from Tori this time. She always rotated where she sat between the two chairs and the couch in the office for the same reason she never read the magazines in the waiting room. Tori had long ago stopped commenting on her actions.

"How's your week been?" Tori asked.

Izzy crossed her legs, resting her ankle on her knee, and leaned back in the chair. She pulled the hem of her khakis to cover her sock.

"Pretty good. Busy," Izzy said. The same answer almost every week.

"Work? Life? Both?" Tori asked. The same response almost every week.

"Both. We're coming up on the next release, so we have a ton of documentation to get out. Plus, I'm working on the book. And I'm still getting used to having Jane at home. I love it, but it's an adjustment." Then there was the worry about Haley, but she'd bring that up later, not as part of the mundane projects in her life. Haley deserved her own mention.

"You now have someone to coordinate things with, adjust to their schedule, etcetera. How's it going?"

Izzy let a wide smile stretch across her face. "Good. I really love having her around. I look forward to coming home. I love waking up each morning with her. It's more comfortable than I thought it would be."

"Good. Good. Do you find anything difficult?"

Difficult? Jane was anything but difficult. Except… "I'm not sure I'd call it difficult, but sometimes, I feel like I have to explain things. I think it's more on me than her, though."

Tori waited a beat before responding to Izzy. "Like what?"

"I don't know. My running is one thing, I guess," Izzy said. Actually, her running was the only thing she'd had to explain.

"Why do you have to explain your running?"

Izzy pinched the crease in her khakis. "She thinks it's excessive to go twice a day."

"What did she say?"

"She just asked me if I always ran twice a day. I told her not always."

Another pause. Izzy was used to it. "Is there a reason you're going twice a day?"

"It helps me stay grounded and dispel extra energy." Izzy repeated Tori's description for why running was good for her when she'd told her she'd started back up several years ago.

"When do you run?"

"In the morning before she gets up. And then again right after work, when she's grading papers."

Tori paused. "How long do you go for?"

"Usually about three miles. Sometimes five. I'm not gone for long."

Tori leaned forward and tented her fingers under her chin. "In the past, you'd go running when you were stressed. Are you feeling stressed?"

"Not in a bad way," Izzy said, picking at the cuff on her pants. "Do you think I might be swinging toward mania?"

"Do you?"

Izzy looked up from picking at her cuff. "You know me. I'm always worried about it."

Tori leaned back in her chair. "But does this time feel different?"

"Everything feels different but in a good way. I'm in love." There, she'd said it out loud. "I feel good. Almost high, excited. I have that Christmassy anticipation feeling I remember from being a kid."

Tori smiled. "It must be a nice feeling. But kids also don't feel wholly in control of their lives. Is it possible you don't feel in control right now?"

Izzy thought about the question before answering. "It's definitely a nice feeling. But I guess I've lost a little control of my emotions. It's expected, right? When you fall in love? Sometimes I wonder if it's too much, though. You know, like I should calm down a little. Like, maybe I'm *too* excited, or *too* high on the feeling."

"Thus, why you run twice a day?"

"Part of it. The other part is just to have some time to let my mind go blank."

"That's right. You tune out when you run."

She linked her fingers together and pulled up on her knee. "Yeah. But don't worry. I'm totally aware of my surroundings."

"Have you thought you might be using running to escape something? Like maybe you're literally running from something?" Tori asked.

"I've thought about it, yeah," Izzy said. And she had. She was always watching out for indications she was veering off her charted path and into bipolar territory. "I don't think I'm trying to escape anything, though. I think it's just my way of resetting. I also know doing anything in excess is probably not a good thing, even if the thing is supposedly a healthy thing, like running. I've run a lot more when I was training for marathons. Five or six miles a day isn't excessive for an avid runner."

Tori tilted her head. "True. The timing of it is interesting, though. Typically, people cut down on things like running and going to the gym when they first enter a relationship so they can spend more time with their partner."

She didn't like the defensive feeling rising within her. "I run when she's asleep or busy. It's not like I'm choosing running over spending time with her."

"Sounds pretty healthy to me."

"It does?" The defensiveness abated. "Good. Because it feels healthy. It's like natural drugs."

"How about sleep? Are you getting enough?"

"Most of the time." Izzy knew that wasn't true as soon as she said it. "A few nights I've stayed up a little later than usual to work on the book." *And have sex*, but she didn't say that.

"How many nights do you think you stay up later than usual?" Tori rested her chin on her hand. She didn't seem too concerned about her sleep, which was a relief. She always worried about going off her sleep schedule.

"A couple times a week." It was more than that, but not by much.

"And when you do, how do you feel?"

Izzy thought about it. "I'm usually tired the next day."

"Being tired is actually a good thing. How do you feel when you're working on the book?"

"You mean, besides feeling completely underqualified to be writing it?" Izzy grimaced.

They'd covered this point several times already, so Tori just laughed. "Aside from the imposter syndrome, yes."

"Pretty focused, actually. I usually stay up later when I'm making progress on it, and I don't want to lose the thread of creative energy."

"How about nutrition?"

"I'm eating well. Probably more than usual because I have someone to eat with, and since I'm running a lot."

"And your meds? Is everything on track with them?"

"Yep. Three times a day like clockwork."

"Well, it sounds like you have the big three under control. You seem aware of what you're doing, and you're managing your sleep, nutrition, and meds. Plus, you're watching out for manic behavior. As long as you have those things in check, even if you are cycling, the meds should keep it from spiraling out of control. I don't think you have anything to worry about. I think you're right. We can chalk this up to the blush of new love and the excitement of a fun project. It will be interesting to see how things are when the newness wears off." Then she dropped the big question Izzy had been waiting for. "Have you told Jane about your bipolar condition yet?"

Izzy stifled a groan. "Not yet. It just never feels like the right time."

"I understand. It's your business." Tori paused.

Izzy waited. There would be more, she knew. She wasn't disappointed.

"I know we've often talked about how being bipolar doesn't define you. Maintaining your privacy is healthy. Think about this, though. It is a big part of who you are. As someone who is significant to you, it's probably something she should know."

Izzy absorbed what Tori said. It was true. "I agree. I feel like I need to tell her. It's only fair."

"I hear a 'but.' Are you afraid of something?"

Izzy uncrossed her legs. "Hell, yes, I'm afraid."

"Tell me what you're afraid of."

Izzy held up her fingers to tick off her fears. "It will scare her off. She'll see me as damaged goods. She'll break up with me." Her heart raced. It had gone through her head a million times, but saying it out loud sounded way scarier, as if it could really happen.

Tori's brow furrowed. "Does she seem like the type to call it quits over something like this?"

It sounded so unlike anything Jane would ever do. Jane was better than that. She wasn't the type to run from an illness.

"Not really."

"Then what are you afraid of?"

Izzy sank into her seat. "I'm also sort of afraid she *won't* break it off with me."

Tori's brow furrowed even more. "What do you mean?"

Izzy laughed and heard how shallow she sounded. "It's like the joke my dad tells all the time: why would I want to date someone who would date *me*?"

"Funny. But don't diminish yourself, Izzy."

Izzy rolled her eyes. "I'm only half-joking."

Tori lifted an eyebrow. "It means you're also half-serious about saying you're not datable because you're bipolar. Do you think it very often?"

She'd tried to not think about it but wasn't always successful. "Not constantly. But it's there."

"Tell me about it." Tori tilted her head.

"Not much to tell. People are uncomfortable with people who aren't one hundred percent stable."

Tori gave her a half-smile. "I know few people who are one hundred percent stable."

She waved a hand. "You know what I mean."

Tori leaned forward. "Our time is up. But before we go, I want to pass something by you that we can pick up on next session. We've spoken quite a bit about the wall you put up around yourself. Most of the time, we talk about how it's there to keep people or events from reaching in to trigger you, to keep you from having another episode. But have you given much thought about how the wall is also keeping *you* from reaching out?"

Izzy stared at the floor. No. She hadn't thought about it at all. And she hadn't talked to her about Haley yet.

❖

Love is hard.

Seriously. So hard.

If you thought putting yourself out there was hard, or finding someone interesting to date was hard, you'll find being in love is even more so. I'm not talking about falling in love. That's actually pretty easy once you meet someone you really click with. I'm talking about being in love, nurturing love, sustaining love. Being in love is one of the most difficult things a person can embark on. It requires true mindfulness and dedication. You have to make accommodations to help your life fit with a new person. You have to consider your partner when you make decisions, even small ones. Sometimes, you'll have to make concessions in order to keep your love in balance. To be fair, your partner needs to do all this, too. It takes work from both of you to make it work.

Sure, it seems easy. At first, you're so besotted and swimming in all the love pheromones, you don't even know you're making slight alterations in your normal routine to fit in this remarkable person you've fallen for. And people will probably tell you they don't work at it, either. It just comes naturally.

Yeah, right.

When was the last time you naturally shaved your legs—or other things—every single day so you'd be silky smooth when you took off your clothes each night? Or how often did you used to leave the last little bit of brownie in the dish just to make another person smile when they came home from a long day at work?

It's not just about doing nice things, either. It's about not doing things, too.

Any book on relationships will tell you relationships require work. While this isn't always the case for those wonderfully lucky souls who find the perfect yin to their yang, it is often the case with the rest of us poor sots who hook up with perfectly human partners. The trick is to be aware of the other person and be concerned with their happiness. Love just makes it worthwhile.

CHAPTER THIRTY-FIVE

The office was quiet; the only sound was the keys clicking under Izzy's fingers. She hit the "Submit for Review" button on the document she'd just finished and reached over to grab a Peanut M&M. The bowl was empty. She looked up, and the office was deserted. The only lights still illuminated on the floor were the ones directly above her head because the motion detector had sensed she was there. She lifted her hands over her head and stretched. A sinking sensation filled her stomach. The clock on her computer said it was after eight p.m.

She picked up her phone, which was face down on the desk beside her laptop. Two missed calls from Jane. Shit. She'd silenced the ringer like she always did when she was at work, but she'd somehow not noticed the vibration, too. It was the second time that week she'd unintentionally worked late, something she'd done countless times before. But now, she had someone waiting for her to get home each night. Guilt soured her stomach.

Jane hadn't said anything the first time, but she'd been a little distant. Izzy felt like a jerk. It wasn't just guilt. She missed Jane when she wasn't with her. Izzy shut down her computer and put it in her computer bag. She collected her phone and considered texting to say she was on her way but decided a call would be better. She'd do that as soon as she got her car out of the garage, where cell service was iffy. She put on her jacket and headed out of the office. On her way out, she stopped by the orange breakroom and filled a cup with Peanut M&M's, thinking it might be a small peace offering.

The campus was nearly deserted as she walked across it, with only a few lights still on in the building where the developers were probably working. Another release was ready for merge, and some teams were undoubtedly burning the midnight oil to work the bugs out of it. Another reason Izzy was working late. But the work would always be there no matter how many hours she put in. Concern about staying late being a sign of pending mania zipped through her mind, but she pushed it away. She'd just gone into the zone and lost track of time. A couple of late nights didn't mean anything.

She pulled her car out of the garage. Would she still have time to go running later? She'd have to test the waters. She pushed the quick dial on her phone, and the computer in the Tesla picked up the call. A ringtone filled the car.

"Hello." Jane's voice sounded flat.

Yep. She was mad. "I'm so, so, so sorry. I lost track of time. I'm on my way home now. I'm so, so sorry."

"I'm just glad you're okay. I tried calling, but you didn't answer."

"I turned the ringer off," she said needlessly because Jane knew she always turned it off at work. "Have I said how sorry I am? Cuz I am."

A sigh came across the line, and the dejection of knowing she was a total loser seeped through her.

"I know you are. I also know your job is demanding, and you have to work late sometimes. I just wish you would call to let me know when you have to."

A flash of anger filled Izzy. Hadn't she just told her she'd lost track of time? If she wasn't aware of time, how could she call to tell her she'd be late?

She had the grace not to react to her anger. "Have you eaten? Do you want me to bring something home?"

"I made dinner. I saved some for you."

Another flash of anger filled Izzy when she found Jane hadn't even waited for her to eat. Almost immediately, guilt replaced the anger. Why should Jane have waited? Jane had every right to eat dinner at a decent hour, and she hadn't known when Izzy would be home. She *had* tried to call.

Her default coping tool kicked in to help with the mood swings. *Fake it 'til you make it.* "Awesome. *You're* awesome. I'll be home in just a few minutes. There's hardly any traffic." It sort of worked.

"Okay. Be safe. I'll see you soon."

Jane's unenthusiastic tone grated against her. She was trying, for Christ's sake. Couldn't Jane meet her halfway?

They hung up, but Izzy continued to repeat the exchange in her mind during the short drive home and as she pulled into the garage. When she turned off the car, she sat in the driver's seat for a minute, trying to settle her emotions and thoughts. Jane was behaving reasonably. She needed to check her own responses. *Don't take it inside. Leave it at the door.* After a few deep breaths, she got out, plugged in the car, and walked into the house. Jane was sitting at the bar in the kitchen grading papers, a glass of white wine on the counter beside her. She looked tired, and Izzy dropped her computer bag on the table and went over to her.

She held the cup of M&M's out in both of her hands and bowed her head.

"I bequeath to you this meager token of my humble apologies, beautiful maiden. I loseth tracketh of time, and it shanteth happen again. I'm thorry."

Jane smiled, and the knots in Izzy's stomach loosened.

"You're a nut."

Izzy hugged her, and Jane hugged her back.

God, I love her, Izzy thought into the top of Jane's head. Tears welled up in her eyes, and she blinked them away. She didn't deserve her.

Jane squeezed her. "There are tamales in the refrigerator."

"You made tamales?"

"My mom did. I got off work a little early and dropped by to see her before my dad got home from work."

"How was she?"

"She was fine when I got there, but then my dad came home early, too, and accused us of talking behind his back, so I left. My mom can usually calm him down better when I'm not there." A shadow clouded Jane's expression.

"He gets mad when you see your own mother without him there?" It came out before Izzy could filter her tone to something less judgy.

"He says it's because any information I pass to my mom doesn't always get back to him." Jane sounded like she knew that wasn't the entire truth. "Anyway, do you want me to heat the tamales for you?"

"I'm not hungry. I had some yogurt and granola at work just before I left," she lied. At least about the yogurt and granola. She really wasn't hungry. "You know what I want to do?"

"Go for a run?" Jane asked.

The look in Jane's eyes was clue enough that going for a run wouldn't go over very well, as much as she wanted to go. Irritation sparked in her even though Jane's answer was a valid guess. She just wanted more credit than that.

She had an idea and flashed what she hoped was a brilliant smile. *Fake it 'til you make it, right?* "I want to sit in the hot tub. Do you have a lot more grading to do? Or can you join me in a delightful soak?"

Jane's shoulders relaxed, and a smile softened her expression. "That sounds lovely. I can finish grading tomorrow."

Proud of herself, Izzy went to the refrigerator and pulled out the bottle of wine Jane had opened and refreshed her glass. She then took a glass from the cupboard and filled one for herself. "Cheers."

Jane tapped the lip of her glass to the glass Izzy held toward her. "I didn't know you liked wine."

Izzy sipped from her glass. "On occasion."

She took Jane's hand and led them through the house out onto the wooden deck just outside their bedroom. A wooden gazebo and lush foliage sheltered the hot tub from the neighbors but gave them a great view of the moonlit mountains to the west. Izzy folded back the top of the tub, and steam rose into the chilly air. They quickly undressed and climbed into the warm water. Izzy's heart sped up at the view of Jane in the moonlight.

Jane eased into the warm water and tucked herself into the arc of Izzy's arm, which was stretched across the top of the tub.

"Aside from the visit with your mom, how was your day?" Izzy asked.

Jane sipped her wine. "It was good. It's always hard to go back for spring term."

"I'll bet." Izzy put her glass on the edge of the hot tub, moved Jane in front of her, and began to massage her shoulders.

"That feels good." Jane placed her glass next to Izzy's and dropped her head forward.

Jane's skin was soft and slick with the warm water, and Izzy worked her fingers over the taut muscles along her shoulders and down her back. The soft sounds Jane made guided her to the areas she needed to spend more time on, and when Jane captured one of Izzy's hands and guided it between her legs, Izzy didn't need to be told she had another kind of tension needing to be addressed. Izzy moved the hair away from Jane's neck and kissed the moist skin as she fluttered her fingers over the folds between Jane's legs. Jane's back pressed against Izzy's breasts, and they slid against each other as Izzy nibbled Jane's neck.

"Rub me around the edges. I want to come fast." Jane dropped her head back so it rested on Izzy's shoulder.

Izzy's center contracted at the request. It turned her on when Jane was direct with how she wanted to be touched.

Jane's eyes were closed, and Izzy kissed her neck, her jawline, and traced a path to her partly open lips. Jane returned the kiss with passion as Izzy continued to touch her.

She traced circles around Jane's swollen center, glancing around the outside edges like Jane liked it. She dipped her fingers inside the silken folds once, twice, three times, eliciting a shiver from Jane, before she resumed the circular motion around the rigid flesh. Jane liked it steady with a firm pressure. If they had been in bed, she would add the tip of her tongue over Jane's clit, soft at first, and then steadily add pressure until Jane came with a hard shudder. But in the hot tub, she held Jane's head above water so Jane could concentrate on her pleasure. Jane moaned, and her breathing hitched. When Izzy slid her fingers inside her again, her muscles spasmed around her fingers.

"Are you ready?" Izzy whispered in Jane's ear, and Jane pressed her mouth to Izzy's lips, sucking on Izzy's tongue.

Izzy circled Jane's clit another time and then flattened her fingers and rubbed them across her clit until Jane arched up, bracing her feet on the hot-tub seat across from them, spreading her legs, seeking more pressure. Izzy watched Jane's breasts heave above the water, her own clit twitching, but she kept her pace, moving her hand in a steady motion. Jane gasped and raised her arms over her head, wrapping around Izzy's head as she climaxed. Izzy ached to put her fingers in her again, but their position didn't give her the right angle. So she rubbed Jane's swollen flesh, making light circles around Jane's clit to prolong her fading orgasm. As Jane relaxed, she sighed, floated into Izzy's lap, and curled up there.

Dizzy with awe about making Jane respond so powerfully, Izzy wrapped her arms around her and nuzzled her neck, which inspired more shivers. Overcome with emotion, Izzy tipped Jane's head back and kissed her deeply. Jane pulled Izzy's hands to her breasts and kissed her in return, arching into Izzy's hands, which were kneading her breasts and pinching her nipples. Breathing hard, Jane pulled away slightly and pivoted in Izzy's lap, facing her, straddling her, pressing into her. The feeling of their breasts pressing together increased the ache between Izzy's legs. She hooked one of her legs around Jane and ground against her, her center pushed against Jane's thigh.

Jane gazed into Izzy's eyes, hypnotizing her with their intensity. "I want you inside me."

Izzy returned the gaze and slid her right arm between them, teasing the outside of Jane's lips. They were swollen, and Izzy drew a long stroke through them. Jane thrust toward her fingers, but Izzy circled her clit and teased some more.

"Like this?" she asked.

"Inside. Please. Deep inside." The plea in Jane's eyes told her Jane didn't want to be teased. She plunged three fingers inside her, and Jane threw her head back, closing her eyes, a deep moan exploding from her throat. Jane's muscles pulsed, and Izzy's did the same. She curled her fingers around and massaged the pad of muscles on the front wall of Jane's tunnel. Jane started to rock and swivel her hips, rubbing her thigh against Izzy's throbbing core just enough to drive her crazy for relief but not giving it. Her wrist grew tired, but she ignored her fatigue, entranced by Jane as she moved above her.

"Oh! Yes! More. Please. I want all of you." Jane grabbed Izzy's wrist and ground against her fingers.

Izzy lifted Jane and pulled her fingers out just far enough so she could curl her fingers together and slowly slide her hand into Jane's warmth. The opening was tight around her hand but opened to accept it.

Jane let out a low, keening sound and gyrated her hips. "God, I feel like I'm going to explode."

"You feel so good."

"Oh! Oh! Oh!" Jane reared up and came down. A wave of water splashed into Izzy's face and over her head. Izzy saw it coming but didn't let it detract from what she was doing, and Jane continued to move until her orgasm was finished, and she collapsed, once more, against Izzy. Izzy gently removed her hand from the warm cocoon of Jane, kissing her while brushing the hair from her face. When Jane opened her eyes, they were unfocused and soft, but she pulled back a little and laughed.

"You're drenched."

"It was the tsunami of passion you unleashed upon me when you came. Next time, I'll just wear my scuba gear."

Jane put her hands over her face and laughed. "I'm so sorry!"

"I'm not. It'll make a good story."

"And who would you tell this story to?"

"Well, for sure the guy who takes care of the hot tub. He'll ask about the missing water. And then there's—"

"You won't tell anyone!" Jane said, putting a hand over Izzy's mouth.

Izzy laughed and took Jane's hand from her mouth. "You sound so mob-bossy! I kind of like it."

"Does it turn you on?" Jane gyrated against her.

"*You* turn me on." Izzy kissed her, and it turned into a long, slow make-out session while a slow pulse beat between her legs.

"Why don't we take this to the bedroom so I can take care of you and so neither one of us drowns in the process?" Jane murmured against her lips.

"I'd gladly drown in the tidal waves of your pleasure, my love."

"That's good. You should be a writer." Jane trailed her lips along Izzy's jaw.

Izzy tilted her head so Jane could kiss her neck. "Right now, I just want to be your pillow princess."

"Take me to bed then!" Jane rose from the water, and the sight of Jane's breasts and the curves of her hips, the roundness of her belly made Izzy gasp.

"God, you're so beautiful."

"You make me feel beautiful."

Izzy rose and kissed her with all the tenderness she felt. Then she helped her from the hot tub and took her to bed.

Jane fell asleep after they made love again, and Izzy pulled the comforter over them to ward off the chill from the cold night air against the perspiration covering their skin. Snuggled under the covers, she held Jane in her arms and pushed her nose against the top of her head, taking in her scent. Izzy's heart rate had just returned to normal after her last shattering orgasm. The taste of Jane was still in her mouth. She and Jane had made love like it was their first time, and they couldn't keep their hands off one another. She loved her so much. She'd have to tell her soon. *I'm so lucky to be with this woman*, she thought, squeezing her, sighing, drifting toward sleep.

This won't last.

The thought whispered through her mind. Barely there, it roused her just as she was about to drift off, planting a cold stone in her stomach, squeezing her chest. She opened her eyes in the dark room. She wasn't sleepy anymore. *It can't last. You're too happy.* The thoughts hissed.

The backs of her eyes stung, and hot tears squeezed from her closed eyes. The tears fell like boiling water on her cheeks, and she struggled to hold in the sob bubbling in her chest. It hurt so much to hold it in that her throat ached with the effort. *It's true. It can't last. She'll leave you. Break your heart.* The thoughts raced through her mind, and she held Jane tight, her face buried in Jane's hair, her throat aching even more from trying to hold back the tears. *Stop it. Stop it! Stopitstopitstopit!* She couldn't breathe.

Loosening Jane's arms from around her, she slid out of bed. Jane barely moved, proof she didn't care about her. *No! She's just sleeping; she doesn't know I got up.* She brushed the hair away from Jane's face, and Jane moved her face toward her hand, smiling. *She loves me.* She took a deep, shuddering breath. *Until she doesn't anymore. It's just a matter of time.* She shook her head. *Shut up! Shut up! You're just overwhelmed. It was a long day. You exchanged a lot of energy with each other. You just need some sleep.* But she wasn't tired, and she couldn't stop crying.

She had to wipe the tears from her eyes to read the clock. Almost one a.m. Anxiety rose in her belly. She needed sleep. But the ache in her chest was too much. Putting on a T-shirt, she shut the bedroom door as quietly as possible and stepped into the hallway, heading to the kitchen for a glass of water.

Tears still streamed down her face. She wiped the snot dripping from her nose with the palm of her hand. She started to sob but covered her mouth. She didn't want to wake Jane. Foregoing the glass of water, she grabbed her phone off the counter and went out to the garage. Gus followed her out and sat next to her on the single stair leading up to the house. He leaned into her as if he knew she needed the contact. Izzy wrapped her arms around him and cried into his neck, the doggy smell of him filling her head, giving her comfort.

"You'll always be there for me, won't you, Gus?" she said into his fur. He licked her cheek, and she smiled. She rubbed the tears from her eyes and wiped her nose on the sleeve of her T-shirt. She looked at the phone in her hand and hit the speed dial for Audie.

The phone rang once, and Izzy almost hung up, but she heard Audie's voice. It was low and gravelly.

"'ello?"

Izzy didn't know what to say and just sat there. Maybe Audie would hang up.

"Izzy? Are you there?"

Of course, she'd seen the caller ID. She cleared her throat.

"Sorry. I didn't mean to wake you up." She sounded stuffy, and her voice cracked as she started to cry again.

"Are you okay?"

"I don't know." Izzy heard rustling on the phone and imagined Audie sitting up in bed.

"What's going on?"

Izzy pressed the palm of her free hand into her eye. "I can't stop crying."

"Why are you crying?"

She leaned against the door and let out a shuddering sigh. "I don't know. I was falling asleep, and then I just started to think about how Jane is going to leave me someday, and I felt my heart break, and I don't know if I can live through it again."

"Okay. Did you guys have a fight or something?"

"No. We're fine. Well, I think we're fine. I stayed at work too late tonight, and I thought she might get mad, but she didn't say anything. And we had a good night. We fell asleep, and that's when the negative thoughts started, and I think I'm going to screw this up, Aud." She pounded her fist against her thigh. "I don't know how to keep from screwing this up."

Audie's voice was gentle but firm. "Hey. Hey. Hey. Iz. Take a few deep breaths. You're not screwing anything up."

She wiped her nose on her sleeve again. "How do you know?"

"I just do." There was rustling on the line as if Audie was readjusting her pillows. "Breathe for a minute."

Izzy closed her eyes and inhaled. It helped. Her thoughts slowed a little. Audie was her rock. She steadied her. Suddenly, she was aware of how chilly it was in the dark garage. Giant goose bumps peppered her bare legs. Gus warmed her side, but the unforgiving cement step beneath her was sending shards of ice into her butt cheeks.

"Thanks, Audie," she said through chattering teeth. Maybe the cold wasn't the only thing causing her to shiver.

"Anytime, kid. Where are you?"

"Sitting in the garage." She pulled up the neck of her T-shirt and wiped away the tears and snot.

"Where's Jane?"

"Sleeping. She doesn't know I'm out here."

Audie chuckled. "You should get back into bed. Go hug on your girl and stop thinking negative thoughts. You're probably just tired."

"Yeah. I'm probably just tired." And she was. The nearly full-on panic attack had taken her adrenaline way up, and now she was feeling the effects of coming down. She could barely keep her eyes open.

Audie yawned across the line. "G'night. I'll see you tomorrow. You can buy me coffee to keep me awake during my staff meeting."

Izzy laughed. She felt a little better. "You got it. Thanks, Audie."

Izzy and Gus went back into the house, and Izzy poured herself a glass of water. She drank it slowly, and the ache in her throat started to ease. Gus stayed close, as if he knew she needed his warm presence to ground her. She blew her nose and took a few more deep breaths. Her headache receded until it was a low ache in the center of her forehead. Her emotions were back in their familiar places, no longer out of control.

She padded through the house, stopping in the laundry room to change from her snot and tear-stained T-shirt before she went back to her room. The door was open when she remembered closing it. Gus jumped up on the foot of the bed before she could stop him, but Jane was already sitting up and hugging her comforter-covered knees to her chest. She sounded angry or scared. "Where'd you go? I went to check on you, and you weren't in the house. Your keys were here, though."

She stopped at the foot of the bed. "I couldn't sleep, so I went for a walk."

"In just a T-shirt?"

Izzy looked down. "Yeah. I didn't get farther than the driveway," she lied.

Jane dropped her knees so she was sitting cross-legged. "Are you okay?"

Jane's tension had switched to worry. Izzy wasn't sure which she preferred. "Yeah. Just super tired." She got into bed, leaving a little room between her and Jane, not sure where she stood with her.

"Me, too," Jane said, sliding down and turning on her side, facing away from her. She scooted her butt into Izzy, which made Izzy feel a little better.

Izzy molded her body around her, spooning her. All of the intimacy they'd shared earlier seemed to have evaporated. When Jane relaxed in her arms and pulled Izzy's arm tightly around her, Izzy wanted to cry again. She nuzzled into the back of Jane's neck, and despite her worries, sleep soon swept her away.

❖

Disagreements are bound to happen even in the best of relationships. It's what happens when two people come together with two sets of perspectives, two sets of expectations, two sets of opinions. In fact, if there isn't some sort of friction, it would be a pretty boring relationship.

Often, when a rift occurs in a relationship and the couple fixes it, the bump makes the relationship stronger by building trust and a shared experience together. It provides a base for them to work from.

A Japanese art form, called Kintsugi, is built upon the idea of making something broken into something beautiful by gluing them together with gold. If you had Kintsugi eyeglasses, you'd see a world full of people with golden lines crisscrossing all over them.

Chapter Thirty-six

Seriously, they need to put a lock on these things." Jane caught the cascade of chocolate-covered peanuts in the cup she held under the dispenser. "I miss these great breakrooms. We're lucky if someone leaves cookies in the coffee nook at the school."

Izzy leaned against the island and stirred the coffee she'd just brewed. "There are probably some doughnuts from this morning's all-hands left in the breakroom on the first floor."

Jane made a face. "The M&M's are bad enough."

Audie entered the orange breakroom with a grin. "Look who's back. Should I tell Hector you're here to help with the quality reviews on the new release? God knows he could use the help." She gave Jane a hug and leaned against the counter.

"I waved at him through the window of the fishbowl when I got up here. I'm sure he'll come find me." The big conference room in the middle of the floor was glass on four sides, so people felt as if they were fish on display when they were attending a meeting there.

Audie grabbed an apple from the fruit bowl and rubbed it on her sleeve before taking a bite. "What are you here for? Just a visit?"

"I had a meeting with the recruiting team to finalize some of our new ideas for student connection between Bay Shores and Gigify. I'm just hanging out here until Izzy gets off so we can ride home together."

Audie looked at her watch and then at Izzy. "Are you actually going home at a decent hour today?"

Izzy took a sip of her coffee and glanced at Jane. "Tonight's the holiday party at the university. Jane's going to show me off to her colleagues."

"Sounds like fun," Audie said.

Jane popped a candy into her mouth. "I'm a little nervous about it."

"Why? Are they going to make you sing karaoke?" Audie joked.

"Ugh! I wouldn't go if they had karaoke," Jane said. "It's just... I've never taken a date to the holiday party before."

Audie's eyebrows rose in surprise. "Are you not out at work?"

Jane pushed her hair back. "I'm out to the other teachers and to my students. I just haven't had the opportunity to be open about it to the higher faculty. I think the dean knows, but we've never talked about it."

"Interesting." Audie tossed her apple core into the composing bin. "I totally had you pegged as a totally out there, flag-waving lesbian."

Jane shrugged. "There's something about authority. It makes me feel like I need to be careful."

"I'm sure it's because of your parents." The words came out before Izzy had a chance to think. She immediately regretted saying anything when Jane flashed a look at her, making her feel like she was a kindergartener who had just said something totally inappropriate. Why had she said it?

Jane put her cup of candy on the counter. "I'm aware of the root of my issues, Izzy."

Izzy stroked Jane's arm. "Sorry."

Jane gave her a half-smile. "*I'm* sorry. I shouldn't have bitten your head off. I'm going to visit the little developer's room before we head home. Be right back."

Izzy still felt bad and watched Jane leave the breakroom.

"You guys are so cute." Audie hopped onto a barstool and was leaning over the counter. She lowered her voice. "How are you doing today? I haven't seen you since your phone call the other night."

"You were right. I was just tired." Izzy wanted to pretend it hadn't happened. It had been a spike of emotion, but she'd been mostly fine since then.

"We can talk about it when you're ready." And that was it. No pressure. One of the million reasons Izzy loved her.

Izzy took an orange from the fruit bowl and tossed it from hand to hand. She checked the doorway before she spoke. "Is it so wrong that I don't want to go to Jane's work party?"

Audie threw her head back and laughed. "Knowing you, no. You don't exactly thrive in hyper-social situations with people you don't know."

"I don't want to come off badly to Jane's boss and peers."

Audie leaned forward. "They'll love you. Everyone loves you. But, I get it. You probably feel like you'll be on display."

Izzy rolled her eyes. "Thanks, Aud. I was hoping for comfort, not a reminder about how people will be sizing us up."

Audie ignored her last comment. "How is it that she's never brought a date to a work thing? She's worked there how long?"

Izzy wasn't sure what Jane would want to divulge. She decided to tell Audie what *she* would have told her. "Her ex is in the closet. In fact, I brought this on myself. She was planning to go alone again this year. I'm the one who asked her why I wasn't going with her. You should have seen her eyes light up when I said it. I immediately regretted it. It was suddenly a Big Deal. And now I'm stuck."

Audie squeezed her shoulder. "You'll do fine. You clean up well. Wear your jacket with the elbow patches to match the scholarly thing. What's Jane wearing?"

Izzy grinned. "A clingy black dress that shows off her entire back."

Audie sucked air in through her teeth. "Sounds sexy as hell."

"You don't even know."

"You get to watch people admiring her all night, and then you get to take her home. Imagine the build-up of sexual tension."

"Are you seriously having fantasies about my girlfriend right in front of me?"

Audie showed no shame. "Are you kidding me? Have you looked at her? I guarantee there isn't a straight male or a lesbian among us who hasn't thought about your girlfriend, Iz. Hell, half the gay guys and most of the straight ladies would probably sample the goods, given the opportunity. She's a bona fide hottie, my friend."

Izzy agreed, but Jane's beauty was only the smallest part of what made her so hot.

Audie shoulder-bumped her. "So, you two are pretty serious. Have you exchanged the L-word yet?"

Izzy groaned and slid a hand down her face. She didn't want to talk about this at work.

"I take it that's a no?"

"I haven't told her I'm bipolar yet. I think I need to do that first."

"What?"

"I know. I know."

The click of Jane's low heels preceded her through the doorway, and they both looked up as she entered the breakroom.

Jane cocked an eyebrow. "You two look like you're conspiring over there."

"We were just talking about what a great time you two will have tonight." Audie was a master at changing the subject.

Jane didn't look convinced, but she didn't say so. "I think we will. I'm probably just being anxious for no reason."

"With this stud on your arm, you're golden." Audie wrapped an arm around Izzy's shoulders and squeezed her.

"Speaking of, why don't we hit the road so we have time to get ready?" Izzy held a hand out to Jane. "I want to get a quick run in before we go."

An expression of irritation flashed across Jane's face so quickly, she wondered if she'd imagined it.

❖

When they arrived home, Izzy went into their room to change into running shorts. It was a little chilly outside, so she wore leggings under them.

Jane leaned against the door frame with her arms crossed and watched her change.

"You look like you want to say something," Izzy said, sitting on the edge of the bed to tie her shoes.

"I've been trying not to be negative about your running because it's something you really like to do. But sometimes, I think there's something more to it than just the exercise. And you going tonight just reinforces the idea. You're going to have to shower and everything, which will make us late to the party."

Izzy finished tying her shoes. "Do we have to be there right at the start time? I thought this was more of a casual tapas-and-mingling kind of thing."

"I wanted to be there close to the start time so we arrive with everyone else and avoid standing out."

Izzy grinned. "Are they going to stop the party and announce us or something?"

Jane crossed her arms over her chest. "Don't try to minimize my discomfort, Izzy."

Izzy was sorry she'd joked. "I wasn't trying to."

"It sounded like you were making fun."

"I honestly wasn't." But she had. Not in a mean way but more to get Jane's mind off whatever was bothering her. But it hadn't come out right, and now she felt as if she couldn't say anything right. She needed to run now, just to get rid of the anxiety she was feeling about it.

"Okay. You weren't. But do you really need to go for a run? Can't you take one night off?"

"I'll be quick. Twenty minutes. Maybe less, if I go faster than normal." Izzy resented having to coax Jane into being okay with her going for a run. She'd already given up her morning runs. She *needed* them. They were keeping her level. She didn't want Jane judging her or being angry about them.

"Fine. I guess it doesn't matter how I feel." Jane pushed herself from the door frame, headed into the bathroom, and shut the door.

Izzy didn't know what to do. Jane was clearly upset. She refused to yell through the door, though. She would wait until she came out. But that would just make them later, and Jane was already angry. And now Izzy's head was spinning with too many thoughts for her to know what she was actually thinking. She *had* to go for a run now, or she'd explode. She leashed Gus and gave Lester a treat for understanding his limitations before she headed out the door.

She fell into a rhythm quickly. Within minutes, she was able to think more clearly. She was feeling better when she completed her route and jogged up the front door steps.

She unhooked Gus's leash, and Lester greeted them at the door. "I'm back! Seventeen minutes! I told you I'd be quick!"

There was no answer, and Jane wasn't in the bedroom or the bathroom when she looked. Her work clothes lay on the bed, and the room smelled like freshly sprayed perfume, but Jane was nowhere to be found. On a hunch, Izzy checked the garage. Jane's car was gone. Jane had left without her.

She'd just left?

She sent a text. *Where did you go?*

Izzy sat on the side of the bed and waited a minute for a response. When one didn't come immediately, she took a Xanax to help calm the anxiety she felt creeping toward the red zone and jumped into the shower.

As the water coursed over her, Izzy vacillated between extreme annoyance, hurt, anger, and concern. This wasn't like Jane. She didn't just shut down. But they'd never had a real argument before, either. She didn't know how to process what had happened. Could she have done something different? But Jane had locked herself in the bathroom and hadn't left any room to continue the conversation. Frustration and irritation started to win the battle within her. By the time Izzy got out of the shower, she was full-on angry, mostly with herself but a little with Jane. She imagined a million different ways their conversation could have gone differently.

She yanked a towel off the towel rack and briskly dried herself off.

Movement out of the corner of her eye startled her. Jane stood in the bathroom doorway looking uncertain.

Relief and confusion rushed through her. She wrapped the towel around herself and felt bad for assuming Jane had just left her. "I thought you left without me."

"I did."

Hurt rose in Izzy. Until Jane confirmed it, she hadn't thought she had *actually* left without her. Sure, she'd started to work herself up about the situation, but in the back of her mind she'd thought Jane had another reason to have not been there and she just forgot to leave a note or text her about it.

"Oh." Izzy was at a loss for words. Not that she didn't have a million of them roiling through her head, but it was too much for her to focus on to figure out what to say next. Without an outlet for all the chaos, she was close to just screaming or rushing from the room to escape the pressure building up. It would just make things worse, though, so she just stood there, staring at the wall above Jane's head.

"Did you hear me? Izzy, you're sort of freaking me out."

"What?" Izzy felt as if she was being reeled back in from a great distance.

Jane looked annoyed. "I asked if you heard what I said, and you just stood there staring."

Izzy searched her mind for the thread of the conversation. "You said you left without me."

Lines appeared between Jane's brows. "I mean after that, when I said I realized I was being a total jackass, so I came back."

"Sorry. I sort of got stuck on the part when you said you left me on purpose." It was weird. She felt sort of numb about it now, like all the thoughts in her head had sort of built a wall around her, and she was just kind of standing there, unaffected. Everything seemed so far away, and she was just observing it now. She didn't like it. She wanted to be present.

Jane leaned against the door frame. "I was a jerk. I'm sorry for leaving. I guess I was just at a loss for how to deal with the situation."

She sighed. "This whole thing about taking you to the party is just so overwhelming, and I don't know why. I mean, I do know why, but I feel like I should have a handle on it by now. I know it's ridiculous."

The weird distance feeling went away, and a muted panic started to set in. The Xanax was kicking in. Izzy just stood there listening to Jane. Could Jane see the turmoil going on within her? Standing there in nothing but a towel, she was trying to listen, but all she could think about was that Jane had left without her. She'd been afraid Jane would leave her, and it had happened.

She'd left.

She'd left.

She'd left.

But she'd come back.

She'd left, but she'd come back.

But she'd left.

"It's not ridiculous." Her lips felt numb.

Jane was looking at her own hands. She didn't seem to notice Izzy was frozen like a statue on the bathroom rug. "It kind of is."

"It's how you feel. It's not ridiculous." She wished she hadn't taken the medication. All she wanted was for the conversation to be over and for them to be okay again. "I don't want to fight."

Jane pushed herself off the door frame. "I don't want to fight either."

Jane wrapped her arms around her and Izzy slid her arms around her waist. Her head was still teeming with words and emotions, and she just let it spin. She tried to concentrate on how their hearts started to beat in time with one another. As she started to relax, her thoughts slowed down, and all the noise and static dissipated. She rested her face against the skin of Jane's neck and felt as if she were floating. The sensation was so strong, she started to worry she'd fall. Slowly, they parted, but Izzy held Jane's hands in hers as she faced her. It was as much to keep from falling as to keep Jane close.

"Now we're really going to be late to the party." She didn't want to go now, but she would for Jane.

Jane dropped her head back and groaned. "So late."

Izzy winked at her, but the move felt wooden. "Let them think we were having sex."

Jane stepped closer. "Sounds way better than going to the party, to be honest."

Even though Izzy felt spacy from the Xanax, a pulse thrummed through her. She shimmied under the towel, and the loose fold keeping it up came undone, making it fall to her feet. "Then why are you wearing all those clothes?"

❖

Jane drifted off to sleep in Izzy's arms as Izzy ran her fingers across the exposed skin of her back. Izzy felt honored to hold her and protect her from the world. She still hadn't been able to bring herself to confess her love to Jane, but it was massive, growing every day. She couldn't try to describe it if she wanted to. But it was bigger than any kind of love she had ever experienced. There was no going back, even if she wanted to now. If anything were to happen to Jane, it would be devastating.

A fear with dark claws grabbed at Izzy's heart. What would she do if anything ever happened to Jane? She couldn't bear the thought, but there it was. She couldn't exist. She'd do anything to protect her. But what if *she* was the bad thing that happened to Jane? Could she leave if it would save her?

A thought, stark and brutal, invaded her thoughts. Would it be better to be with Jane a short time, knowing her sickness would probably eventually drive Jane away and possibly break Jane? Or would it be better to let Jane go, knowing Jane was still in one piece, not broken? Izzy couldn't make up her mind. One path was selfish. One path was unselfish. Indecision welled up in her, and she imagined Jane hurt by her inability to pick a path. Izzy convinced herself that, no matter what she did, she was going to hurt Jane and, in the process, destroy her own life.

Tears streamed down Izzy's face. She tried to contain the grief building inside her. Not wanting to wake Jane with the shaking of her sobs, she held her breath and carefully rolled out of bed. The act of holding it together made her light-headed, and when she finally stood beside the bed and watched Jane sleep so innocently, she thought she might pass out from the physical reaction of holding in her tears mixed with the overwhelming amount of love and fear rampaging through her.

Izzy stumbled from the bedroom. Once she made it to the living room, she collapsed on the couch and rolled into a tight ball, crying. She was barely aware of Gus following her and jumping up on the couch, curling against her. Her entire body shook with sobs. A low keening escaped her, and she couldn't stop it. She pulled a throw pillow to her mouth and held it there to stifle the sound, but it just grew louder. Her head filled with pressure. Her grief and exhaustion built until she thought she'd explode.

"Izzy?" Jane's voice was miles away. Warm hands rested on her back. "What's wrong, honey?"

Izzy felt Jane sit next to her on the couch, and she allowed Jane to pull her head into her lap. Gus pressed tightly against her stomach. The warmth of Jane's body seeped into Izzy where they touched, and Izzy didn't know she had started to freeze. Jane's warmth was thawing her. Izzy wrapped her arms around Jane and buried her face in Jane's stomach. She continued to cry, but the sobs didn't threaten to shatter her anymore. Jane stroked her hair and pulled a blanket over her.

"Izzy, honey, what is it? Why are you crying?"

Izzy wanted to answer, but she was so, so tired, and she didn't trust her tight throat to work enough to answer. She only squeezed Jane tighter.

Izzy wasn't aware she had fallen asleep until Jane was helping her sit up and guiding her back to the bedroom. Jane helped her into bed and lay beside her, pulling Izzy close to her.

"Thank you," Izzy whispered. Her throat was tight and painful.

Jane stroked her hair. "Oh, Izzy. What's wrong?"

Izzy swallowed. "I just started thinking about losing you, and I couldn't bear it."

Jane held Izzy tightly. "You aren't losing me. I'm right here. I'm right here and I'm not going anywhere."

❖

"Hi, Izzy. How has your week been?" Tori asked as Izzy took a seat across from her.

"It's been good," Izzy said, and then she shook her head. "I don't know why I said that. It hasn't been good. It's been pretty difficult, actually. It's like the universe opened up and decided to take a crap on me, to be honest." The words came out in a rush, as if she couldn't keep up with her thoughts. "You know what I mean? Life saves up a huge pile of shit and just pounds you with it? I don't believe in fate, but if I did, I'd think someone was royally messing with me, you know?" She didn't wait for an answer. "It's been a true shit-storm of epic proportions." She slid her hands under her thighs, not sure what to do with them. "I can barely sit still because I've just been dealing with it, and it feels like it's just creating this energy ball deep within me, and I'm not sure if I'm going to just fall over from exhaustion because of it or explode. Do you ever feel that way? I can't even describe it adequately. I hate the feeling, though. I can't wait to go running tonight to get rid of all of this energy. You know, to ground myself. Running is the only thing that grounds me. I wish Jane understood. But she doesn't, and it's a problem."

Izzy forced herself to stop talking. After her breakdown on Friday night, she'd had a hard time talking at all. It had rained all weekend, and she and Jane had spent the weekend at home, barely talking. She knew Jane wanted to know more about the episode, but she hadn't pushed, and Izzy hadn't offered more. Now, Monday morning, Izzy couldn't seem to stop talking.

Tori paused as if to make sure Izzy was done. "You seem a little keyed up. Is that why you made this extra appointment?"

She laughed. What an understatement. "Is keyed up the clinical definition for symptoms of my bipolar disorder?"

"Is it what you think you're doing?"

"Definitely. And the sad thing is, I'm trying so hard not to. You know, trying to keep my behavior within the confines of social norms? And I know I'm not being successful, making me want to try even harder, which makes me act weirder. It's a vicious cycle. Or is it viscous circle? It's vicious cycle, because a viscous circle implies a thick liquid, which is just a little moist for my tastes. Not to mention it's just pornographic. See? That was weird. I knew it was weird when I was saying it, but I didn't stop, because stopping midsentence would be even weirder." She threw her hands up. "I can't win."

Tori tilted her head. "You're probably aware you're exhibiting forced talking."

She tilted her own head. "Yeah. I know I'm a bit of a chatterbox. I only have fifty minutes with you, and it goes by so fast sometimes so I want to get it all out."

"How have you been sleeping?"

"Well, it's hard to stick to a specific bedtime when you have a beautiful woman right next to you. Plus, we're new, and you know how it is."

"But do you think you're getting at least eight hours of sleep each night?"

God. She wished people would stop policing her sleeping patterns. She *knew* it was important. She did her best to manage it, but life wasn't always so neat and tidy. "I wasn't for a while, when I was running in the mornings, too. But after the session where we talked about it, I've cut it back to running just after work, so I've been getting a little more sleep each night. I shoot for eight hours, but sometimes, it's just six or seven."

"You know eight hours is the magic number for you, though."

Izzy ran a hand through her hair. "I know. I know. I know. I need to work on it. I *will* work on it."

"How about nutrition?"

Okay. They were going to check all the boxes. God, this was tedious. "I've been eating fine. I've been taking my meds. We've already established I'm getting exercise. I'm watching my impulse control. I'm aware of the forced talking."

Tori smiled. "You mentioned you've adjusted your running schedule. It seems like you're still a little fixated on it."

"Running has always been my happy place. I think it's as important as my medication. It grounds me."

"Tell me a little more about what you need grounding for."

Izzy forced herself not to roll her eyes. Tori knew what she needed grounding for. She knew Tori was just trying to get her to talk more about it, but it was all academic. Her issues were all on the table. She had a chemical imbalance called bipolarism, and all the talking in the world wouldn't fix it. Still, like running, her sessions helped ground her. She'd play the game. She sighed. "I've had some changes in my life lately. I think I'm just adjusting."

"Do you think there's other stuff going on?"

Izzy realized she was shaking her knee. She put her hand on it and told herself to stop. "Like what?"

Tori tilted her head. "I don't know. I just wonder if the changes have brought up stuff you need to work on. You've spent a big part of your adult life holding people at a distance because you're afraid potential pain caused by being vulnerable may trigger a bipolar episode. Maybe you're subconsciously causing it to happen."

Izzy hadn't thought of that. "Like a self-fulfilling prophecy?"

"Kind of. It could be you sense you're losing control. Maybe running is one thing you can control. How's work going?"

Interesting about the control thing. "It's the same as always."

"Are you putting in more hours than normal?"

"Yeah. I am. But there is so much work to be done." No revelation there. They'd talked about her tendency to work long hours to death over the years. She had to do something to fill her days, right?

"Has anything changed?"

"Not really. There's always more work to be done."

"Are you avoiding going home at night?"

She laughed. "Actually, the opposite. Especially since Jane moved in. I can't wait to see her every night. It's just, I lose track of time sometimes. When I realize I've stayed late, I always pack up and go home."

"To run?"

It was hard to explain how the stronger she felt about Jane, the more important the running was for her. It helped balance things. "Partly, but more to get home to Jane."

"How are things with Jane?"

She started to shake her knee again, and she didn't bother to stop it. "Up until this week, I would have said great. But we had a fight Friday."

Tori raised an eyebrow. "What was it about?"

Thoughts started to spin around in Izzy's head. She told Tori about their fight, how it had started because she'd wanted to go running before the party, about the panic attack she had after Jane fell asleep.

"You said you *needed* to go running even though Jane was concerned about being late to the party."

She was tired of defending her need to run. It grounded her. How hard was it to understand? "I run to think, to clear up my thoughts. It calms me down."

"Do you think you run because it's something you can control?"

"Maybe. It helps me control my thoughts."

"I meant more about you being able to control the running, the whole thing, all aspects. From the scheduling of it to the route you take and the pace you set for yourself. It's your thing. You're in charge of it. You can't control your workload or even your sleep schedule, but you can control your running. So, when Jane suggested you not go running that night, it may have upset your balance."

Izzy considered the possibility. It made a lot of sense. It would explain how irritable she felt any time someone suggested she change her running schedule. "You may have a point there."

"Tell me a little more about your panic attack."

Izzy's chest grew tight just thinking about it. "It's not the first time it happened. A couple weeks ago, I got home late, and I knew Jane was sort of angry, so I tried to make it up to her, and we went in the hot tub, and we ended up making love. After she fell asleep, I kept thinking how our happiness was finite, and she would end up leaving me. I just started bawling. I couldn't stop. I called Audie, and she talked me through it. This last time was basically the same thing. Jane found me crying on the couch and comforted me."

"Why do you think she's going to leave you?"

"It's not like I think about it all the time. It's only been those two times, and I was stressed."

"Have you told Jane about being bipolar yet?"

"Not yet. I want to get it under control before I do."

"It might be helpful to take away the stress of withholding it from her. Just a thought."

Easier said than done. "I'm going to get on a solid schedule and get my sleep under control first. Once I do that, I think I can manage the racing thoughts and mania."

Tori leaned forward in her chair. "Izzy, I just want you to know how proud I am of you for being so responsible about your health. So many people don't take it seriously, and then they lose the ability to manage the illness themselves."

The positive affirmation made some of the tightness in her chest go away. "I know from experience: medicine helps only so far. Unless I want to be drugged into submission, I need to control my environment."

Tori smiled. "True, but remember, part of controlling your environment is building a support system around you to help you through the hard parts. You don't have to do this alone. Don't you feel better when you have Audie to lean on?"

She thought about Audie. She couldn't ask for a better friend. "Yes."

"Jane can be someone you lean on, too."

"I plan on telling her soon. I promise."

❖

One of the biggest mistakes people make when they enter a relationship is losing their own identity when they become a couple. It's important for people to maintain their individuality.

Not to put a shadow over the happiness of love, but sometimes, things don't always go well. It's during those times you have to rely on yourself to make it through the tough times. It doesn't hurt to have your own friends and a support system to help you get through it.

Chapter Thirty-seven

W hat's all that?" Jane sipped her coffee and leaned her hip against Izzy's desk in their home office.

Izzy rested a large whiteboard against the wall next to her desk and set the small box of office supplies that had just been delivered next to it. She leaned over and gave Jane a quick kiss.

"I ordered some stuff to help with scheduling."

"Can't you do it all online?"

"I do. But I think I need to have a physical reminder." Izzy pulled a desk calendar, a notebook planner, colored pens, and some other things from the box. She may have gone a little overboard.

"It looks like you're pretty serious about this project."

"It's more of a way of life than a project." Izzy flipped through the planner. "Tori suggested I might have a lot going on in my life, and since I want to be fair to you and I also need to make sure I get enough sleep and exercise, I decided I needed a visual to make sure I adhere to my needs."

Jane inspected a package of colored pens. "I totally get the idea. I'm visual, too."

"I didn't realize how visual I was until I met you." Izzy sidled up to Jane, resting her hands on her hips, pulling her close.

Jane put her coffee cup on the desk and melted into Izzy's arms. A warm flare of love rose in Izzy every time Jane surrendered like that.

"I was thinking. Maybe I can try to sync your writing schedule with my grading schedule," Jane said. "Maybe it will help you remember to go to sleep at a decent hour."

Izzy liked Jane's idea. "I planned to set an alarm on my phone, but syncing schedules seems nicer. Writing and grading are such solitary pursuits, but it would be nice to at least share space with you while we're doing it. I'm also going to cut my running down to just three evenings during the work week and one long run on the weekend."

Jane pulled back to look at her. "You don't need to cut your running down. I know you love it."

Izzy kissed her nose. "I do. But I like spending time with you more."

"Maybe I can start running with you sometimes."

Jane's suggestion hit her squarely in the heart. "I'd love it." She squeezed her. "I'm still going to cut back, though. Too much of a good thing is still a problem."

Jane kissed the corner of her mouth. "Too much of some things but definitely not this." And then her lips pressed over Izzy's mouth.

Fat Bob purred on the bed beside Izzy, and Romeo and Juliet were curled around each other on the other side of her. Her face was illuminated in the darkness of the room by the light of the phone she held in her hands as she scrolled through the day-planner app. She was pleased with herself for having adhered to her schedule all week long, and for the seventh day in a row, she was in bed by her eleven p.m. bedtime, with fifteen minutes to spare. She had quickly replaced the physical day planner when she realized the visual was just as good in the electronic version, and it didn't require toting a book around with her everywhere she went.

She set the phone on the nightstand beside her and eased under the covers, trying not to disturb the sleeping cats. Just as she pulled the comforter over her and settled on her side, the bathroom door opened, and Jane stepped out with a billow of steam. With nothing but a white towel wrapped around her body and her hair pinned on top of her head, she looked like a galactic goddess in the sliver of light and the dissipating clouds.

"Don't move. I want to stare at you for a million hours."

Jane stopped and smiled at her. "Your wish is my command."

"You always say the exact right thing."

Izzy drank in the perfect sculpture before her. Jane dropped the towel, and her breath stuck in her throat. She watched as Jane walked slowly to the bed, her body in silhouette. Tightness filled Izzy's belly, and her sex clenched.

Jane slipped under the covers and pressed against her. Fat Bob reluctantly rose and waddled to the foot of the bed, dropping over the edge onto the floor. Izzy lifted her head and propped it on her hand as she ran the other along the curves of Jane's body. The skin under her fingertips was soft and slightly moist from the shower. The scent of citrus body wash filled the space under the covers. Izzy kissed Jane while she ran her hands along her back. Her lips trailed over to her jaw and then to her neck as she scooted down and rolled Jane onto her back.

Her mind was on one thing while she sucked each of Jane's nipples and continued her journey across Jane's body. Jane moved beneath her, responding to each new place Izzy placed her mouth, and she spread her legs as Izzy lowered herself, leaving a chain of small kisses on her belly, along her inner thighs, and finally in the cleft between her legs. Jane was wet and swollen, and Izzy slid her tongue over the glistening flesh. Izzy wrapped her arms under Jane's legs and around her hips, laying her hands on the soft mound of Jane's belly, burying her face in the succulent space in front of her. Soon, her tongue found the firm knot of skin housing Jane's most sensitive spot, and she wrapped her lips around it, first running her tongue around and over it and then flicking it rhythmically until Jane moaned in pleasure.

Jane's voice was gravely and low. "God. Right there. Just keep doing exactly what you're doing."

Izzy complied with pleasure, relishing the throbbing of the flesh in her mouth. Jane's hips rose and fell until she came with a shudder, and Izzy slowed the movements of her tongue until Jane's hips relaxed onto the bed. She slowly licked around Jane's clit and ran her tongue through Jane's folds one more time before she kissed the swollen lips and crawled up to lay her head on the pillow next to Jane to pull her into her arms. Jane's pliant body wrapped around Izzy in a soft embrace.

"You turned me to mush. I can't move."

A pulse shot between Izzy's legs as Jane's soft lips moved against her sensitive skin.

She rolled onto her back and removed her panties. Then she took Jane's hand and put it between her legs.

"You just stay relaxed and put your fingers here," she said, sliding two of Jane's fingers inside. Don't move. Just keep your fingers inside me."

Izzy began to rub her clit. Jane hooked her fingers and pressed on her inner wall, and a pulse rolled through Izzy. An orgasm was building.

"Perfect…"

Jane nuzzled Izzy's throat and lightly bit it. Another pulse shot through her, and she throbbed around Jane's fingers. She pressed harder against her clit, and her orgasm exploded, lifting her hips. "Oh my God, yes!"

Jane's mouth descended upon hers, and they kissed as Izzy worked her clit until the last of her orgasm ebbed away. Jane ran a trail of kisses from Izzy's mouth to her throat and then slowly removed her fingers, settling into the crook of Izzy's arm. Izzy stretched like a sated cat as all of her muscles began to relax.

"You're amazing," she said, burying her face in Jane's hair and inhaling her scent.

"You were so sexy. It was erotic to just have my fingers in you as you made yourself come. Usually, I'm distracted by what's happening to me. I want to watch you come like that a million times."

"And we finished before eleven." Izzy was proud of herself for keeping to the schedule.

Jane grew tense in her arms. "I wasn't aware you were timing us."

Izzy kissed her shoulders. "I wasn't. I just noticed the time, and we've been talking about getting to sleep at a reasonable time."

Jane relaxed a little. "Glad I could accommodate you."

Izzy couldn't tell if her response was good or bad, so she went with good.

"Hey, sister-friend!" Audie dropped onto the bench beside her at the table next to the Traveling Bean coffee cart.

Izzy looked up from her phone and smiled. Audie was full of her normal high-octane energy since it wasn't Monday. Izzy pushed the steaming mocha she had already bought toward her.

"You're a goddess! Whip and sprinkles?"

Izzy pretended to be offended. "You act like I don't know you!"

Audie sipped her drink and moaned. "So good! Well, it's been a minute since we had coffee together."

"Work has been crazy lately."

Audie tilted her head at Izzy's phone and took another sip. "You were frowning at your phone. Catching up on politics?"

Izzy laughed. "I totally avoid politics and the news these days. It was a text from Jane."

Audie rested her elbows on the table behind her. "Lovers' quarrel? I have to say it gives me relief to see even perfect couples have their moments."

Izzy wasn't sure she wanted to tell Audie about it, but she needed a friend on this one. "Well, not really, but sort of."

"Spit it out, Iz."

She didn't know how to say it without the intimate details. "It's stupid. Okay, so last night, Jane and I, um, we, well, we sort of—"

"You fucked?"

She laughed. "I wouldn't use the word fucked, but yeah."

"And then what?"

"Well, it was nice. We both had a good time, and we didn't stay up too late, which was good."

"Right. You need your beauty rest."

Izzy picked at a splinter on the table. "Right. Well, this morning, Jane is a little upset because I said something about how nice it was to…to be intimate and still get to bed at a reasonable time."

Audie squinted at her. "I'm not sure I follow. Was it the way you said it?"

"I don't know. She said it made her feel like an afterthought."

Audie shoulder-bumped her. "You said you both had a good time. Are you sure?"

"Oh, absolutely. I am one hundred percent sure she had a good time."

"You're a stud." Audie gave her another shoulder bump.

Izzy pushed her. "Shut up!"

Audie sat back up and laughed. "Okay, so it had to be something you said or did. Did you fall asleep immediately?"

"We both did."

Audie paused, considering the info so far. "Sounds like you need to talk it out."

"Yeah." She wished she could just let it drop, but Audie was right.

Audie turned, straddling the bench and facing Izzy. "Speaking of which, I've been meaning to check in with you about the night you called. How are you doing?"

Izzy sighed. She knew it would come up sometime, and if she was honest with herself, avoiding it was one reason she and Audie hadn't been hanging out recently. "I think my issue was mostly about not getting enough sleep and just trying to figure out how to deal with all these new emotions. I was pretty overwhelmed. I think I have it under control." She hoped that explanation sounded plausible to Audie. It was the same story she was trying to believe herself.

"Are you talking to your therapist about it?"

"She says I probably just need to settle in and get used to all the new things in my life now."

Audie made a sound of agreement. "Makes sense."

Izzy rolled her coffee cup between her hands. "One thing she said was really interesting. She said falling in love makes normal people kind of crazy."

"Interesting. It's true, but did she actually use the word crazy? Cuz it's kind of insensitive, given her profession."

"No. That's mine. She probably used some psychological word. But she said all the emotions love stirs up are bound to make anyone feel like they don't know which end is up. Then there's all the overthinking and going outside your routine to fit a new person in. The things that come with a new relationship feel exceptionally good, but it can make someone like me worry about whether they're getting out of control." Relating Tori's observation renewed Izzy's sense of normalcy, whatever normal was.

Audie looked at her for a minute before answering. "Control is important to you."

She was tempted to make a smart-ass response but refrained. "I would like to say it isn't, but it is. I need control in order to know when I might lose it."

Audie bobbed her head. "I get it."

"So, I've put together a schedule for everything—running, meal times, work, bedtime. I think it will help."

Audie shot her a half-smile. "Don't tell me. You penciled in sex, too."

The remark made her grumpy. Why was it so hard for people to understand how important it was for her to keep to a normal schedule? "No. Maybe I should, though."

Audie gave her a light shove. "Don't get all pissy. You said Jane got upset about a comment you made about getting to bed at a reasonable time. I'm just trying to figure out why. Does Jane know about your schedule?"

Audie was trying to help. She tried not to be so grumpy. "Yeah."

"Does she know why you have it?"

Izzy looked away. "If you're asking if I've told her about being bipolar, it hasn't come up yet. But it will."

Audie set her cup aside. "I think I know what Jane might be upset about now."

Izzy looked at her expectantly.

"You might have implied having sex with her was just another thing you needed to check off on your checklist."

"But it wasn't on the list."

Audie raised her eyebrows. "Maybe that's part of it, too. She needs to feel like she's the *only* thing on your list. At the very least, the most important thing."

Izzy kept shaking her head. "Seriously?"

"Chicks are sensitive, Iz." Audie patted her on the back.

Izzy looked at her. "Hey. I'm a chick."

Audie laughed. "Yeah, well, other chicks."

"You suck." But in reality, she knew *she* sucked. How did she not get these things?

Audie pretended to hook her fingers around invisible suspenders. "That's why the chicks dig me."

❖

There's a saying about the only way to really understand someone: walk a mile in their shoes. This means you have to try to see things from the perspective of someone else in order to understand them. Nowhere is it more necessary than in a romantic relationship. It's not just about being sensitive to your partner and anticipating their needs; it's also about making sure you communicate your needs and feelings so your partner doesn't have to read your mind. In my experience, the latter is the hardest part and probably where most relationships are the most difficult. When someone has to guess about something, there's a huge chance they won't get it right, which just sets everyone up for disappointment.

To take the guesswork out of the equation, you need to be open to your partner, and in order to be open, you have to be vulnerable. It can be hard for some people. You have to feel safe. It's up to both of you to protect one another and make it okay to be vulnerable. And you have to operate by the same rules. When one of you is open and the other isn't, it can cause an imbalance in the relationship.

In the beginning, you overlook the little things that might drive you nuts because you're into your partner, enthralled by all the millions of wonderful things about them. It doesn't bother you when they forget to replace the empty toilet-paper roll.

But over time, when the newness starts to fade and you get used to all the wonderful things about them, some of the little things become bigger things, and it's hard to bring them up because you don't want to hurt their feelings or start to nag them. But holding all of it in just makes the little things into bigger things, and then all the things start to collect. Eventually, you will have a bad day. One of you is tired or sick, and being nice is too hard. The littlest thing just gets on your nerves, and then suddenly, you're listing all the minuscule grievances you've collected because you were being too nice to mention the dirty socks on the kitchen counter. And a tiny little thing becomes a huge monster of a thing.

That's when you have to remember to put yourself in the other person's shoes, take a moment to get some perspective.

Have I mentioned relationships are hard?

Chapter Thirty-eight

Izzy tossed her keys onto the counter and wrapped her arms around Jane from behind. She was proud of herself for adhering to her schedule. She'd left work at the right time, and she looked forward to going on a run while Jane made dinner. Her run was the only thing on her schedule tonight. Jane would be happy. She planned to take a break from writing and any work-related stuff, so after her run, the evening would be all about her and Jane. Maybe she'd suggest a long soak in the hot tub.

Jane set her red pen on the pile of papers she was grading and leaned back against her.

"How was your day?" Izzy nuzzled Jane's neck. God, she always smelled so good, and her skin was so soft.

Jane hummed her pleasure. "A bit crazy. How about yours?"

"The same. Did you go by your parents' house?"

Jane tensed. "Yes."

Izzy wanted to ask how the visit went, but it was obvious she didn't want to talk about it, just like every other time.

Jane swiveled the barstool around to face Izzy, and she took her hands. "I know it's my night to make dinner, but can we go out tonight? I'm just not into cooking."

And...the inevitable change of topic. Jane always looked beautiful, but tonight, she also looked tired. Her shoulders drooped, and her smile didn't quite make it to her eyes. Izzy saw she was done with this day and done with the subject of her parents.

"I can cook, if you want. You can just relax and tell me about it." Izzy massaged Jane's hands and kissed her palms.

"Won't it mess up your schedule?" Jane didn't look as relieved by the suggestion as Izzy had hoped, which was disappointing.

There was a hint of something in Jane's voice, too. Izzy couldn't place what it was, but it made her feel disconnected from her. The conversation with Audie replayed in her mind. She needed to let Jane know she was the only thing on her list tonight and the most important thing all the time.

"I can shift things around. Unless you truly want to go out to eat."

Jane relaxed a little. Her brow smoothed and she smiled. "I'd truly love to just go out. No dishes. No fuss."

"Okay. Let me just get my run in. You pick the place." Izzy peeled off her jacket.

Jane's shoulders stiffened a bit. "Oh. Okay." She didn't sound enthused.

"I can pick the place, if you want." Jane usually liked to pick the place. She was more of a foodie than Izzy.

"No, it's okay. I'll do it." Izzy wondered what had happened at her parents' house to make Jane so low-energy.

Izzy kept her run short so she could get home to take a shower before they left for dinner. When she got out of the shower, Jane told her they had reservations at a casual Italian restaurant they both liked. Izzy wasn't terribly excited about having a heavy meal, but she figured she'd eat a salad rather than suggest a different place. Tonight was all about Jane.

Dinner was nice, but Jane was still quieter than usual.

"Did something happen at work today? You're not saying much."

The waiter brought the check to their table, and Jane waited to reply. "It was just busy. I have some projects I need to catch up on. My sister didn't help, either." Jane added the last almost as an afterthought.

Jane didn't talk about her family much, but when she did, Izzy was always interested. "Leticia called you?"

"We went to lunch." Jane picked up her purse and started looking for something.

"Oh. She's in town?" Maybe Jane would invite her to their house so they could finally meet.

"I didn't tell you?" Jane continued to dig around in her purse.

Izzy wished Jane would look at her. Her distraction was frustrating. "Nope."

"Well, it was a surprise. She came to have lunch with me, and she was her typical self. Just tiring."

"Will she be in town long enough to come over so I can meet her?"

Jane looked up from her purse. "Um. She's pretty busy. Maybe next time?"

Izzy didn't know how to respond. She felt left out and unimportant. She tried not take it personally, but she couldn't help it. She paid the bill and helped Jane put on her jacket.

Izzy took her hand as they walked back to the car. "Do you want to take a soak in the hot tub when we get back home?" Memories of their last soak in the hot tub played through her mind, making her heart beat a little harder. She tried not to think about the freak-out afterward.

"Not really. I just want to tune out with TV." The letdown Izzy felt surprised her. Tonight was a her-and-Jane night. But maybe they could watch a movie together.

She hid her disappointment. "Sounds good."

The drive home was quiet and short. Izzy held Jane's hand, and Jane kissed her knuckles like she always did when Izzy reached over and took it. The sense of disconnect receded just a little.

They parked in the garage, and the dogs greeted them with excited dances when they entered through the kitchen door. Jane knelt and loved on them like she always did when she came home to them, and the disconnect seemed to recede a little.

Jane finished petting the dogs and went into the living room and turned on a light. She kicked off her shoes, turned on the news, and then walked down the hall to the bedroom. Izzy was tempted to follow her but didn't want Jane to feel like she was clinging. She sat on the couch and thumbed through a running magazine. Her thoughts were on Jane's sister being in town. She knew Jane had issues with her family, but it seemed as if she and Leticia got along well, even if they were a bit distant. Why wouldn't Jane want to introduce them?

Jane emerged from the bedroom in a pair of old sweats and a T-shirt. Without a word, she sank into the corner of the couch. She looked wiped out, so Izzy tried to forget about her sister. They could talk about it some other time, when Jane wasn't having such a rough day. Izzy took Jane's feet, placed them in her lap, and began to rub them. Jane let out a grateful sigh.

The news was so depressing. Izzy normally picked her news input carefully since it had a negative effect on her mood. So much political anger on the national level and only stories about tragedy on the local level. Tonight was no different. But she wanted to be with Jane.

"Do you want something to drink or some popcorn or something?" Izzy asked.

"I'm fine, but thanks." Jane's eyes didn't leave the television.

Izzy rubbed her feet for a few more seconds and then stood. "I'm going to get a cup of decaf. Let me know if you change your mind."

While the coffee dripped, she retrieved her laptop from the office, along with a pair of headphones. When her coffee was done, she went back to the couch and kicked her shoes off and pulled her feet up onto the couch. Her toes touched Jane's, and she wiggled them together a second before opening her laptop. She preferred to work in her office, but she figured they could be in the same room even if they were doing two different things.

"Working on the book?" Jane's eyes stayed on the television.

Izzy smiled at her. "Yeah. I'm not much for the news."

"It'll be over soon."

They were quiet for a while, and Izzy put her headphones on with some music to block out the noise from the television.

Several minutes later, Izzy heard Jane speak but didn't hear what she said, so she pulled out one of the earbuds.

"Where are you in the book?" Jane repeated.

Izzy grimaced. "In the third section. It's not going so well." She'd been stuck on this part for a few weeks. She'd started it several times, but each time, the words just seemed so wooden. They didn't flow like they had in the first two sections.

Jane lowered the volume on the television, which was playing commercials. "What are you having trouble with?"

"This is the part about making love last." The part I have no experience with, she thought.

Jane sounded more interested in this conversation than she had all night. "But this is the part you do so well at when giving advice to your friends."

"It's different when you're talking to someone about their specific situation. But I find it's harder to write about it in general terms."

"Maybe if you think about examples you've talked about with others."

"I have. And when I write my thoughts down, they feel so trite."

"I'm sure you'll figure it out." The commercials ended, the news started up again, and Jane's attention returned to the television.

❖

Izzy parked her car and jaywalked to the coffee shop across the street. She'd left work a little early to meet Haley, and the café was just a couple miles from work. Traffic had been bad, though, like always in San Jose, and it had taken her almost a half hour to get there. She hated driving in rush hour. But if she wanted to get home at a reasonable hour to be with Jane, she would do it.

Before she even entered the shop, she smelled fresh-ground coffee and something chocolaty being baked. Maybe brownies. If it was brownies, she was going to take one home to Jane.

Haley was sitting on a bench right outside the front door. She looked well-rested and in a good mood—a contrast with the last time Izzy had seen her, when dark circles under her eyes and uncombed hair had worried Izzy. The yellow dress she wore was a nice change from the baggy jeans and sweatshirts Izzy had come to expect.

"How's my favorite niece doing?" Izzy gave Haley a big hug when she stood.

"You know you have other nieces, right?" Haley said as she entered the door Izzy held open for her.

Izzy winked at her. "And I say the same thing to them when I see them."

"But you only mean it with me, right?"

"Absolutely." It was true, though. She could admit it to herself even if she wouldn't dream of telling anyone else.

It was great to see Haley in a good mood. Izzy didn't mention it, though. She knew how hard it was to try to conform to what people thought you should feel. Haley was Haley, no matter what mood she was in. She'd just enjoy it.

After they ordered their coffee along with three fresh brownies, one wrapped to go, they found a table in the farthest corner so they could talk.

"How are things going, Hale-Bopp?" Izzy used the nickname she'd given her as a child when the comet by the same name was lighting up the skies during its journey through space.

Haley's smile faded a little, and she tore little pieces from her napkin. "It's all so overwhelming. So many appointments. Managing medication. Trying to figure out what feelings are real and what are part of this whole…thing."

Izzy put her hand over Haley's. "You're doing so well with all of it. I'm proud of you."

"What else am I supposed to do?"

Haley's response reminded her of herself. "You'd be surprised at how many people *don't* manage it well," Izzy said. "You may think there's just one right path, and it might be easy for you to see it, but other people have a hard time acknowledging what they have to deal with, and they let their illness control them."

Haley shook her head vigorously. "That's not an option. I have a baby and a husband to take care of. Simone needs me."

Izzy was relieved to hear the resolve in Haley's voice. "It helps to have something to motivate you when you have hard things to deal with. Something that was hard for me was figuring out I was important, too, and I was doing it for me as much as anyone else. You are, too, Haley. Even if you didn't have Simone, Josh, your mom and dad, me, your friends—anyone else to do it for. You have yourself to think about. I hope you know how important you are."

Haley stared into her cup. "I do. But it's hard to remember sometimes." Then she looked up. "Before the medication, though, it was impossible to remember. So, there's that."

It had been such a long time ago for Izzy, but it was still difficult to think about the inky darkness that used to fill her mind, even all these years later. "How's the medicine working for you?"

Haley looked at the ceiling as if she were taking stock. "It's helping. I don't feel so out of control." Her shoulders sagged. "But it makes me so *tired*. And I miss having real feelings."

"What do you mean, real feelings?"

"You know, feeling strongly about things. I miss laughing so hard I almost pee. I can't even get pissed off about politics lately, and believe me, I know there's a lot to be pissed off there."

Izzy laughed. "Yeah, definitely. I remember the feeling of being almost numb."

Haley leaned forward, gripping her cup in her hands. "What did you do to help with it?"

Izzy paused. She didn't know. She'd just adjusted. "Well, it was a long time ago, and it's been a while since I've had to adjust them. I've been on my current meds for several years. But back when I first had to start taking them, it was a mess. I was on so much lithium I was a zombie. I needed it to help me stabilize, though. Then they worked with my mood stabilizer until we found the right combination of antipsychotic, mood stabilizer, and antianxiety meds. I'll probably have to tweak it sometime in the future, but it's stable now."

Haley studied the liquid in her cup. "I did genetic tests to figure out what meds should be effective and what meds to avoid. So far, they're working. I just have to figure out coping skills."

"Coping skills are important. They can do genetic tests now? I wish they'd had them when I was first diagnosed. A few meds I tried in the beginning messed with me quite a bit." Izzy remembered the one that made her not care about anything so she didn't shower for weeks at a time. And the one that made her sleep so hard, she'd wet the bed. Embarrassment filled her now. But those meds were nothing compared to the ones that just didn't work, and she'd cycle through depression and manic episodes at the drop of a hat, taking her rapidly cycling moods out on everyone around her. Her family lost patience with her time and again but wouldn't tell her. She knew, though. She knew exactly what she put her family through, and she couldn't do a thing to stop it. She still felt pangs of regret. But they were always there for her. She was so grateful for them. She'd tell Haley this stuff later. It was too fresh for her now. "Getting my meds right was one reason I was in-patient for so long."

Haley slumped back in her chair. "I can't even imagine being locked up."

"It wasn't a cake walk, that's for sure. Someday, I'll tell you what went on in my hospitalization."

"I can't wait." Haley smiled ruefully.

She didn't want Haley to build a negative perception around her illness, at least not more negative than it was. It was an illness, after all, and she had every right to feel whatever she did about it. But still… "It wasn't as awful as it sounds. My state of mind was the worst part, and it would have only gotten worse if I hadn't been in the hospital. You'll feel better once they get your meds straightened out. You have a lot of input there, and it'll help if you make an effort to be genuinely open with your doctor about it."

"I've been more than open." Haley grimaced, and Izzy remembered how she had focused so much of her pain and confusion at her doctors back then. She should look them up and send them some flowers or candy or something.

She patted Haley's hand. "Your doctor is used to it, Haley. Don't worry about hurting her feelings."

"That's what Dr. Ishikara said. She's nice, but I don't like everything she says."

Oh, jeez. She remembered some of the hard things her doctors made her deal with. A lifetime of meds, a lifetime of personal responsibility, a world of worry she'd somehow learned to live with. Izzy knew exactly what it was like. "I totally understand what you're going through. It's a lot to deal with. I promise it gets easier. The important thing is for you to be engaged in and committed to your treatment."

"I'm trying to be." Haley looked up at her. "Part of me wants to just say fuck it all sometimes. You know?"

Izzy knew all too well.

"I have to admit it even if it's hard to say out loud." Haley frowned. "I have to remember Simone needs me."

"Simone is a good reminder." What she remembered back then, when she was coming to terms with her own illness, was her mother. Her mother was her rock, and she'd do anything to keep it together for her. Now it was herself. She was worth it, and she knew it. Jane factored into it now, too.

Haley took her hand. "You're fine, though. You've been the most stable person I've ever known. You give me hope. Will I ever get there?"

Izzy's heart swelled along with Haley's words. Hearing them was the best motivation to stay on track she could get. "I love you. You know that, right?"

"I love you, too, Aunt Iz. I don't know how I could do this without you." Haley's eyes misted up, and Izzy's followed.

"I think you'll be fine. I *know* you'll be fine, as long as you commit to taking care of yourself. It's a lifelong thing, Haley. It's an illness you have to manage."

Haley frowned. "I didn't ask for this. Fucking genetics."

Haley's hand balled into a fist, and Izzy squeezed it. "I know. No one asks for an illness like this. But I promise, it won't ruin your life if you manage it correctly. It's a part of you, but it doesn't define you." Her own voice echoed through her mind: *Listen to your own words. It doesn't define you.*

"I have to remember that." She put her other hand over Izzy's hand. "I don't want to tell people about it. I don't want them to judge me."

Been there, done that. "You don't have to tell anyone if you don't want to. It's your business. But I will say that it will make your life easier if you're more open about it—when you're ready. Maybe right now, you just take time to get used to it. But when you're ready, you might want to pick a few people you feel safe enough to share it with."

"Do you?" Haley asked.

Izzy was taken aback. Not the question actually, but by the real answer. Yes, she had shared with a few people, but not with Jane. She felt like a hypocrite.

"Not as well as I should, I admit. I need to work on that."

Haley smiled. "I'm so glad I have you to work this out with, Aunt Iz. I don't know what I would do without you."

❖

Relationships are often defined by the way we respond to the most difficult circumstances. This is true in friendships and family ties, as well as in romantic partnerships. It's inevitable. Bad times are going to happen, but they don't have to destroy us.

At the risk of sounding repetitive, the best tool we have to deal with hard times is good communication. Communication won't prevent the hard times, but it will help to keep things from getting worse by limiting bad responses.

And remember there is strength in numbers. Joining forces with your partner to get through the bad times will make the bad times easier to manage, not to mention that you won't be so lonely. Plus, the relief of getting through a tough time is kind of an aphrodisiac, and the sex can be pretty amazing! I'm just saying.

CHAPTER THIRTY-NINE

"Hey, guys! I missed you, too." Gus wagged his tail as he greeted Izzy at the door, and Lester promptly sat on her foot, a sign he missed her, too. "Where's Jane?"

A quick look determined she wasn't at the counter grading papers like usual. Izzy tossed the brownie she'd brought home for Jane onto the counter and wandered through the house, finally finding her on the back porch, drinking a glass of wine. The dogs settled around Jane's feet, probably in the positions they'd been in when they'd heard the car pull into the garage.

Izzy leaned against the door frame and looked at her—so beautiful in the late afternoon sunshine. She rubbed at her goose bumps. "Hey, you. It's chilly out here."

Jane was bundled up in a hoodie and her warm slippers. It was weird to find her outside drinking wine by herself. A distant wood fire, probably in a fireplace, scented the cold, light breeze.

Jane looked tired again. Izzy wanted to make the weariness go away, but Jane hadn't been too talkative lately. The disconnect lingered. "It feels kind of good. Lester nearly tore the doggy door out when he heard you come in."

"Maybe we should get a bigger one. You know, one to accommodate all his bulging muscles." Izzy laughed at her own joke.

Jane shrugged and barely smiled. Izzy pulled up a chair close to hers and sat. The cast-iron seat cold even through her jeans.

"Why are you out here?" Izzy took her hand, and Jane squeezed it.

"Just thinking. How's Haley?"

"She's doing a lot better." Izzy unrolled her long sleeves. She'd explained Haley's condition as postpartum depression. The earlier feeling of hypocrisy returned.

"Did you get to see the baby?"

"She left Simone home with Josh."

"Then I'm not so jealous." Jane's eyes focused on the tops of some nearby trees, a group of crows dotting the gently swaying branches.

"I'll ask her to bring the baby by this weekend."

Jane didn't answer.

"Are you okay?"

Jane glanced at her but moved her eyes quickly away. "Yeah. Why?"

"You seem a little quiet."

"I'm in a quiet mood."

It was Izzy's night to cook, but she wanted to tell Jane about being bipolar. Her talk with Haley reinforced the knowledge that she should have done it months ago.

"A glass of wine sounds good. Do you mind if I sit out here with you and have a few sips before I start dinner?"

"Sure. I'm not too hungry anyway."

Izzy went inside and poured herself a glass of wine. As always, she questioned drinking alcohol. The ingrained warnings about it not being a good mix with her meds or her condition ran through her mind. She poured half a glass, grabbed a jacket, and carried her glass and the bottle back out to the deck to see if Jane wanted a refill.

On the short walk back to Jane, she tried to summon words, but they wouldn't come. None had come on the drive home from the coffee shop, either. *I'm bipolar. I'm bipolar. I'm bipolar.* The phrase resounded in her mind. They were the only words she could think of. Though they were true, they were artless. Overly direct. Sterile. She wanted the declaration to be less of a declaration and more a natural part of a conversation. But it took a conversation to make it happen, and Jane was far from conversational this evening.

Still, without a way to speak her truth, she moved the cast-iron chair back to the patio table and settled in the Adirondack chair on the other side of Jane. It wasn't as close to Jane as the other chair was, but she wanted to see her face. She followed Jane's gaze, which was still on the crows.

"How was your day?" she asked after a minute.

"Okay." Jane accepted a little more wine.

"Mine was pretty good." Izzy put the bottle on the table between them.

"That's nice." Jane sounded distracted, and Izzy wondered why.

They were quiet for a few more minutes, and Izzy still hadn't figured out how to bring up the topic of her illness. Her stomach started to churn. She wanted to chicken out, but she refused. She finished off her wine and put the glass on the table. She wanted another glass for courage, but the last one was sitting like a vat of acid in her stomach already.

She leaned forward, clasping her hands between her knees. "Hey, so, there's something I want to talk to you about."

Jane looked at her for the first time since the glance when she'd arrived. "Oh, yeah?"

"Yeah." She cleared her throat. "I've wanted to talk to you about it for a long time. Since I met you, actually." Jane's glance wandered over her face as if she was searching for something. It made what she had to say more difficult.

"I'm listening." Jane rested her wine glass on the arm of her chair.

"I wanted to tell you before, but the longer I didn't, the harder it got," she said. "And now, it seems like a super huge thing, but it isn't."

"It sounds pretty serious." Jane switched her gaze from Izzy's face to her wineglass.

"It isn't." Izzy paused. "Well, it is, but it isn't."

"Just say what you need to say." Jane sounded resigned.

"Well, the thing is, I'm bipolar." God. She'd said it. Her heart sped up. "I have been pretty much all my life, and I have it managed, but it's still part of who I am, and I thought I should tell you, but how do you bring something like that up in conversation? So, I could never figure out a good time, and…" She was babbling. She let the sentence die. The silence unnerved her. She looked up at Jane, who was still staring at her wineglass. "Anyway, I thought I would let you know and see if you wanted to talk about it. I'm not sure what more I can say, but maybe you have questions or something?"

Jane continued staring at her glass, and Izzy wondered if she would even respond.

The crows in the tree silently scattered into the sky, flew over them, and disappeared over the house.

"That's a pretty big thing," Jane finally said.

"It is, but it isn't." She was relieved, but Jane was just sitting there, and she didn't know what to do. "I was afraid to tell you early on because I didn't want to scare you away. And then, like I said, the longer I didn't say anything, the harder it was to bring up. But there it is. I'm bipolar, and I hope it doesn't change how you feel about me."

Jane looked at her, and her eyes weren't so distant anymore. Izzy felt as if Jane was seeing her for the first time in several days—not just her outside but all of her. A small flare of elation rose in her.

"You being bipolar doesn't change a thing about the way I feel about you. You are *you,* and I fell in love with *you.*" Jane's words landed like a ball of sunlight in Izzy's chest. She'd said the L-word! "Being bipolar, well, I guess it's just a part of the wonderful woman I know and only one facet of who you are."

Izzy felt such relief she almost started to cry. "I was so scared to tell you." She wanted to tell her she loved her, too, but she didn't want to tangle it up in this discussion.

"I'm sorry it was so hard for you." Jane leaned forward in her chair, leaving her glass on the arm and clasping her hands together between her knees. "It's bad timing, but I have something to tell you, too." Jane stared at her hands.

"Okay." Jane's demeanor didn't bode well for whatever it was, and the sun that had risen in Izzy started to sink.

"I need a little space for a while. I think I need to move out and get my head together." Jane's voice cracked on the last word.

Everything around Izzy receded. Nothing made sense. She watched Jane wipe away tears with both hands and stare at her hands again.

"What?" She managed to get the word out through lips that had become numb, much like the rest of her.

"This has nothing to do with what you just told me." Jane wrung her hands. "But things haven't been working out very well lately, and I don't like how I feel."

Izzy was dumbfounded. Where had this come from? How had it happened? "What? Um…why?"

"I do know I love you. I love you so much."

She said it again. She loved her. But those words weren't syncing up with the other words.

"I don't understand." Izzy wanted to cry. A howl was creeping up her throat. She couldn't speak or it might come crashing out.

Jane stared at her hands; her white knuckles were stark in the deepening dusky light. "It's all my fault. I feel like we aren't connecting. You have all your things going on, and I feel like a distraction." Jane rose and picked up her glass and the bottle. She looked at Izzy for a moment with a broken expression in her eyes and then walked to the door.

She couldn't just say what she said and walk away! Izzy wanted to stop her, tell her they could work things out, explain that her illness wouldn't be an issue, but she couldn't get up. She was still too numb. Jane tucked the bottle under her arm and opened the door. She paused before going in.

"I already have my stuff in my car. Just a suitcase for now. I'll take Lester, but I'll have to leave the cats here until I figure things out."

Jane watched her as if she expected a response, but Izzy didn't know what to say. The howl was inches away from exploding from her throat. She could only stare at her with her mouth open. Hot tears streamed down her face. Some trailed into her mouth. But she couldn't move.

Jane watched her for a few minutes and then turned into the house and shut the door.

Izzy's chest was tight, and her limbs were numb. She didn't know how long she sat there.

She's leaving!

She hadn't even said where she was going.

She pushed herself out of the chair and stumbled to the door. The house was silent. Gus was lying by himself near the door to the garage. Lester wasn't with him. It was as if he knew Jane's leaving was not just a trip to the store. She was gone. She stumbled to a barstool and fell into it, resting her arms on the counter and crumbled forward onto them. Jane was gone, and the tears wouldn't stop.

You know when you get on an airplane and they do the safety briefing no one listens to? There's a part where the flight attendant shows you how to affix your oxygen mask and says you have to put yours on before trying to help someone else. This advice also applies to issues in a relationship. No matter how hard you try to fix someone else, if you have your own issues, they will always get in the way. So, you have to address your own issues first before you address your partner's.

Chapter Forty

Tori's office looked different in the morning light. Direct sunlight into the waiting room gave it a cheery definition, contrasting with the light of late afternoon when the sunlight hit the other side of the building. Izzy wasn't sure she liked seeing the office this way, especially in the mood she was in, but she couldn't go to work. Not today. She was grateful Tori had an opening in her schedule. She cringed, remembering the panicked call she'd made to Tori's emergency line the night before.

Izzy picked at the cardboard sleeve on her to-go coffee cup. She was groggy. She hadn't even been able to drag herself out of bed to go running, and it was all she could do to take a shower and put on clothes. Gus hadn't left her side since Jane left the night before. He lay at her feet now, her good boy keeping her grounded.

She stared at the quick blurt of texts she'd received last night on her phone.

I'm so sorry
I love you
I'm at a friend's house
I'll call you once I get my head clear
How long do you think you need? she'd texted back.
The response took a while to come.
I don't know. But don't call me. I'll call you when I'm ready.
        I love you. I just need time.

If you loved me, you wouldn't have left, she thought. No. That wasn't fair. She owed Jane the space she needed. But why hadn't she seen it coming? How had she been so blind?

"Izzy? Come in. And you brought Gus." Tori bent to scratch Gus behind the ears.

Izzy stood in front of her chair before sitting. Gus sat next to her, leaning against her leg. "I told Jane."

"Oh?" Tori put her cup down without taking the sip she was just about to take. She didn't mention the hysterical call Izzy had placed at two a.m.

Izzy wanted to ask her if she had erased the initial message after listening to it. She didn't want the embarrassing recording sitting in the Cloud, even if it was accessible only by the one person she trusted more than herself. It had been almost two decades since she'd used the emergency line Tori had given her, and she'd never been hysterical. Embarrassment aside, Izzy was grateful for the almost-immediate response. Just hearing Tori's voice had calmed her. They agreed on a seven a.m. slot the next morning. Izzy knew by now that Tori wasn't a morning person, so she appreciated the accommodation. Izzy was exhausted from a sleepless night. She sat heavily in the chair across from Tori. The couch might have been a better choice, but she wanted to see Tori's reactions.

"She left me." Her voice sounded far away. Gus rested his head on her leg.

"She left you." It was a statement, not a question. Tori already knew from the call last night.

Izzy wanted to hear outrage, even though she knew she wouldn't. "You're not surprised."

Tori tilted her head. "I'm just absorbing. Tell me how *you* are."

"I'm not anything." Izzy slumped in her chair and absently scratched Gus's head.

Tori leaned forward in her chair. "What do you mean?"

"I thought I'd be devastated, that I'd fall over the edge or something."

Tori made a motion for more. "Tell me more about that. You were pretty upset last night when we talked."

Izzy grimaced. Shame washed over her. "I should have waited a little before calling you. All the ugly emotion sort of evaporated after I got off the phone with you last night."

"Izzy, it's not ugly. It's pain. Justifiable pain. Did all of it evaporate? Or just the anguish?"

Izzy didn't feel like analyzing her current emotions. She knew what was causing them. She just wanted to be told things would be okay, maybe get some tools for losing the woman she loved. "I don't feel anything. It's all quiet in there." She'd expected her inner voice to say I told you so or something. But even it was quiet.

"Your body language tells me you have something major going on. Maybe it's quiet in there, but you must feel something. Do you think you're just tired?"

"I think being tired is part of it, but I've also been protecting myself all this time. After I talked with you, I must have just activated a shutdown switch or something."

"Interesting. We've never spoken about a switch. Can you explain?"

Izzy searched for words. "I seriously thought I might go crazy again. Since the start, I was worried that, if my heart got broken again, I would land in the hospital. So maybe I've somehow built up some sort of protective shield against going crazy."

"Is that what you've been thinking about since last night? Not going crazy?"

"Not at all. It's sort of an observation in hindsight. At first, all I did was obsess about how I didn't see this coming." A few tears slipped from her eyes, and she wiped them away.

"Tell me about the protective-shield thing."

Izzy threw her hands up and let them drop into her lap. "It's pretty much what I said. I think I've been so afraid of something major or devastating like this happening and sending me over the edge of sanity, I've somehow built up a barrier against it actually happening."

Tori seemed to consider her explanation. "It's true we do hone our coping skills. We've spoken before about how the worst thing that could happen to you is to lose control again and getting admitted to a hospital. What are your thoughts about how you're coping?"

Izzy thought about it. "I suppose it's a positive thing, right? It's only been a few hours, though. The initial shock is supposed to be the worst part, right?"

Tori held her hand out. "I don't know. It's unique for everyone. What do you think?"

She pondered the question. "I guess it proves I can handle hard things. I don't need to live in fear that I have this hairpin trigger just waiting to push me into the deep end. Or maybe I still do, but the meds keep it from triggering. Whatever it is, I don't have to keep protecting myself from doing things that might result in bad endings. I can deal with bad things. Who seriously wants bad things to happen, actually? No one. But if they do, they won't kill me."

Tori's brow furrowed. "You say they won't kill you. Have you been worried they will?"

"Well, maybe not *kill* me." She paused. That wasn't true. "Actually, yes. I did think they would kill me. Not directly, but yeah. If things got bad enough, I have worried I might consider trying to kill myself again."

She felt the shadow of the cold, dark chill that always descended upon her when she thought of the terrible time just before she was admitted to the behavioral-health hospital. It didn't envelop her, though. She watched it like it was a movie: Kelly telling her she was getting back with her ex-girlfriend, tearing through her roommate's cosmetics bag to find the pill bottles, and swallowing every pill she found. Thank God the bottles were mostly laxatives and only a couple of sleeping pills. But the intent had been real. She hadn't wanted to live. All the feelings of worthlessness haunting her since before her adolescence had reached a brutal crescendo. No one needed her. Her family was big, and she wouldn't be missed. Her friends didn't understand her. And finally, Kelly, the love of her life, didn't love her. Why try to get through it when she could just end it?

Tori's voice brought her back from that dark time.

"We haven't talked about suicidal thoughts in a while."

"I haven't had any in a while. Longer than I can remember. Not the planning or wanting to do it kind of suicidal thoughts, anyway. More like thoughts that I *don't* want to kill myself. There's a difference."

"I agree. A pretty big difference. Do you see the way your thoughts have transformed over time?"

Izzy gave a half-smile. "Yeah. I think I have a more rational perspective. It's kind of cool."

Tori made another gesture for more. "Explain this new perspective."

Izzy sat up in the chair. "Well, I know for a fact my family loves me, and they would be devastated. Haley, especially. We have a bond. Plus, she's in a fragile state. I could never let her go through something like that. I need to be a role model for her in this situation. In everything, but this especially. She needs to know lots of people learn to live with our illness."

Tori smiled. "Good point. What else?"

"I want to watch Simone grow up and see what kind of human

she becomes. All my nieces and nephews, actually. I can't imagine not being around for their graduations and other milestones."

Tori rested her chin on her fist. "Remember how ambivalent you were about your own graduation?"

"I was ambivalent until I finally did it. It took so many years."

"You had a lot on your plate."

"I did." Some years she'd been able to take only one class a semester. Even the meds couldn't manage the overwhelming sense of anxiety too much responsibility gave her. Without some of the amazing faculty at the college, she probably would never have graduated.

Tori gestured at her. "You have a lot of friends and family who depend on you."

Izzy made a sound of agreement. "I wouldn't say depend, but yeah, I do."

"Depend can mean a lot of things," Tori said with a smile. "I'd say they depend on you. Who would manage the bowling league? Who would give excellent relationship advice? Who would find themselves in trouble with HR for shenanigans with interns?"

Izzy couldn't help but return Tori's smile. Oh boy! Audie would kill her if she knew how much of Audie's over-sexed life she'd shared with Tori. "I get what you're saying."

"You are intertwined with so many lives, Izzy. It must feel good."

"It does." Izzy had to admit it did. "Once I didn't see or feel the good. I saw the intertwining as a negative thing full of pain and eventual heartache."

"Do you see it that way now?"

Izzy paused. "Not the way I used to. But loving people does invite pain."

"Yet it also invites a lot of positive things, too, right?"

"For sure. But is it worth it?"

"You tell me."

Izzy glanced around the room. "I think so. I used to feel afraid that heartbreak would send me careening into the abyss. But now I know it won't. And it sort of changes everything."

"Does it?"

Izzy tipped her head to the side. "It still hurts like hell, but I would say it's still worth it."

"So, back to what you said about the protective shield. You said you weren't anything, which I took to mean you weren't feeling anything about what happened with Jane. Is that true? Do you think your protective shield has been keeping you from feeling what you should?"

Izzy paused. "I don't know. I don't think so. I'm not going crazy, which is a good thing."

"What are you feeling now?"

She had a hard time answering the question. Her feelings were all knotted up. Hurt. Confusion. Longing. Regret. Anger. "I'm sad," she finally said.

"Explain."

A huge wave of impotent longing surged through her. Her eyes stung with imminent tears. "I miss her. I miss everything about having her around. It was so lonely getting ready this morning and not doing our little dance around the sink when we brush our teeth." She paused to let the stone in her throat ease so she could continue. "I missed waking up with her. I stayed in bed and hugged her pillow."

Izzy began to cry. She took the box of tissue Tori handed her.

"Tell me how it happened."

Izzy wiped her eyes. "I had a cup of coffee with Haley after work to check in with her. Jane knew I was going to see her and that I left work early so I wouldn't be cutting into our time together. I thought she'd be happy. While I was with Haley, something we talked about made me realize I had to stop hiding my bipolar disorder from her. Because that's what I was doing by not telling her. I realized the person I needed to be open with first was Jane. I decided I would never find a good time to bring it up, so I would tell her when I got home."

"And this was her reaction? To leave?"

"Well, she said she wasn't leaving because I told her I was bipolar." Izzy blew her nose, the pressure in her head intense. She hadn't cried this much since Kelly left her. "I believe her, too. She was surprised. But she didn't freak out."

Tori leaned forward. "Do you think she left because you kept it from her?"

"She said it was because she thought she was a distraction."

Tori tilted her head to the side. "From what?"

"I'm not sure. She just said she knew I had a lot of things going on, and she felt like a distraction."

"We've spoken about this before, but do you think she felt like maybe you weren't giving her enough time?"

Izzy didn't know what she thought anymore. "Maybe. I don't know. I've been super conscious of that specific thing. You know, the schedule and all? I told you I even left work early to see Haley so I wouldn't be late getting home."

They were quiet for a moment. Izzy stared at the floor but didn't see it.

"What are you thinking?"

Izzy looked up, exhausted. "That I want her back." She leaned forward in her chair. "I will do anything required to make her feel like she's the most important thing in my life."

Tori tilted her head. "More important than your mental health?"

The answer came easily. "In order to be anything to anyone else, especially Jane, I need to make my mental health a priority. I have to let her be part of it, too. I don't want to make it a huge focus for us, but I need to let her in on it."

"Is it scary?"

"Hell, yes, it's scary. But I think I can be open about all of it with her." Izzy paused. "If she'll let me."

❖

"You look like shit."

Izzy looked up from her laptop. Audie was standing against the cubical wall with her chin resting on her arms. Izzy leaned back in her chair and stretched. She was so tired. It had been two days since Jane left, and she couldn't sleep without her. Or maybe it was the not knowing. Since she'd honored Jane's request to give her space, she hadn't talked to her except to send a text that simply said, *I miss you.* There had been no response.

"Thanks. It's lovely to see you, too." She threw a red candy at her. She'd been eating way too many M&M's. It was only seven thirty a.m., and the bowl was half empty. She didn't want to think about how many she'd eaten the day before. After her session with Tori, she'd gone to work and buried herself in work and Peanut M&M's.

Audie caught the candy and popped it into her mouth. "If it makes you feel any better, Jane looks like shit, too."

"How do you know?" Izzy sat up in her chair. Had she spoken to Jane?

Audie stared at the ceiling for a second and then looked at her again. "She's staying with me."

What? Izzy stood. She didn't know whether to be mad or relieved. It also occurred to her that Audie's place was so small, Jane couldn't possibly stay there for long. Maybe this whole thing truly was temporary. "She is?"

"Yeah." Audie stepped back and walked around to the opening in Izzy's cubicle. For a moment, Audie's outfit distracted Izzy. Was she wearing lederhosen? "She asked me not to tell you she's staying with me, but this morning, she had a change of heart. She thought it wasn't fair to you not to let you know. I totally agreed. It killed me not to tell you yesterday."

Anger flared in Izzy, then jealousy. Her stomach churned with it. She didn't know if she was jealous about Audie being so friendly to Jane or that Jane had highjacked her best friend. It didn't fucking matter. It wasn't cool.

"How did it happen?" She worked to control her voice.

"She called me when she left your house. She wanted to know if she was making a terrible mistake." Audie put a hand on her arm.

Izzy fought back the urge to shake her off. She thought about tossing Audie backward and imagined all the cubicles falling like dominoes under her. The image of her lying on the fallen structure in her lederhosen would have made her laugh if she wasn't so pissed off.

"She was a wreck, Iz. A total wreck." Concern etched Audie's face. "She originally planned to stay at her parents' house but said she wasn't ready to deal with them. I wasn't sure what to make of it, so I agreed to meet her and ended up offering her my couch. For the record, I tried to convince her to go back home to you."

That made her feel a little better. She was still pissed, though.

"I'm not sure how I feel about this. You're *my* best friend."

Audie smiled. "I am?"

Izzy rolled her eyes. "You already knew."

Audie looked at her boot-clad feet. "I always assumed, but we never actually clarified it."

"What is this, high school?" Izzy laughed. "We're adults. We don't go around declaring people our best friends. But, yes, for the record, you are my best friend. And I don't like the fact you're harboring—"

"The enemy?" Audie finished it for her.

What? Jane was far from the enemy. "Not even close."

Audie leaned against the cubicle. "What's this all about then?"

"Jane is the woman I love and miss and..." Izzy rubbed her face. She didn't know she'd been so close to tears. And now she was embarrassed to be crying at work. At least people didn't start rolling in until nine-ish, and they were pretty much alone.

"Hey. Let's go get a coffee." Audie searched the nearest cubicles and finally found a box of tissue.

Izzy blew her nose and got herself together at her desk before she followed Audie to the elevator. On the way, they passed Hector at his office door. He still had his backpack slung over one shoulder, having just arrived. He took one look at Izzy, dropped his backpack inside his door, and fell into step with them.

He bumped her lightly. "You look like shit."

"What is this? Make-Izzy-feel-beautiful day?" She glared at the floor.

"You know I've been exactly where you are, Iz." Hector pushed the button to the first floor. She'd told him everything yesterday at lunch. Audie had been there, too. Did he know Jane was staying with Audie, too? The anger flared again. Not so hot, but it was there.

"True." Izzy wiped her hands down her face. At least no one else was in the elevator with them.

A few early-bird Gigify employees were arriving, and the three of them walked against the flow of pedestrian traffic into the building. Izzy kept her eyes averted. She was sure her nose was red, and her eyes were red-rimmed from crying, in addition to the dark circles under her eyes. Her appearance meant nothing to her, but she didn't like people wondering why she'd been crying. Or telling her she looked like shit. *A girl still has feelings, after all.*

They got to the coffee cart, and a table was free. Hector went to order their coffee.

"What am I gonna do?" She dropped her chin onto her arms, which were crossed on the table in front of her.

Audie rubbed her back. "She misses you, Iz."

Izzy sat up. "Then tell her to come home."

"I'm trying not to get in the middle. You two need to work it out."

It was a good answer, even though Jane was staying with her, and she was still pretty much as in the middle as it got.

"I'm not sure I like you being able to see her when I can't." She knew she sounded like a three-year-old.

Audie rapped a quick tempo on the top of the table. "Have you asked her to come home?"

Panic rose in Izzy. What if Jane's leaving was a test? "Should I have? I don't know the rules! I'm trying to honor her request for time to let her figure things out."

Hector walked up holding three coffee cups. "You haven't called her? Holy shit, woman! I called Jillian about twenty times a day when she moved out." He placed a cup in front of each of them.

"How'd that work out for you?" Izzy sniffed the steam rising from the hole in the lid. Chai latte, her favorite.

"She told me she'd call the cops." Hector slurped his black coffee loudly, and Izzy wanted to poke his eyes out. Why did all the chicks dig him? Ugh!

She shot him a look. "Exactly. I'm not gonna make her hate me."

Audie took a quiet sip of her coffee, and Izzy was grateful. "You should call her, Iz."

"Did *she* say I should?" Izzy took a careful sip of her very hot latte. A half dozen taste buds sacrificed themselves for the attempt.

"As a matter of fact, she did."

Izzy set her cup down, thankful for the lid since the lava inside would have splashed across her hands without it. "What else did she say?"

Audie raised a hand to ward off the questions. "I really don't want to be in the middle."

"Too late, my friend." Hector took another loud slurp.

Izzy didn't even care. She had to know. "What else did she say?"

Her grasp on the strap of Audie's lederhosen might have been too fierce because Audie pried her fingers from around the embroidered leather. "She misses you. She loves you. She's bummed you haven't called. That's all I know, except she hasn't gone to work in two days, and she's been watching Meg Ryan movies nonstop. Just freakin' call her."

Izzy walked back to her desk and stared at her phone. She had her finger poised over the speed dial, and her stomach was in knots. Audie had said Jane wanted her to call. It was eight thirty a.m., and she had her daily team meeting in thirty minutes. After the first meeting, she had back-to-back meetings until noon. If she didn't call her now, she'd be thinking about calling her the entire time, and what good would she be? But if she called now and the call didn't go well, she'd be in worse shape for the remainder of the day.

"Just call her already! Jeez!" Hector stood in front of her cubicle balancing his laptop on the top of the wall.

"Go away." She waved her hand. "Shoo!"

He backed away slowly. "Tell me how it goes at lunch."

She inhaled and pushed the speed dial. The phone rang once, and Jane's voice filled her ear.

"Hello?" Jane sounded tired but artificially peppy at the same time. It was the way she answered the phone when she knew it was her parents. It was fake hospitality masking stress and uncertainty about how the call would go. Izzy hated that she was on the receiving end of it.

Izzy cleared her throat. "Hi." She heard Jane breathing, but neither of them said anything for a few seconds. "How are you feeling?"

"Miserable." Jane sounded real. Heartbreakingly unhappy, but real. Izzy wanted nothing more than to hold her.

"Me, too," she whispered.

Jane sighed. "I miss you."

I bet I miss you more, thought Izzy, but it was something she would have said before. It would have been teasing, and she would have expected Jane to refute it, and they would play-argue until they laughed and carried on with their conversation. But this was not the time for teasing.

"I miss you, too. Very, very, very much." There was no teasing. Just the truth. The knot in her stomach loosened a little.

"I'm glad you called."

Izzy sighed. "It's good to hear your voice. I wish I'd called sooner." She slumped back into her chair.

"I asked you not to."

The person in the cubicle next to hers arrived at work. Izzy leaned forward so her elbows were on her desk and spoke more quietly. "I probably shouldn't have listened to you, but I didn't want to push you further away."

"It wouldn't have pushed me further away, but you aren't a mind reader."

"Where are you?" Audie had said she had been staying home from work.

"At Audie's. Sorry I didn't tell you where I was. She texted me and told me she told you."

Izzy imagined Jane sitting on Audie's orange leather sofa. "Yeah, she did. I'm just glad you're somewhere comfortable."

"You mean not at my mom and dad's." Jane coughed out a hollow laugh.

Izzy smiled. "Yeah."

"I was afraid you'd be mad. I didn't intend to go to Audie's. I don't know why I called her when I left our house. I just did."

She said our house. Not *the* house. Not *your* house. *Our* house. It had to mean something. Izzy tried not to get her hopes up. "I was mad at first. But I'm glad you went there now."

There was a long pause during which Izzy had to keep from asking Jane to come back.

Jane broke the silence. "Don't you have the morning meeting right now?"

Izzy check the time on her computer. Two minutes after nine. Damn it. "Yeah. I need to go. I'm presenting today." She didn't want to hang up.

"Izzy?"

"Yeah?" Who cared if she was late? No one would die.

Jane's voice was soft. "I'm glad you called."

"Me, too." *When will I see you again?* The question was on her lips, but she couldn't say it. "Bye."

The call ended, and Izzy looked at her phone. They hadn't talked about next steps or when she could call again. She stood and picked up her laptop. As she hurried down the hall to the meeting room, her phone buzzed.

I love you. I'll call you tonight.

The words blurred on the screen, and she smiled through the sting of unshed tears.

She opened the door to the meeting room and was halfway to an empty seat when she realized none of the people in the room were on her team. She stopped in her tracks and stared back at all of the eyes on her.

"Are you here to go over the code merge scheduled for this afternoon, Izzy?" Hector asked, with a smile. "Otherwise, I think you're looking for the documentation daily meeting next door."

❖

You know how they say your mistakes don't define you, that it's your response to them that does? Or something like that. I told you, I'm terrible at remembering quotes. But you get the idea, right? The point is, people are going to make mistakes in their relationships. We all do. But when we do, it's important to own up to them and try to make things right. So, when you make a mistake—and, like I said, you will make mistakes—the best thing you can do is learn how to say you're sorry. Don't just say it. Mean it. Be sorry you hurt someone you care about. Be sorry your actions had an undesired effect on someone else. The worst kind of apology is when it's obvious you don't mean it.

The simple steps to a successful apology: recognize the other person is upset, acknowledge what they are upset about, and apologize from the heart. That's it. Nothing else. If you want to do additional nice things like buy them flowers, that's cool, too.

CHAPTER FORTY-ONE

Izzy fed the animals and noted she wasn't hungry, but she had to eat. Three pounds of M&M's and a few cups of coffee over the course of a couple of days was not what she'd consider a nutritious balance. Between not eating well and not sleeping more than a few hours each night, she was starting to feel run down. Between miserable nutrition and her depression over Jane's absence, she was headed in a very unhealthy direction.

Amid the gluttonous crunching of kibble going on in the corner of the kitchen, she opened the freezer and stared into it. With the door still wide open, she looked behind her at the phone sitting on the counter. Its silence screamed at her. She would not call Jane. Jane said she would call her. She turned back to the freezer. Nothing looked good, and after five minutes of staring, she still hadn't decided and the phone hadn't rung. Sigh. She wasn't going to call. What would be the easiest thing to make, then? Uninspired, she selected a tray of frozen enchiladas. And with just her to eat it, she'd have leftovers for a few days. Eating the same thing for four or five meals in a row didn't matter if she didn't care if she ate or not.

Izzy turned on the oven to preheat and removed the plastic wrap from the frozen dinner. She was contemplating whether the plastic wrap went into the recycling or the garbage when Gus did something entirely unheard of. He left his meal half-finished and ran into the living room. The doorbell rang a second later.

When Izzy reached the living room, Gus was dancing near the front door.

"Are you expecting a package, young man?" He barely paid attention to her, and she pulled him back and blocked him from the door as she opened it.

Jane was standing on the doorstep with Lester, who ran forward, nearly knocking Izzy off her feet. She still had Gus by the collar, but he pulled out of her hands, and the two dogs immediately started to play in the middle of the living room.

But Izzy's eyes were only on Jane. "Hi."

"Hi." Jane's eyes were sad, but she was still beautiful. Izzy ached at the sight of her. Her immediate response was to hug her, but she didn't dare.

Izzy realized she was staring, and she stepped back. "Come in." It was a weird situation. Jane lived here. At least most of her stuff was still here. She shouldn't have to be invited in.

"I should have called." Jane walked in and stopped a few steps away.

"I'm just making dinner." Izzy shut the door and walked around her. She hoped Jane would follow her into the kitchen. "Enchiladas."

Jane gave a little laugh. "Déjà vu."

Izzy was suddenly aware of the contrast between the first time Jane had been to her house and now. Except she felt as if land mines were peppering the landscape. Sadness stabbed her.

"There's more than enough for two if you want to stay."

"Do you want me to?" Jane followed her through the living room, sounding so unsure.

"I'd love it." *I wish you'd stay forever.*

"Then I will."

"Good." She wanted to dance. "I was just preheating the oven."

Jane followed her to the kitchen, dropping her bag and keys on the same part of the counter she always did, and sat on one of the stools at the counter while Izzy put the enchiladas in the oven.

"So…how have you been?" Izzy leaned against the kitchen island. Two days felt like a year.

Jane looked like she might cry. "Lonely."

Izzy wrestled with an overpowering urge to go around the counter to hug her, but she wasn't sure Jane would welcome her.

"And I miss you," Jane added.

She turned around to set the timer because she suddenly wanted to cry. "I miss you, too," she said with her back to her.

She heard a sob. Izzy couldn't do anything else. She came around the counter, spun Jane's stool around so she faced her, and pulled her into her arms.

"I miss you so much," Jane whispered into her chest.

Izzy squeezed her tighter, unable to speak through the lump in her throat. All she wanted to say was come back.

"I was a jerk. I shouldn't have left." Jane's words were hard to understand through her sobs.

Izzy found her voice. "I get it. You have to figure things out. You need space."

"I should have talked to you. Tried to work it out. But I left instead." Jane held onto her with a desperate tightness Izzy found wonderful. She wanted her. She needed her. The pain in Jane's voice broke her heart, though. She had to fix it.

"Do you…do you want to talk about things? Work it out?"

Jane leaned back and her face was wet with tears. "I want to go back to where we left off and pretend it didn't happen."

As much as Izzy wanted that to be a real option, she knew it wasn't. "While it tempts me to try, I'm not sure we can just declare a do-over. But I'm open to figuring things out."

Jane's face crumpled. "Did I break things too much?"

Izzy regretted how she'd shut Jane out of an important facet of her life. It had left an invisible barrier between them. "If anyone broke things, it was me. I should have told you about things way before."

"I should have told you I already knew."

Izzy pulled back slightly, surprised. "You knew what?" She must have misunderstood.

Jane wiped tears from her eyes. "About your bipolar disorder."

Izzy took a step back, confused. "When?" She eased onto the other stool.

"The first night I stayed over here. I went into your medicine cabinet to find some toothpaste and saw your medicine."

Izzy blew out her breath. "You knew."

"I didn't know how to tell you. I didn't want you to think I intentionally went snooping. I didn't mean to. I swear. But when I saw them, I was concerned for you. I looked them up. I felt so guilty."

"I wouldn't have cared if you had." That wasn't true, she immediately chided herself. She'd been self-conscious about it all along, hiding it.

"But it was your business. If I had just said something then, but I didn't. I never do. I've spent my life not saying anything." Jane wiped her eyes.

"What do you mean?"

"With my parents. With my siblings. With my coworkers. With

my exes. I avoid things, and I ruin things." Jane turned her stool toward the counter and put her head in her hands.

Izzy had spent so much time dissecting herself, she had never guessed Jane was struggling with anything other than the secret Izzy had kept. Izzy felt even more guilty for not having been aware of Jane's struggle. She gently spun the chair back so Jane faced her and took her hands again. "We're not ruined. At least, I don't think we are." She kissed her hands.

Jane ran her fingers down Izzy's cheek. "I don't want us to be ruined."

"Then we aren't." Izzy leaned forward, staring into Jane's eyes. She needed her to see how strongly she believed what she was saying. "We can get through this."

Jane clasped Izzy's hands and pulled them to her chest. "I want us to be okay. You don't know how badly I want it."

Izzy had never seen Jane look so intense—and so vulnerable. She needed to protect her. "I'm absolutely positive we can fix this. We just need to talk it out."

Jane looked away. "I don't know how to. I've spent so much of my life avoiding hard conversations."

Izzy decided to go first. "Well, I can start." She straightened in her chair. "I'm bipolar, and I hid that fact from you, or at least, I tried to. And by hiding it from you, I acted weird instead of just telling you I need to have a regular sleep schedule, and I exercise when I'm trying to maintain control of myself. And when I feel like I'm losing control, I sometimes get single focused on things like stupid schedules."

Jane sighed. "I knew how important the schedule was to you. I just didn't stop to think there might be more to it."

Izzy pushed a lock of hair behind Jane's ear. "If I had been open about my illness, you wouldn't have felt like just another task on a checklist. You're more important than anything on a list."

Jane took a deep, shuddering breath and rested her head against Izzy's chest. "I've been miserable without you." Izzy wrapped her arms around Jane. They sat that way for a few minutes, and their breathing synchronized. Peace settled over Izzy even though they hadn't finished talking things out. They'd get through this. She knew it.

Jane sighed and sat up. Her gaze searched Izzy's, and Izzy wanted her to see that nothing she said or did would drive them apart again.

"I guess it's my turn." Jane seemed to steady herself. "I'm a master at compartmentalizing the hard things in my life."

Izzy furrowed her brow. "Is that so terrible?"

"It is when you compartmentalize and don't deal."

"What do you mean?"

"My sister moved back to town."

Izzy wondered what that had to do with anything. "Interesting." And now she sounded like Tori. Might as well go for broke. "Tell me more about it."

"She said she wanted to be closer to our family."

Izzy still didn't understand how her sister moving back factored into anything. Jane never talked about her family except for a few stories about her father and to say she wished she and her siblings were closer. "Well, I know you missed her. When did she get back?"

"A couple of months ago."

"Oh." That long? Why hadn't she said anything? It seemed like something she'd have told her casually, maybe even have been excited about. Especially considering the situation between Jane and her parents. Did Jane not want her to meet *any* of her family? Her feelings were hurt. Some of the disconnection she'd felt in the days leading up to when Jane left came back. Her chest felt heavy. She didn't know what to say.

Jane looked at her hands. "I know. I should have told you."

"Why didn't you? You don't have to tell me everything, but this is obviously a thing you don't feel comfortable about, and I want to understand."

Jane rubbed her temple. "It's this whole thing with my parents."

"But this is your sister. She's supportive of you."

Jane frowned and wrinkled her nose, which was a lot more emotion about this topic than she'd shown before. "I told you it didn't go well when I came out." Jane unconsciously cradled her left arm as she spoke. "My sister and brother always stood up for me, even when I wouldn't stand up for myself. I always felt guilty about it, but they understood. When Leticia decided to move back, she told me she wasn't going to let Mom and Dad ruin my life."

"Okay…" She still wasn't tracking.

Jane raised an eyebrow. "You don't know Leticia."

True. She didn't know any of Jane's family. "You're right. I don't."

"She can get a bit pushy."

"Why would she feel the need to get pushy with me?"

"I wasn't afraid she'd get pushy with you, but that she'd use you to confront my parents. She'd have no problem with pulling you right into the middle of it."

"Is that really what you're afraid of? Because I can deal with whatever comes up."

Jane was adamant. "Not this, Izzy. You're a wonderful, strong woman, but I don't think you know what you'd be faced with."

Jane was cradling her arm again.

"Explain it to me."

"I…I…" Jane started to cry. Izzy stood and wrapped her arms around her, and Jane leaned into her.

"Sorry. I actually don't get emotional about it anymore. I think this," she gestured to her tears, "is more about you and me than my awful childhood. I just don't want to subject you to it."

Izzy smoothed her hair. "Tell me what you're afraid of."

"My dad isn't a reasonable man. I never told you about him and what it was like to grow up around him."

Izzy ran her hand up and down Jane's left arm. "Did he hurt you?"

Jane paused before she spoke, telling Izzy what she needed to know. A stone of anger lodged in her stomach.

"I thought it was normal. All kids got spankings when I was a kid—worse if it was something super bad. It was always worse with us, and I always thought it was because we were worse kids than normal. But no. We weren't worse than normal kids. My dad was…well, my dad has a short temper."

"Why are you holding your arm?"

Jane looked at her arm and dropped it. "I didn't realize I was."

"Did he hurt you?"

Jane blew out a breath. "It's a long story."

"I have time."

Jane seemed to gather her thoughts. "I was a sophomore in high school. My dad caught me kissing someone. A girl." Jane grimaced.

"I gather from the look on your face he didn't have a good response?"

"You gather right. I'd asked to stay home from a family outing to do homework with a classmate. It really did start out as an innocent study session. I'd kept my fascination with girls a secret, and I had no idea Amy was like me. But we ended up kissing. It wasn't even close to passionate. Neither of us had ever kissed anyone before, so we were just learning. But he came back to check on me—he never trusted any of us—and when he saw us, he threw her out of our house. Physically picked her up and threw her. She landed on the sidewalk and got pretty scraped up. I was horrified, but I didn't do anything. I just stood there, until he came for me."

Izzy felt her jaw twitch. "Did he hurt you?"

Jane's eyes got a faraway look. "I don't remember what happened after he shoved my mom out of the way so hard, she hit the wall and slid down..." Izzy waited. "I woke in the hospital. My jaw was wired shut, and my arm was in a cast. It hurt to move because some of my ribs were broken. The doctors never told me the extent of my injuries. My dad did all the talking. I couldn't because of my jaw. I wouldn't have if I could, anyway. I barely talked for a year, even after they unwired my jaw. But from what I was told, I had a concussion, and they had put me in a medical coma to wait for the swelling in my brain to go down."

Anger boiled in Izzy's gut. "Didn't the hospital report it? Did they tell the police?"

"My dad told them a gang of kids attacked me."

"Didn't they ask you? What about the other girl? Surely, she reported him."

"She was just as scared of her parents as I was of my parents finding out. Even if my jaw hadn't been wired shut, I wouldn't have told anyone what happened. My dad would have—" She didn't finish her sentence, but Izzy knew what she couldn't say.

Rage stewed in Izzy, and she squeezed her hand. "God. I can't even imagine what you went through."

"I learned not to rock the boat. He never hurt me as badly again. None of us. Well, there was the one time my brother got in trouble for fighting at school, and my dad took him out back...I think it scared him, too, because we just got normal spankings and smacks after I got out of the hospital."

There is no such thing as normal spankings or smacks, Izzy wanted to tell her. But now was not the time.

Izzy struggled to connect this horrific story of Jane's past with their current conversation. Then it hit her. "Are you afraid your sister will stir some of it up again?"

"I was. She moved away to escape it. My brother, too. But she went to counseling, and she came back because she says she's done with running."

"When I told you I was bipolar—"

"I already knew about—"

Izzy needed to know. "But when I told you, you left. Why? Were you afraid I couldn't deal with something like this?"

Jane squeezed her hands. "Not at all. I wouldn't have moved in if I was worried about it."

But why? Why did she leave? Without a reason why, she didn't know what to say. She let her heart speak. "Why did you run? I need to know. I want to fix us."

"I do, too." Jane's voice was just a whisper.

She needed to know. "Why did you leave, then?"

Jane stared at their hands. "I got scared."

Izzy was getting frustrated. "Of what?"

"I was afraid of her pulling you into it. Afraid my father would…" Jane's eyes grew distant.

It dawned on her then. "Were you protecting me from your father?"

Jane nodded and dropped her head. "It turns out I was right."

"What do you mean?" A cold current washed over her.

"Yesterday evening, my sister went to see my parents because her kids, Marcus and Tricia, wanted to see their grandparents. Leticia told me what happened. Everything was good at first. My nephew looks just like my dad, so my dad was strutting around about that. But then he said something about what a disappointment I was by not giving them any grandchildren. Of course, Leticia couldn't keep her mouth shut, and she reminded him that due to his homophobia, I couldn't keep a relationship, let alone plan children."

The expression of sadness that swept across Jane's face made Izzy want to cry. "Wow. That's harsh."

"Yeah. That's Leticia. Things got heated after that. My dad spewed a bunch of typical bigoted crap and said something about how it was against God's law for me to love another woman, let alone have children with one. That's when Leticia told him I was living with you. I'm not sure what her point was other than to piss him off. He flew into a total rage."

Izzy's anger at Jane's father was boiling. "Did he threaten you?"

Jane's eyes filled with fear. "He said he'd kill both of us."

"If he lays a finger on you…"

Jane shook her head. "He won't."

"I won't let him."

"He won't," Jane repeated. "The kids were crying, and Leticia said she refused to let her kids be around such an awful person. That's when my mother got angry. I wish I had been there. She never stands up to him." Jane took a shuddering breath. "But she did. She told him she was done with his anger. She wouldn't allow him to threaten her daughter, and he wasn't going to be the reason she didn't see her grandchildren."

"And he just backed down?" Izzy asked.

"Not at all. He pushed her and knocked her to the floor."

Izzy clenched her fists. "Is she okay?"

"She's okay, but…"

Izzy wasn't sure she wanted to hear more.

"…he went to kick her and collapsed. He had a stroke. A severe one. The doctors don't think he'll regain use of his left side."

Izzy was ashamed. She'd never met the man, but she was glad he'd been struck down. More than anything, she was worried about Jane and took her hand. "Are you okay?"

"I don't know. I've spent my entire life wishing bad things would happen to my father. Lately, I've been filled with such hatred knowing he was capable of hurting you. I feel like a stroke is nicer than many of the awful things I wished on him. Does that make me a bad person?"

Izzy kissed Jane's hand. "Not at all. It makes you a strong person."

The buzzer on the oven went off, making them both jump. Izzy let go of Jane's hands, and Jane let out a nervous laugh. She pushed her hair behind her ears when Izzy got up to check the enchiladas.

"I'm not going to burn dinner this time."

Jane shut her eyes and inhaled when Izzy opened the oven. "Smells delicious. I haven't had much of an appetite the last few days."

Izzy put on oven mitts and took the enchiladas out, placing them on the stove. "They need to sit for fifteen minutes, according to the instructions."

"I've really missed you, you know." Jane's voice was thick with emotion.

Izzy turned to look at Jane, who traced the whorls of dark color in the marble countertop.

Izzy played with the quilted oven mitt. "You know, when I came home and told you I was bipolar, I had just realized I needed to be open about who I am. I was terrified you would reject me. I thought my worst fear had come true when you left. But I was wrong. My worst fear was that I would lose all the control I have been trying so desperately to hold on to for all these years. But I didn't. I was devastated, but I didn't lose myself."

"I'm so sorry I hurt you." Jane wiped her tears away.

"It taught me I can deal with hard things, though. Thinking that I'd lost you was the most difficult thing I've ever gone through. But I did it. I survived." Izzy stepped forward and propped her elbows on the counter.

Jane reached across and took one of Izzy's hands. "I wish I had tried to talk to you sooner. I just hope you can forgive me."

Izzy rounded the counter to be closer to Jane. "I feel like I'm the one who needs to be forgiven."

"How about we just forgive each other and try to do better this time." Jane stroked Izzy's face, and Izzy closed her eyes. "Will there be a this time?"

Izzy's eyes flew open. "God, I hope so."

"I've missed you so much." Jane buried her head in Izzy's chest.

Izzy lifted Jane's head. Their eyes met, and Izzy wiped the tears from Jane's cheeks. "You're beautiful even when you cry, you know."

Jane tried to bury her face in Izzy's chest again. "Shut up."

"I mean it. I hate it when you cry, but even when you do, you're beautiful." Izzy kissed her. "And I love you."

Jane froze and Izzy pulled back, searching her face.

Jane stroked Izzy's cheek. "I love you, too."

Their kiss felt like a first kiss, exciting and new. Izzy held Jane's face and kissed her with all of the longing she'd drowned in over the last few days. She felt like a miracle had just happened. For once, she didn't question her grasp on reality.

❖

Being with someone you love can sometimes be so easy, it doesn't feel like you have to try. Other times, it requires a major effort. But no matter what, if you keep your mind on the prize and cherish the results of your hard work, it's quite possibly the most rewarding and worthwhile thing you'll ever do.

Think about a cherished possession. Maybe you have a trophy or a set of silver your grandmother handed down to you or an old car you've restored from scratch. Each one of those things will gather dust, start to lose their luster, if you don't keep up with them. At the very least, you need to wipe the dust off. But to really keep the shine on, you're going to have to put some elbow grease into it.

CHAPTER FORTY-TWO

The sun was warm on Izzy's back as she nailed down the last shingle on the roof of the tiny house.

Izzy got off the ladder and backed up to survey her work, stopping next to the lounge chair where Jane reclined, reading a book. A glass of lemonade sat on the table next to Jane, and Izzy picked it up, drinking half of it before placing the glass back on the table. Haley strolled across the backyard lawn toward them with Simone in her arms.

"Where's Josh, Uncle Max, and Uncle Teddy?" Haley pulled alongside Izzy and stopped to look at the playhouse.

Jane held her hands out for the baby, and Haley handed her off.

Izzy shook her head with a smile at her baby-hungry lover. "They went to grab beer and some food to put on the barbeque."

Haley dropped into the other lounge chair. "Thank God. I wasn't looking forward to figuring out dinner tonight."

"You and me both, sister." Jane held up her hand.

Haley slapped it for a weak high five. Izzy just shook her head again.

"Why do you look so serious, Aunt Iz?" Haley followed Izzy's gaze to see what Izzy was staring at.

"It's missing something." Izzy frowned at the playhouse.

"It's perfect. A miniature replica of Grandma Sophia's house."

Izzy hooked a thumb in her tool belt. "Something's missing. I just can't figure it out."

"It has everything. You even put in a sink with real running water. Simone is going to love it."

Izzy figured it out. "It needs a welcome mat with cats on it." Izzy pulled her phone out of her pocket so she could add it to the list of things she needed to buy for the playhouse. Top of the list was a real ceramic tea set so she and Simone could play tea party.

Haley laughed. "She's not even a year old, Aunt Iz. She won't know the difference."

Izzy finished updating the list. "I will. It'll give us some time to build some furniture for it."

Haley laughed. "You're crazy."

"Takes one to know one!" Izzy pointed at her and made a face.

Haley made a face. "Ouch!"

"Too soon?" Izzy asked.

Haley scrunched her face. "You're the only one who's allowed."

"It's like our own little club." Izzy gave Haley a high five. She looked over at Jane. "I hope you don't feel left out."

Jane looked up from kissing the baby's toes. "To be honest, I'm grateful not to be a part of your club, but I'm glad to be an ally." She continued to nibble on Simone's toes and talk baby talk with her. Simone ate it up.

Izzy and Haley exchanged a look.

"Jane looks like she has a little baby fever." Haley spoke so only Izzy could hear.

"God, I hope not." Izzy didn't mean for her words to come out as quickly or emphatically as they had.

"I thought you liked babies. You're always the first to cuddle with the new ones in the family."

Izzy made a face. "I like them fine when I can just hand them back to their parents. I have enough trouble taking care of myself, let alone a baby."

"You'd be an excellent mother. You've always done a good job with me."

Izzy pushed her shoulder. "Like I said, it's because I could give you back to your mom when you got on my nerves…or pooped."

Haley pushed back. "I never got on your nerves."

"But you don't deny the pooping." Izzy pretended to push but tickled Haley's ribs instead.

"Everyone poops!" Haley laughed and squirmed out of her reach.

Izzy assumed a terrible British accent. "Some of us are spared the indignity of bodily functions."

"Yeah, right. And I was a perfect child."

Izzy pretended to think back. "I seem to remember the years between eleven and thirteen were particularly horrendous."

Haley dodged another push and stopped with her hands on her hips. "Who? Me?"

"You never came out of your room, and when you did, you acted as if it was a chore to be around your family. Including me," Izzy said.

"I was never embarrassed to be around you."

Izzy put a finger to her chin. "Hmm. I seem to remember a kid who refused to take a ride from me after school one day."

"I was just having a bad day."

Izzy waved a hand. "A bad couple of years, more like it."

Haley put a hand on Izzy's shoulder, sincerity shimmering in her eyes. "I apologize for being a jerk."

"Apology accepted." Izzy patted her hand.

"Haley seemed to be doing well today." Jane pulled on her robe, steam from the shower she'd just left billowing around her in the bathroom.

Izzy finished rinsing out her toothbrush, desire filling her at the sight of Jane pulling her damp hair out of the collar of the robe and shaking it out. She wanted her again, even though they'd just made love.

"Stop looking at me like that." Jane grabbed a tube of lotion from the counter and kissed Izzy as she passed on her way back to the bedroom.

"I can't help it when you keep seducing me in the shower. It's become a Pavlovian response. In fact, I think I'm starting to get a shower fetish." Izzy put her toothbrush away and followed her into the bedroom.

"I'm totally okay with you having a shower fetish. There are a lot of things way worse." Jane stood by the bed, squirted lotion from the tube into her hand, and rubbed it over her arms.

"What were we discussing when you started talking dirty to me?" Izzy sat on the bed next to Jane and lifted the hem of her robe.

"You're the dirty one!" Jane slapped her hand away. "I said Haley looked better today."

"Oh, yeah." Izzy tried not to get distracted again. "Her meds are finally at the right levels, and she's finding a balance."

"I'm glad. She finally seems to be enjoying being a mother." A little line furrowed her forehead.

"I was pretty worried there for a while." Izzy felt bad saying it, but Haley was doing better now, and she didn't feel as if she was jinxing her ability to cope.

The worry line grew deeper. "For little Simone? Or for Haley?"

Izzy scooted back and leaned against the headboard, thinking about it. Who *had* she been more worried about? "Both, actually. Simone has a huge family. None of us would let anything happen to her. But Haley is a grown woman, and we couldn't force her to do anything she didn't want to do. If she hadn't been committed to her own health, it could have gone badly."

Jane climbed onto the bed. "I hate to think about that."

"Me, too."

"Would you have taken in Simone if it had come to it?" Jane asked.

Izzy laughed and grasped Jane's hand. "I'm pretty sure I'd have to fight Josh, her mother, and my other sisters for her if it came down to it. But if it were only me, I would definitely do it."

"Have you ever thought about being a mother?" Jane asked, playing with Izzy's fingers.

Izzy's earlier conversation with Haley came back to her. She didn't want to come off so vehemently this time. "Not really."

"I think you'd be great."

"You're the second person today to bring up the subject of having a baby."

"Who else said it?"

"Haley. She saw you with Simone and said she thought you had baby fever."

"She did?"

"Yeah." Izzy laughed. "Do you?"

Jane was quiet for a moment, and Izzy began to wonder. "I've thought about it, yeah."

Izzy sat forward. This felt like an important discussion. "Recently?"

"In the past, mostly. But being around Simone, it's hard not to think about how nice it would be to have a baby."

Izzy tried to summon a light tone. "In a general way or in a, you know, longing sort of way?"

"Oh, I don't know." Jane sighed and leaned back against the headrest. Because they were side by side, Izzy couldn't see her eyes. "Would *you* want to have a baby?"

"Personally? No. I can't even imagine carrying a baby. Plus, despite what you and Haley say, I don't think I'd be a good mother."

Without seeing Jane, Izzy thought she could feel what felt like disappointment exuding from her. But Jane didn't say anything more about it, and Izzy was relieved to let it drop.

❖

The CrossFit instructor called out instructions to the group of sweaty people doing burpees over in the grassy area behind the West building. The group dropped and did a pushup and stood again before they dropped again, over and over. Izzy's back ached just watching them.

Audie watched them intently. "I'd let her yell at me all day if she wanted to. I'm a giver like that."

Izzy sipped her coffee. "Are you ever going to ask her out, or are you planning to just stare at her for the rest of your life?"

Audie grinned. "I want to keep her hoping for a while longer."

"You're afraid of her." Izzy shoulder-bumped her.

Audie looked at Izzy with wide eyes. "Terrified."

"You might be passing up a pretty good thing if you don't give it a shot."

"True."

"Maybe tomorrow, then?"

Audie shifted her gaze back to the group working out in the golden sunshine. "Maybe."

They both watched for a few minutes.

"You're never gonna do it."

Audie sighed. "*Never* seems so permanent."

The instructor had the group switch to touch-and-goes. Izzy sipped her coffee. It was still too hot, and it burned her tongue. "I think Jane wants to have a baby." She pressed her tongue to the back of her teeth. Yep, definitely scalded.

Audie swung around to face Izzy. "Seriously?"

Izzy grimaced. "Yeah, seriously."

"What about you?"

"You know how terrified you are of Captain Pain over there?" Izzy nodded toward the instructor.

"Yeah."

"Times that by infinity."

"What's so scary about it?" Audie asked. "Besides the small detail of you being almost fifty?"

Izzy glared at her. "Thanks for reminding me. I have three years to go, thank you!"

Audie held her hands up. "Hey, I'm not calling you old. I have you by a year, remember? But you *are* pretty much at the top side of the childbearing years. Not my rules. I'm just saying."

"Jane's younger. Lots of women have babies in their early forties."

"Gotcha. So, what are you terrified of if she's the one who would carry it?"

Izzy stared at Audie with her mouth hanging open. "Just screwing up a human, for one. What if I don't know how to do it right?"

Audie waved her hand as if shooing the question away. "You'd be a better parent than the majority of the human race. It's not like you haven't been around a ton of kids. Your family alone is the size of a small town."

"It's different when you're the sole person responsible for the successful development of another person." Just discussing it made Izzy panic.

Audie poked a finger into Izzy's chest. "Don't forget that Jane would have a hand in this endeavor, too."

"Jane would be an excellent mother."

"I agree." Audie's brow furrowed. "Are you afraid of the whole bipolar thing? Does it play a role in this hesitancy to be a mom?"

Izzy thought about it. "It used to. But not so much anymore. When Jane moved out, I found out I was lot stronger than I thought."

"So, what's holding you back?"

Izzy pushed her hands through her hair. "I don't know. I just never thought I was the parent type."

"Maybe you should rethink it."

❖

When I first started writing this book, I was the biggest idiot you'd ever seen, at least as far as love went. Interestingly enough, I was exceptionally good at giving other people advice about their love lives. However, when it came to me, not so much. I was a disaster at relationships, a mess when it came to meeting potential girlfriends, and clueless about dating. In fact, I actively went out of my way to avoid it all because I believed I was better off single.

Then, one day, my best friend, Audie—the one I have so lovingly used in example after example in this book—talked me into writing this. She thought I should package some of the advice I was giving and spread it to a larger audience. She thought I needed to help others. I thought she was nuts. But to shut her up, I wrote a few chapters. They turned out pretty well, so I kept going.

Interestingly enough, as I was compiling the chapters, I did some major introspection and found that, even though I was telling other people how they should approach the whole love thing, I wasn't doing any of it myself. I decided, in order to be credible, I should follow my own advice. Of course, my efforts were for pure research. Or so I thought. Guess who found the love of her life. This idiot!

Now, I'm not saying I have all the answers about love. Honestly, who really does? But, if my advice can help a few people work out some of the issues preventing them from finding their Happily Ever After, well, then I guess this book is worth the effort.

So, relax a little. Give yourself a break. Give your partner a break. Let each other mess up sometimes. And then try to figure out the next step.

All I can tell you is, it's worth it.

Chapter Forty-three

Izzy held Jane's foot in her hand and rubbed the arch. She wasn't much of a foot person, but poor Jane had been on her feet all day at the freshman-orientation meeting at school and had gone by to see her dad at the nursing home after work.

Jane moaned and closed her eyes. "God, that feels good."

Izzy smiled. "I'm glad m'lady approves. How was your dad today?"

"The same. I think he might outlive us all."

It had been touch-and-go after the initial stroke. It had affected his entire left side, leaving him confined to a wheelchair, and his cognitive functions had been grossly affected, but they couldn't tell how much since he was unable to speak and didn't seem to understand language. The interesting thing was, nothing seemed to bother him. He seemed content, and he enjoyed seeing his family. The staff loved his happy demeanor, and Jane looked forward to seeing him. Izzy still hadn't met him, but she'd met the others.

She rubbed Jane's foot and thought about how things had a way of changing in interesting and unforeseen ways.

The doorbell rang.

Jane opened her eyes. "It's after six. Who could it be? Is Audie coming over tonight?"

"Who knows? That woman is as predictable as a box of monkeys." Izzy raised Jane's foot from her lap and placed it gently on the cushion she'd just risen from. "I'm not done."

"Yes, mistress." Jane stretched like a sated cat. "I'll be right here when you come back."

Izzy opened the front door, and a large box sat on the front doorstep. The delivery person was running back to the big brown truck parked in the street in front of the house.

"Thanks, Heidi!" Izzy yelled at the back of the tall woman who'd delivered packages to houses on her street for over ten years.

"See you at the alley tomorrow. We need you to bring your A game!" Heidi shouted back.

"I'll be there!" Izzy shouted back.

Heidi mounted the steps to her truck, and Izzy waved as the truck roared down the street.

Izzy lifted the box. It was heavy, the return address unfamiliar.

"We need to have Heidi and Remy over for dinner or something," Jane said when Izzy came back into the house.

"If we invite them, we have to invite the whole crew. I'd never hear the end of it from the bowling team if they thought I was playing favorites."

"Let's have a barbecue, then. Invite them all."

"You know me. I love any excuse to fire up the grill." Izzy walked toward the couch where Jane was still sitting.

"What's in the box?" Jane sat up.

"I don't know. I didn't order anything." Izzy placed the box on the coffee table, pulled her pocket knife out, and started to break the seal. A familiar title appeared in the box.

"Oh, wow." Excitement bubbled in her stomach.

"What?" Jane stood to see inside.

Izzy picked up one of the books and held it aloft. "It's here."

"Oh my gosh!" Jane hugged her. "This is awesome! Your book is a real book. How incredible does this make you feel?"

Izzy stared at the volume in her hand. "I have no words."

Jane patted her on the belly. "And you call yourself a writer!"

"I never thought of myself as a writer until this very minute. Not until I held this."

Jane grabbed her phone from the arm of the couch. "Let me take a picture of you with it. I'm going to send it to everyone I know."

Jane positioned her with the book facing her, and Izzy couldn't help but give a goofy, excited smile. Jane snapped a picture and then picked a copy of the book out of the box. "This is good-looking. I'd buy it."

Izzy flipped through it. "I saw the cover during pre-production, but it looks so much better in person."

"It's gorgeous," Jane said. "This calls for a celebration. Where do you want to go?"

Izzy didn't know what to do with her excitement. "I want to go out, but we have work tomorrow."

Jane popped her on the shoulder. "So what? This is a good excuse to call in well tomorrow. I can't think of a better reason."

Izzy mentally flipped through tomorrow's calendar. The goofy smile didn't want to go away. She hugged the book to her. "Okay. I'm calling in. We can celebrate with a day of doing anything we want."

"That sounds awesome!" Jane flipped through the pages. "It's so professional."

Watching Jane, Izzy's heart rate went up. Jane had already seen the dedication that Izzy had written to her. She'd stupidly left the page up on her computer, so she'd ruined that particular surprise. But there was something else on the last page she hadn't seen. Maybe she wouldn't see it or she'd flip past it. But Jane stopped when she reached the back cover and turned again through the pages publishers mysteriously leave blank at the end of some books. She stopped on the last printed page. Izzy saw disbelief and then something else in her expression. Izzy hoped it was happiness.

Jane looked up.

"What does this mean?" Jane pointed at the words on the otherwise blank page.

"What does what mean?" Izzy knew exactly what she was asking about.

"This. What is this?" Jane turned the book so Izzy could read the words Izzy already knew by heart. "Coming soon?"

"Oh. I'm writing another book." The tumult in her stomach increased.

"*An Idiot's Guide to Lesbian Pregnancy?*"

Izzy's mouth was dry. She swallowed hard. "Yeah. My publisher thinks it's a great idea."

"And why would they think you're an expert on this topic?"

Izzy cleared her throat. "I wasn't an expert at love, but here's the book I wrote about it." She held up the book.

Jane looked at her suspiciously. "This is a little different, I think."

"Yeah. I'll need a little help."

"I'd say. Who were you planning to get help from?" Jane's brows were furrowed as if she was trying to figure something out.

Izzy was too nervous to help her connect the dots. She needed to just come out and say what was on her mind, what had been on her mind for months. But she was afraid she'd have a heart attack instead. Her voice was faint when she finally forced the words out. "I was thinking of working it out with you."

"Me?" Jane looked confused.

Izzy smiled. "Yeah, you. If you're still thinking you'd like to give it a try, that is. Otherwise, I'm going to be a little hard-pressed to get the information I'll need in order to write the next one."

Jane's eyes grew wide. "Wait. Are you saying what I think you're saying?"

Izzy felt like giggling. "I think I am."

Jane grabbed Izzy's sleeve. "Are you sure?"

If she started laughing, she might not stop. "Hell, no. But I'm willing." Relief began to swell within her just because she was talking about it.

"You are?" Jane didn't look convinced.

"I am." Izzy smiled, and then she did laugh. "I seriously am."

Jane let go of her death grip on Izzy's sleeve. Her shoulders relaxed, and a huge smile lit up her face. She covered the lower part of her face with her hands and then dropped both of them.

"Oh my God, I'm…I don't know what I am! This is crazy." Jane threw her arms around Izzy and buried her face in her neck. Izzy couldn't tell if Jane was laughing or crying. She didn't know if *she* was laughing or crying. It was both. Her body shook with all this tension. She buried her face in Jane's hair, taking in the wonderful scent of the woman she loved.

"Believe me, I know." Her voice cracked.

Jane looked up with tears on her face. "Are you okay? Are you sure about this? Seriously sure?"

Izzy wiped the tears from Jane's face with the front of her T-shirt. "I have never been more serious about anything in my life."

"What made you…how did you decide to do this?"

Izzy wasn't sure how she'd decided. When she'd written the words in the back of the book a few months earlier, she'd done it almost out of determination more than anything else. She hadn't been sure then. But she was now.

"I could tell you wanted it, and I did a lot of soul-searching. I realized all of the reasons I'd always had about not having a kid didn't seem right anymore, especially now that you're in my life. And then all the fears I've had about my illness just didn't make sense anymore. I've learned what I was afraid of might never actually happen. It's hard to explain, but I'm just not afraid anymore."

Jane's brow furrowed again, and Izzy wanted desperately for Jane to understand. "I know this isn't something to experiment with. Not at all. But I've thought about it. A lot. Most of all, I see how much it means to you. And I want to give you everything you want. This is a big deal, and I want to do this with you. I want to share a big deal with you. I want to see a little you in this world. I want to have a baby with you, Jane. I really, really do. More than anything else I've ever wanted."

Jane kissed her. She wasn't sure if it was to shut her up or what, but she didn't care. She kissed her back, and all the feeling she had for Jane welled up and flowed through their kiss. Jane must have felt it, too, because the kiss she gave Izzy back was different, bigger, more open, more everything. The scope of their love exploded beyond the space they occupied.

Eventually, Izzy gently broke the kiss. She held Jane's face in her hands and stared into her eyes. It seemed the gaze Jane returned was a physical path between them.

"I love you so much," Izzy whispered.

"I love you, too. It's impossible to tell you how much."

"I feel it."

"So…"

"Are you ready to do this thing?" Izzy asked.

"I think I am."

Izzy smiled. "Good, because I've been doing some research."

Jane looked skeptical. "Already?"

"I have a book to write, remember?"

"Oh, yeah. Well, where do we start?"

"Well, duh. You know how babies are made. We practice. Tons of practice."

Jane laughed. "You do realize we're both women?"

"You don't say!" Izzy pretended to be surprised.

"Well…"

"Don't worry. I've started the homework. I have a stash of books I've been gathering to figure this whole thing out. You and I have a lot of planning to do. And practice. Lots of practice."

About the Author

Kimberly Cooper Griffin is a software engineer by day and a romance novelist by night. Born in San Diego, California, Kimberly joined the Air Force, traveled the world, and eventually settled down in Denver, Colorado, where she lives with her wife, the youngest of her three daughters, and a menagerie of dogs and cats. When Kimberly isn't working or writing, she enjoys a variety of interests, but at the core of it all she has an insatiable desire to connect with people and experience life to its fullest. Every moment is collected and archived into memory, a candidate for being woven into the fabric of the tales she tells. Her novels explore the complexities of building relationships and finding balance when life has a tendency of getting in the way.

Books Available From Bold Strokes Books

30 Dates in 30 Days by Elle Spencer. In this sophisticated contemporary romance, Veronica Welch is a busy lawyer who tries to find love the fast way—thirty dates in thirty days. (978-1-63555-498-4)

Finding Sky by Cass Sellars. Skylar Addison's search for a career intersects with her new boss's search for butterflies, but Skylar can't forgive Jess's intrusion into her life. Romance is the last thing they expect. (978-1-63555-521-9)

Hammers, Strings, and Beautiful Things by Morgan Lee Miller. While on tour with the biggest pop star in the world, rising musician Blair Bennett falls in love for the first time while coping with loss and depression. (978-1-63555-538-7)

Heart of a Killer by Yolanda Wallace. Contract killer Santana Masters's only interest is her next assignment—until a chance meeting with a beautiful stranger tempts her to change her ways. (978-1-63555-547-9)

Leading the Witness by Carsen Taite. When defense attorney Catherine Landauer reluctantly becomes the key witness in prosecutor Starr Rio's latest criminal trial, their hearts, careers, and lives may be at risk. (978-1-63555-512-7)

No Experience Required by Kimberly Cooper Griffin. Izzy Treadway has resigned herself to a life without romance because of her bipolar illness but wonders what she's gotten herself into when she agrees to write a book about love. (978-1-63555-561-5)

One Walk in Winter by Georgia Beers. Olivia Santini and Hayley Boyd Markham might be rivals at work, but they discover that lonely hearts often find company in the most unexpected of places. (978-1-63555-541-7)

The Inn at Netherfield Green by Aurora Rey. Advertising executive Lauren Montgomery and gin distiller Camden Crawley don't agree on anything except saving the Rose & Crown, the old English pub that's brought them together. (978-1-63555-445-8)

Top of Her Game by M. Ullrich. When it comes to life on the field and matters of the heart, losing isn't an option for pro athletes Kenzie Shaw and Sutton Flores. (978-1-63555-500-4)

Vanished by Eden Darry. First came the storm, and then the blinding white light that made everyone in town disappear. Another storm is coming, and Ellery and Loveday must find the chosen one or they won't survive. (978-1-63555-437-3)

All She Wants by Larkin Rose. Marci Jones and Tessa Dalton get more than they bargained for when their plans for a one-night stand turn into an opportunity for love. (978-1-63555-476-2)

Beautiful Accidents by Erin Zak. Stevie Adams doesn't believe in fate, not after losing her parents in a car crash. But she's about to discover that sometimes the best things in life happen purely by accident. (978-1-63555-497-7)

Before Now by Joy Argento. The instant Delaney Peyton and Jade Taylor meet, they sense a connection neither can explain. Can they overcome a betrayal that spans the centuries to reignite a love that can't be broken? (978-1-63555-525-7)

Breathe by Cari Hunter. Paramedic Jemima Pardon's chronic bad luck seems to be improving when she meets police officer Rosie Jones. But they face a battle to survive before they can find love. (978-1-63555-523-3)

Double-Crossed by Ali Vali. Hired thief and killer Reed Gable finds something in her scope that will change her life forever when she gets a contract to end casino accountant Brinley Myers's life. (978-1-63555-302-4)

False Horizons by CJ Birch. Jordan and Ash struggle with different views on the alien agenda and must find their way back to each other before they're swallowed up by a centuries-old war. Third in the New Horizons series. (978-1-63555-519-6)

Legacy by Charlotte Greene. In this paranormal mystery, five women hike to a remote cabin deep inside a national park—and unsettling events suggest that they should have stayed home. (978-1-63555-490-8)

Somewhere Along the Way by Kathleen Knowles. When Maxine Cooper moves to San Francisco during the summer of 1981, she learns that wherever you run, you cannot escape yourself. (978-1-63555-383-3)

Blood of the Pack by Jenny Frame. When Alpha of the Scottish pack Kenrick Wulver visits the Wolfgangs, she falls for Zaria Lupa, a wolf on the run. (978-1-63555-431-1)

Cause of Death by Sheri Lewis Wohl. Medical student Vi Akiak and K9 Search and Rescue officer Kate Renard must work together to find a killer before they end up the next targets. In the race for survival, they discover that love may be the biggest risk of all. (978-1-63555-441-0)

Chasing Sunset by Missouri Vaun. Hijinks and mishaps ensue as Iris and Finn set off on a road trip adventure, chasing the sunset, and falling in love along the way. (978-1-63555-454-0)

Double Down by MB Austin. When an unlikely friendship with Spanish pop star Erlea turns deeper, Celeste, in-house physician for the hotel hosting Erlea's show, has a choice to make—run or double down on love. (978-1-63555-423-6)

Party of Three by Sandy Lowe. Three friends are in for a wild night at billionaire heiress Eleanor McGregor's twenty-fifth birthday party. Love, lust, and doing the right thing, even when it hurts, turn the evening into one that will change their lives forever. (978-1-63555-246-1)

Sit. Stay. Love. by Karis Walsh. City girl Alana Brendt and country vet Tegan Evans both know they don't belong together. Only problem is, they're falling in love. (978-1-63555-439-7)

Where the Lies Hide by Renee Roman. As P.I. Camdyn Stark gets closer to solving the case, will her dark secrets and the lies she's buried jeopardize her future with the quietly beautiful Sarah Peters? (978-1-63555-371-0)

Beautiful Dreamer by Melissa Brayden. With love on the line, can Devyn Winters find it in her heart to stay in the small town of Dreamer's Bay, the one place she swore she'd never remain? (978-1-63555-305-5)

Create a Life to Love by Erin Zak. When sixteen-year-old Beth shows up at her birth mother's door, three lives will change forever. (978-1-63555-425-0)

Deadeye by Meredith Doench. Stranded while hunting the serial predator Deadeye, Special Agent Luce Hansen fights for survival while her lover, forensic pathologist Harper Bennett, hunts for clues to Hansen's disappearance along the killer's trail. (978-1-63555-253-9)

Endangered by Michelle Larkin. Shapeshifters Officer Aspen Wolfe and Dr. Tora Madigan fight their growing attraction as they work together to destroy a secret government agency that exterminates their kind. (978-1-63555-377-2)

Incognito by VK Powell. The only thing Evan Spears is focused on is capturing a fleeing murder suspect until wild card Frankie Strong is added to her team and causes chaos on and off the job. (978-1-63555-389-5)

Insult to Injury by Gun Brooke. After losing everything, Gail Owen withdraws to her old farmhouse and finds a destitute young woman, Romi Shepherd, living in a secret room. (978-1-63555-323-9)

Just One Moment by Dena Blake. If you were given the chance to have the love of your life back, could you ignore everything that went wrong and start over again? (978-1-63555-387-1)

Scene of the Crime by MJ Williamz. Cullen Mathew finds herself caught between the woman she thinks she loves but can no longer trust and a beautiful detective she can't stop thinking about who will stop at nothing to find the truth. (978-1-63555-405-2)

Fear of Falling by Georgia Beers. Singer Sophie James is ready to shake up her career, but her new manager, the gorgeous Dana Landon, has other ideas. (978-1-63555-443-4)

Daughter of No One by Sam Ledel. When their worlds are threatened, a princess and a village outcast must overcome their differences and embrace a budding attraction if they want to survive. (978-1-63555-427-4)